AND THE

BOOK 4
HEALING FATE SERIES

ASHA NYR

ISBN: 979-8-9924739-1-9 (ebook)
ISBN: 979-8-9924739-0-2 (paperback)
ISBN: 979-8-9885350-9-6 (hardback case laminate)
ISBN: 979-8-9885350-8-9 (hardback dust jacket)

Copyediting by Misha Carlstedt, Verity Ink Editorial

This novel is dedicated to Mogget. He kept me alive from 2010 to now and continues to hold my head above the water. He doesn't know how critical he is, but to him I show it with endless love, and to the humans I show it by immortalizing him in text with this publishing.

Thank you, my wonderful and sweet Mogget.

Content Warning

Dear new readers, this novel contains adult content with scenes describing explicit language, explicit sex, violence, human trafficking, and sexual assault. Reader discretion is strongly advised.

The Tiger Pariah and the Runaway was originally exposure therapy for the sexual assault and abuse I survived. Due to popular demand, I've decided to publish it. More information is provided in the Author's Notes about why this was written. Please note that includes spoilers.

More information can also be found in the Author's Notes of *The Mistake and the Lycan King*, *The Dragon Knight and the Coveted*, and *The Packless and the Fae Prince*, the first three books of Healing Fate.

Acknowledgments

The list of people to thank grows almost by the day, but this time, I will keep it short.

With my history, always is my fear of abandonment. Such is its strength that when I have to say or do something, I'm nigh paralyzed by fear, worried that a crossroads I didn't see right in front of my feet will result in a loss. I struggle to trust my judgment, worrying I'm not yet normal enough to make good decisions, even though I know full well there is no normal.

Even though I labor to make additional progress, my social worker, doctors, therapists, psychiatrists, readers, street team, and other supporters have not wavered. Writing these novels has opened my mind to so many ideas, trails to explore for further healing, but becoming a relatively public figure has also made me more vulnerable than I've ever been in my life. The invisible crossroads are more consequential too.

Saying that I'm doing the best I can only helps so much, but now that people continue to stick by my side, it's been enough to convince me that… perhaps… I may just be doing something right.

Thank you to *everyone* who helped nudge my compass in the right direction. Thank you to those who've kept a vigilant watch. The nights may have been starless, but you haven't let go of my hand.

Because of you, I can still move forward—that is, until April the cat darts in front of me when I'm walking and trips me. She's really quite good at that.

Love,
Author, artist, musician, and unyielding survivor,
Asha Nyr

Chapter 1

Niusha

My home had once been a place of comfort… or at least held the illusion of such a notion. One would've expected that a village so focused on adopting orphans would be a place of pure goodwill. The mothers and fathers referred to themselves as such—pure—but after my blind, innocent eyes grew into adult ones, the pure parents became eerie. My entire village had turned eerie.

For some reason, my friends continued to turn a blind eye to it, even after the oldest of us disappeared. Perhaps it was because some of the orphans did end up staying in the village. Upon turning eighteen, we'd either be paired up with a significant other or vanish with nary a goodbye. There were theories the other orphans had moved to another village, but none of us who'd left had ever returned. It unsettled me enough to keep my eyes and ears wide open, regardless of explanations offered. Something within my body warned me to not be a fool.

So, I did three things.

Just before turning eighteen, the very first thing I did was to stop drinking the 'purity,' a potion they forced us to consume with every dinner. Supposedly, it drove the monsters away from our souls, especially the dreakshasa demons, but when I finally noticed that our sharp-minded leaders weren't imbibing the liquid at mealtime, I stopped… secretly. And I had to be stealthy about it; being caught emptying my chalice would only have them forcing it down my throat, such was their fervor.

The discontinuation of the purity changed everything, more than I could have expected. I thought I'd been thinking clearly my whole life, but it turned out that I'd been living in a fog thicker than the most choking, humid evenings. The resulting clarity had taken me weeks to get used to, and though it frightened me at first, the enhanced state of mind became addicting, precious. I couldn't lose it ever again.

My second task was to sneak into the pure elder's office and change my birth year. If I never turned eighteen on paper, they couldn't make me disappear. I knew that'd only work for so long, and it relied upon the pure parents' inattention, but I hadn't solidified my plan just yet. To be honest, I was scared to even consider a different life. Perhaps this was as good as it was going to get. Perhaps it was much worse out there... in the depths of the jungle.

And finally, the third item was to get my friend, Mehr, to promise to lie and vouch for taking my virginity if my true age was discovered. If they thought I was touched, they wouldn't be able to force me into a spousing to make me a pure mother.

I stared down at my meal, nervously pushing the last of my rice around the plate. Though I appreciated that Mehr was taking such a huge risk for me, and I hoped we'd never have to spin that thorny yarn, I didn't think it would happen. Years had passed since I'd come of age, but recently, I'd heard things I shouldn't have, and now I had a much larger concern. Time was running out for a different reason.

"Did you take your purity, Niusha?" a pure mother asked tersely, and I nodded before showing her my empty tin chalice. The liquid had long since been dumped into the small jars I kept in my pockets, ready to water the weeds by my hut in the dark of the night. I stuffed the last piece of bread into my mouth and watched the rigid woman depart the dining hall, pausing only briefly to stack several cups and plates onto a tray. I wrapped my wool shawl around my shoulders and left the stone temple, the balmy evening breeze a welcome change to the flat indoor air.

My cotton skirts swished through the weed-ridden, neglected path as I made my way home—a shelter barely more than a hut. We slept beneath clay and twigs until we came of age. It wasn't so bad inside, but I did have to fix the roofing quite often, especially after long downpours. Little Tahmina, my hutmate, certainly wasn't going to do it; the fragile seven-year-old could barely open the door.

I sighed and turned to watch the gloomy grey clouds catch the last light of the setting sun. The golden-brown haze stretched from the horizon to the emerald world below, quiet and heavy. We lived high up in the mountains and could view the jungle's expanse as well as any bird. I couldn't smell it or touch it, but I heard its wildness. Both below and above, the creatures of the night stirred, including the irritating insects that were addicted to the taste of blood. I cursed inwardly, forgetting that I needed to find extra oils to keep them at bay.

I'd taken care of my entire escape checklist, but I continued to recall important things I'd left out on accident, and that frightened me. There would be no returning once we departed this poisonous place, and I wasn't talking about the insects this time.

The children are little and few; perhaps the small amount we need to take won't be as obvious, the demon said to me. The being had slowly begun its possession of my mind a little after I'd stopped taking the purity, but I strongly believed that the trade had been worth it. If I lost a little of my soul to keep a sharp mind, so be it. It was what the potion was supposed to prevent, but I really didn't see why this demon was such a danger. Perhaps it was only a matter of time until it ate my entire soul, but I thought that saving the children was more important. It was a better fate than my two alternatives.

"I hope so," I muttered to reply to the demon. It had only ever been helpful, and sometimes, I wondered if 'demon' was the right name for it.

I stretched skyward as I studied the canopy below the village, making it look like I was about to go on a casual stroll instead of raiding the communal storage. The only way to dissolve suspicion was to live the lie. I never assumed I wasn't being watched, and as exhausting as that was, it never failed to keep me out of trouble.

I broke Tahmina's and my jars of oil. I broke Tahmina's and my jars of oil. I broke Tahmina's and my jars of oil, I chanted in my head until I almost started believing it. *I'm just getting extras. I'm such a stupid, clumsy fool. I'll need rags too.*

Two pure fathers were already in the storage room, so I forced a bleak look on my face. "Niusha," one inquired, frowning at me, "what has you coming here?"

I scuffed the dusty wooden floor with my embroidered slipper and looked away for a moment. "I-I'm sorry, pure father. I was moving some things around to fix a part of the roof, and I broke Tahmina's and my jars of ward oil…" I pasted an angry look on my face and hissed, "Stupid, stupid mistake. I know we don't have much to spare now, but I also need so—"

"Quiet and take the oils, Niusha," he interrupted, gesturing me away from him. "You are forgiven."

"Did you take your purity?" the other asked as I turned away from them, sniffing quietly.

"Yes, Pure Father. I was late taking it, though, and my head hurts a little…" I answered like it was a confession. I waited for it as I walked to where the ward oils were stored; I always let them fill in the last half of the lie themselves.

"That's probably how you got so clumsy as to break those jars," he admonished, and satisfaction coursed through me. "You need to take your potion on time."

"I know… I'm sorry." I moped, dragging my feet out with two extra jars of oil. "I will try harder, Pure Father." I trudged all the way home, and I felt an echo of delight from the demon.

You did well. Perhaps that was the last ingredient. We should ready the bags tonight when Tahmina sleeps, the demon said.

I hummed as I opened the door to the hut. A cotton curtain separated my half of the hut from Tahmina's, a critical piece of privacy to have once I'd started crafting the children's backpacks. Tahmina was inquisitive even with the purity in her system, and if I didn't have the divider up, she'd be asking too many questions. Too many questions meant too many lies. Too many lies made it too hard to keep up the act.

Sometimes, I'd have moments where I wasn't sure what the truth was anymore, and that was when the demon would set me right. It truly pinched my heart that I had to lie to survive. I could only hope that if I lived through our foray into the jungle, I'd never have be false again.

I lit a candle to the sound of Tahmina prying open the creaky hut door. The small thing padded to her bed and asked me to read to her again. I could barely read myself, but I knew enough to understand what was being said. Our favorite story was the one on survival where it explained how to build animal traps. It had very nice drawings, Tahmina's favorites being the animal illustrations.

After I read through a handful of pages, she rubbed her sleepy eyes and mumbled, "When're we going on the secret surprise trip, Nini?"

"In two days, I think," I answered, putting the book aside and tucking the cover under her chin. "Remember, it's a secret. Hush, hush."

I retreated to my side of the hut, making sure the curtain was drawn all the way so Tahmina wouldn't see me opening the false floor to pack the extra oils. All seven drawstring backpacks sat there, safe and secure. The large bag was mine, and there were six smaller ones for Tahmina, Anaitis, Fulco, Gerhard, Sam and

Jam. These canvas backpacks were precious; it'd taken over a year of cautiously scrounging supplies to make them all, and I'd have a nervous breakdown if someone found and confiscated them.

Just two more days, then we'd be gone.

I woke to a harsh rapping, and I nearly fell out of bed in my haste to answer the door, my mouth drying from sheer nervousness.

Don't look anxious! If they think something's up, you're going to make them more suspicious! the demon snapped. It was right.

I forced another yawn out of me as I opened the door. "Good morning, Pure Elder Vimal," I greeted, stifling another yawn. "Do you need me or Tahmina?"

The tall, willowy man with faded brown hair gestured toward the temple. "You, Niusha," he ordered hoarsely. His seemingly endless preaching often cost him his voice, a casualty in the war against the demons, fighting the ones who wanted his words. I worried no one else but me found that complete nonsense.

I followed the pure elder to his study in the temple where he gestured for me to sit… next to Mehr. I tilted my head at him in mild surprise, but he didn't meet my eyes. The young man just sat in his seat, facing straight ahead.

"Are you ok, Mehr?" I asked, but before he could even blink, the pure elder interrupted.

"A pure father saw you last night," Vimal wheezed, leaning forward in his chair as I kept my violent heart attack to myself, "and he came to ask me if you'd been mothered yet. He could have sworn you were of age by now."

It's remarkable that we fooled them for so long, the demon muttered in disappointment.

I plastered a look of confusion on my face and asked, "No one mentioned I'd turned eighteen yet… am I eighteen?" I swung my legs casually from the chair. "And why is Mehr here?"

"Someone changed the birthdate on your records," he said, pulling out a roll of parchment. "I don't know who did it, but what's done is done." He didn't look at me, and I chose to just wait him out in silence with a confused expression. "Anyway, we've clearly neglected you for too long, so you will be mothered."

It's fine; we'll be gone before th—

"Which will be tonight," he announced.

The hairs on the back of my neck stiffened in alarm, prickling like wandering spiders. I turned to give Mehr a meaningful look, waiting for him to say that I wasn't fit to be a spouse—that I was touched already. But Mehr, once again, did not meet my gaze, and my worry increased threefold.

"So why is Mehr here?" I inquired, still shooting looks at him.

"He will be your pure father."

"I am honored to have been chosen," Mehr said solemnly, and I gaped. We'd had a plan! How could he betray me like this? Even if he'd been the one to touch me, the ceremony would still be ruined!

"I am not fit to b—" I started saying, initiating the lie for him if he wasn't going to be brave enough.

"Yes, you are," Mehr argued, suddenly acting like a complete stranger to me. "You are untouched and pure, and I'm honored to become your spouse." Then he did something strange; he glanced down at my breasts.

I stood up immediately, so thrown off guard that I wasn't able to think straight. The room greyed from a head rush, not helping my immediate confusion, and I groped for the back of the chair to stay steady. What was happening here?

"Ignore her odd behavior," the pure elder dismissed. "She's been late with her potions, apparently. Her mind isn't right."

"That means the ceremony will wait until I'm better?" I asked, grabbing onto a fragile ray of hope.

"No. We've waited too long."

The ray of hope snapped under my grip, and reality caught up to me. I'd been betrayed, and I'd run out of time. I swallowed heavily as my eyes darted between the pure elder and the man I'd thought was my friend. If I stayed in the village, Mehr could force me into his bed tonight. Even though all our newborns died upon delivery, we were still pressured to make them. My friend Gerlind was due any day now, and we'd already dug the small grave.

You're not thinking about anything helpful, the demon warned. *Focus on getting us out of this mess.*

"You are excused, Niusha. A pure mother will find you later to prepare you for the ceremony."

I did what I could to suppress my reeling so I could continue my act, curtseying with just a pinch of anger. If I appeared complacent, it'd be just as suspicious. It was a fine line to walk, but shock thickened the path. "It will be as you say," I replied bitterly, turned on my heel, and did my best to look defeated. It wasn't that much of a deception.

Leaving the temple had my mind rushing for solutions. Even the wind swaying my hair felt a touch panicked. Escaping in broad daylight with six children sounded impossible, and I wouldn't put it past the pure elder to have me watched until the evening ceremony.

We should go before midmeal. Everyone will be at the temple, and they'll assume we're running late, at least for a few precious minutes, the demon suggested.

I frowned at the idea, knowing it might be the best opportunity, but it didn't leave me a lot of time to quietly gather the children. At least the orphan huts were all in one spot, which meant I didn't have to go traipsing suspiciously all over the village. What excuse could I give if I was caught herding the small ones to the jungle?

A scream pierced the walls of one of the pure mother's houses, startling my already upset body. It sounded like it had come from Gerlind's home. When murmuring and shouting followed her cry, I had to assume she'd gone into labor. My heart sank, knowing I wouldn't be around to comfort her after she lost this child.

As I neared my hut, anxious and distressed, footsteps swished through the weeds from behind me. I whirled and scowled to find Mehr following. What did he want? I certainly did not want to talk to him! I rushed to enter my home, but he grabbed my arm. I stared up at him to find his calm face flushed and his eyes dilated more than what the purity wrought.

"Don't touch me!" I hissed, yanking my wrist out of his grip. "You betrayed me! I trusted you!" I bared my teeth in fury, seething from the depths of my soul.

Mehr raised his hands in bland supplication. "Forgive me, Niusha," he said with a shrug. "I would have done it if you'd been mothered to someone else."

"You were supposed to do it, period!" I retorted furiously, trying not to shriek and attract attention.

"Isn't it better to be mothered to someone you like?" he drawled, stepping closer to me.

"I don't like liars!" Well, I didn't like people who lied with bad intentions. I took a step back, not liking the eager gleam in his eyes. How had I not seen it?

"You hear the screaming and yelling all the time. I think you'll forgive me once you realize I won't abuse you like the others do," he articulated slowly, like I was misunderstanding and overreacting.

"So you won't touch me tonight?" I asked, narrowing my eyes. My hand drifted to the wrist he'd grabbed.

He laughed and shook his head. "No. I plan on touching every inch of you." He raised his hand and brushed his knuckles over the rise of my right breast. "I've wanted you for so many years."

I hadn't expected him to ever get that close to me. Cold, repulsive electricity had me recoiling just as he cupped my breast through my clothes. Every inch of me prickled with violation, and though my mind threatened to freeze on me, I had enough sense to slap away his hand. The violent act spurred my outrage. I couldn't believe he'd touched me!

“How dare you? You had no right!” I hissed shrilly, trying not to scream at him.

I reached for the doorknob with a shaking hand, but he pulled me back and planted his lips on mine. Never would I have expected Mehr to force my first kiss upon me. I grimaced in disgust, stretched my lips flat, and turned my head away to escape his cold kiss. His hand found my breast again, squeezed it, then released me. My last shove against him—suddenly met with no resistance—threw me into the door. Stunned and almost blind with fury, I swung my fist at him, but he retreated enough to make me miss.

He laughed lazily as he returned to the path, unbothered by my fuming. “I’ll see you tonight, Nini,” he called with a grin and sent me a friendly wave, as if he’d done nothing wrong. “Don’t be so upset. You’ll come around. Remember, we’re friends, right?”

I didn’t watch him leave. I could not live a second longer with his spit on my skin. Horror-struck, I ducked into my hut, slammed the door, and rubbed feverishly at my mouth, trying to get every part of him off me. Tears blurred my vision as I grabbed some soap and washed my lips, but I worried I wouldn’t have enough soap in the world to make him go away. When bitter suds found their way into my mouth, I gagged and leaned over the basin, now at risk of vomiting. A tiny sob escaped along with the tears trickling down my face, but I bit back the rest that bubbled up into my throat. I had to get control over myself. I didn’t have time for this!

“Nini?” Tahmina inquired, and I jerked my gaze over to find her sitting up in bed with a scared frown. “What’s wrong, Nini? I heard Mehr out there, but I didn’t understand what the fight was about.”

Oh no, what should I say? I swallowed hard, closed my eyes, and took a deep breath. My body trembled uncontrollably, and my nerves sat on the precipice of panic, but I couldn’t allow my brain to remain stunned like this. I almost felt like I’d imbibed an entire bowl of the purity. I hadn’t felt this weak in a long time.

"I… I was mad that… Uh, he told me that a pure father predicted a storm in a couple nights, which will ruin our secret surprise trip! We have to leave today if we're to go at all. The rain's supposed to last over a week!" I lied, praying that Tahmina wouldn't parade around telling everyone about the looming change in weather. "I was mad because I was the last one to find out. Then the fight turned into something else... but it's not important," I finished with a wavering smile and the wave of a hand. Oh, I was crumbling. I was crumbling hard.

Amazingly, Tahmina's face lit up, and she stood to jump on her sleeping pallet. "Yes, yes, yes! When are we going, Nini?" she cried, clapping in delight.

"Hush, hush," I cautioned, making her eyes go wide, and she clamped her hands over her mouth. "We'll leave right before lunch because… I'm taking us on a picnic first!"

"Do the others know? Can I tell them? Please, please, please?" she squealed quietly, placing her fists over her grin and displaying a gap left by a recently departed baby tooth.

It's less suspicious than you running around gathering them, the demon mused. *Risky, though, if they get too excited and someone overhears.*

I wished I could reply, but I couldn't in front of Tahmina. I sighed, ran my fingers through my hair, and said, "Ok, but remember that it's a secret! Only the young orphans know so we can surprise the adults who took us into their homes. You want to bring them back little unexpected treasures to show your gratitude, yes? They've done so much for us."

"Yes, yes, yes! I'll be so careful! I'll tell them to be here before the mid-meal bell!" she squeaked happily and skipped out of the hut. I winced and rested my face in my palms, needing a moment to just breathe. Oh, I was taking such a huge risk.

Knowing the risk still needed taking, I solidified my resolve, changed clothes, checked the bags to make sure everything was packed, and hid them once more. The only thing I removed from my bag was the dinner knife I'd stolen ages ago, and I placed it on the small table next to my bed. All I had to do was wait for the young ones.

I wrapped my arms around myself and shuddered. Now that I was alone with my thoughts, I kept feeling Mehr's hands and lips on me. Cold lips. Not even the knife next to me was a comfort. What would I even do with it? Would a knife even scare a man?

No, no, I couldn't be alone right now. Maybe I should check on Gerlind. I still had some time.

Hoping that Mehr wasn't nearby, I left the hut and walked quietly to Gerlind's house. This would be her third attempt to deliver a living child, and I couldn't imagine what must be going through her mind—what she must be feeling. It seemed so painful, so pointless, to be a pure mother, doomed to suffer hours of agony just to bring a corpse into the world. Usually, I stayed away from the delivering pure mothers to give them space in their grief, but I desperately needed a distraction. There'd be no harm in lingering nearby, right? I could pray for Gerlind, her pure father, and her stillborn from a distance.

I didn't pray with the village's religion anymore, but rather my own. I prayed to the sun that warmed my skin, the stars that told me where I was, and the moon that made the night paths glow. I prayed to the earth beneath my feet as well, thanking them for nourishing the crops that we used to feed the other orphans.

Hours passed, and as it drew close to mid-meal, I drooped in my prayer, saddened that I might have to leave before Gerlind delivered. Before I could get to my feet, however, her cries stopped and were followed by relieved noises. I perked up and peeked into a side window, spying a pure mother walking away from a crying Gerlind, carrying a bloody… creature. I blanched at the wretched sight. I'd never seen a baby before, but that couldn't possibly be a baby… could it? It had tiny humanlike hands and feet, humanlike puffy legs, and a humanlike belly. It might be a small person, but it was horribly ugly, wrinkly. Was this why all our babies died? Were they all deformed? It certainly didn't look like a small version of Tahmina; that was a certainty.

Curious, I followed the pure mother's march into another room where she ended up slapping the dead thing. When it started screaming and crying, I nearly fell dead myself. What was happening? What was I witnessing? I glanced over into the other room to find the pure father attempting to comfort Gerlind.

"You know how it is," he said to his sobbing Gerlind, putting his hands over her ears with a pained expression. "Don't listen to her soul leaving her body."

I frowned and ducked over to see what the pure mother was doing to the deformed baby. It was dead? It certainly didn't look dead. Its limbs jerked as it wailed, reminding me of one of Tahmina's tantrums. Continuing as if she wasn't handling a dead body, the pure mother cleaned the baby, wrapped a cloth around its bottom, and placed it in a padded case. It was still screaming.

Why would they put a diaper on a dead child? the demon asked, sounding as befuddled as I felt. I dropped under the window with my back to the wall and chewed on a nail while I thought about it. We were either matched with a spouse or made to disappear. Maybe they took all the babies to the same place the missing adult orphans went?

They were stealing children. Sure, they were deformed... but perhaps they thought they were possessed by demons? It certainly wasn't their fault they were ugly. I wasn't deformed, and I had a demon inside of me. I placed a hand to my forehead and swept it over my head, making a disheveled mess of my hair.

Deeply confused and unsettled, I pondered to myself, *If I told Gerlind about the baby being alive, would they let her keep it?*

Not likely, the demon said, reading my mind, which always startled me. It'd been getting better at that lately. *It would raise too many questions about the other babies.*

The more I thought about the strange infant, the more panic seeped into my chest. Then the bell signifying the mid-meal hour tolled, and I gasped. I was late! With a reluctant heart, I snuck away from poor Gerlind's house and hurried to my hut to find six orphans sitting in a circle, passing a ball of yarn back and forth. They looked up at me with grinning faces and put their fingers to their lips, except for Jam, whose finger was currently up one of his nostrils.

"Gross!" Anaitis exclaimed, wrinkling her freckled nose. Sam slapped his twin's arm, who withdrew his digit with a sigh that sounded far too world-weary for someone his age. I glanced at them all while checking for adults in my peripheral vision, but I didn't notice anyone else. I stepped into the hut that I'd never call home again and handed the backpacks to the children.

"Run on down to the edge of the jungle and wait for me! Stay together and don't let anyone see you! Remember we're on a secret quest!" I grinned and tickled Fulco's side. He doubled over, giggling and squirming away from me. It was so hard to smile right now. My stomach twisted into knots, my heart pounded, and a lump in my throat fought to keep me from swallowing.

The children ran off to the jungle. The eldest, Gerhard, was barely ten years old, and the youngest, Anaitis, was only six. I squeezed my nervous, clammy hands together, attempting to warm them as I fumbled over the hardest decision yet. I didn't know how to take care of a baby; the youngest orphans I'd ever met were out of diapers and fairly competent.

Wherever that infant is going cannot be good if they're faking its death, the demon pointed out with distaste.

"How odd for a demon to care about a baby's fate," I whispered to it. "You truly surprise me."

Maybe demons have babies too? I don't know any more about it than you.

I stared at my backpack and set my brows. If I was going to do this, I might as well be thorough about it. I placed the backpack at the door and walked calmly to Gerlind's home. When I peeked through the windows, I found the other pure mothers hovering over the poor woman.

"Why do they keep dying?" she wailed. Her face was as red, scrunched, and swollen as what she'd birthed not that long ago. It broke my heart to see her in such a state.

"You'll try again, Gerlind. You must pray harder this time. You can't give up. We're fighting the good fight, you know," a pure mother urged, patting her hand.

I scowled and snuck to the back door, opening it quietly to steal the wicker case housing the infant. I slipped out, holding the case as still as possible, but worried over its silence. The baby was quiet now; maybe it had died after all. I didn't open the case until I got to the hut, and when I did, I discovered that the baby was merely asleep. It was definitely breathing.

"Oh, you're still alive!" I nearly fell to my knees in relief. With renewed purpose, I threw my backpack on and left to find the children in the jungle, praying that the small bundle would stay quiet.

"Niusha?" someone called in the distance, and lightning crackled through my skin. I walked faster, assuming I hadn't been spotted yet. I couldn't look behind me.

"Niusha? Niusha?" That was Mehr's voice now, which was closer. I must be missed. My swishing skirts suddenly sounded too loud as I rushed down the hill toward the dense underbrush and vine-covered trees. Thick roots and loose dirt threatened to send me tumbling with every nervous step.

I cringed as more people from the village began calling my name, but as soon as I stepped into the overgrown, steep decline of the jungle's entrance, I put on a broad smile for the waiting orphans. We were out of sight but we had to keep moving.

"Are you all ready?" I asked in an excited whisper, and the little orphans nodded, barely able to contain their squeals. "Let's go find some treasure then! We'll eat in a little bit, I promise!"

They lined up to follow me, giggling quietly like they'd gotten into sugarcane juice. I was glad they were behind me; it meant they couldn't see the terror I was trying to fight off my face.

Chapter 2

Javed

I stopped counting everything but the days now. I stopped counting the endless push-ups, pull-ups, and squats that I did obsessively to stay stronger than the other exiles. I stopped counting the meals I ate because mealtimes didn't really matter anymore. I definitely stopped counting the number of times I almost died out here… in the great southern jungle of our cat-shifter kingdom.

It was great in size, that was—not fantastic or anything. I supposed it'd make for a good time if one enjoyed the constant threat of death. Dangerous animals, diseases, and criminals made for a thrill-seeker's delight. Surviving in the wild was one thing, but the odds overwhelmingly stacked against the average person here.

Staying hydrated was probably one of the biggest challenges I'd had when I was first exiled. Water was everywhere, but so were bacteria and poisons. By now I'd gotten into a rhythm with my water sources, but it'd been a struggle the first year out here. Mistakes… had been made. The tiger in me was fairly resistant to things like dysentery, but we weren't immune to poison. The jungle had as many poisons as a dandy had outfits—one for every occasion.

I wrapped my leg around a stiff cluster of vines and leaned out to collect the container I'd situated under a palm's cut flower stalk. It looked like I'd collected almost a liter this time, and even though the liquid was a little on the sweet side, it was safe to drink. I poured the precious resource into my dented canteen, cut another thin slice off the stalk, and put the container back under to continue its collection.

Shall I try to catch that boar again today? my tiger, Convict, asked.

What do you mean? I was the one who did the chasing, I replied, adjusting the canteen's strap while I strolled across a thick tree branch covered in lichen.

That's exactly my point. You were a real idiot about it.

Uh, no, that boar had exceptional reflexes, I disagreed, jumping down to a lower branch, not really sure where I was going.

Oh puh-lease, he was a snooze-fest. There's a reason why they're called boars, Convict argued.

It's truly sad that I can't tell if your wordplay is intentional or if you're actually that daft, I retorted. Convict and I might bicker, but it was a painful kind of fun… or perhaps the isolation out here was starting to get to us.

Speaking of boring, I'd like to bury my nose in that smell. What is that? Convict asked. I tilted my head around, scenting something different, but it was too faint to tell what it was. I stayed up in the trees as I chased the smell, not wanting to encounter danger on the jungle floor if it ended up being a baited trap. Convict's been fooled before by poisoned meat. That wasn't an experience I was willing to repeat.

I still smell it, I said distantly, digging my claws into a tree to make my way around it. *I also smell more shifters. It's a group.*

Careful, Convict said unnecessarily.

I released a derisive snort. Of course I was going to be careful. We were farther south than usual. I heard chattering now, and the pitch of the voices immediately concerned me.

Am I hearing cubs, Javed? Convict blurted in surprise.

I was about to ask you that...

I slowed my approach to a crawl, barely feeling the hard bark dig into the thick callouses of my palms and feet, and peered through the leaves to find an adult female making her way down a trail with six cubs. I barely registered the young ones because all my attention was centered on the female. She was...

Mine.

I swallowed heavily, staring down at the impossible sight. This couldn't be real. This couldn't be happening. There was no way my fated mate was here, in the jungle, seconds away from where I'd been wandering. I must have swallowed some kind of hallucinogen. Perhaps I'd bled the wrong vine?

Can you hallucinate smells? Convict asked, shaken.

I... I don't know! I soundlessly pushed a thin branch aside to get a better look at her.

The graceful cat moved cautiously through the underbrush, pushing strands of thick dark blond hair away from her sweet oval face. Her tresses reminded me of that perfect moment whenever I'd pour heavy cream into a cup of rich, dark coffee—the moment when the colors first swirled into a hypnotizing dance of yellows and browns. My fingers flexed slightly, wanting to know what those soft waves felt like under my caress.

Her humidity-soaked skin was a warm beige, and I shifted uncomfortably when my eyes followed a trail of sweat down her chest. I swallowed hard again as saliva flooded my mouth and forced my eyes back to her face. I wanted to memorize every single feature. I wanted to be able to close my eyes at night and see it in all its perfection. I wanted to raise my hand and imagine that I was stroking her soft, gentle cheekbones.

Her dark brown brows were drawn in focus over a pair of stunning eyes. They were framed in long, curled, dark lashes, and the blue-grey color of her irises was as cool as her skin was warm. They darted around the landscape, looking for trouble.

She seemed as fiercely protective as any female great cat. The firm press of her full pursed lips gave off the impression that she was holding a great many things in, and that seemed so lonely that my heartache almost overcame my growing lust. Loneliness was something I could relate to—even with Convict keeping me company.

Mate... Convict verified in awe.

As alert as the female was being, she was checking everywhere but over their heads. If she had glanced up, she'd have spied my shocked face.

What was a female doing out here with six cubs? Was this her litter? That thought sent rage pulsing through my veins, and I dug my claws into the bark of the tree, hissing soundlessly. My canines lengthened in my fight to retain control, but the thought of some other male claiming what was mine was unbearable. I squeezed my eyes shut as Convict tried to talk me back to sanity. My blood was boiling, and it was a miracle I could even hear him.

You're moving too fast! I don't think they're hers. They look too different, and the scents are all mixed up. They're not from a singular home, Convict insisted. *We can take a closer scent when they're asleep tonight.*

I followed the group from the treetops, struggling to pay attention to Convict's words. I was mesmerized by the female but couldn't understand what they were doing out here. The jungle was especially dangerous for females due to the number of criminals who'd been dropped off here. It was almost impossible to leave, and it wasn't like the jungle was regularly stocked with willing females. Criminals would take what they could get—by force if necessary.

This sprawling green jail was sandwiched by the mountain cliffs past the southern slaver dens and a massive river too dangerous to cross. One could head east and try to escape into dragon territory, or go west and be stopped by the ocean. They didn't even bother posting guards because so many of the exiles died at each other's hands. The jungle wasn't without opportunities, but failure brought brutal consequences.

So where did this female think she was going? Sure, there were a couple villages north of here and some sketchy nomadic traders, but that was it. The villages were very private and suspicious of outsiders. Maybe she was headed as far as the ferry, but the price for passage was… steep. I wasn't sure if this beautiful creature in the simple cotton dress had the small fortune to transport seven people.

Then I heard the sound of a newborn crying.

Eight, Convict amended.

Where the fuck did that come from? I asked him, surveying the group. My eyes landed back on the case that the female was carrying. She'd frozen in her steps and looked back at the cubs, who started and stepped away, visibly frightened by the noise. Did they not know there was a newborn amongst them?

I watched as the female bit her lip and sat down with the case in her lap. The cubs crowded her when she lifted the top but then scurried back when that made the screaming louder.

"What is that?" a little male asked, pointing at the newborn. "It's making the dying sound!"

The female took a deep breath, and she appeared to struggle with an answer. "It's… a… baby. I think?" she answered, looking down at it with a pouting, dubious expression.

It's a cub, not a baby, Convict muttered, offended. *Can't tell what type. There're too many scents down there.*

"A baby?" the older girl squealed. "But all the babies die!"

"This one didn't… but… it looks deformed, don't you think?" the female asked, tilting her head and placing a finger in the newborn's little hand.

No... that's a normal cub. What the fuck is going on? They're acting like they've never seen a newborn before, I sputtered, leaning forward to make sure I didn't miss anything strange. Nope, that was a perfectly healthy little thing.

"Where did it come from, Nini?" another cub asked, reaching over to remove his twin's finger from his nose.

Nini... I sighed dreamily. Her name was Nini.

Nini... Cute. Like her.

She's more than cute... I replied, trying to slow my thrumming heart. Nini...

My fated mate scrambled for an answer and ultimately said, "It's Gerlind's. When she finally birthed a live baby, I volunteered to bring her to the… sacred jungle spring. T-to clear out the demons that deformed her."

That was a lie. Why would she lie about that? Not to mention its strangeness. What was all this nonsense about sacred springs and demons?

Convict remarked, *There is something extremely weird about this. More bizarre than just coming across a female with cubs in the jungle. They look like they've been traveling north. Do you think they're slaver den escapees?*

No... they don't look malnourished or scarred. The cubs seem to be healthy, I answered thoughtfully, studying their little forms.

The cubs, abuzz from her words, jumped up and down with excitement. As excited as they were, they also sounded a little... lethargic. Their words were somewhat slurred, like they were slightly tipsy. It was a weird combination. They almost seemed drugged.

"We get to bring back gifts for the pure parents and see a sacred spring?" one exclaimed so loudly that my mate, Nini, winced.

"And be one of the first to see a living baby!"

"I guess… even though it's a mutant…"

"The right word is deformed, Jam!"

"Whatever…"

"It is pretty ugly, though. There's no way I ever looked like that!"

"Don't be mean! It's not its fault it's possessed!"

"Is it going to kill us in our sleep?" the youngest, a female, asked, her large eyes wide with fear.

"It's going to eat your toes, Anaitis! Then you can't escape it!"

"Fulco!" My mate gasped, gaping at the cub. "You apologize to her right now! She's going to have nightmares for a week! Would you want nightmares for a week? Are you that unkind? I don't think you are. Orphans are supposed to stick together!"

The little black-haired cub pouted, wrinkled his nose, and scuffed the floor with a sandal. "I'm sorry," he muttered quietly, and Anaitis started bawling, which made the newborn join her wails. My mate looked helplessly at it, not knowing what to do. So were they all orphans? Was my mate an orphan or did she work at an orphanage?

I have too many questions; they're hurting my brain, I murmured to myself.

Thank the Sky Gods for that piece of evidence. I thought you'd lost your mind ages ago.

Shut the fuck up, you tabby, I snapped, not that I was particularly angry. Convict just chuckled, unoffended by the insult. He sobered the same time I did as we watched my mate try to hush the newborn. *She doesn't know what she's doing, Convict,* I said quietly. *Look how lost she is.*

We need to go down and help them.

You know we can't, I replied, and I felt him wither in my mind. He would probably fight me on it later, but we'd have to do what we could from a distance. I clutched at my chest, embracing the sting of claws sinking into skin. I'd make sure they survived. I'd keep the males away and leave food in convenient spots for them to find. I'd scout ahead and remove dangerous predators and poisonous creatures. I just couldn't bring myself to make my presence known… for so many painful reasons.

This was going to hurt like fuck.

I stared at my mate while she told the cubs to sit in a circle and grab some snacks from their backpacks. When they moved behind her, Nini drew a deep breath, and her eyes watered. She stared down at the newborn with a strained, worried expression. She pulled some fruit from her bag, looked at the fragile little thing, then slumped. She didn't know how to feed it. It tore at me. It absolutely gutted me that I couldn't go down there.

Javed, Convict grunted. *Javed. We have work to do. Hey, snap out of it.*

I sat back on my haunches and placed a hand to my forehead. Right... I needed to come up with a list of priorities. *The newborn needs to be fed, I need to clear their path of dangerous creatures, I need to keep an eye out for other exiles, I need to sneakily leave resources for them to find but in a way that's not suspicious...* I listed off to Convict.

Newborn food first. It's too young for solids or mash. Needs some kind of milk.

We won't find any cows or goats here. I thought hard and scrubbed a hand through my hair. *If you tell me to try to milk a monkey, it's not happening.*

Convict chuckled in a low rumble. *Then a substitute... anything to keep it alive until they reach a village. They will have to stop there. We must herd them, Javed.*

I agree... I replied with a sigh, standing and stalking off to think about what was available and safe. Shit, we'd just eaten meat and the occasional fruit. *What about rice? No one touches the stuff, but we're pretty much all carnivores. There's plenty to make rice milk...*

I think that might keep it alive, Convict agreed. *It's better than nothing. Let's harvest some.*

We rushed through the jungle, knowing exactly where the rice was. I squatted and used my claws to slash at the grass, then bundled the clumps together so I could pull the seeds off elsewhere. Once I had enough, I raced ahead of Nini's litter of orphans and dug a firepit in a little clearing I was pretty certain they'd run across.

I did everything I could to make it look like it'd been an abandoned site; I started a fire, then put it out after the wood charred, made some imprints where one would walk and sleep, and even dragged a log over to the firepit. I scattered some of the rice grass, then harvested the rest, putting them in a messy pile on the log.

Shit, I need something to write on. I placed my hands on the sides of my head, not quite panicking but definitely feeling anxious. She'd see the rice, but she wouldn't know what to do with it.

I spied some thin, peeling bark curling from a tree trunk, and I ripped off the largest piece. The inside was smooth and tan... I supposed it would have to do.

Charred wood... try writing with that. Convict reminded me that I'd already made some, and I scrambled to break a chunk off the firewood. I hissed as I burned my fingers. The fucking thing was still hot... I was such an idiot. Convict sighed and started putting our energy into healing my dumb ass.

I blew on the piece of wood until it cooled and wrote a rough recipe on the bark. *It's amazing what we took for granted before,* I told Convict, my throat tightening with emotion. *There was always food, tools... company.* He didn't reply right away, but his feelings echoed mine.

Best write another recipe, so it seems more random that this would all be here, he suggested, changing the subject uncomfortably. I sighed and snagged another piece of bark and wrote a list of what was edible. I jotted one more down that was a random diary entry about someone who was bringing their newborn back to their northern village.

I put the charred wood down and scattered the bark, then made footprints headed north. I looked behind me and sighed. I hated this. I used to be outspoken. I used to live in the open with everyone else. I used to bask under the starlight with friends. Now I was hiding and doing everything from the shadows—even hiding from my mate. I was pathetic.

I scowled and clawed my way up a tree to stalk Nini's group again. I still needed to figure out what kind of cat she was. There were too many scents, and one in particular overwhelmed all others.

It reminds me of acpoama… or netacaria, I said to Convict. *Don't you think so?*

Both of which are illegal, and I can't fathom why cubs would be dosed with it. I don't think our mate is dosed with it. She speaks clearly, and her eyes are sharp.

More questions… I replied vacantly, staring down at my mate, who was busy mashing a banana. *Wait…*

She's not going to try to feed it banana, is she? Convict asked.

Fuck.

I jumped up silently and stalked south of the group, hating that I couldn't think of an alternative. I crouched, kept myself well-hidden and shook the foliage violently. The cubs and Nini froze, except for their wide eyes, which were scanning the jungle for the source of the noise. Nini slowly closed the case that carried the newborn, stood, and beckoned for the cubs to gather behind her.

I shook the foliage more violently and released a low, feral growl of warning. I hoped it came across as a 'get away' instead of an 'I'm going to attack and eat you.' I held my breath as my mate backed up the trail that would lead them to the prepared site.

Though terrified, she kept herself steady for the cubs, murmuring sounds of comfort to them. "Don't be afraid; we'll be ok," she said confidently, but her face made it clear that she was anything but confident. "Just back up slowly. I bet you we're just standing on someone's doorstep, that's all. Just a grumpy neighbor who doesn't like little troublemakers like you guys," she added, forcing a smile into her playful words. It seemed to calm the cubs, making them more wary than terrified, which was good. I made sure they kept moving until they disappeared around the corner, then I clambered up a tree to follow them from a distance.

They never broke into a run—just stayed huddled together as they moved down the trail. They traveled at a painfully slow pace, but I didn't care so long as they were going in the right direction, which they were. Nini melted in relief when they came to the small clearing. She told the cubs to stay where they were and investigated the little site, looking around for any sign that someone might still be using it.

She found the scattered pieces of bark and shifted her weight as her eyes scanned over them. She frowned and twisted her lips, seeming confused for a long while, like she didn't understand what she was reading. Holding on to the notes, she picked up some of the seeds and frowned, then studied the recipe again. It took a long time for realization to set in, but eventually, her eyes widened, and she clamped a hand over her mouth to muffle a sob. She tilted her head back, closed her eyes, and mouthed some kind of silent prayer.

I was fucking glowing, though. I didn't realize I was grinning until a small breeze hit my teeth. I had tricked her into accepting my gift. I had managed to help my mate from the shadows.

I collapsed on the branch and let an arm swing lazily as I watched them settle around the firepit. My heart was full. I hoped this gave the newborn a chance to hang in there until I could herd them toward a village. It was not a good replacement for breast milk, but it was the only thing I could think of to keep it alive for a couple more days.

Nini pulled out a book and skimmed through it until she found what she was looking for, then set to making a fire. She struggled with it, but after fifteen minutes of sweating over the firepit, she got a blaze going. I adored the victorious grin that spread across her pretty face as the cubs clapped for her. They were being a bit too loud, but I was here. I'd keep them safe and let them celebrate a little bit. Morale was important in survival situations.

This is a significant challenge just to get 'little treasures' for the pure whatevers, Convict pondered.

Well, she's already lying to them. There is no fountain or demon. She has a newborn she's not prepared to care for, and the cubs are drugged. I'm starting to think this is a rescue.

Or a kidnapping, he said, but it was delivered reluctantly. I scowled, and he knew very well that I was offended on her behalf. *I don't think so either! I'm just saying something that had to be said...* he apologized—kind of.

Someone's rescue is another person's kidnapping, I thought philosophically. *No doubt whoever she may be saving them from would consider it a kidnapping. She may end up with someone on her paws.*

We'll kill them. Convict casually dismissed the worry.

We sure will.

Convict and I, smitten, watched Nini boil some water and prepare the rice. I grew a little concerned when she didn't seem to be following the recipe at all, but what she'd produced would be acceptable... for now.

When they all settled, Convict and I left to scout the area for threats. We destroyed anything that was dangerous without a shred of mercy. I didn't like killing things I wouldn't eat, but I had a female and cubs to protect. That brought a pitiless beast out of me.

I smashed giant centipedes, knocked spiders out of banana bunches, and slayed a colossal snake—which I was actually planning on cooking later.

Oh shit, Convict said in a hush.

We'd stumbled upon our biggest nightmare and I froze. My face chilled as the blood drained from it. I bit my lip with my long canine in anxiety, almost provoking a bleed. This thing had nearly killed us once, but I couldn't let it stay here.

What do I do? I asked him nervously, pumping my clammy fists and getting ready to move at a moment's notice.

I don't know! he sputtered.

Should I let you handle it? I asked, stepping away slowly.

Fuck no!

But you have fur!

What the fuck do you think will happen when I shift back? You think it's just going to fix everything?

No...

And you're the one with hands!

I fucking know that!

It's not like I ca— Aaah! Convict screamed like a cub when the golden frog jumped at us. Both his shriek and the amphibian startled the fuck out of me, so I jerked, stumbled back, and tripped over a root. I pinwheeled my arms as I fell tail over head and rolled several feet. When I looked up through my strands, I discovered the frog a foot away from my face, glued to a bobbing leaf.

I held my breath.

Does it see us? Convict whispered.

What does that matter? Frogs don't hunt shifters!

Great Sky Gods, are there frog-shifters?

What? No, don't be stupid.

You're st— Aah! Convict screamed again when the frog performed an encore. This time it brushed past my hair on its way to the next leaf. A shudder raked over me when I spied a strand of my dark ginger hair stuck to its poisonous body.

We're going to die.

The cubs will want to play with it. Look how colorful it is! It needs to go!

Convict was silent as I grabbed a giant palm frond. I held it in front of me like a shield and jerked it toward the frog. Instead of hopping away, it jumped onto the frond.

Convict screamed a third time, and I just fuckin' ran. I reached a ledge and tossed the frond off the side. It floated down and settled on a branch where the frog slowly crawled off—no shits given.

Chapter 3

Niusha

Perhaps I've chosen the right gods to pray to after all, I thought as I let the baby suck on the fabric soaked with rice milk. I pulled it away, poured more milk onto the cloth, and let the baby continue to drink. I had no idea if I was doing anything right. Once I discovered that I'd been lied to my whole life, I questioned everything I'd been taught. Who knew if this rice milk was even a good idea? The note looked like a recipe, and the pure mothers occasionally made rice milk, so I figured that maybe it'd be good for babies? Was I making a mistake? I knew about breastfeeding, but milk was milk, right?

I kept my eyes and ears open while feeding the baby. Aside from some odd crashing noises earlier, all seemed to be well. I didn't know much about what lived in the jungle, but leopards were something we'd occasionally have to chase from the village. I shuddered and looked over my shoulder. It was probably a good idea to stay here tonight. We already had a fire going, and the clearing felt… safe. Yes, it felt safe for some reason. I couldn't put my finger on it, though. Even earlier when something was warning us away, the message to leave was clear, but I didn't feel like we were actually going to be attacked. Maybe one of my gods was watching over us.

"Niusha?" The only child who didn't call me 'Nini'—because he was a self-declared very mature ten-year-old—tugged on my sleeve, and I smiled up at him.

"What is it, Gerhard?" I asked, repositioning the newborn on my lap.

"What about our purity? We'll be late taking it." He scrunched up his nose. "The pure parents will be mad if we miss it…"

"Ah." I glanced away and cleared my throat to buy some time. "It's ok to miss a dose or two. You'll be fine. We're protected on our way to the s-sacred spring." I rubbed his arm to comfort him, but he hung his head.

"Okay, if you say so. I don't want to be punished again for missing it," he mumbled crankily and wandered back to the other children.

"These lies are getting harder to keep track of," I whispered to the baby, who opened her mouth and gawked at me like I'd insulted her. "Oh, don't you judge me! Drink your milk," I huffed with a smirk and replenished the cloth.

The little deformed thing was growing on me, seeming less foreign as the day progressed. I felt sad that her mother was missing out on this. The baby was still a person. She still deserved love. She didn't deserve to be shipped off to gods know where. Then again, she didn't deserve to be killed on accident by a young woman who didn't know anything about babies…

Perhaps I should have tossed a coin before taking her.

I placed the newborn back in the case and tried to control a wave of stress that washed over me. I wished I wasn't alone with this. I wished there was someone here who knew what they were doing—definitely not a pure father. I wanted… I didn't know what I wanted. I wanted someone genuine at my side to fill in the gaps and help guide me. I wanted other things, but…

I didn't exactly know what. It was like not knowing enough of a language to speak it, but the language was actually my life. I felt like I didn't know how to speak 'life.'

There were seven other people here, but I somehow felt completely alone. It was a slow countdown to a severe depression. At some point, they'd realize we were never going back to our village. They'd either wise up in a couple days or upon reaching the next village.

They'd feel betrayed—not just once but twice. They might not even believe me. All they'd know was that I lured them away from their homes with a lie. They'd hate me, and I was going to have to face that wall of pain when it happened. I just had to keep reminding myself that their safety was worth it.

A breeze met with the sweat on my skin, pebbling goose bumps along my arms. The cool evening barely moved the humidity around, but it reminded me that the insects would be prowling soon. I grabbed the jar of ward oil and reminded the children to cover up as well.

I know we worked to get this stuff, but... do we really need it? It makes me feel like I can't breathe, the demon in me said.

"How can you breathe when I'm the one doing it for both of us, demon?" I muttered under my breath as quietly as possible.

It's like the purity but milder. I can feel it try to push me away.

"You never mentioned this before." I frowned and glanced over at the children, who were slathering the oils on their arms, legs, feet, and necks.

Being away from that village has changed something. It's clean out here. At the village... the purity was everywhere. It was coming out of people's pores. Maybe you couldn't sense it, but I could. I just didn't realize how much was there until we got real, fresh air.

I grew slightly alarmed at the words 'changed something.' "You're not going to manifest and eat me now, are you?"

And have to be the one to feed the baby? No, thank you.

"You get stranger by the day, demon," I replied in a hush and shook my head, bewildered. I then stared down at the jar of oil in my hands. "So you think this has the same ingredient in it?"

I opened it, brought it to my nose, and took a delicate sniff. It'd been years since I last partook of the purity, but there was some familiarity in the pungent, minty scent. Perhaps it was wise to stop using it, not that I was thrilled about bugs partaking of me in the middle of the night.

I put the jar back in the bag, not quite willing to throw it away yet, then added more wood to the fire and got everyone settled in their blankets to sleep. They fell asleep as quickly as expected, though I had to remove Jam's finger from his nose. I laughed quietly at his obsessive habit. Perhaps a bug had flown up there once, and he never wanted to leave it unguarded again.

When the baby started crying, I winced, worried that it was going to disturb the children. I didn't know what was wrong with her. I'd cleaned her cloth diaper once I figured out how to take it off, then I'd fed her, but she was still fussy. I sighed miserably when she rejected more milk, so I just held her close to me, shushing and swaying a little like how I'd sometimes hug Tahmina when she was upset.

It hadn't helped much, but her cries did get a little quieter. I grimaced and rose to take her away from the campsite, just for a couple minutes. I rocked her as I walked, feeling a little odd as I did so. Several feelings were growing inside me, but I didn't know what to make of them. Something was telling me to coo and sing to the baby, which was like learning a language out of nowhere. Once I did, it seemed to help and she calmed more.

Then I had the strangest desire to make a baby of my own, which made no sense because there was absolutely no way I was ever letting a pure father touch me. How could holding a crying infant make me feel such odd things? I frowned and stood there in the dark, feeling more confused and lost than ever. Though I'd never seen it done—and I had no idea how it was even possible—I thought about what it'd be like to breastfeed my own child, but bile threatened to crawl up my throat. All I could feel were Mehr's hands on my breast instead. Had he ruined that for me as well? I shuddered and held the small thing close until she fully quieted. Bad memories churned my stomach and left me cold.

Suddenly, I was quite tired. I trudged back and placed the newborn in the case, leaving it cracked so she could tell I was nearby. I curled up into a blanket and fell into an uneasy sleep.

I was in the temple at last meal. I needed to empty my chalice of purity without anyone seeing me, and the only way I could get away with it was if I escaped to the jungle. I grabbed my dinner plate, lifted my cup, and scooted several feet over, jumping into someone else's seat and conversation to hide my motive.

After a couple minutes, I sank under the table to move to the other side. I pretended to see someone who needed me, waved, and moved several more seats down the table. I stared wistfully at the exit and looked around to see if any of the pure mothers or fathers were watching.

The pure elder, sitting at the front, was being addressed by a baby who hadn't been born yet. She was complaining that her parents had already dug her grave, and she wanted to speak to the leader.

The pure elder just stared past the baby. He either didn't notice it was there, didn't care it was there, or simply had nothing to say. It pained me to see such neglect, and I wanted to go back for the baby, but if I did, I'd get caught. I couldn't very well steal a baby from a person's womb either. I didn't have that kind of dexterity.

So I kept moving down the table, which took forever, until I was able to slip out the squeaky door. I agonized over how to climb onto one of the roofs so I could maybe hop from roof to roof, but when I finally got to the top of a hut, I realized that the other homes were too far away, and I'd just lost a lot of time.

People were leaving the temple now, so I dodged them and snuck around the backs of houses. Terror shot up my spine and splintered through my ribs when I saw the pure elder near my hut, which was the last bit of cover before the jungle. If I stood any chance of getting to the jungle with my plate and cup, I had to keep the hut between us.

As the pure elder began to wander around it, I darted to keep myself out of his line of sight. I backed up toward the jungle, terrified I'd be seen any second. My mind screamed at me to turn and run, but if I did, I wouldn't know if I'd been spotted or not.

It doesn't matter! If they don't reach us in time, they can't stop us!

The demon was right. I'd just been too afraid to see it. I sprinted for the jungle, swearing that my back was covered in eyes. I wanted to look and see if I'd been seen, but I couldn't risk it losing speed.

Just keep running! There's a turn in the jungle, and if we can reach it, we'll be free! Just get to that turn! Freedom is so close! Just twenty more feet! Five more feet!

I was free! I was free, but I couldn't stop running. The goal hadn't been enough. I should be safe, but what if I wasn't? I needed a new home. I needed… something more. There had to be more. Parts of myself were somewhere else, but at the same time, something was under my skin, trying to burst free and show me where to go. Where was I supposed to go?

I woke to find myself upright and dewy with sweat. I hadn't woken up screaming, but my heart was racing. I held a palm to my breast and took in a steadying breath.

When my emotions caught up to me, the first thing I felt was disappointment. I'd had a small hope that once I left the village, the recurring nightmare would stop. Maybe I needed to give it more time. Though the details were different each time, it was always about escaping the village.

The baby was new... for obvious reasons, but it was also the first time the demon had manifested. It spoke then like it spoke when I was awake.

That was new, the demon commented weakly. It sounded distressed, which was unlike it.

"Did you dream too?" I whispered, staring into the pitch of the midnight jungle. The fire had dwindled into glowing red char. Condensation dripped from the leaves around me like rainfall. Or maybe it was raining. I'd never been beneath the canopy.

The demon finally replied. *I did. We did. I was the thing trying to burst out of you.*

Both of us shuddered at the thought. We were both very comfortable with our current arrangement. For the first time, I wasn't even sure I wanted the demon to leave. It would be all that remained once the children learned of my lies.

Javed

Niusha... I repeated in my head for the hundredth time as I watched her go back to sleep. *Niusha, Niusha, Niusha.* The nickname 'Nini' was cute, but the beautiful name suited her much better. Oh, how I yearned to climb down there and hold her in my arms until she fell back asleep. She'd obviously had a nightmare, and I suffered an incredible pull—almost painful—to go down and comfort her. It was as though she had yanked on a tether attached to my heart.

I couldn't wait until she fell back asleep, but wait I must.

The cubs are obviously familiar with her, Convict pointed out while we watched over the orphans. *Nini is their nickname for her. That means she didn't just show up and lure them into the jungle. They all left together. They are running from something together.*

That's a reasonable theory, I replied, tucking a knee under my chin while the other swung freely off the branch. *I almost hope they come after her so we can kill them.*

And get answers.

Better get answers before I kill them, Convict. I grinned, but then my face fell.

Not sure I'll ever get used to it, he murmured, then he changed the subject, thank the Sky Gods. *Did you notice how she never showed any signs of shifting today? She never used her claws when they could have helped with so many things.*

You're right. I thought about what I'd overheard her say earlier. *She sounded like she was talking to her cat earlier, but she kept referring to it as a demon. I doubt that's her name.*

If my counterpart's name is Demon, I'm in for it.

Just don't go running off screaming, you big cub, you.

Shut it, furless.

I smiled into my knee and continued with my thought. *She mentioned her manifesting and eating her. I'm starting to think she... Convict, is it possible they don't know about their kind?*

I don't know. She definitely looks older than eighteen. You can't really prevent your first shift...

I frowned. *We'll have to try to catch more of their conversations. So bizarre.*

I think she's asleep now, Convict said, and I focused my senses on her. Her breathing was calm and even, and her heart rate had slowed by a third. She was definitely out cold. I might not have a lot of time, though, if that newborn cub woke and started screaming.

I climbed quietly down and moved about the cubs to identify and memorize their scents. If they got separated, it'd help me track them. I leaned down to identify each one, wrinkling my nose at the oil's smell. I had watched them apply it, but now I could tell that it was made from netacaria. Yes, it could act as an insect repellent, but I was still suspicious of it because they'd clearly already been exposed to a higher dose. For all I knew, whoever was drugging them thought this was a fine little booster.

Collect the jars. We need to get rid of them. They don't need it anyway. Cubs are not vulnerable to the bloodsuckers, Convict demanded, offended on the orphans' behalf. Human children might get diseases from them, but not big cats, and being dosed with netacaria was so much more harmful than a little bite.

I quietly searched through all the bags, including Niusha's, and buried them far away from the campsite. I curled up a lip in disgust as I flattened the soil with an angry foot. Not even this oil would help them through the psychological withdrawals they were going to encounter. I couldn't believe anyone could drug cubs like this. They deserved to be skinned alive. For drugging my mate, they deserved to be tortured for all eternity. A deep growl threatened to rumble in my chest, and I fought to suppress it. I was just so fucking enraged.

I took some deep breaths, pumped my fists at my sides, and returned to the campsite. I crouched and returned to memorizing the cubs. The littlest was a clouded leopard, the twins were a pair of cheetahs, the slightly older boy was a black leopard, the eldest girl was a jaguar, and the eldest boy was an ocelot. Yes, my Niusha was definitely not their mother. Except for the twins, none of them were related.

I crept over to the wicker case that the newborn was in and panicked when I saw her open eyes. The little she-cub began to fuss when she saw me, so I did something incredibly stupid. I pulled her out of the case and tried to quiet her myself. Gods, I should have run.

I walked away with her like an idiot, bringing our noses together and releasing a little chuff to comfort her. I took in another rumbling breath and forced it out my nose to chuff again. The newborn quieted and closed her eyes, lulled by the soft, rolling sound. I sighed in relief and cradled her, snorting again but this time in amusement. This little one was a tiger too, just like me.

That sent a pang of loneliness into my chest.

I returned back to the campsite and placed the little tiger back in her case, then I swiveled my head to study my mate. Ah, fuck. She was too beautiful. I gazed down at the female's sweet face while I took in her scent. Oh Sky Gods, she was utterly delectable, and I had to swallow several times to get the flood of saliva down my throat.

She smelled like figs and oud wood—like the sun hitting fresh, sweet hay and warming it into a luxurious bed, a bed I wanted to pull her into with me. Continuing my tradition of acting like an idiot, I leaned in closer to take a deeper inhale of her neck and upper chest where the scent was the strongest. I held back a thrilled groan and squeezed my eyes tight. This was a whole new kind of torture. I loved it, and I hated it. It felt so good, and it hurt so bad.

My nose and lips hung mere inches from her skin, and it was killing me that I couldn't claim her this very second. The canines in my mouth, already extended, itched at the base. I wanted to bite her marking spot, and it cut me that I wasn't enough of an asshole to try to do it in her sleep. I'd been alone for so fucking long, and she was right here.

I wanted her so badly. I wanted her like I needed my flesh and bones, but I knew better. Though I was aching with need, I was here to watch over them until they got to safety. After that, I had no plan. I couldn't even think about it because I'd likely go mad.

I pulled back and studied her sleeping face, wanting to memorize everything about this picture. I didn't know why I was torturing myself like this. Why come down here and agonize over her rapturous, sweet aroma?

Because we were going to identify her, Convict said suddenly, like he'd awoken from the same trance that'd enthralled me.

Right...

I took another deep breath of her fragrance, trying not to get distracted by the decadence, then froze.

Oh... Convict whispered.

Oh, I agreed quietly. *This changes everything.*

This is going to complicate things.

And put a target on her back. I sat on my haunches while I examined her.

The village might take the cubs, but they won't accept her.

I know. I honestly... I don't know what to do. We have to get her out of the jungle, Convict.

She's going to be so confused, my tiger said darkly.

I snapped, irritated. *You think I don't know that? I don't fucking know how to get around it!*

We could mark her, he suggested, and I stood abruptly, quickly removing my footprints before escaping up a tree.

And take away her choice? Forget it, I snarled at him.

Not if it keeps her alive.

Fuck! I moved away from the campsite to take my rage out on an unsuspecting tree. I carved out chunks with my claws, sharpening them while I vented. *Fuck! That will just cause her more problems!*

But it will keep her alive.

I turned to fall back into the tree and slid down until I was sitting, my head tilted up and a pained grimace straining my face. *I'm... going to do what I can from the shadows, Convict. That's all I can promise right now. She wouldn't understand it if we marked her, and when she finally does, she'll never forgive us.*

But she'd be alive.

I groaned and buried my face in my hands, almost wishing I'd never scented her at all.

I'd gotten what sleep I could, and though I was physically fine by morning, I was an emotional mess. The cubs weren't faring much better now that they'd missed a dose of the netacaria. They were all reacting differently, but Niusha seemed to be unsurprised. She was being extremely patient with the cubs, who were excessively anxious and uncomfortable. All the complaints were absorbed without reprimand. If anything, she looked guilty about it. I suspected she'd gone through this herself and knew exactly what those cubs were facing.

I grew to admire her more by the moment. Whatever she was doing, it was for those cubs at her expense. I truly couldn't imagine being in her paws. She was extraordinarily strong-willed. By the bleeding skies, I wished I knew more about her situation.

I traveled ahead of them throughout the day, making sure they stayed on the right trails. At a fork, I placed a tapir's bloody body on the trail I didn't want her taking, making sure to spread blood and intestines everywhere in a violent mess. She'd ushered the cubs up the other northern trail, keeping her hand over the youngest's eyes as she did so.

Maybe I could've thought of something less disturbing, but it was all that'd come to me in such short notice, and there'd happened to be a tapir in the area. I sadly regarded the creature, harvested what meat I had time to cut, and continued my stalking.

After a relatively uneventful day, I caught the scent of other shifters and hissed silently. *Convict. Exiles.*

Northeast, he verified. *Three? I think it's three.*

I curled my lip and moved farther ahead of Niusha's litter to intercept them. I didn't want them even laying eyes on my mate.

Or the cubs, Convict hissed. I threw off what little clothes and gear I had and let Convict take control. He shifted and bounded to head off the three exiles who were fast approaching. Three shifters appeared out of the tangled, dense underbrush. Two tigers and one bobcat, all in their human forms, slowed to size up Convict. They spread out in an attempt to flank him, but Convict released a sudden, startling, and ear-rattling growl, then swatted at the closest tiger to make him retreat.

"What're you hiding, brother?" the bobcat asked with a tilt of his head. "Smells... forbidden," he added with a grin.

"Cubs," one of the tigers noted, chin raised and nostrils flaring. "The fuck are cubs doing out here?"

"Just take 'em to the trader. Maybe they're still buying slaves somewhere," the other tiger grunted, crossing his thick arms. "Kill our brother here, share the female."

Convict lost his fucking mind, and I was swept right along into his madness.

Chapter 4

Javed

Convict was well over seven hundred pounds of rampaging muscles, and it was only because there were three of them that they'd gotten so fucking cocky. First of all, they hadn't expected his roar to be as paralyzing as it was. The infrasound rattled them, and the tiger who'd suggested selling the cubs and sharing our mate found his neck in Convict's jaws. When he tried to shift, it merely increased the pressure on both his windpipe and the blood flow to his brain, and the shifter expired in about ten seconds.

Convict let the dead exile drop from his maw, and he sprang toward the next tiger, who managed to free himself from his shock and jumped up into a tree. The noise of scrambling feet, shuffling dirt, and rustling leaves told the both of us that the bobcat had made a run for it. Convict jumped up and climbed into the tree to chase the remaining tiger, who was also trying to flee.

His panicked breathing did nothing to tug at Convict's heartstrings. The male would have forced himself upon our mate. He would have sold the cubs that she obviously loved. The longer

Convict chased him, the more he ruminated on those thoughts and became more enraged by the resounding slam of each paw.

When we both returned to the forest floor at a dead run, my raging mind separated a little from Convict's, and clarity turned into concern.

Convict, I urged, trying to get his attention. *Convict! We're getting too far away from them. We need to let him go and turn back!*

Convict roared in fury and pushed all his energy into his run, gaining slowly on the smaller, terrified tiger. He was ignoring me, trying to catch our prey before I took back control.

Convict! I snarled at him as loudly as I could. *The bobcat could be attacking our mate right now! Turn the fuck back! Now!*

Fear dropped on him like ice water. He skittered to a stop across a slippery patch of leaves, panting as the other tiger disappeared into the tangled green wild. His anger vibrated through his bones, and I was fucking livid too, but it was my job right now to slap sense into him. We lost control too easily, so we had to make sure one of us was always thinking straight.

Without saying anything, Convict turned back the way we came and kept his senses open for other exiles. I'd never seen him this agitated before, but we'd obviously never had a mate before now. I'd seen others with the fated bond, but I never could've been prepared for how it felt. The territoriality, the yearning for closeness, and the pull of lust wasn't something I could put into words. I'd fought against the lust particularly hard, trying my best not to think about sex when there were so many cubs around her.

Shouting up ahead alerted us that the cubs and our mate weren't alone, and when we exploded onto their trail, we discovered absolute chaos. My mate, Niusha, had hopped onto the bobcat-shifter's back and was... well, I wasn't sure what she was trying to do. She was going from scratching at his face to punching the side of his head, then trying to choke him. Once again, she wasn't using her claws or shifting...

The cubs were going wild, beating the bobcat with sticks and grabbing onto his legs because he'd grabbed the eldest female cub and was trying to abscond with her. Once the bobcat saw my approach, he redoubled his efforts, threw off everyone, and fled with the she-cub. My mate released a shriek when Convict ran past, and she scrambled to pull the cubs behind her. My tiger made every effort not to growl, snarl, or roar as he flew by, not wanting to frighten the precious things any more.

"No! Tahmina!" I heard her scream through a sob as I chased down the bobcat. He was smaller and more agile, so it took us longer to gain on him. However, out of nowhere, he screamed a shrill, garbled, and gut-churning wail, and I grinned from inside Convict's mind.

Should have picked any other cub but that one, you fucking idiot. I laughed darkly. He'd grabbed the jaguar cub, which had been an incredibly bad call on his part. He probably had thought she'd be worth more in the slave market as the older female cub, but I doubted it was worth whatever bit of flesh he'd just lost.

There was a reason why there were so many jokes about jaguars avoiding breastfeeding like the plague. Tigers had about double the bite force of a lion, but jaguars had three times that. Little Tahmina might not have shifted yet, but she wasn't a human child. She was a full-bred jaguar cub. She wouldn't need to crush throats to suffocate prey when she got older—she'd go straight into crushing skulls.

Whatever Tahmina had done, it allowed Convict to reach the bobcat within seconds. The rancid scent of him pissing himself hit our nose, and he threw Tahmina away, thinking we'd go catch her instead of chasing him. The fucking bastard was right.

I shifted back into my human form and lunged to snatch her out of the air before she landed. If she broke a bone, it'd take forever to heal and would bog down their traveling speed. The sooner they could get to a village, the better.

I caught the little jaguar and cradled her to my chest, stroking her hair to let her know I wasn't the bad guy. Her gaze wildly darted about, then popped up to gawk at me. A small swell of pride warmed me at the sight of blood all over her mouth and dress from her attack on the bobcat, but that feeling evaporated when she erupted into tears. The cub collapsed into me, crying her heart out.

She probably doesn't understand why she bit him so viciously. From the looks of it, she may have torn out some of his throat, Convict said.

I know she's upset and will be in shock, but I can't stop feeling so proud of her. I wonder if this is what it's like to have a cub of your own, I said thoughtfully, hoisting her up closer and nestling the cub under my chin while I turned to walk her back to Niusha. I'd been around cubs before, but perhaps my time in exile had me cherishing them more. I released several chuffs into the top of her head to comfort and calm. She stiffened at first from the foreign sound, but when I repeated it, she relaxed, and it wasn't long before she fell asleep.

I took a moment to memorize this feeling, pretending this was my cub in my arms. When my life more than likely returned to solitude, I'd like to remember this moment well. I cradled her warm little body and made silent promises to see her and her loved ones to safety. I would have never expected to be so emotionally moved by a cub. I didn't know if it was something that'd come with age or from our years of loneliness. I supposed it could be both.

I could hear Niusha's frantic shouts a mile away now, so I woke Tahmina. I then gently set her down on the jungle floor and pointed to where the calls originated. She was frozen as she looked ahead, biting her lip nervously and picking at her fingers. Once I gave her bottom a gentle little nudge with my foot, she broke into a run and disappeared into the underbrush, headed straight for Niusha's calls. I followed at a distance to make sure they reunited, and I grunted in approval when my mate ripped Tahmina right off her feet and pulled her into a crushing hug.

I retrieved my clothes and gear, then went back to following my mate, who was trying to backtrack to the trail they'd been on before the attack. Tahmina was no longer crying, but Niusha's face had become pale and tear-stained.

"—nd just threw me!" Tahmina babbled, holding on to Niusha's hand while my mate's other arm was wrapped around the case with the newborn. I wanted to go down there and carry it for her. Fuck. I wanted to help. I wanted to keep helping her every second of every day.

Tahmina continued her story. "Then a big, big, big man came out of nowhere and caught me!"

"Another man?" She gasped, staring down at the she-cub. "How did you get away, Tahmina?"

"Get away? No, he saved me! He caught me right out of the air and brought me back! I fell asleep for most of the walk back, though…" she mumbled the last part, like she regretted missing out on the return trip. There hadn't been much to miss; we'd walked by green, green, and some more green.

"I don't understand. Why didn't he come speak to us? Did he say anything to you? I wish we could thank him…" she said worriedly, looking around as though she could spot me. Wasn't happening.

"Maybe he was a demon!" the black leopard cub said, grinning at the tiny clouded leopard, who looked like she was going to start crying.

Our poor mate, Convict noted, appreciating the mischief she must be constantly juggling. Niusha didn't look like she'd even heard him, though.

Tahmina exclaimed, "Nope, nope! He just brought me here! He was very nice!"

"Everyone wants something, though," she murmured under her breath, frowning. "What…"

Before I had a chance to be hurt by those words, Convict said, *She's not wrong to think that. We do want something. We want them to be safe. That's our ulterior motive.*

Deep down, we want her too, I guess. I sighed miserably.

It's not that deep down. Convict snorted, but his amusement lacked authenticity. He was suffering just as much.

"What'd he look like? You'd recognize him if you saw him again?" Niusha asked.

Tahmina nodded, staring soberly up at her. "He was like a mountain, but he had a strange hair color! It was like a dark orange color." She pinched a lock of her hair and looked through it at Niusha, making a funny face.

Apparently, they don't have redheads where they come from, Convict said wryly.

They don't seem to have a lot of things...

"And his arms were as big as me! He's much better looking than Mehr too!" the jaguar continued to prattle.

"Nuh-uh! Mehr is the handsomest! Only Niusha'd be spoused with the best!" the ocelot cub argued.

Both Niusha and I froze midstride.

Who the fuck is Mehr? Convict snapped.

"You knew, Gerhard?" Niusha asked and left her mouth agape in shock.

Gerhard's confidence drained, and his eyes darted about the trail like he was looking for an escape route. "Uh... he was bragging to everyone."

My mate closed her eyes and put a hand to her chest, obviously fighting for calm. I was having a much harder time with it because I wanted fucking answers. While I slowly cut out curls of bark from the branch under me, the cubs reacted differently. Most of them congratulated Niusha, but Gerhard and Tahmina remained silent—both clearly old enough to know better.

"I-it won't b-be so bad, Niusha. You know he's my hutmate... He s-said he'll take good care of you," Gerhard stammered.

So maybe she's running from a forced mating? Convict wondered.

I gripped my arms and willed my shaking to cease. I couldn't keep losing control like this. It was getting worse.

Keep it together, Javed.

I'm trying, I seethed with a painfully clenched jaw. *When they sent us into exile, I had no idea that would include torture. That's what this is, Convict. Fucking. Torture.*

Niusha

In my shock, I didn't know what to say to Gerhard at first. I couldn't bring myself to tell them that we weren't going back to our old village—the village of pure lies. Why had no one warned me? Had it happened that fast? How long had Mehr been planning on having me as his pure mother? How long had he pretended to be just my friend while looking at me in a different way?

I wrapped my arms around my breasts, unable to keep the disgusted grimace off my face. It was too violating. I'd only ever trusted the orphans, and he… Not even he'd been worthy of that trust.

"I'll… do my best to please him when we return," I muttered, unable to speak in any other way than through my teeth. The words rebelled with the taste of acid as I forced them from my throat, but at least the acknowledgment seemed to calm the children. Even the gums around my teeth ached.

A hissing growl came from somewhere far away, and my skin pebbled from fear. I rubbed my goose bumps and picked up the baby's case. "Let's go," I prompted quietly. "I don't know what that big cat was, but it might still be nearby. Let's not make the kitty cranky, ok?"

"What did happen to that big orange kitty?" Sam asked, scratching the back of his head while walking next to Tahmina. "Did you see him?"

She shook her head. "No… that bad man shoved my face in his shoulder while he ran. Grabbed my neck. I couldn't see anything at all."

I stared worriedly down at her. I'd wiped her face the best I could, but I needed to boil water to clean it more thoroughly. I needed to ask about the blood, but that was best done with her in private. It obviously wasn't hers, and it looked like she'd...

Can't blame her if she bit him, the demon said. *She's otherwise powerless. Don't you go conveniently forgetting that we were a second away from biting him too.*

Something struck me in the way they said 'we' this time. It sounded unified, as though they were just as much a part of my body as I was. Like they had a natural right to be inside me. Like my body was their body. Disoriented, I stumbled, then palmed my head as the jungle tilted. My brain buzzed with a new sense, like the demon and I were actually sharing the same space instead of them enveloping my mind like an intruder.

Something is changing... the demon noted nervously. Yes, something was changing. It felt like more than simply coming down with some odd jungle disease, and that newness frightened me.

The demon had been right; I'd gone a touch crazy when the short, stocky, one-eyed man had burst into the trail to wrap an arm around my little friend. The demon inside of me almost melted into my—as much as I loathed to admit it—bloodlust. I'd never felt anything like it before, not even when Mehr had touched me. I felt like at my very roots, I had some strength to rip him to pieces, but it wasn't available to me. As much as I tried to analyze it in silence, with the children at my heels, the feeling didn't make sense. It was real, but... simultaneously impossible.

The day on the trail otherwise went smoothly. An hour before sunset, I discovered a little clear patch a short walk from a stream where I set about digging a firepit.

Once the shock from Tahmina's kidnapping had worn off, the children returned to being tired, cranky, and depressed. Some were anxious and restless, and those ones chose to help find firewood while the others curled up to nap or pout. I'd been prodded multiple times about their concerns over missing purity doses, but I continued to insist it'd be ok, pointing out that I wasn't taking it either, and I was just fine. I hoped that since they were still young, it'd clear from their bodies faster than it had for me. I prayed to all my new gods that they'd be fine in a day or two. I knew full well it wasn't fun to come off that poison.

"Nini?" Jam asked, tugging on my clothes while I prepared another day's worth of rice milk for the baby. I hummed in response and waited for his question. "I can't find my ward oil. Can I have some of yours?"

"That's odd; did you leave it behind?" I asked him, standing and brushing my hands on my skirts.

"I don't have mine either…" Fulco said.

"Me neither, Nini…"

A chill ran down my spine, and I searched my own bag. When I'd finished digging through my belongings, I stilled.

Gone, the demon said quietly, echoing my finding. *Can you lean forward for me?* I frowned and leaned forward, not sure why it was asking me to do that. *Do you smell something?*

I sniffed a couple times, then inhaled deeply. There was a new smell. "What is that?" I leaned so far forward my head was almost in the bag. "What is that smell?" I whispered.

It was subtle. There was something sweet and tart… like mango, but it was thicker, headier. It had a salty and musky quality that made the hairs on my body stand on end. I just couldn't identify what I was smelling. Had I picked a fruit that fermented or…? No, it didn't smell fermented, but it was making me salivate for some reason. What…

"Nini?"

I hadn't realized that my entire head had disappeared into the bag until Tahmina called my name. I jerked my head out, wild-eyed, and looked up at her with a red face. Why was I embarrassed? I wasn't doing anything wrong. I brushed my hair back and glanced at the cloth she was holding. Oh right, I was going to wash her face!

I poured some of the boiled water over the cloth, let it cool for a moment, then started wiping down her face and neck. When I turned her around to make sure I got everything from her neck and shoulders, I got a stronger whiff of that new scent. Her hair was saturated with it.

Woah! the demon in me exclaimed, sounding more thrown than ever.

The dizziness returned, and I placed the back of my hand to my forehead before closing my eyes. Something about the smell tugged at me. It came from the same deep root that I shared with the demon—from where the bloodlust had originated.

"Tahmina…" I asked carefully, licking my dry lips and working hard to swallow the extra saliva made by the smell. "Did anything touch your hair today?"

"The man who saved me petted it like I was a kitten," she answered. "He had big hands! It was like wearing a helmet." She laughed and rocked, pivoting on her ankles. I wrinkled my nose in frustration and turned her around again to dab at her dress. I couldn't do anything about the blood there. It'd be stained.

"So the bad man who first took you didn't touch your hair?" I asked casually, and she shook her head. "Just your neck?"

Nothing else is missing. Had he taken our oils? Only the oils? the demon asked thoughtfully.

"Very strange smell," I murmured to myself as I let Tahmina go, telling her to let the others know we'd have to go without the bug repellent. I should be thinking about why the oils were taken, but I was obsessing over why the smell… smelled so good.

I cleaned the baby's cloth diaper and kept the bag in my lap while we ate dinner. I hugged it, kept it tucked under my chin, and continued to sniff it. It was an obsession, a mystery, and I couldn't stop. When I'd breathe in, I'd feel a rush and taste an incredible flavor, but when I'd exhale, I'd feel a loss. What was I smelling, and why did it make me feel such things? New things…

I didn't know what the new things were; they were just different. They weren't unpleasant—no, far from it. It made me feel warm and achy in some rather odd places. It reminded me of some instances in the past where I'd wake up from a dream with damp underwear and pulsing between my legs. I couldn't remember the dreams, but the pulsing had always been memorable. I had so many questions, and no one could answer them.

"Maybe he is a demon," I whispered as the children curled into their blankets to sleep. "Maybe it's some kind of spell."

If he's a demon, he's a benevolent one—like me. Maybe he required a sacrifice to help us, so he took the oils, the demon mused.

"That actually could be the case," I whispered, standing up to walk toward the stream. "You have a very good idea there, demon." Yes, a sacrifice did make sense for saving Tahmina.

The stream wasn't wide, but it was plenty deep, and I wandered a little farther upstream to find a slightly less muddy section of the bank. It was hard to see in the dark, as the moonlight barely passed through the thick canopy, but I didn't bother with a torch. Perhaps it was the additional separation from the purity, but I felt like my vision had sharpened too.

I was about to step into the water to scrub more blood from Tahmina's ruined dress when an arm shot around my waist and a hand clamped over my mouth. I started and bucked in their hold, screaming into a palm that was too intentionally cupped for me to bite. Despite my thrashing and kicking, they simply stood behind me in silence, like a parent waiting for their child's tantrum to conclude.

I didn't know why I didn't notice it right away—perhaps it was the rush of alarm—but that salty, musky, mango scent seeped into my nostrils and curled around my tongue. It was the man, or demon, who'd brought Tahmina back to us. It had to be him. I took a risk and offered him my calmness, letting my arms fall to my side and closing my mouth. Still, I was unable to stop taking deep breaths. He was the pure, unfiltered source of the scent, and I was nearly intoxicated from it. Was this a different kind of purity? If so… I wasn't sure I wanted to come off of it.

The broad hand fell from my mouth, and the man behind me walked me toward the edge of the water. With a palm pushing down on my head, he made me crouch with him. I stared wide-eyed at the muscular, ginger-dusted thighs that appeared on either side of me. A mountain indeed. If these were his thighs, how tall was he?

D-definitely a demon, Niusha, my own demon said.

I swallowed heavily. Too many sensations, too many emotions, flooded me. His right hand went out of sight for a second, then came back into my vision, but this time his index finger was bleeding. He rubbed the blood with his thumb to show me, then plunged his hand into the water. There was an instant thrashing and bubbling where his hand had disappeared, and he yanked out a mean-looking fish. I gasped in surprise and recoiled back into a rock wall. No, not a wall. A hard demon's chest.

The demon held the agitated fish in one hand and opened its mouth with the other, showing me a horrifying row of sharp teeth that certainly didn't belong in the mouth of any fish. I scooted more aggressively against the immovable chest, needing to get away from the nightmarish creature.

We were about to step in there! the demon exclaimed, then noticed something I hadn't. *Niusha, he has claws!*

My gaze moved past the awful fish to see that there were indeed claws coming from his fingertips. Demon. There was a demon, but he'd saved Tahmina. There was a demon, but he'd taken the oils. There was a demon, but his scent drugged me. There was a demon, but he kept me from dangerous waters.

There was a demon, and he had me in his clutches.

Chapter 5

Niusha

I stayed pushed back against the demon's chest as he quickly tossed the knife-mouthed fish back into the stream. Those giant, white, conical teeth were going to join my nightmares. I shuddered violently at just the memory of them, and my toes curled in their own cringe. I could have lost a toe in seconds!

The demon brought both hands to my arms and rubbed them up and down in a soothing motion. I stiffened at the sweeping, intimate gesture, having not expected a gentle touch. And no one had *ever* touched me like that before, not even any of the pure mothers who'd helped raise me. A hand tightened on my arm in response to my freeze, and the other moved to my head to stroke my hair.

That was also intimate. This demon was touching me… differently. I couldn't tell if I was being soothed, or if I was being caressed like a pet. I knew I had questions, but the knot in my throat seemed to have extended all the way to my brain. I couldn't put a sentence together to save my life.

I took stock of my body because it was going crazy. My heart ran dangerously fast, and my breathing became too rapid, but the latter was my fault; my continuous sniffing of the air was making me lightheaded. Still… I couldn't stop. There was more information out there, but my nose just wasn't letting me detect it yet.

When my head began to swim, I was forced to slow my breathing. Simultaneously, he placed a calloused palm on my chest and tapped it, like he was telling me to calm down too. I froze again and glanced down, wondering if he was going to do what Mehr did, but the hand didn't wander down my body. His palm stayed affixed to my chest over my collarbone and above my breasts. My brows drew in as a confusing thought occurred to me. I kind of… wanted his hand to wander. Why would I want that? The idea both revolted and excited me.

Maybe there was something about his touch that was different. His skin… there was almost a vibration where we met. No, vibration wasn't the right word. I shifted uncomfortably against him as some kind of hard bulge pressed against my lower back. Not vibration… Perhaps I'd call it a slight tingle? It wasn't like the tingling I'd get after a limb fell asleep, though. Oh, why was this so hard to describe? Everything about this demon was… hard to describe. I continued to feel like I didn't have the language of life yet. The resignation, however, brought some calmness, and I managed to push out two quiet words.

"Thank you." I had enough of my mind sorted to at least be grateful, and I slowly gained momentum. "Thank you for saving Tahmina. For preventing… that." I jerked my foot toward the water, but he simply remained silent and continued to stroke my tresses, occasionally untangling a snag. My brain nearly stopped working again when the thumb that was resting on my chest started stroking my skin in little caresses. This demon was so honest with his touches. It was like he knew something I didn't. I imagined most demons did, though my own personal demon seemed to be a little lacking…

Hey now, my demon protested, but it sounded just as dazed.

I heard the demon behind me inhale, and his rib cage slowly expanded against my back. When he breathed deeply several more times, I started to wonder if he was sniffing me like I'd been with him. I leaned away a little, saying, "I haven't bathed in days. Maybe don—" but he interrupted me by pulling me back against him once more. I felt his nose and mouth brush against the top of my head. The sensations of his breaths and skin moving my hair sent a shiver skittering up my spine.

A moan lingered on the tip of my tongue, but I didn't know why it was there. Warmth seeped in between every rib in my chest and dripped down into my belly. Whatever I was feeling felt… good. It felt more than good. The sound of his deep, curious breaths just above my ear sent the heat swirling around my abdomen where it eventually drifted down to pool somewhere intimate. It was as though a scalding hand had landed over my… well, the spot between my legs. My crotch?

A throb that matched the beating of my heart joined the heat. It wasn't the pulsing that I'd experienced after waking in bed. This one was achy, and it was awful, needy. It made me feel empty, and I pressed my thighs together, feeling confused and vulnerable but not actually wanting to go anywhere.

"What's happening?" I whispered to myself. I tried to turn my head to see what the demon looked like, but he stopped me with a hand. "What do you want?" I asked. I didn't ask it aggressively; I asked it with genuine curiosity. He'd helped us, so he must want something.

He didn't answer. He just heaved a sigh, and it felt like he'd placed his forehead against the back of my head. A hand slid up my arm to trace a spot where my shoulder met my neck. He tapped it a couple of times, but I couldn't figure out if he was asking a question or answering mine.

"You have my attention, demon…" I said nervously. "What… Do you want an offering? To keep protecting us?"

The demon stiffened, and I cringed, worried that I'd made him mad somehow. He palmed my shoulders, though, lowering them to force me to relax again.

"It's ok," I said quietly. "What do you want? If I can give it, it's yours. Tahmina could have been killed." I nearly choked on those words. I'd tried not to think about it, but it was true. I'd put these children in a very dangerous situation. Part of me was wondering if running away had been worth it. The abduction had been a brutal slap in the face for me. I was in over my head, and I needed all the help I could get. I couldn't believe I'd forgotten my knife. How naive, how careless I'd been.

A rumbling, breathy sound came from the demon after I spoke. I'd never heard anything like it. It was another first for me. The sound rolled up his chest and through his nose like a short rumble, but it had a sweet note to it. I imagined it was like a demon's version of a soothing hum. He made the noise again, and I just barely felt his breath move several strands on the back of my neck. Something feral in that sound called to something deep inside me, down to my very roots.

Something in me gave way to that call. I convulsed unexpectedly, arching back into the demon's chest. I gasped, and my hands flew to my heart, which had lurched beneath my ribs from the sound he'd made. Something felt like it'd awakened inside of me, overwhelming me. My lips parted, and a whimper escaped through them.

When pain blossomed into my clenched fists, I shouted. The demon grabbed my hands and pried them open. For just a second, I could have sworn I saw claws retracting into my nails. I shook my head and bit my lip. No, I'd seen them. They'd been there. If there hadn't been fresh cuts on my palms, I wouldn't have believed it.

"What's happening to me?" I sobbed, staring at my palms in disbelief. A dull, metallic pop came from behind, and the demon brought out a container that he tilted over my hands to wash away the blood. I stared as this creature continued to care for me. What was happening? What was going on? What were we to this demon? What was I to this demon? Why fixate on us?

"I'm so confused. Just tell me what you want!" I begged. This was all too much, too bizarre, too much like a dream. Leaving the village, I hadn't expected to feel like I'd entered a completely different world.

"Are you making me like him?" I asked my own demon.

I'm not actively doing... anything. Nothing about who we are has changed that I can see. Not from in here. You have... claws. I didn't... mean to do that. It just slipped. I'm... I didn't mean to hurt you.

"What?" I asked, breathless. "You did this? But..." I put a hand to my head, suffering another wave of dizziness. I groaned and fell back against the demon, who supported me. This was like having the purity drained from me all over again, and I remained limp in the demon's arms, trying to recover.

At some point, he moved us so he could sit and lean against a tree, still keeping me faced away. As I rested against his chest, staring up at the dark canopy with weary eyes, he started some kind of grooming. I heard him swipe at his upper chest with both his hands, then he'd drag his palms and fingers over every inch of exposed skin on my body. It took me a while to figure out what he was doing, and had I not discovered how potent his scent was, I never would have solved the mystery.

He was covering me in his smell. The demon was swiping sweat or something from his skin and was spreading it all the way from my fingertips to my upper arms where my dress stopped. He did the same with my other arm before addressing my neck and shoulders.

When his hands swept over my upper chest, he buried his face into the side of my head. Seemingly done, his thumb lazily traced my collarbone, like he was lost in thought. At this point, his touch only warmed and comforted. It was... more. Something continued to change, but it was like the entire jungle would find out before me.

"You covered me in your smell. Do all demons do that?" I asked quietly, but once again, he didn't reply. I didn't think he would. His fingers idled gently along my upper chest, never going farther than where the swells of my breasts began.

I sighed. Mehr had been more barbaric than a demon. Imagine that. He'd ruined my first kiss too.

Dung pile, my demon muttered.

"What can I give you?" I tried asking again. "For you to keep us safe. I'm afraid I can't let you possess me. I already have a demon in me." That last part, as utterly bizarre as it was to say, especially out loud for the first time, came out apologetically.

The rock wall—the demon's chest—bobbed a couple of times, like he was silently laughing. A rough hand slid to my shoulder, and he thumbed that spot again, that spot where my shoulder met my neck. This time it sent a tingle straight between my legs, and a massive shudder rattled my body, raking me from the top of my head to my tailbone. My underwear dampened horrifically, making my face burn with embarrassment. That definitely wasn't pee, I didn't think. Had that ever happened before? I couldn't think for the life of me.

I didn't know my body anymore. He'd made me feel so many new things in such a short span of time that it was like my body had also become a new world, a strange jungle. I sighed and shifted under my skirts, not liking how the accumulating wetness made the cloth glue to my skin. A new world indeed… and as wretchedly damp as this humid jungle. Humiliating. Thank my gods he wouldn't know, not that a demon would care about me soiling myself.

After a sharp breath, the demon tensed and promptly sat me upright to lean me forward. What was going on? I allowed him to situate me but jerked in surprise when I felt his face next to mine. I couldn't see it, but he lowered his lips to rest on that sensitive spot. My pulse accelerated and echoed between my legs, a merciless beating. I squirmed uncomfortably underneath his mouth, practically holding my breath. What was he going to do?

He tapped the spot with his finger again, like he was asking a question.

"O-ok… just… don't eat me," I stammered, some nervous sweat trickling down my temple. He wouldn't hurt me. He'd protected me. It wouldn't make sense for him to eat me.

I was startled by a warm, soft, and wet surface sliding against my skin. Oh my multiple gods of the sky and the ground! Was that his tongue? I couldn't hold it. It fought too hard to get out, and it burst raggedly from my lips. I arched sharply, released a long, pleased moan, and shivered violently from the shooting sensations he'd sent deep into my flesh. Each lap of his tongue had me convulsing from an entirely new physical pleasure, one that threatened to boil my insides.

"Aaah…" I gasped and tilted my head to give the hungry demon more room to take his strange payment. My fingers twitched, and I felt the urge to touch… something. Was it me? Him? What did I want to touch? I wanted the ache to go away from between my legs. My breasts also felt neglected, which was odd. I wanted someone to touch them—not Mehr, though. That thought was like a splash from a bucket of cold water. It jarred me, but it wasn't enough to put out whatever was growing in this moment. He was feasting on me but eating nothing. Why?

The demon released a new sound. He started growling as he licked, and though that noise was meant to terrify, it only stoked the sensations eating me alive. His tongue flicked once, twice, and then…

His maw must have opened because his teeth pressed into his obsession. Four razor-sharp canines pushed harder until my elastic skin gave. His teeth punctured me but didn't dig any deeper. He clamped a hand over my mouth as I groaned and was swept away by the most unique, rapturous pleasure I'd ever experienced.

The heat built just before I felt a release between my legs, and a gush of incredible sensations rocked me back into the demon. Rhythmic moans I'd never imagined making were ripped from my throat, and the demon's hands slid down my hips to grab fistfuls of my skirts. His muscular arms trembled as uncontrollably as me.

I wanted more, but I didn't know what 'more' was. Whatever he'd taken as my sacrifice for his protection felt like more of a gift than anything else. My body calmed, and I collapsed against him, but this time it was from a surreal satisfaction. I swallowed heavily as he released his bite and returned to cleaning my neck with his tongue. Perhaps it was a foolish thought, but whatever it was he got from it… I'd gladly give it again.

I wasn't sure how I kept myself from biting harder while her lush body undulated, writhed, in a sensual dance. Her moans of pleasure and the explosion of her scent from her climax had all my muscles trembling as I fought for control. I fisted her skirts to keep my hands from groping her, and my knuckles blanched from the effort.

Oh Sky Gods, grant me the strength to get through this, I prayed through the exquisite torture.

I had only wanted to perform a partial marking—a shallow, incomplete mark that'd last for a couple days, something that'd allow me to guide her without taking away her choice of another mate someday. That thought wasn't doing me any good in the moment, though. Picturing her writhing like this under someone else very nearly collapsed the last of my restraint. Both Convict and I knew that our temperance in general was lacking.

I let my marking venom seep in a second more, then pulled from her, causing some of her blood and my venom to leak out of the punctures. My cock swelled further from the sight of my saliva mingling with our mixture, but I released one last frustrated growl and lapped at the injury to clean it. I put pressure on it with my tongue until the holes stopped bleeding, then removed my mouth from her addicting skin, already missing how my flesh tingled when I touched her. Fuck... it made me want to kneel at her feet in worship.

I tilted my head as I regarded the mark, fairly certain I'd done it correctly. The venom would sit superficially and allow a bit of myself to leak through for a while, but her soul would eventually recognize the shallow invasion as an injury instead of a marking and heal it—I just wasn't sure when. From what I'd heard, partial markings were unpredictable at best.

Niusha, can you hear me? I asked, prodding at the tenuous one-way link I'd created.

She scooted up a little, still breathing hard and trembling from her orgasm. I put a steadying hand on her shoulder as her head turned slightly in the dark, her eyes scanning the jungle.

Niusha, I tried again. *Can you hear me? I'm calling to you.*

"Demon," she said in a breathy voice. "I hear my demon clearly, but I feel you... inside my head. Are you trying to communicate?"

Half of me was filled with excitement but the other half... trepidation.

Yes, I am trying to speak to you. What are you hearing?

Her head bowed forward, like she was thinking. "You're inquiring about... are you asking what my experience is like? I don't hear words, demon. I feel ideas, I think? Is this from you biting me?"

I tilted my head back only for it to thunk against the tree. Shit. I was hoping it'd be more substantial than this. My heart squeezed in pain, and I scrubbed a hand over my face, feeling so very tired now. How was I going to explain to her what she was? There was so much I needed to tell her.

"You seem disappointed... upset," she added hesitantly, and I glanced down to see her worrying at her skirts. My slow breathing stopped at those words, and I narrowed my eyes.

She shouldn't be feeling your emotions, Convict said in alarm.

Am I just... sending her fuck all everything except for words? I snapped and bristled at the implications.

Think about it. Your words are bundled into ideas. Thoughts or feelings aren't that different from communicating an idea, I guess.

Fuck! I cringed. Normally she'd have to mark me as well to feel my emotions. This was not turning out at all how I'd hoped.

I'll take what I can get, I'll take what I can get, I'll take what I can get, I chanted to myself. This was supposed to be a tool to communicate from the shadows. What mattered was getting her and the cubs to safety. At least I had some means of guiding her from a distance. I could still warn her.

"I'm sorry whatever it was didn't turn out like you'd hoped. Is there any other payment I can offer?" she asked quietly. It was almost enough to make me laugh. She was too innocent, and there were too many males who'd take advantage of that. I tried desperately not to think of what I'd like to do if I was a lesser male. No, I couldn't get any ideas around her because it might be possible that she'd just fucking feel it.

Thank the gods we found her first, Convict grunted.

Niusha, I thought clearly and firmly, *I am protecting you and the cubs.* I kept it simple since I had no idea how hard it was for her to discern what she was receiving. I also had no idea if the concept of a cub would come across differently than a child. If it had, she didn't say anything.

She seemed to relax, and I encouraged her to stand so I could escort her back to camp. When she tried to look at me a couple of times, I gave a warning growl and gently turned her head away. Once we arrived at her campsite, I disappeared up a tree. She turned to look for me, realizing I'd left, then slumped her shoulders.

When she'd finally retired and fallen asleep, I went from cub to cub and ran my hands over their backpacks, leaving my scent for their protection as well. Any exiles would know that these cubs were part of my territory as well. Those who knew me were aware that no one fucked with me. What I was more worried about were the males who didn't know my scent—who'd never heard of me.

We must remain vigilant, Convict murmured as I carefully lifted the newborn tiger cub from her padded wicker case. I chuffed quietly to keep her calm and held her to my upper chest, making sure she'd smell strongly of me. I sighed again, feeling that deep ache in my heart to have a cub of my own, and placed her back in her case before the feeling worsened.

We're going to have to be in better control of our emotions, I told Convict as I searched for a decent branch to sleep on tonight. I felt his amusement, but it was quickly overshadowed by bitterness.

It's going to become more of a challenge over time, he said shortly. *Worse when her beast emerges. I think it will be soon, Javed. You saw how her claws came out for a second or two. Our presence as her mate must be speeding up the process. Do you think the netacaria drugged and buried her beast? She wasn't dosed with it, but that doesn't mean she's never been.*

I have no idea, Convict, I muttered absently, letting an arm and a leg sling off the branch to cool down as I stared down at my charges. They were my responsibility, and I had to stay focused on their well-being. Their safety, health, and happiness were my priority. My needs came last, and my personal wants didn't even belong here—even if it put me in sheer misery.

It didn't matter that I wanted to slide my hands into her bodice to fondle the smooth, fatty globes of her bosom. It didn't matter that I wanted to wrestle her to the ground, lift her skirts, and clamp my teeth on her neck to show her whose fated mate she was. It didn't matter that I wanted to wet my dick with her heat while she kneeled in lordosis. It didn't matter that I wanted to be buried gum-and-balls-deep in her flesh—to not only give her cubs, but a permanent mate as well. It didn't matter that I wanted to curl up afterward and provide for her with all the affection in my heart. I had to shut it down so she wouldn't know, so she wouldn't be afraid of me.

I knew there was no muting my territoriality, but I could at least try to make her not feel hunted by my lustful thoughts. I folded my arms and buried my face in them. Had the partial marking been a mistake?

I was such an idiot.

I met the next day with dedication to my purpose. I kept a straight brow and a firm grip on my emotions as I scouted around Niusha and the orphans, keeping myself hidden from them as well. Convict and I noticed more exile scents in the area, so we stayed focused on intercepting any that would come within range of our senses. The bobcat and the tiger had gotten away from us, and I was under no illusion that we'd been forgotten about for a single second. The exiles would be chattering soon enough about a beautiful new female in the jungle.

If they thought she was worth joining forces to take me down, it'd make traveling a challenge. Anyone catching sight of us had to be killed immediately before they could report our whereabouts. Convict and I were strung tight, but it was a welcome distraction. Looking for a fight was a lot easier than dealing with heartache. I'd rather Niusha get a hint of tension from us than yearning. She didn't need to be any more confused about me than she already was.

I'd occasionally have to send Niusha a thought to pause their progress so I could deal with problems down the trail. I chased off a few predators and knocked a tree down to bridge a stream, allowing safer passage. There were more dangers in these waters than just hungry piranha.

Once, I'd returned to find Niusha wrestling a twenty-pound eagle off of Anaitis. I wasn't sure why that bird thought it could carry twice what it was capable of lifting, but I was certain it regretted its decision. I wanted to jump in and help, but she quickly took care of the situation.

She's toughening up, I said to Convict, staring at my mate's own developing territoriality with the cubs.

Her instincts are blooming, yes, he replied thoughtfully. *We need to warn her about frogs...*

My mate's nostrils flared angrily as she stared at the bird she'd finally conquered, and I could have sworn I heard a small growl escape her before she walked away and mercifully released it. Both pride and my cock swelled at her feral victory. Any time I'd catch the smallest glimpse of her cat emerging, I'd struggle horribly with my attraction to her. I placed a firm hand on my erection, pressing down and willing it to go away so I could focus.

I tilted my head in curiosity when Niusha's head snapped up and her eyes searched the trees. A blushing glow spread across her cheeks, and I had to wonder if my arousal had seeped through our tenuous connection. If so, that was... extremely inconvenient. Wrestling that bird hadn't been enough of a distraction during my slip in discipline. Well, shit.

Maybe that reaction was just from our pride in her. We should test that later, Convict muttered. *Because if that's the case, we're going to have to act like fuckin' emotionless rocks to keep your cock at rest.*

I'm not sure that's a great idea, I replied dryly. *I'm already at my limits for being tested. I don't think my cock listens to me either.*

Niusha and the cubs continued their march, but the older male cubs now formed a protective circle around a teary-eyed, snotty, and traumatized Anaitis. The one who was always teasing her, Fulco, made sure to keep her hand in a firm grip. I was glad to see the cubs pulling what weight they could despite their netacaria withdrawals. Niusha had her own hands full with the newborn, and I had to remind her to stop more often to feed and clean it. So far, the communication over the temporary bond worked well enough. Perhaps I was only a half-idiot.

I rubbed at my chest, feeling a little comfort from the gratitude I'd occasionally sense from her. There were moments throughout the day when she'd look up at the branches, and I'd feel a slight taste of her relief, like it took a burden off her shoulders to know that I was around and watching.

I'm here, Niusha. I'm watching, I thought to myself and kept the usual longing out of my purposely blank mind.

Chapter 6

We didn't get as far today as the first couple days. Not only were the children becoming tired, cranky, and sore, but Anaitis was very upset. She'd received a couple good scratches from the eagle, but it wasn't anything that a dab of ointment and a bandage couldn't handle. Fulco, Jam, and Gerhard had done well to surround her after the attack, while Sam and Tahmina stayed closer to me and the baby.

I was becoming extremely proud of the little orphans. They'd shown a lot more bravery than I had expected. It was a little hard to tell how they were feeling coming off the purity because our trek through the jungle was grueling—for all of us. Blisters had formed on our heels, and there was a leg cramp or two every handful of hours. I'd tried to be generous with the breaks, but after the attack, I was desperate to get them to a village.

The demon whom I'd paid—I think—to protect us must have been sent by the gods because he cleared a safe path forward like a scythe through crops. The children and I would occasionally be startled by one of his explosive growls when he scared off animals, but we became used to it. I had a hard time explaining why the demon was protecting us since we were raised to be afraid of them, but they were pretty accepting of the situation.

The demon was a master at staying hidden, but I would occasionally feel his presence from a small emotion that'd trickle into the back of my mind. Whenever Tahmina would babble and pout about how much she wanted to see her giant friend again, I'd feel a small flare of his amusement. Sometimes I'd feel fondness as well, which surprised me. I had no idea that demons were so similar to us in how they expressed themselves. He had an unexpected depth to his emotions.

As I started looking for a place to set up camp for the night, I also searched for reasons why he kept himself hidden. Why couldn't I look at him? Why wouldn't he talk to me? Was he hideous and didn't want to scare us? Was his voice gravelly and terrifying? I hoped he didn't think we were that judgmental.

Maybe if we look at him, we'll be cursed or something, my demon guessed.

"That would be a terrible thing to have to be alone for," I said under my breath. I placed my hands on my hips and stood in place for a minute, trying to decide whether to keep going or settle for the smaller clearing here. I looked up at the ceiling of vines, branches, and leaves, then listened closely for the demon. All I could hear was the buzzing of insects, the plipping of moisture from one leaf to another, and the distant sounds of monkeys hooting. He was so quiet and so stealthy.

My cheeks flushed, and I became flustered. Why did it… excite me to think of his prowess? Was excite even the right word? I cleared my throat and raised my voice to ask the demon a question. "Is there any water nearby? I was hoping to get the children clean tonight." I waited, searching for any sign of him. I was becoming increasingly more curious about what he looked like. I knew what his arms and legs looked like… and what his torso felt like. No man in the village was built like him. I shuddered and placed a palm to my forehead.

Great gods of the sky and stars, get control of your body! I thought vehemently.

I finally heard back from the demon who sent me the general idea of continuing down the trail. It was like a nudge and a sensation of encouragement. After about ten more minutes, I got a sense that he wanted me to turn left off the path, so I marched through the thicker underbrush until we reached a better spot to spend the night. I was urged to leave my bag and follow his directions to a short waterfall that fed into a little pool. The pool spilled over into a small stream that wandered off into the depths of the dimming undergrowth.

I beamed, unable to picture anything better than what he'd found for us. "This is perfect! Thank you!" I exclaimed in bone-deep gratitude. I cautiously tiptoed to the edge of the pool and wondered if it was safe to bathe in. There were large rocks at the bottom that could host any number of teeth with creatures attached to them.

When I took a last step to the edge of the water, the demon expressed a firm order to stop. I didn't get any details as to why I shouldn't go in, but I trusted him after my close call with the wicked fish. I certainly hoped there weren't any of those in the water. Even if I was only scooping water out, I could still imagine one of them jumping out to get me. What else lived in the jungle that had sharp teeth that didn't belong on them? I pictured a snail with fangs and didn't know whether to laugh or grimace.

Perhaps he noticed my disquiet because he reminded me that I was safe and under his protection. I put my cool palms to my hot face, not knowing how he pulled such strong reactions from my body. His comfort was… it felt…

I frowned and stood up to return to the campsite where I'd left the children. It was so frustrating to not have the right words! Something about his peaceful dedication tugged at my heart too, but I knew that to be affection. I was growing fond of the care he gave us, even though it was paid for—I think.

"Nini, this is the one! When are we going back?" Jam asked, holding up an interesting teal feather he'd discovered off the trail.

"That's a very pretty gift, Jam! Well done," I praised, smiling as I unpacked the cookware. I pretended to get distracted by pulling out items, but they were not willing to let the question go unanswered.

"I found this dead, dried lizard…" Sam announced, wrinkling his nose and holding up a shriveled brown object that might have been alive at some point. I wasn't willing to go closer to check. "So are we going home now?"

I winced at the tired whine in his voice. "I-I…" I stammered and nearly dropped the pot I used for boiling water, "th-think we're going to have to take the long way back... because of that man who attacked us…" I swallowed nervously and strode out of the site to collect water from the pool. Unfortunately, the children followed, showing their little treasures and asking questions.

"But that demon's protecting us now," Gerhard pointed out, leaning over the edge of the water to watch me dip the pot.

That reminded me of the better excuse. "Well, we can't forget about the spring! The sacred jungle spring. We still need to go there for the baby."

"Maybe this is it?" he asked and poked his finger into the pool. Worried about hungry fish, I smacked his hand away, and a growl escaped my mouth. I blanched and tried to cover it with a hacking cough. Though Gerhard had started at the unexpected sound, the coughing seemed to placate his alarm.

We did it again... my demon said. *I swear I didn't do anything!* They sounded like they were telling the truth. I'd known this demon for years, and I didn't think they'd ever lied to me.

I directed the children away from the water once my fake coughing fit had subsided. A thought occurred to me, and I idly traced around the bite mark the demon had left. Was this injury the cause of my growling? I told him I already had a demon, so it wasn't like he could turn me into one… could he? I glanced down at my fingers, making sure I had nails and not claws. Whatever was happening, I just had to stay focused and distracted. If I turned into some kind of creature, it didn't mean I had to stop helping the children.

I trudged back to camp with the heavy pot of water and took stock of the remaining rations. We were going to run out of food soon, so I needed to start setting traps. I pulled a book, some string, and carved wooden pieces from my bag, then left to find a place to set a snare. I thumbed through the book while walking, noting that I needed to find a spot that animals were likely to pass through, especially if there was a water source nearby.

"Oh gods," I muttered to myself, "what if this doesn't work? I have eight mouths to feed..." When I didn't see a spot that the book described, panic welled in my chest, and I palmed it, struggling against the tight pain of worry. The jungle floor was so dense, creatures could be passing all over the place, and I'd never be able to find a trail.

The demon's presence entered my mind, and his curiosity probed at my activity. He seemed to want to know what I was doing. I supposed a demon wouldn't need a trap to catch prey.

I straightened and looked around for him, but like usual, he was invisible. "I'm just setting a snare trap... for food. You know." I brushed a strand of hair from my sweaty face and searched about for a springy sapling to use—maybe I'd get lucky. I felt his eyes on me as I struggled to put the trap together. The illustrations in the book weren't that helpful, but I had an idea of how it was supposed to work.

I got a feeling from the demon that he wanted me to stop and return to the camp.

"I can't yet. Let me set this up," I replied.

He repeated his order, and I caved, scooping up the trap materials to use another time. I asked for his protection, so I had to listen. Maybe I wasn't doing something right... or maybe there was a predator nearby. Not for the first time, and certainly not the last, I wished he could just talk to me.

The longer we're out here, the more embarrassed I feel, my demon said. *We were completely unprepared.*

"I'd pictured a nice long hike that was peaceful and relaxing," I admitted, then burst into laughter now that I'd heard my thoughts out loud. It sounded so incredibly idiotic.

I focused on boiling water for letting the children wash and for making the rice milk. I pressed my lips together at my dwindling supply of rice, feeling stress eat at me. At least I knew what the plant looked like, so maybe I could find some myself. An urge to cry nearly overwhelmed me because I was struggling to keep us going. I deeply hated myself for not keeping an eye out for the plant this entire time. Why had I not done that? I should have been constantly working to replenish supplies. Was I going to be the death of us all?

No, we're learning! We've never left the village. There was always food, and it was always prepared for us. We won't make this mistake again! my demon snarled at me. *We will not fail them! We just need to get creative to catch up, that's all.*

I nodded, humming my acknowledgment of their words, but still struggled to restrain the tears brimming in my eyes. Anxiety cramped my stomach and worked to sicken me. I hated my mistakes. I wished I hadn't been so unprepared. I wished I'd stopped taking the purity when I was much younger. I wished I had worked harder to convince my grown friends to leave with me. I wished I had realized Mehr's intentions sooner. I wished I had kept him from touching me and ruining how I felt about my chest and mouth. Everything was making me sick, coming down on me like a suffocating blanket that was weighted at the corners.

Suddenly, a rustling came from above, followed by a warning from the demon. When a dead boar fell through the trees and thudded five feet from me, I started, shrieking like a baby. The children screamed too, but some of them recovered faster than the others. Sam edged forward and poked the fresh kill with a stick.

"Awesome!" he exclaimed, and the children crowded the dead animal in fascination. I released a short, crazed laugh and took some calming breaths. I tilted my head up to stare at the swaying branches and vines that had birthed the gift of food.

I supposed not everything was making me sick. He'd provided for us as well? I wiped a watery eye and simply choked out my gratitude. "Thank you." It wasn't nearly enough, but it'd have to do for now.

When I poured over the survival book to figure out how to cook the boar, I felt another horrifying wave of failure. That was right. I didn't have my knife. I couldn't skin it or remove the meat. I closed the book and stared vacantly out into the jungle, trembling from shot nerves. The sensation of failure turned into one of shock. It clawed its way inside me to hold all my muscles hostage. I knew I was capable of moving, but I just couldn't.

When some of the children asked what was wrong, I used all my willpower to address them, ordering the boys to go bathe with the soap and water I'd prepared. I told Tahmina to look after Anaitis and feed the baby while I went to do something quickly.

I wrapped my arms around myself and found a quiet place to cry. I let it all out as silently as I could, screaming into the soft flesh of my forearm to muffle the agony of my ongoing failures. I couldn't keep us safe, I couldn't find us food outside of what we could safely forage, and I couldn't even cook the bountiful gift the demon had provided.

My sobs chipped away at my body. It wasn't long before the crying wore my throat raw, and a headache pounded my skull. I gripped my knees through my skirts and wished I was a better person. I wished I was more reliable. Had this all been a delusion?

I felt a tug in my chest, and I realized that the demon was approaching before I felt him settle behind me. Once again, he placed his legs on either side of my thighs so he could pull me up to his chest. He released that soft, rolling huff and stroked my hair again, like I was his pet.

I felt an inquiry, and I figured he probably wanted to know why I was crying. I clenched my teeth, already neck-deep in self-loathing and unsure about my ability to admit to my failures.

I was humiliated. I must seem like such a weak, dumb woman to this demon, a woman so ill-prepared for survival she'd starve before she was able to figure out how to cook food. I cringed, unable to think of a more disgraceful way to die.

I think your reaction may not be proportionate to the problem... the demon murmured hesitantly, tactfully. It was a nice way to tell me that I was overreacting, and I tried to take their words to heart, but the failure seared. Why did emotional pain have to hurt so much?

I took a wavering breath and confessed in a mutter, "I don't have a knife, so I can't skin and cut the boar. I am mad at myself for being so poorly prepared for the jungle. I can't let these children suffer because of my mistakes." I hadn't planned on saying more than one sentence, but he got three out of me.

He released his rolling huff again, and his large, warm hands slid down my arms to cover mine. I flushed at how sensual the movement was and my heart skipped. I tried not to pay attention to his pleasant, balmy breaths on the back of my ear as he grabbed my hands and turned them palms up in his. The skipping of my heart dropped down between my legs. Oh gods, not again.

When one of his nails grew into a long, razor-sharp claw, I tensed. Showing it off, he expressed that I always had a knife on me. He expressed that he was as I was. A twinge of fear caused me to stiffen further.

"So you are turning me into a demon?" I pressed.

There was denial from him. He repeated that he was as I was. Not a demon but a... something. It was the most complicated idea I'd ever received from him, and I had a hard time pulling it apart. It was something like a cat being in a person, then that person was a cat. Sometimes that person wasn't a cat, but they were always a cat. Cats also had cats in them. Sometimes they could borrow the cat in pieces.

Something must be wrong with how we were communicating because none of that was understandable. I whimpered, feeling another hefty dose of panic coming. Was he telling me the answer, and I was just failing to grasp the concept?

"I don't understand what you're talking about. Cats within cats? People are cats?" I tried my best to keep a level tone, but I was exhausted, I felt too vulnerable, and I was afraid of coming across as a child.

The demon grunted, and mild frustration dripped from him. He took my right hand with both of his and gestured to my finger. He pointed to his claw, which he retracted and then regrew. He tapped on my index finger, and I felt a push from him in my mind. He expressed the notion of trying.

"I-I'm not a demon," I protested, but that only seemed to irritate him. He tapped my finger emphatically and nudged me once more. He repeated the ideas of trying and encouragement. "What do you think?" I asked my own demon miserably.

We did it before... they answered dubiously. *I guess we try to think of claws?*

I grimaced at my finger. I'd never wanted to see a claw come out of it again, but if I had tools, I should use them. A bewildered laugh nearly escaped my lips. I could hardly believe any of this.

For the children, I thought and stared at my finger. I pictured the claws how I recalled them, though it had happened so fast. I glanced at his claw while I focused, using it as a reference. It did look like a cat's claw. Dog claws were darker and stubbier if I correctly recalled the strays from our village.

The demon's left hand went to my arm as I focused—or tried to focus. He rubbed and squeezed encouragingly while he released little soothing noises into the back of my head. I bit my lip hard to keep my body from shuddering. It was happening again; my body was reacting to him, and I had to wrestle my mind back to my task.

He leaned down to inhale by my ear, and the breath he let out caused me to buck from an excessively pleasant shooting sensation that traveled up my spine. It echoed hot, damp, and warm between my legs, and an excited cry burst out of my lips.

The tips of my fingers became hot for a moment, and I bit back a shriek when I saw them. All my nails had turned into brown and tan claws, darker than his, and I scrambled back into his chest, like I was trying to escape from my own hands.

Happiness and satisfaction bloomed from the demon, and he nuzzled the back of my head—a very intimate gesture. It seemed like… perhaps he was getting attached to me? I didn't know what to think, but what I felt was the shock of having claws while my body became overwhelmed by the demon's touch. After I blinked away a brief wave of dizziness, he encouraged me to retract my claws, which seemed easier than growing them. All I had to do was scream at the gods to get them off my hands.

Once I was able to grow and retract them, he stood me up and turned us around to face the tree. He placed my hands on the bark and pressed up against my back so he could do the same. My stomach knotted from our continuing closeness, and I shifted uncomfortably from the ache between my thighs. It was becoming too distracting, and I felt an absurd, yet intolerable, urge to rub up against something.

Trying to force myself into focusing, I snorted through my nose and furrowed my brows, waiting for his direction. He grew a claw and ran it up my forearm. He wanted me to notice. I wasn't sure what he wanted me to notice, but I paid attention to him. Yes, that claw was sharp.

He reached for the bark of the tree again and scratched down it with all his claws. I watched tiny pieces of wood drift to the jungle floor as he repeated the movement. He shook the splinters away and ran his claw more gently up my arm. Oh… that was a lot sharper!

I cringed as moisture seeped into my underwear, and I bit back a number of curses. This was all extreme. His gentleness and deadliness were too potent, absurdly so. He was too thrilling, too forbidden, and much too exciting. I tried to slow my breathing and my fluttering heart, but my whole body ached. There were too many fires to extinguish.

An agonized grunt squeaked out of me as I repeated what he'd shown me. Though I looked at the tree I was clawing, I paid more attention to the broad body against my back and its deep breathing. His left hand found its way back to my upper arm to return to its slow rubbing, making my breath catch. I didn't know if I'd ever get used to it.

I really must not have been paying attention because I felt a sudden bobbing from behind, like he was laughing. I blinked heavily and he pulled my hand from the inch-deep hole I'd dug into the poor tree. I stared wide-eyed at the damage I'd inflicted and tested one of my claws.

Ow! Yes, I think we can skin that boar now... the demon said with amazement. *This feels incredible. There's something so familiar about this.*

I was more fascinated now than scared, and I scratched with my left hand, wanting to sharpen the other claws. The demon, pleased with my progress, moved both his hands to my shoulders now, massaging them while I prepared my knives. Part of me felt like a new person, and the other part of me remained in shock. The claws were horrifying, but beautiful. My mind felt like it had split in half, but whatever I was becoming, my goal still stood firm. I would do anything to get those children to safety. If I had to embrace some strange inner demon, I'd do it.

Speaking of embracing demons, the one behind me had moved closer. When his body pressed into my upper back and bottom, I fumbled to brace myself against the tree, gasping quietly. Just him shifting his weight back there, reminding me of his closeness, nearly took the wind from me. I felt a burning need to have his teeth on my neck again, and I fought the urge to curve my back and stick out my bottom. More moisture leaked into my underwear, and my face heated in embarrassment. What was that?

Something faltered in his silence, and there was a wave of... wanting coming from him. Whatever I was feeling, it seemed like he was feeling it too, but it was much stronger. I whimpered as he pushed me up against the tree and held me there. My claws had hooked into the wood, and his large, calloused hands locked over mine to do the same.

One of his rolling huffs turned into a low growl, sending curls of breath into the side of my neck. I couldn't contain the violent shudder, and a tiny, weak growl puffed from my lips. I didn't think about it because my mind was trying to deal with too many other fires.

The demon's entire body clenched after that sound leaked from my throat. He nudged his hips into my body, pushing something hard against me. I didn't know what it was, and I continued to fight the urge to push back into him. I didn't understand any of this, and my body was in agony.

"It's too much," I sobbed just above a whisper. "Make it go away." I couldn't fight it. I couldn't fight what I didn't understand. "It's driving me crazy."

He jerked his right hand from the tree, tossed my hair aside, and bit into the same spot he bit last time. It was exactly the same—the pain, the pleasure, and the whirling sensation of him inside me. His hands flew to my hips as my knees attempted to buckle.

It happened as it had before—the heat, the flare, and the release. The rolls of pleasure crashed down onto me like a flood, over and over. I moaned and gasped into the bark of the tree as he kept me pushed against it. This time around, his hips rolled subtly in response to my undulations, and I barely made out his own quiet grunting and faltering groans. His noises vibrated into his bite, which brightened the blinding ripples of satisfaction swimming through me.

On the last releasing throb, he removed his canines from my neck, laved the punctures with his tongue, and stepped away, leaving only a hand on my shoulder to make sure I could stand on my own two feet after that. I felt something like shame come from him before it was quickly cut off and replaced by a message. He urged me to go make food and conveyed a sense of pride in me.

His hand slipped away, and I knew that when I turned around, he wouldn't be there.

There was a moment of silence between my demon and me as we tried to process what'd happened. When my demon finally spoke, it was with confusion, disbelief, and restrained delight.

Was that a payment or a reward?

Chapter 7

Niusha

I didn't know what the demon kept doing to me, but I could see myself getting dangerously addicted to it. Pleasing was the best word I had to describe it because it was better than stepping into a hot bath or releasing a really pent-up sneeze. Perhaps that last example wasn't quite right... but my brain was in too thick of a delighted fog to come up with a better comparison.

When I arrived at the campsite, I told the girls to bathe when the boys returned. I perused the survival guide until I found the right section, then followed the instructions until I finished skinning the pig and had eight sections of muscle carved out for cooking. I kept my back to Tahmina and Anaitis whenever I had to use a claw, though. I was already pushing my luck with the explanations I'd given the children regarding this trip, and I didn't need to foster any distrust if they thought I was actually a demon luring them away from home.

I was determined to keep my changes to myself—well, me and the baby. I smiled over at the newborn in the case and tickled her nose with the back of a freshly washed claw.

"You and I can be weird together," I whispered to her curious face, chuckling.

With the help of the boys gathering fresh, green wood, I built a grill to cook the meat. I felt a different flush of pleasure watching the meat drip and sizzle over the fire. I couldn't remember the last time I was this proud of myself. Yes, it happened because of my strange new demon claws, but they were my demon claws, and I'd put the work into extracting a meal from the beast. If only I could hunt like the demon, then I could be self-sufficient!

Though I didn't have any seasoning, the children raved about the grilled meat. I claimed the one that was slightly more burned than the others and saved the last steak for the demon. After all, he was the reason we were eating right now.

With an oddly satisfied body, my demon said with approval.

I nodded subtly and wandered over to the waterfall to place the humble meal on a rock. "Thank you for the boar," I called up into the crowded, sprawling canopy. "If you want some of it, it's here for you. Just don't let the bugs get to it first!"

There was a notion of appreciation, and I let out a relieved breath, glad that he'd been around to hear me. I'd hate for him to find it covered in ants later.

When we went to wash up after dinner, I noticed that the steak was gone and hoped it was a decent enough gesture of gratitude. I still had a guilty feeling that he wasn't getting that much out of this arrangement. I wished I knew more about the biting. I especially wanted to know why it did… what it did to me.

I shooed the children away so I could finally bathe. I felt like I was wearing sweat and mud like an additional layer of clothing, and I couldn't wait another second to slough it off like snakeskin. I ended up scrubbing my skin so hard that I was flushed pink everywhere.

I felt slightly shy at first because I knew the demon was around, but I couldn't do anything about it. If he was going to watch, he could easily do that without me knowing. A small part of me was thrilled, but I still asked my demon, "Do demons care about nudity?"

I don't… know. I imagine not? I don't feel particularly weird about being naked right now.

I frowned. Why was my demon speaking like they were me? "I'm the one that's naked. You're just in my head."

Right. Us. I meant us. Or rather, I meant you. The demon sounded flustered, confused, but I let it drop. We were both probably tired.

Strangely enough, I smelled the demon before I felt his thoughts. The breeze blew it toward me, and I sniffed happily while lathering my hair. It was a good scent. Salty, musky mango filled my lungs and caressed my tongue. It was another way for him to be inside me, which was an excessively provocative thought. Why did that twist my insides the way it did?

I clamped my jaw and my thighs shut as I rinsed my soapy tresses. Just the memories had me aching again, and I fought fiercely against the moan that wanted to force its way out—to call to the demon. My fingers twitched as an embarrassing question came to me. What would happen if I soaped my body up again while he watched?

I reached up and slapped my face.

What was I thinking? Was I really thinking about luring a demon? Could cleaning myself even be that exciting? I rinsed my hair one more time but finally felt something from him, a faint sense of wanting. It was the same feeling I'd noticed when he pinned me to the tree earlier. The notion was quashed as quickly as it'd come, and it was followed by some kind of emotional pain. I couldn't tell if it was from anger or sadness, but it was fairly potent. The fading of his scent made me realize he'd left me to my privacy, and my heart sank from both his disappearance and pain. I sat there for a little while, trying to make sense of his reactions.

Minutes later, the peace of the night shattered. A squeal of alarm made the hairs on the back of my neck stand, and I jumped to my feet, fumbling to get my dress over my head. The sounds of a scuffle came from the camp, and I raced back, my heart in my throat. When I saw three large men looming over the children, a rage like I'd never known set my blood boiling. Like the first man we'd encountered, they were dressed in loincloths, but the third wore one in a different style, a belted leather skirt missing the side panels. The largest aggressor had grabbed Anaitis and had a claw pressed to her throat—a claw?

More demons? my demon choked out.

I tried to duck into the thick undergrowth before I was seen, planning to sneak around and surprise them, but I was already spotted. The other two men had grabbed Sam and Jam by the throats, making it obvious they could strangle the children if they wanted.

"Seems like your male left the area," the olive-skinned demon with the dark brown hair snarled. "When's he returning?"

Our male? I mean, your male? my demon echoed, though I could barely hear her over the sound of my heart trying to break my rib cage. My eyes flickered to the children, who were staring at me with wide-eyed terror. I'd failed to protect them.

I thrust my hands behind my back when I noticed my fingernails itching. My agitation, anger, and fear were slowly forcing them out; I just knew it. I didn't want the children to see my claws. I didn't even know if I could bring myself to cut into another person, but if the moment presented itself, I'd have to do it—anything to keep the children safe.

It didn't change the fact that I was outnumbered. I wasn't convinced I could handle even one of them. And they had claws too.

I licked my lips nervously, still needing to answer their question. When one of them tightened their hand around Jam's neck, I fumbled to perform my best lying. Telling them that he'd be back soon would make them think he'd be gone for a while. Telling them he'd left for good would make them worry that he was closer than they thought. These men—these demons—had to expect lying in this situation.

I let my eyes dart to the trees behind them and stammered, "H-he l-left for good!" I clenched my jaw and began babbling nervously. "H-he said that it w-was too much work to c-care for us. He's never coming back!" I squirmed and stopped meeting their gaze.

Unfortunately, some of the children actually believed me and started crying.

Ah, poop.

The demon with the cedar-brown skin and black hair looked over and murmured, "We should hurry up."

"N-no!" I exclaimed nervously and gestured to the raw boar meat. "I'll c-cook for you if you leave us alone…" I continued avoiding their eyes and gestured slightly with a finger, like I was signaling someone.

The third man, shorter, pink, and freckled, looked over at his slightly spooked friends and snapped, "Just grab her and go! Forget the cubs; she's worth more than them combined."

No, no, no, no, no, my demon sputtered in horror.

I'd wanted them to panic and run! I hadn't wanted them to panic, grab me, and run! It took all of my remaining cool to look over their approaching shoulders and let a delighted and relieved smile spread across my face. When they all stiffened and looked back, I ran to the smallest one and raked my claws across his freckled jaw.

He hissed in pain and cupped his bleeding cheek. The other two laughed and rounded on me before I could get in a second swipe. I shrieked furiously when I was slung over the brunet's shoulder, and they ran off with me.

I glanced up, seeing Gerhard and Fulco falling into brave pursuit, so I screamed, "Stay together!" They froze, their horrified, firelit faces staring back at me, and it was only a couple seconds more before they were all taken from my sight.

I released a frustrated scream through my teeth and tried to kick the one who was carrying me. It wasn't to escape; it was to vent my fury. At any rate, the kicking was futile from this position, so I tried to think before all the blood rushed into my head. I writhed my hands as the blood drained from them, squeezed tight by the demon's crushing one-handed grip on my wrists.

At least the children are safe, the demon snarled, and I agreed with the same fervor.

"He'll take care of them," I whispered as quietly as possible.

The demon carrying me barked out a laugh. "Tigers don't give a shit about their offspring. He definitely won't give a shit about those cubs."

"Tiger? Cubs?" I wheezed. Why was everyone talking about cats? It was all I'd heard since entering the jungle. The demon and these men have all mentioned cats in one way or another. We did see a tiger, but a tiger was a tiger, a demon was a demon, and a man was a man. It made the back of my brain tickle—or maybe that was just the blood filling my head. I wrinkled my nose and pursed my lips, trying to get rid of an itch on my gums.

The demon carrying me guffawed. "Your nose must be broken if you thought he was one of you, rag-puss." He said that last word like it was a slur, but it didn't mean anything to me. My list of swear words was extremely short, though. I usually had to get creative.

He can hear everything you say, the demon said nervously. *You can't talk to me.*

I huffed out an angry breath and pondered the problem. Ok, I couldn't talk, but my demon had heard my thoughts on occasion. What would happen if I thought really loudly? Could I communicate that way?

Can. You. Hear. Me? I asked, shouting one word at a time into my brain. I felt like I was flexing a muscle I'd never used before, so it was awkward and hard to maintain throughout the entirety of the message.

Woah! my demon exclaimed. *Yes, I can! Turn it down a little, though!*

We can communicate! I replied in disbelief. It took some effort to stay focused, but I could manage it.

Ok, ok, ok, my demon said, gathering their thoughts. *We can't overpower them, so we'll have to use either trickery or stealth.*

I'm not sure how stealthy I can be, I responded with a great deal of insecurity.

Let's just take this one step at a time...

I frowned worriedly as I continued to suffer the bumpy gait of the demon carrying me. The prickling energy that'd sparked from fighting had now worn off and was replaced by stress, fear, and illness. My heart thudded in my head, unbearably heavy, and my vision blurred. The trip was torture, and I just wanted to be upright again, even if I was to be shoved in a cell or tied up.

At least the children were safe. The demon would care for them—or was he a tiger somehow? Tiger demon? Either way, I kept chanting it in my head for comfort. I swallowed, choked briefly on my saliva, and blinked away tears that trickled up my temples instead of down my cheeks. I coughed and repeated the thought. The children were safe. I just had to get back to them.

The sense of relief I felt when I was eventually placed on a floor, right side up, wasn't as pleasant as I'd hoped. The pressure in my head faded as my blood returned to the rest of me, but the entire experience left me ill and reeling. Wooziness and a mild headache lingered well after my eyesight recovered.

The black-haired demon approached with some thin vines and reached for my wrists while the brunet restrained me. I fought them weakly, like a woman who'd pretty much given up the fight. I was trying to think as far ahead as possible, but lies landed more successfully when you knew the individual's personality. What they'd said further unsettled me, and I needed to give my brain a moment to catch up after being upside down for so long.

"There we go," the black-haired demon said as he tightened the vines around my ankles. I fumed at their thoroughness. I was hoping I could maybe try to grow claws from my toes so I could free my wrists later. I thought I'd been really clever to come up with that idea. However, it seemed like my body held no secrets from them, and the self-loathing returned. Whatever power I'd felt before had been an illusion. Being able to skin a boar was nothing if I couldn't even defend myself against one person.

I did start panicking when the brunet wrapped the last vine around my throat. "Don't even think about shifting. You do, and you'll strangle yourself," he grunted.

I paused in my fuming. *What did he mean by shift? Certainly I could shift about if I got uncomfortable. How would that strangle me?*

It wouldn't. It's a weird thing to say, my demon dismissed.

I pursed my lips, suffering the bitter combination of frustration and fear. The anxiety of not knowing what to say ate at me. Once I opened my mouth, my path of lies would start, and I didn't know enough of what was happening to even begin.

I took a moment to glance around the space. It looked like we were inside a domed wooden hut. From the looks of the dry moss stuffed in between the woven sticks, the shelter was well hidden. Several grass mats surrounded the central firepit and some cloaks hung on a hook. Another hook had pheasant hanging from it. There was random junk as well—moldy bags, broken pottery, bits and pieces of traps. It smelled too, reeking of three sweaty demons.

"Go work on hiding our scents, Dash," the black-haired demon said to the freckled one. He turned back to look at me and grunted, "She's a quiet one, isn't she?"

I kept my face blank and did my best impression of someone in shock. Actually, I think I was in a little bit of shock, so it didn't require a lot of acting. I hadn't decided whether to play aggressively or passively yet.

"She should be screaming. She should be suffering like how her kind treats the rest o' us!" the brunet sneered, leaning forward to slap the side of my head. I saw white. My head snapped to the side, and a stinging pain washed over my face and skull.

More newness. I hadn't seen that coming. I didn't know that blows to the head hurt that bad or were as stunning. I didn't know it made ears ring. I'd never felt anything like it. I knew that some of the pure fathers got a little heated and occasionally struck their spouses, but if it was anything like this… why did they allow it?

St-stay focused, my demon said, sounding rattled.

R-right, I stammered, wishing I could touch my face with my cold hand. Would it bruise?

"Not even a shriek or a moan," the black-haired one said, shaking his head. "Do it again."

I ducked my head, but it didn't matter. His hand swung faster this time, and pain exploded in my cheekbone and brow. I gritted my teeth and hissed, trying to ride out the terrible reeling sensation.

"Well, at least we got a hiss that time," the brunet said. "I bet you've never even felt pain before, have you?" I glared at up at him through my brows, too angry, afraid, and humiliated to speak.

"This isn't any fun at all, is it? Rip her top; that'll make her loud."

That broke my focus. Thoughts of strategies escaped, and I panicked. My eyes snapped open wide, and I leaned away from the approaching demon. "I'll talk! I'll sing! I'll tell you stories! Stop! No!" I struggled, shrieked, and cried like all the demons from the village were coming out of me, but his claws found their way to my dress and shredded the front. He yanked the fabric aside to expose my breasts, and all I could do was fall deeper into shock, hang my head, and try to curl in on myself.

"Wow, pretty for a rag-puss. She should make us more than enough to get on that ferry now," the black-haired demon said, reaching under his clothes to rub at something.

"All rag-pusses are pretty. Breed 'em that way. Don't know why she's all the way out here, though. They keep 'em all under lock and key at the capital."

"So selfish. Save some for the rest of us."

"They're all dead inside. You wouldn't want one. Rumor has it the new king did a culling."

"We're in exile, in the middle of the jungle. Where the fuck do you even hear this shit?"

"Rubble."

"Yeah, and where does he hear it?"

"Dunno. He gets around, you know that."

What are they talking about? the demon snarled, growing progressively more worked up since my exposure. I was the opposite. I wanted to hide and crawl away in disgrace. I wanted to leave my body behind and never come back to it.

Ask them what they're talking about! my demon demanded, growling.

What if they hit me again? I asked, feeling my nerves start to catch up to me. My body shook like it was freezing, but I wasn't that cold.

Then they'll die! My demon released an unhinged roar. The situation had brutally snapped its mind.

For the first time, I felt the demon scrabbling at the inside of my head. It was like they were trying to find a way out to kill these demons—for humiliating me into accepting defeat. The urgent scraping harshened the more feral it became, and I winced at several pinpricks in my temples.

Something new flooded my veins, muscles, and bones like a rush of hot air. The sensation overcame everything I was, and I lost control. The tethers to my own body were yanked from me, and my form convulsed in response.

"What the fuck is happening?"

"Why does that look like a first shift?"

"How old is she?"

"Shit. Get the acpoama before she chokes herself!"

The vine around my neck tightened, and my lungs couldn't pull in air. No, it wasn't even my neck and lungs. It wasn't my body. I felt thicker, heavier. I writhed in my binding, unable to scream through my closed throat. Tears poured down my cheeks, and my confused mind barely noticed the herb being brushed across my nostrils.

"Loosen it."

The pressure on my throat released, but as soon as I pulled in a lungful of air, I inhaled the pure scent of the plant. My body continued to fight against the demon holding me until it was drowned with both familiar and unfamiliar sensations. Heat spread from the center of my body to my extremities, forcing sweat to stream down my skin. My heart tripped, then started running. Soon it felt like it was racing through my chest, dragging iron chains. Rattling. Vibrating.

The flat ground under me was no longer flat. The floor swelled as it breathed, and I laughed at first, but then I started bawling. It was scary. I was so scared. Why was the floor breathing? Had I been eaten? I looked down at my legs to see blond fur and choked on another sob. What was happening to me?

The demons stepped back and regarded me with wary eyes.

"Don't let me get eaten, please!" I yelled, begging for mercy.

"Looks like a bad trip this time," the now-green demon muttered. "That's going to be annoying."

"She'll get no sympathy from me," the demon with the giant hands said. His claws hung like massive metal hooks from his fingers. Little birds were hanging from them to dry.

"Also, been a while since we heard from Dash. Should go check on him." The green one pulled on a cloak and marched out, leaving me alone with the sadistic claw monster.

"It'll eat you too," I cried. "If you let me go, we can escape through its mouth!" Why wasn't he scared? Did he live in stomachs? This was a harsh, cruel demon, so a harsh environment must be like home. The floor breathed less and began to churn, which made sense because it was evil and wanted to fold me into it. The firepit breathed as well, stoked and fed by the swirling.

"Need to find a gag," the claw monster mumbled and turned toward a pile of cast iron pots that hid a litter of kittens.

The other demon returned but didn't remove his cloak. Instead, he reached for his friend's head, grabbed his hair, and slit his throat. Blood poured on the floor, a gory end to a demonic sacrifice. I tried to turn to get a better look. I was afraid the kittens would drown, but maybe the floor would rather accept the blood.

"Save the kittens," I sobbed as the ground took me. The blood had soaked into the quicksand. "Don't let the floor get them!"

The cloaked figure ran over to me and destroyed the vines numbing my hands. Behind my eyes, in my skull, was a nudging, but it was far too foggy, a muffled bid for my attention. I tossed my head and wailed, too terrified to focus as I sank deeper into the ground.

My body lurched, and I flew up into the air to be surrounded by warm rocks. A cloth draped me, and the world fell into a rhythmic jostling. I spent all my tears into the hard surface, laughed a couple times, then returned to crying. Noises and vibrations pushed against me, demanding to be heard. All had turned into a tangled mess, endlessly changing whether my eyes were open or closed.

Occasionally, I'd get a calming whiff of a fruit. The name was faint in my mind, but it was the one thing I recognized—mango. Its presence surged more frequently the longer I was nestled in the rocks. By the time the lurching slowed, my face was buried, coveting the one pleasant sensation available.

I was placed on the ground again, but this time, a soft object cushioned my head. My clothes over my chest were tugged at, and the cold sweat sluicing down my chest warmed. Small voices piped up, timid but urgent. Were those the kittens? These were bigger than the ones in the pots.

"Saved the kittens," I mumbled out, not sure if I was smiling or not. All I could feel on my face was heat and perspiration. More familiar smells surrounded me, but I didn't know what was so familiar about them. I'd just known them for a very long time.

"Is Nini going to be ok, demon?" a kitten asked and received a grunt as an answer.

"We don't speak grunt," I mumbled, then cackled uncontrollably. That was the funniest thing I'd ever said in my life. Nervous giggles peppered about the kittens, but I mostly just heard popping and crackling. There was another fire breathing somewhere around here. It seemed to be coughing. Someone should make it tea.

"I'm worried about Nini."

"Will she be better in the morning?"

"You're tall."

"Should I get water? Ok, I'll be back!"

"I'm so proud of my kittens," I murmured. Fresh tears tickled my cheeks. "They're so brave. So much better than me."

"Nini, stop…"

"It'll be ok, Nini."

"We'll make you feel all better!"

"Jam, get your finger out of your nose."

A large, warm hand tilted my head, and a cold lip of metal was pressed to mine. A sweet liquid poured down my throat, and I swallowed thirstily, feeling intolerably parched all of a sudden. A soothing sound urged me further, and I drank until nothing remained.

I tried opening my eyes a couple times, but the sights were so horrific that I closed them again with a whimper. Everything had slanted and stretched thin, tall. My kittens no longer looked like kittens, and I couldn't bear the visions before me.

"What's your name?" a kitten asked and was met with silence.

"He doesn't have one…"

"We should give him one!" a kitten squealed in excitement. Sharp, eager clapping assaulted my ears.

"What about Mountain?"

"Ginger Muscles!"

"Rooster!"

"Cloak!"

The kittens continued to babble, and I covered my ears to muffle the strangely shifting pitches. A soft growl quieted the kittens, and there was a great deal of shuffling before a last piping of voices.

They all said good night in one form or another and finally quieted. A large, warm body settled behind me and another layer of fabric was draped over me. The hard surface that smelled of mangoes—and now bamboo too—dragged me back against it. I could smell more now. The scent richened, and I turned so I could escape into it again.

The breathing skin under my fingers tingled pleasantly, and I hung on to everything inside this private bubble. This was a surface that was supposed to be breathing this time. This was safe. It smelled good, it felt good, and it sounded good. I held on to the rhythm of its pulse under my palm—its reliable ticking cradled and rocked me into calmness.

The rocks around me relaxed, softened, and an arm pulled me into a snug embrace. I thought I'd be awake for hours with whatever poison thrummed through my body, but there was something healing me right now. I fell asleep, encouraged into oblivion by soft, rolling huffs.

Chapter 8

Javed

I'm slowly losing control, I confessed to Convict, who was still seething over our mate's assault. He thought we'd been far too lenient in giving the exiles a quick death, going so far as to suggest filling their mouths with poisonous frogs while we slowly disemboweled them, then replacing their guts with more frogs. Needless to say, Convict's rage was almost as frightening as my fear of losing control.

Don't think I haven't noticed. I'll probably go wild the next time I see her shift completely. I hope she likes pain... If not, I'll swear celibacy. Promise you'll stop me, Javed. He didn't say that part as a threat; it was just a well-known fact that tigers had spines on their penises to induce ovulation. He was actually pretty worried about it and insecure about his mate's… receptivity.

So… we both had concerns on our minds.

I think you'll stop yourself, but sure, I promise, I swore as I looked down at my sleeping mate. I hadn't planned on sleeping by her side when we returned, but I recalled that the mate touch helped speed up healing, and I wanted to try to expedite the purging of the acpoama from her system. She'd reacted poorly—probably due to the stress of her abduction—and experienced an extremely bad trip. It'd take about twelve hours for it to clear, and the last hour approached.

She was soaked in sweat, and I'd make sure she bathed before they started moving again today. If she wasn't awake, I'd try to communicate to Tahmina and Anaitis to wash her by the pool. I wanted to do it, but there were too many reasons to resist that temptation.

I couldn't even teach her how to grow and sharpen her claws without risking a mating, and the more awake her cat became, the more she'd react to our fated attraction. I hadn't planned on renewing her partial mark so soon, but I'd heard partials were almost as pleasurable as full markings, and she'd been begging for release. It'd certainly been enough to make her orgasm the first time I'd done it.

It was also painfully obvious she'd never been with a male. I could see how she resisted her instincts, and I craved a way to explain it all to her. Even if I could teach her everything I knew, she'd have to be approached with caution. I wasn't in control of her destiny, though. Whoever claimed first dibs on her likely wouldn't care to be gentle. I wouldn't even have the right to kill them for it. If I went mad from all this, perhaps it'd be for the best. Maybe an old friend would be kind enough to put me down for good.

At that thought, tears threatened to pass through the threshold of my eyelids, and I clenched my teeth at the agonizing pain. It had me pull her closer, bury my face in her hair, and pretend that this could last forever.

I pictured her cooking all the kills I brought home, like the wild boar she set aside for me. I'd gladly cook for her if she brought anything home. She'd make a fine huntress once I trai— I paused that thought, choking back a sob as I struggled to pretend. Reality kept interrupting my escape.

I switched my thoughts back to her bathing. I hadn't planned on watching, but when I went to guard her while she was naked and vulnerable, she'd pulled like a lodestone. I hadn't been able to move my eyes from a body as lush and wet as the jungle around me.

She'd crouched so gracefully on the rocks, like the cat she was, as she poured water over her soapy blond tresses. I could only restrain my emotions and reactions for so long—she'd captivated me so. I'd wanted to climb down there so badly and court her in the manner she deserved. I wanted to help her finish her cleaning and groom her like a proper mate should. I wanted to croon soft chuffs into her neck and make her melt the way she had the last time I sank my canines into her.

Then I'd pleasure her. I'd pamper and celebrate every inch of her skin. I'd make her feel as special and as priceless as she was. I'd start with massaging her back, maybe working my way down to her beautifully round butt and slender legs because she must be so sore from traveling. If she was receptive, I'd slide my hands around to feel the soft curves of her hips, her smooth belly, and her ribs. Maybe she'd let me hold her full breasts and play with her nipples—stiff and alert from the cold water and my loving touch.

I nearly released a growl when I recalled that the exiles had seen her breasts. One of the reasons why I'd killed them so quickly was because I couldn't handle them living one more second knowing what they looked like. They were for my eyes onl—

Once again, reality slapped me in the face. Great Sky Gods, why was I torturing myself? I needed to get some distance. I couldn't grow any more attached than I already was. She had me wrapped tightly in her vines and didn't even know.

I think it's too fucking late for that, Convict said flatly. *We're in too deep, and when we return her to her family, it's going to rip us to pieces. Not because we're starting to fall, but also because no one will treasure her like we do—not even close. She'll just be 'another one.'*

This time I did growl lowly. *Don't fucking call her that. I can barely... We need to stop talking about this, Convict. I'm about to lose my mind, and we can't afford to let that happen.*

Let's get up, then. We can feed the cubs and get them ready for the last day of their march.

Should get there by early afternoon, thank the gods. These cubs must be on their last legs, I replied, gently untangling myself from Niusha so I could wake the young ones. Cubs were easily roused by the smell of food, so I cooked one last round of the wild boar and smirked when they came clambering out of their blankets.

Could I change our destinies? I thought hopelessly to myself.

Convict chuckled at the sight of ravenous cubs. Working like fuck to distract us, he said, *What cute, tiny predators. Always hard to believe they'll grow into fierce, great cats.*

Especially Tahmina, I said with a fond smile. *She's already drawn first blood. She'll be crushing skulls in no time at all.*

I ignored the pang in my heart of wanting my own offspring and gave the cubs their piping hot steaks. They delivered their thanks with their own names for me, which was an endless font of entertainment. I couldn't tell which one amused me the most—Ginger Muscles or Rooster. They had added Volcano to the list because they all agreed that I was like a fire-headed mountain. I was going to miss them, but they'd end up in a much better home, and I couldn't ask for more than that.

After breakfast, I carried Niusha to the pool and mimed instructions for Tahmina and Anaitis to wash her. Niusha, fortunately, had a spare dress in her bag, so I left it with them and departed.

"Is Niusha going to be ok?" Gerhard asked, coming up to me while biting his fingernail. I gently pushed his hand from his mouth. It was a bad habit. As the eldest, he needed to start learning restraint.

I nodded a 'yes' to Gerhard's question, and he looked down at his feet. I could tell the cubs felt guilty they hadn't been able to protect her, but they'd have to learn that guilt did nothing but weaken the soul. I tilted Gerhard's chin up, lifted my own, and stood tall so he'd understand he needed to do the same. I thumped a fist on my chest and nodded for him to imitate.

The cub—hardly more than nine or ten—sobered, straightened, and copied my gesture, thumping his own chest. The other young males crowded around me and stood at attention like little warriors, hitting their scrawny torsos in youthful copycatting. I grinned in approval and decided that now was a good time to attempt swearing them to secrecy.

I took a step back and pointed at each cub, then brought my fingers up to my lips, miming a shutting of the mouth. Lastly, I gestured to my face, then pulled the hood over my head.

"You want us to wear cloaks?" Sam asked, tilting his head. I shook mine, then repeated it more slowly.

"You want us to decorate your cloak," Jam proclaimed, nodding in understanding. I held a laugh back and shook my head again. I mimed the first part until they understood the secret portion, then I mimed the second part where I wanted them to keep my face a secret. When they finally understood it, they hopped around in excitement at being included in a secret—except for Gerhard, who crossed his arms in an imitation of me. Hopefully they'd clue Tahmina and Anaitis in, but who knew?

"Is that because you're embarrassed about your injuries?" Fulco asked with a frown. My smile faltered for a second, and I just shrugged. I wasn't actually prepared for that question. I certainly didn't want to teach them about shame at such a young age. I stood tall again and thumped my chest, which they repeated, and I nodded a last time, indicating a job well done.

When I went to pack up Niusha's belongings, the cubs did the same, eager to imitate everything I did now. They would have plenty of strong role models at the village, of that I had no doubt. The locals were hardy; they had to be with the influx of exiles.

I salvaged what meat I could from the boar and wrapped the cuts in broad leaves. I'd gift these to the village in thanks for taking the orphans. I'd provided for them before, and they were always grateful.

A rustling and footsteps told me that three cats were coming. The scent of figs and oud wood filling my nostrils and making my dick twitch told me that one of them was my mate. I tugged anxiously on the hood of my cloak, knowing this would be the first time she'd lay eyes on me. Convict and I agreed that we'd have to stay closer now, not wanting to repeat our stupid failure to protect her, especially with the exiles growing bolder. We just needed to stay as covered as possible.

I stood after wrapping the packages of meat in the extra cloak and briskly walked past my exhausted, stunned female. I tilted my head to acknowledge Niusha's presence, released a very short, formal chuff of greeting, and went to wash my hands at the pool.

Now would be a good time to change our behavior—keep our distance, touch less, build our resilience, Convict uttered, forcing the bitter words out with substantial effort.

My gut twisted in pain, and I spent a much longer time washing my hands than necessary. When I'd return to her side, it would begin, and I didn't want it to begin. I didn't want to lose her. I wanted her so badly that I couldn't compare the need to anything else—not even food or air. It went well beyond our physical existence. Our souls were meant to journey through the rest of eternity together, hand in hand.

I put a fist to my chest in an attempt to keep from hyperventilating. I'd never been so affected by someone before Niusha. She was supposed to be my beginning and ending, but she could be neither.

Niusha

I stopped breathing when I returned to camp, seeing a large man in a cloak hunched over a bundle he was tightening. My eyes

immediately darted to the children, but they were all relaxed, done packing up their bags and waiting patiently to get back on the trail. This was not a stranger to them. The wind then explained it, sending the aromata of mangoes and bamboo home to my lungs.

The demon had finally made his appearance! He wasn't hiding anymore—well, not completely. I just froze, wide-eyed as he walked toward me, but instead of stopping, he nodded, released his signature huffing sound, and moved right on past me. My expression drew tight in shock, and several of the boys grabbed Anaitis and Tahmina to whisper something into their ears.

I didn't even try to overhear what they were saying. I was just trying to process that he'd been here, right in front of me. Yes, he was quite tall, and whatever I could see under the cloak was… very muscular. His warm, tanned skin—almost bronzed—appeared oiled from the humidity, and my underwear suffered yet another flooding of something. My face flamed as it trickled down my thigh, but I couldn't put any energy into questioning it.

I'd caught sight of the only other piece of clothing he wore, which was a wide leather belt that had a flap of leather hanging down the front. It was like what the other demon had worn—a leather skirt that was missing the sides. I had to wonder if there was anything underneath it.

I'd barely caught a glimpse of his face. The hood went down pretty low, and I was barely able to see the tip of his nose, a strong, sharp jawline dusted in fine mahogany stubble, and a tensed mouth that I could only describe as sensual. I grew weak in the knees and stumbled over to my bag to crouch by it, placing a hand over my heart to make sure it hadn't beaten its way out of my chest.

W-wow, my demon said, laughing weakly.

I… I tried to say something, but I was at a loss for words.

I know.

I made a weird choking noise and squeezed my legs together. I liked him. I liked him a lot. Was there a word for this? Was it ok for someone like me to like someone like him? I reached for my backpack, but it was picked up by a large, calloused hand before I could get to it.

I received the notion of him helping me, but at the same time, a new voice popped into my head. *I have,* the voice said. It was rich and charismatic, just as alluring as the body that housed it. Though the tone was pleasant, the communication was stilted, like I was only receiving some of the words he was sending.

"I heard a couple words!" I gasped and looked up at the cloaked demon, who stepped back and tugged slightly on his hood. I sensed some surprise and nervousness from him, which was odd for someone his size. He cocked his head, and I was then prodded with a questioning sensation.

"You said, 'I have!'" I reported, a thrill rushing through my belly. He stood still for a moment with his head turned thoughtfully.

Second, he said. It sounded like a guess. He gestured to my shoulder where his bite mark was. I blushed furiously at the reminder of what he'd done, especially now that I knew what he looked like.

"Biting me twice made me hear you better?" I asked, and he nodded. His shoulders relaxed in relief, and he gestured for me to stand.

Time. There today, he said. Another thrill went through me as I stood, realizing that the children might arrive at their new home today! I sent a quick prayer to all my gods that they'd be taken in so I didn't have to worry about their safety again. I wanted them to be happy, and I wanted them to have a better future with better opportunities. I knew nothing of those things, but anything had to be better than where we came from… right?

Maybe he can... bite us again, my demon uttered. *So we can hear him... even better...*

I... agree, I replied dazedly.

I reached to take my bag from him and said, "I can carry my own bag. I appreciate the offer, though." He merely shook his head and slung it on under his cloak. The motion lifted the fabric, revealing the exposed side of his hip. A flap of leather also fell down to cover his buttocks, but I could see the slight ripple of muscles shifting with his movement, and I swallowed hard, sensing I was likely to faint if I stared for too long.

Muscles everywhere, my demon choked.

Time for you to move out, I said absently. *I'm ok with this one possessing me.*

I promise I'll stay quiet!

My mouth ran dry, and I coughed into a hand when my throat tickled. "Gods help my eyes," I wheezed. When I realized I'd said that out loud, my face ignited. The demon didn't seem to react to my very smooth, incredibly calm demeanor, and he turned to grab the bundle he'd wrapped earlier. I tripped on a root because I couldn't stop looking at him and whimpered another prayer when I successfully caught myself, thanking the gods he hadn't seen that.

You're doing great, my demon reassured.

Thank you.

I picked up the case with the newborn and followed the demon back onto the jungle trail, the orphans falling behind like ducklings. I let them pass me so I could keep an eye on all of them. I didn't want an eagle descending upon Anaitis again while my back was turned.

The entire time we marched through the jungle, I felt a vicious pull to be at the demon's side. The children had apparently spent a little time with the demon before but still didn't know his name. It was a relief to find that he didn't mind being called 'Ginger Muscles.' He was actually quite gentle with them, and every time I saw that being exhibited, more moisture would run down my thighs. I hoped the village had a doctor because I was starting to worry about leaking so much.

Early afternoon slowly dragged the dim sunspots across the undergrowth, and it wasn't long before the jungle started looking a little more… groomed. The path was now completely cleared of plants, jutting stones, and evened, obviously the work of people and not animals. Some of the higher brush had been trimmed as well, improving visibility.

When we rounded a bend in the trail, a village appeared in the distance. The sights, the sounds; they shook me to the core. I nearly fell to my knees in piety.

The demon and the orphans never broke stride, but I slowed, unable to process the jovial atmosphere. From a distance, I could see that the children were playing, and the adults were chatting, laughing, or working hard on one task or another. Everyone was dressed beautifully. No one was in plain or threadbare clothing. A man walked by with some lumber in only a cloth, but it was of a superior, glossy material and lovingly embroidered. Beads clacked at the hips. Even the clothes thrived here.

The homes seemed to have been built with love and decorated with a zest for life. I didn't see any clay and straw huts that would need tending to every time it rained. There were no overgrown patches. All the plants in the village were either part of a garden or purely decorative.

Tears pricked my eyes when we all stopped at the village entrance. I still couldn't hear anything the orphans were saying because my mind was buzzing. I had no idea anything like this place could exist. The people here were happy. They were actually happy. The adults… the adults had friends. They actually socialized, and I could easily pick out the ones who were spoused because they were openly affectionate with each other. The women didn't have bruises on their faces or arms.

No one looked drugged. They all seemed bright-eyed and healthy. Happy and healthy.

That was when I finally fell to my knees. I had known that there must have been somewhere better, but this was beyond foreign to me. I almost didn't understand it. Something in my mind, some expectation, shattered, and I couldn't even see the pieces on the ground.

The demon waved to the woman approaching us. Her stride was strong, decisive, and she radiated both power and confidence.

Her eyes flickered to mine, and she scowled, but when she looked back to the demon, she smiled in greeting.

"Welcome, tiger. Starlight preserve you. It is good to see you still live. What has you coming to our doorstep?" she asked.

Her scowl had shaken me, sent a pang into my heart, and I made myself smaller, hoping not to draw her attention again. The village had seemed so friendly at first. Had my assessment been wrong?

The demon who'd escorted us made a series of gestures and eventually crouched to write in the dirt. The woman's eyes followed his message, widened, and darted toward the children. After he finished explaining, he passed the bundle over, and the woman took it gingerly, still wearing a surprised expression.

Some of the other villagers approached, animatedly discussing the children. The commotion loudened, and one voice rang out, so sharp that it cut through all the other voices. I almost thought she was calling me at first.

"Nisha!" the voice screamed, and a woman came running up to us. "Nisha! Nisha, my cub!" She sobbed wildly, scooping Anaitis up and holding her close. A man jogged up to her and palmed the little orphan's face.

"Nisha, you've come back to us," he croaked in a thick voice as his own eyes flooded with tears.

Two more adults descended on Fulco, pulling him into a similar emotional embrace and calling him by a different name.

"Raju, where have you been?" the woman cried, and her husband pulled them both into a possessive hug.

The other children watched, stunned. They'd just witnessed that a couple of them had actually found their families. The bittersweet scene had us all in some kind of shock, and it was Gerhard who freed himself from it first. He turned to me and asked the question I'd been dreading this entire time.

"Niusha?" His brows furrowed in worry and confusion. "Why are we here?"

The children who were not being worried over by parents turned to me with the same questioning look. Both the demon and the woman—who appeared to be the leader of the village—also looked down at me, waiting to hear my answer.

I felt myself drift away as I opened my mouth. I'd just let it all come out and let the truth do what it willed. "The pure parents and elder were drugging us to keep us complacent. The purity is… bad. It's bad for you. When my friends started disappearing—our friends—I kept my eyes and ears open, noticing a pattern." I averted my eyes to the jungle because there'd be no looks of betrayal there. "I eventually overheard you were all going to be sold, so I took you from your homes to keep you from disappearing like everyone else. I don't know what you were to be sold for… but I decided that you weren't safe. You're not going back to the village and n-neither am I." I closed my eyes, unable to say more.

"Oh…" came Gerhard's quiet voice. I didn't even know if he understood my answer. I didn't know if any of them would truly understand it until they got older.

The village leader spoke up. "We will take the cubs and the newborn. Maybe we can find their original families." She raised her chin. "But you cannot stay. Your species is not welcome here. They've tried to settle our territory but have settled for sending us their criminals instead. To allow you in would go against all we've fought."

I was too numb to process that, so I just nodded and stared at the dirt by my feet. This was too much. Still, my goal was reached. That was all that mattered. The children were safe.

The woman's voice softened. "It is clear you are not bad, but there will be unrest. Many in the village will not be able to restrain their prejudice."

"What is it about me?" I asked, my need to know finally breaking through the numbness. The children began protesting the village's rejection of me, and the demon made some gestures to the leader. He drew on the dirt again, and though I didn't know what he was saying, I could sense his sadness and frustration.

She glanced from him to me in bewilderment. "She is unshifted? She does not know?"

That word again. Shifted, my demon noted, and we watched him go through another round of gestures and drawings.

The leader nodded thoughtfully as they came to an understanding. "Then you'll bring her back anyway. That is good, but do not get caught. She'll be… with her own kind." The last sentence was spoken with a hint of loathing, like she was tasting something rancid.

Chapter 9

Niusha

I brought the orphans to sit just outside the village so I could properly say goodbye. They settled into a half-circle before me with all their little knees drawn up to their chins. Gerhard was trying to put on a tough shell, but I could tell that he was feeling lost.

"It's ok to be mad at me for lying to you," I said quietly, picking a flower from the soil and playing with its petals. I was going to say that it was ok for them to hate me too, but the last thing I wanted to do was guilt-trip them on accident. "I've lied a lot, and I took a choice away from you. But it was my responsibility as an adult to make that choice."

I dropped the flower and opened the case to pull the newborn into my lap. "Did you know that they told Gerlind her baby died?" I asked them, cradling the infant for the last time. The children's gazes widened and darted to the baby. "I watched Gerlind deliver her, and as they took this little one, they told her she was dead but went into the next room to put a diaper on her. They lied to Gerlind. I have no idea how many babies they've taken from the pure mothers, but I can guarantee you that they haven't all died like we've been told."

"Why didn't you tell Gerlind her baby was alive?" Sam asked, tilting his head to rest his cheek on his knee.

I sighed and answered, "So many reasons, Sam. First, I didn't have much time to escape with you all. And… they were probably going to sell this baby too. I can't imagine they would have let Gerlind keep her own child, not after the decades of lies they've built our old community on." The children probably wouldn't understand the nuances of manipulation. "All the other mothers would ask questions and beg to get their own children back. They'd dig up all the old graves to find them empty. The village would turn into chaos. People would get hurt. I don't know if that makes sense to you all…"

It had me wondering, though, if maybe I should have stayed and tried to… An uncomfortable mix of confusion and guilt settled within my very being, as if I'd abandoned people I shouldn't have.

The newborn started bawling, bringing me back to the moment, and the children fell into mumbles. The demon's large hands startled me, appearing from the corner of my vision to take the baby. He strolled off, making soothing noises until she quieted. I swallowed hard at the touching sight and tried to force my heart back down my throat and into my chest.

Tahmina crawled over to cuddle up against me, and I gently addressed the orphans again. "I'd like you all to stay here and live a better life. I'd like you to do that for me," I said, placing my hand on the grass between us. "You don't need to forgive me. All I ask is that you thrive and look after each other. You'll be able to do so much more here. You feel better after you've stopped taking the purity, right?"

"Yes, Nini…" most of them said. Some looked like they'd only just realized it, like Jam who was scratching his head in amazement.

"I'm so proud of you all," I said and released a laughing sob. "You're all so strong and so, so brave. I love you all so much. Be good and be brave." I wiped away tears before they could drip onto Tahmina's nuzzled head, then helped her stand so I could give them all one last hug, if they wished it.

They all wished it. The orphans huddled around me, and I wrapped my shaking arms around them. I tried not to cry, but they were crying, and that made it all the harder to keep it together. I kissed their foreheads fiercely and guided them back to the village. Nisha's and Raju's parents received the children and guided them to wherever they were going to live now. They all looked back at me except for Gerhard, who stood tall and proud. I smiled and sniffled at his attempt to project confidence. Gerhard would take it on himself to be their protector now.

The demon returned the newborn to me, and I embraced her for a long moment before placing her back in her wicker case. With a heavy heart, I handed the case to the leader, who carefully passed it to another woman.

"Her name?" the leader asked me, raising a brow.

"She doesn't have one. Her mother's was Gerlind. They lied to her and said she was dead, so… give her a name that means 'life.' I think that would be good for her," I said with a quivering chin. I wiped a tear from it that was about to drip.

"It shall be so," the leader replied, tilting her head to study me. I couldn't read her facial expression, but the quiet moment allowed me to remember my own question.

"Is there a doctor in your village I could talk to?" I asked, shifting nervously. Rejection hurt so bad; I hoped she wouldn't decline.

"I will go get a doctor to see to you before you leave. Good luck on your journey," she said, but before she could fully turn, I shouted for her to wait. She raised her brow again, regarding me with a cool expression.

"P-please," I begged, this taking all my courage to communicate, "d-don't teach them to h-hate…" My plea had her eyes narrowing, her gaze so razor-sharp that my eyes shot to the dirt by my feet.

"It shall be so," she eventually said, and I blew out a colossal exhale. She took one last glance at the demon and muttered, "Brave mate," before turning and leaving—hopefully to fetch a doctor.

The demon stared daggers at the woman's back, angry for some reason. I sighed wearily and plopped down onto a soft patch of grass while I waited. My mind was flooded with so many thoughts, questions, and mixed emotions.

Sick? the demon inquired. I shrugged unhelpfully. I certainly wasn't going to tell him about my strange incontinence. The gods knew what was happening, and hopefully I'd know soon too. It definitely wasn't menstruation. I wrapped my arms around my legs and rested my head on my knees.

"Someone requested a healer?" an older man with a long grey ponytail said, and I winced slightly. I'd hoped it would be a woman.

"Ah, yes… I have some… questions." I eyed the demon at my side, and the healer shooed him away with a hand. He turned back to me, waiting for my question. There was no hate in his gaze. He just maintained a kindly countenance.

I took in a deep breath to gather my nerves and whispered my inquiry to him, worried about being overheard and simply unable to say something so embarrassing in a normal voice. He stood up straight, like a startled bird, and said, "Oh, there's nothing wrong with you. That's arousal fluid. When a female is aroused, it's produced to lubricate the vagina for sexual intercourse."

"Vagina? Intercourse?" I croaked out, feeling like my one question just led to a plethora of others. The doctor explained both, but that only introduced more new words. It led me to asking about penises and sperm. With each additional question and answer, my face became more inflamed. By the time my last question was answered, I'd buried most of my face in my palms, with just my eyes peeking through my fingers. My voice was little more than a squeak, and my mind was more than a little thunderstruck.

"Your mate should have explained all of this to you," the doctor said, bemused.

"Mate?" I asked, and he pointed to the demon's bite mark on my shoulder.

"O-oh! No, I think you misunderstood. He only did that so we could communicate," I replied, though this was the second time that word had been mentioned. Mate.

"Ah, so it's a partial," he said, still frowning a little. "Yes, that'll go away, then."

"What's a mate, though?" I asked, and he blew out a long breath.

"Shifters can have two types of mates—fated mates or chosen mates," he began, but I interrupted him with another question.

"What's a shifter?"

The doctor clapped his hands together, put them to his mouth, and just stared at me. I fidgeted under his scrutiny, embarrassed about my incomplete education. It looked like he was trying extremely hard to put his next words together, but my courage finally failed.

"It's ok, it's ok," I said quickly, waving my hands in an attempt to placate him. "I got my urgent question answered. I'll learn about all this later… I'm overwhelmed anyway." I laughed nervously and took a step back. "I'm really sorry for all the questions, but I really appreciate it."

"Are you sure?" he inquired. It touched me that he genuinely wanted to know what I needed, but I just nodded aggressively and faked the biggest smile I could, making my cheeks hurt. I doubted I convinced him, but he just wished me luck from the bottom of his heart and left. The older man walked back to the village, but when he entered one of the buildings, he started laughing.

How mortifying.

Ok? the demon asked, approaching me now that I was alone. I couldn't face him now that I knew what lurked beneath his leathers—a penis. He was smuggling a penis and a pair of testicles.

I buried my face in my hands and raised my voice. "I'm all good! Everything is good! Everything is great!" I figured that if I yelled it loud enough, I might even convince myself of that.

I couldn't look him in the… half-face. I'd just learned that my body wanted his demon penis in my vagina, and my brain couldn't function. I wanted to complete the rest of my existence with my hands over my face, not caring what I bumped into so long as I never had to look at the source of my embarrassment. I didn't care—I'd walk across a rickety rope bridge that spanned a river full of tooth-fish before I'd take my hands off my eyes.

A messy mixture of amusement, confusion, and suspicion came from the demon as I floundered for my next course of action.

"Stop thinking about it," I muttered and slapped my face lightly. I winced when my slap hit a bruise on my cheek and last night came back to me in a rush. I stilled and rubbed my cheek with a cold hand. I wished it had only been a nightmare.

The demon came to my side and pulled my hand from my face. He leaned down a bit as he traced the sore spot with a thumb, then growled quietly. He expressed his anger about my bruise.

"You saved me," I murmured, staring straight ahead. My memories were hazy, but I believed I recalled all the important parts. "I'd forgotten about that. I never thanked you… so, thank you."

He straightened and crossed his arms. *Fault,* he said. He was blaming himself.

I shook my head, "No. It was their fault."

Dead, he said with finality, but he was still angry. Yes, I did recall him spilling a lot of blood.

"I need to find my own home now, I guess," I noted vacantly. "Where in the name of all the gods is that supposed to be? I didn't even know that"—I jerked a finger back at the village—"was truly possible until now. What other surprises does life have in store for me?"

A stab of pain came from the demon, and I glanced over at him. He was experiencing a lot more emotions now. I wondered if he was missing the children too.

"I guess we'll go our separate ways then," I said with a sigh. "Thanks for your help. I don't… think we could have made it without you, to be honest. I owe you so much; I just don't know how to repay you."

The demon growled and shook his head sharply. He jerked a thumb violently toward himself, then pointed a finger at me.

No. Home. He sent me a notion that he would take me, and his tone left no room for argument.

"I don't have a home for you to take me to," I said with a short laugh.

Yes, he insisted, pointing at me again, then pointing north. *Family.*

My face fell, and my lips parted in slack-jawed shock. "I have a family? H-how could you possibly know that about me? I don't even know that about me!"

One place, he communicated, telling me that there was only one place.

"One place where…?" My heart thrummed uncomfortably.

Where found. He repeated the gestures.

"Only one place where you can find what?" I pressed, growing agitated. I wished there was a better way to communicate than this!

The demon's shoulders fell, and he raised both his hands helplessly. Something in him seemed to crumble. I didn't know how I felt it, but the pain echoed into the very marrow of my bones as he managed to communicate a single word over to me.

Lions.

It was out now, and there was no going back from here. My heart shattered to say the one word that meant we could never be. For the first time, as I thought of destiny, I wondered why the Moon Goddess would do this. Why would She pair us together when She knew lionesses weren't free to choose? I knew from my own failures what was possible and what was not. This was simply not.

Unsurprisingly, Niusha's beautiful face went from shocked to perplexed. I didn't know how I was going to explain all of this. No one in the village would volunteer, that was a certainty. I understood their prejudice. I didn't like it, but I understood it. Their pain came from experience, and now they were on the defensive. They had a lot to lose, and almost anyone who'd trusted a lion had been clawed in the back.

"What's a lion?" she asked.

Oh my fuck, Convict moaned pathetically.

This is going to be as overwhelming to her as that conversation with that doctor, I replied to him with a sigh. I scrubbed my hands over my face, careful not to dislodge my hood. This wasn't going to be a quick chat, so I wanted to get us settled first.

Camp first, I said to her, making my sentences short so the odds of a word getting left out were smaller. *Near village.* I pointed a distance away from its entrance. They were ok with letting us stay nearby tonight where it was safer. All things considered, that was fairly generous.

I guided us downhill toward the sound of running water, which turned out to be a creek. When the chorus of frogs hit our ears, Convict bristled, and I backed up a few paces, spooked.

Nope, I muttered to Convict and took us back up the hill to set up camp. Niusha didn't comment about the pointless hike, which worked for me. I'd explain that nightmare another day.

I placed her bag on the ground, dug a pit for the fire, and got a good blaze going. It was late afternoon, so there were some daylight hours left. I tensed when Niusha stood with a pot, knowing she'd be going down to the creek to fetch water. I reached out to grab her wrist, and the mate touch flared between us both, tingling and generating comfort. She jerked in surprise, and I immediately loosened my grip so she could wrest her hand from mine.

Before she could address the incident, I pointed down to the creek and said, *Frogs.* I paused and added, *No touch.* Lastly, I emphasized with a severe insistence, *Poison. Understand?*

She swallowed and brushed a trembling blond strand from her eyes. "Don't touch the frogs. I understand." She left, and I was only able to relax when she returned without incident. Realization had seemed to hit her, and she nodded in understanding. "That's why we're camping up here."

When we were both seated and ready, I started explaining her nature from the beginning.

Lions. I raised my hand up to show her how tall they were. *Big cats. Bigger than leopard. Smaller than tiger.* I made sure to pause between each sentence and forced her to repeat it so I knew she was hearing everything I was saying. It was exhausting, but it was all we had.

Tan fur. Males mane. I gestured around my head. *Long fur. Females no.* I sighed and rested an arm on one bent knee, gesturing to her with the other. *Female lion. Lioness.*

She frowned and stared at the pot of water that wasn't boiling yet. Bringing a hand to her face, she released her claws, and her lower lip trembled. I wanted to comfort her, but I kept my distance.

"Demon cat?" she asked in a whisper.

No. Not demon, I said fiercely, really needing her to stop using that word. *Demons don't exist!* I clapped to emphasize the importance.

She winced from my reaction. "Then what?"

Lioness-shifter, I asserted. I pointed to myself and said, *Tiger-shifter. Wait here.*

I strode off to shift where her eyes couldn't find what I kept hidden. Leaving my clothes and gear in a pile, I gave control to Convict, who left our hiding place to slowly approach her. My tiger moved carefully, and I spoke to her again through our weak connection.

My tiger, I explained. *Safe.* At those words, Convict stopped ten feet from her and lay down on the jungle floor. He did everything he could to seem gentle, which was hard because of his monstrous size.

Niusha just stared at him for a while, her soft lips parted in an expression that was hard to read. Fear reflected in her eyes, but so did wonder. Convict's sudden sneeze broke her trance, and a nervous laugh trickled from her throat.

"So it was you..." she murmured, putting a hand to her soft lips. Convict shook his head. It wasn't something he did normally, but he knew she'd understand the movement.

No. He's... I hesitated, not sure how to explain the shifter's beast half. *My beast. Other half. Own mind.*

"So this isn't you?" she asked, pointing at my tiger.

Augh, Convict said, *let me try.*

Go slowly.

Convict sat up, bowed his head, and released a soft chuff. *I'm other. Name Convict. You have beast. Head voice?*

She didn't seem to be able to hear him. Maybe that would require a third bite? I repeated his words to her, explaining that they were messages from Convict. Niusha paled at first, but then her eyes flickered back and forth, like she was talking to her own beast. Her breathing and heart rate accelerated, but it wasn't from fright. She was excited and amazed, as if everything she'd ever known suddenly made sense to her.

She leaned forward in her sitting position, and the corners of her parted lips curled up ever so slightly. After a moment, she blurted, "I have a voice in my head too! I've had one for... five years? Has it been five years? I've always called them a demon, though."

Not demon! Convict snapped. *Lioness! You! She is you. You are her. Same! Shifter! Lioness-shifter!* I parroted this back to her with equal intensity.

"I-I'm sorry, th-this is all so new!" she stammered and drew her knees in to hug them.

I was frustrated. I was so fucking frustrated. As much as she'd physically freed herself from her toxic village, she had a lot to unlearn. This was not starting from a blank slate; this was starting from a blank slate that was covered in vines and poisonous frogs.

Simple, Convict said, which I repeated. *You shifter. Two parts. Lioness and Niusha. Lioness name?*

"I didn't even know she was a she..." Niusha said, and Convict merely grunted at that. "I don't know. She doesn't know."

You will. She will. You shift first. I go shift. Convict stood and retreated to where we'd left our clothes. I returned to my human body, dressed, and rejoined Niusha by the fire. Her cheeks pinkened when she glanced up at me, and I did my best to keep my emotions buried. It was hard to be brusque with her. It went against all my instincts, but I didn't know how else to control my growing feelings and attraction. I was on a slippery slope.

You'll shift soon, I said, softening my tone. *You'll learn.*

"So what do I call you? I've been referring to you as... the wrong thing this entire time. You have a name, don't you? Your tiger has one," she asked, pushing hard for information I didn't want to offer. Once I freed her from the jungle, she might...

On the other hand, if I died without ever hearing my name on her lips...

I pulled the cloak tight around me and looked away, sick to my stomach. I didn't know what to do. I clenched my teeth as my intestines writhed and cramped from indecision.

"It's ok." Her tone gentled as well. "You don't have to. It's clear th—"

Javed, I said and frowned. I hadn't planned on saying my name. It just popped out, like she'd pulled it from me.

"Javed," she echoed. "It's a handsome name. I like it."

Fuck, the way she said it was like honey spilling from her tongue. I wanted to hear her say it again. I wanted to hear her moan it. I wanted to hear her scream it while I fucked her into a climax.

Lightning skittered through me from my mounting desire. I groaned and rubbed my brow. Definitely not possible. I brought a knee up and stealthily placed a hand over the erection that was starting to tent my leather loincloth, telling it to calm the fuck down with an adamant palm.

Secret name, I asserted, trying to tamp down my arousal before she noticed it. *Don't share.*

She drew her brows in and twisted her lips. "Alright. I'll keep it a secret. You can trust me." She laughed suddenly, which caught me off guard. "From what I've heard so far, my kind doesn't have a good reputation. It means a lot that you trust me." She snorted in self-deprecation, but then sent me a shy smile.

Trying to not let her smile affect me, I waved a hand in dismissal. *Doesn't bother.*

"I still don't understand why you're helping me. Won't helping me put you in danger?" she asked, moving the pot from the fire now that the water had boiled.

I set my jaw and answered, *Someone has to. Dangerous.*

She looked anything but convinced. "Doesn't make sense..." she muttered and wrapped her arms around her waist. "It's lopsided..."

We sat in uncomfortable silence for a while, and I poured some of the water into my canteen. I picked up a piece of bark, sharpened a claw, and started shaving the stubble off my jaw. Niusha glanced up at me through her curled lashes and handed me some soap from her bag. I took it with a nod of gratitude and gave myself a closer shave with the hot water and soap at my disposal.

The sky dimmed and she began to speak again. "I know you're keeping things from me."

Low chirps and shuffling rose from the jungle around us. The evening shift had begun, and the air gradually took on the sounds of different creatures starting their nightly survival. Niusha drew her hair closer to her neck as a chill settled around us. I stoked the fire, making it pop and crackle.

"I grew up in a village built on lies and secrets, Javed," she murmured, gazing into the flames but likely staring at her youth. "It's instinct now. You can keep your privacy, but if it's about me… I won't live another minute of my life being kept in the dark."

Well fuck. Convict grunted. *Now what?*

I flicked some soap off my claw and rinsed it with warm water, then looked off to the side, not knowing what to say. When I took too long to answer, she snarled and stood like she was trying to loom over me.

She hissed, "Don't be like them! Don't do this to me or I'm going by myself!" Something had changed. Her voice carried a feral edge that immediately put me on the alert. Her claws were out and tan fur rippled out of her skin.

I jumped to my feet and pulled at her dress. *Shifting. Undress or rip,* I snapped and held her arm up so she could see it. She released a strange, shrieking whimper and hastily untied the back of her dress. I pulled her skirts up and over her head, trying not to lose my mind at the sight of her naked flesh. She doubled over in pain, and I laid her down, hurrying to pull off her underwear and slippers.

Several villagers came to see what was causing the commotion, and I waved them off, hoping they'd understand it was a first shift. Niusha then screamed, and I rolled her onto her belly to take the pressure off her joints. She stretched and contracted as her bones shrank, elongated, fused, or broke to make new bones. I kept a hand on one shoulder and another on her hip to hold her in place, letting the comfort of the mate bond try to dampen some of the pain.

My heart clenched to see her in agony, but we all had to go through this. This was supposed to have happened when she turned eighteen, but that netacaria had kept it from initiating. I cursed her old village, wishing I could go back and set them straight in the most vicious way possible.

Let go, I soothed. *Let her out. Free her.*

Niusha's cries turned into snarls as she crossed a threshold. She was more lioness than human now, and I put more weight into restraining her. Once her tail lengthened and her spine finished its last alignment, the lioness collapsed in exhaustion, panting and licking her chops.

Big for a lioness, Convict noted, and I nodded, stunned and breathless by the suddenness of her shift. Niusha's high emotions had kept prying at her chains, and the lioness finally broke free. I settled to rest her large, warm head on my lap while petting her neck.

Beautiful lioness, I complimented her. *It's ok. You're safe. Just rest.*

Chapter 10

Niusha

He… he called me beautiful, my demon—I mean—my lioness said. She giggled crazily from exhaustion and exhilaration.

Yes. I pouted, a bit jealous. *He did, didn't he?*

Oh puh-lease, he's given you two good times. You can give me this.

Out of a need to talk, I mumbled, but she just laughed.

Look, he's amazing, but I want him to bring that tiger back out. I have a vagina too, you know. I think.

I would have blushed had I been in my human body, and realizing that made me snap back to the moment. I had switched places with my lioness.

I feel like we're inside out, she said, scooting a little to get more comfortable while Javed cradled her head. *I feel exposed. It's uncomfortable.*

Well, I have over two decades of practice over you. You'll get used to it, I promised, realizing I should be more supportive right now. *Have you remembered your name yet?*

Oh! My name... is Field! she recalled with a tone full of delight. *Five years I've lived not knowing my name. Well, I suppose you gave me the lovely nickname 'demon.'*

I... I didn't know who you were! You didn't know who you were, I protested. *Maybe I'll bring it out whenever you're being difficult.*

I have never! She gasped, faking being appalled.

She eventually lifted her head from Javed's hold, groaning in a voice louder than I expected. Even I was slightly intimidated for a moment by the power in her chest. When she sat up and stared into the jungle, she let out a huff in surprise.

Wow. My eyes are so much better than yours, she said, but I detected the tease in her tone. Even if she wasn't teasing, I wouldn't have been put off by her words. The dark jungle was no longer this encroaching black void. It was obviously night, but she could see so much farther and clearer. Her eyes fixated on the smallest movement of a rodent well past the creek.

Great gods, she murmured. *I can see. We can see. This is so exciting!* She sat up and continued looking around the jungle, her heart pounding from a burst of energy. *We should try to make a kill next time! I want to put these eyes to use!*

Field, can you look at those flowers for me? I asked, nudging her to turn toward the right. *I could have sworn they were red.*

Oh yes, she acquiesced but had to turn her head because her eyes didn't have as much of a range of motion as mine. The color of the flowers was hard for her to focus on, but they slowly adjusted to red. *This doesn't feel normal,* she noted. *I think that's from you. I don't think I can see red by myself.*

Wild, I breathed. *This feels so surreal.*

Better nose too. She turned to take a deep breath of Javed's scent. The mangoes and bamboo smells were still gloriously present. *I think your nose has improved. I think that's from me. You might be able to keep some of this when we shift back...*

She leaned toward Javed to sniff him, and I nearly melted when I saw his sensual lips curl into a genuine, pleased smile.

He lifted a hand to scratch behind her ear, and this time, Field melted.

Oh gods, oh gods, oh gods. That's the spot. Don't stop, she begged and leaned into his moving fingers.

Why is this making me jealous? I moaned. She tilted her head down in her leaning, and looking through her eyes, I stared unashamedly at how his abdominal muscles shifted with his movements. Oh gods, I wanted to lick them. I'd never wanted to lick anyone before in my entire life. What was I thinking? Was I going mad?

Field snorted. *Because you want to be scratched somewhere else.*

It's true. I'll admit that, but I can't be sure why! Just don't embarrass us! You're being very forward.

She broke into laughter. *Can't be forward with the wrong species,* she cackled. *You can't tell me you wouldn't want to cuddle and scratch behind Convict's ears.*

She had a point. He was a little intimidating, but…

Field exhaled a sound that was similar to a purr, though throaty and quite a bit thicker. She butted her head against Javed's shoulder, and he laughed silently, moving both hands to scratch her. I allowed myself to enjoy it through Field's body. I could feel everything she could, and I let myself relax under the care of his deft fingers. I still wanted to feel them on my human skin. I wanted to make him smile and laugh too.

Ah, I was turning into a desirous woman. I couldn't help it. I'd never met anyone like him, and he'd awakened something inside of me. Damn him and his penis.

Field and I were startled by the sound of two growling cats tumbling through the undergrowth a good distance away—closer to the village. When they shifted to their human forms and moved on to a new, intimate activity, I nearly fainted... if that was possible to do from inside Field.

Javed placed a firm but soothing hand on my lioness's shoulder and said, *Calm. Just shifters. Just mating. Harmless. Can't tell. Likely mates.*

More shifters? They were both very naked and seemed to be ok with that out in the jungle. Their collision was shockingly passionate, moving like they wanted to melt into one being, and mashed their mouths together. I'd seen a pure father kiss a pure mother on the mouth during their ceremony, but it was only for a second. This… this was nothing like that. They looked like they were swallowing each other's tongues.

I felt like I should be scandalized, but I wasn't. If anything, it seemed to chip a tiny piece off of my sense of propriety. Maybe it was because he wasn't hitting her or forcing her. That lack of violence and her willingness made it seem… beautiful. It struck me in a profound way. Could making babies actually be pleasant?

You should try that with Javed, Field encouraged, less impacted by the performance than me.

No way in the world I'd be brave enough to even ask!

You just need a little inspiration, she said mischievously and stood to trot away from the campfire.

What are you doing, Field? I asked, alarmed. *Go back.*

Nothing, she replied evasively.

You ok? Javed's voice called out to us.

No, Javed, I don't know if I'm ok, I said to myself as Field slowed and turned to face the campfire, which was now maybe forty feet away from us.

You see your dress? Field asked, and I spied it on the other side of the campfire with my underwear and shoes.

Yes... I answered warily. *Why?*

Go get it! She laughed and shifted back to me, which was painful but not as slow this time. I scrambled to my feet, completely nude and thoroughly horrified. Yes, I'd been naked at the pool, but I'd had a right to be naked while bathing! She'd just dumped me away from my clothes, and for the first time, I really wanted to punch her.

You demon! I hissed. I tried to shift back into her, but she fought me, laughing wickedly at every one of my attempts. I gave up and made a run for it, ignoring Javed's gaping mouth. I had an arm wrapped over my breasts and a hand over my privates.

"Damn you, damn you, damn you!" I hissed under my breath at her while I ran, trying to minimize the embarrassing jiggling of my feminine parts. My face heated as I eventually passed the man who I'd not planned on seeing me in such an undignified state. I fumbled for my dress, shoved it over my head and wriggled it down until I was properly covered. Then, scowling, I slipped on my shoes and grabbed my underwear to put it on behind a tree.

What... Javed, sounding bewildered, repeated, *You ok?*

I leaned against the tree, panting and fuming. Oh gods, that had been so mortifying. I smoothed my skirts and returned to the campfire with a pinched face. He repeated his question, and I just nodded, sat, and drew my knees up to my chin.

What happened? he asked, more curious than confused now.

"My awful lioness pulled a prank on me," I muttered into my arms. I could tell that he was a little excited, but that was probably because of the shifters rolling around in the jungle. To make matters worse, their moans of pleasure had gotten louder. I buried my face in my arms as if that'd make them go away, but I could still hear them quite clearly.

Nudity natural, he said in a generous attempt to console me. *Shifters comfortable.*

"They certainly seem to be," I muttered, then gestured blindly to the couple while keeping my face buried. "Is... that normal?"

Often do. In nature? Natural. Normal, he answered, sounding a little distracted. The couple had quieted, and I took a peek to see if they were done. They were not. She had crawled onto all fours, breathing heavily, and arched her back to stick her butt into the air. When he kneeled behind her and gripped her hips, I caught sight of something I'd never seen before and couldn't even bring myself to blink.

"Oh my own personal gods, that's a penis," I wheezed and slapped both my hands over my mouth. "It's huge." I nearly shrieked as he made it disappear between her legs, though even if I had, it would have been buried under her cry of pleasure.

A small growl came from Javed, and I whipped my head around to look at him. His jaw tightened, and the side of an upper lip twitched, like he was fighting a snarl. Some firelight flickered under the shadow of his hood and reflected sharply on a partially hidden eye. He was looking at me like… like… I don't know! His stare narrowed with tension, like he was about to pounce. His crossed arms twitched, and he sat unnervingly still, as on edge as I felt.

My stomach was writhing in knots, and the arousal in the air became unbearable. The slapping and moaning of the two shifters increased in pace, and I desperately searched for something to say—something to break the tension.

"D-do they kn-kn-know we're h-here?" I stammered quietly, almost unable to handle his hooded gaze. His head tilted ever so slightly as he examined me. I adjusted my seating uncomfortably as my underwear dampened again. Just looking at his smooth lips put me in a state of wanting.

They know. Don't care. Or show off, he explained tersely.

"O-oh…" I swallowed hard and grimaced when the man started talking to the woman through his grunts and gasps. I didn't understand half of it, but what I did made my face erupt into flames.

"Why are they talking about cocks and pussy cats?" I asked weakly. "N-never mind. Maybe I don't want to know."

Slang. Sex organs, Javed said, still watching me with an intensity I couldn't escape. *Cock's penis. Pussy's vagina.*

I was going to die. It was vulgar, it was embarrassing, and it was amazing. I was getting thrown into the waters of sex education, and I couldn't find air to breathe. I whimpered and drew my legs closer, like that'd slow the flood of my arousal. Everything ached and pulsed. My breasts ached, my clit ached, and I suffered that deep feeling of emptiness all over again.

My eyes flickered around our campsite because I didn't know where to look. I couldn't look at Javed because he was still staring at me, breathing deeply with an arm slung over his lap. I could hear his heart pounding, though. I'd give anything to know what he was thinking.

They were moaning, crying, and slapping together now. Javed cracked his knuckles as his body appeared to tauten. Why were we just sitting here listening to them? I should be doing something. I fumbled for my bag, shaking almost violently from nerves and excitement. I had half a mind to turn and get on all fours myself, and that was a sign that I definitely needed a distraction.

I froze, though, when the man yelled and the woman screamed. If I hadn't known any better, I would have thought they were dying. My eyes had locked unwillingly onto what I could see of Javed's eyes, and the crowded muscles of his tight abdomen contracted at their cries, like he was holding his breath. I just realized I was holding onto mine and released it with a huge, embarrassing exhale. Their noises subsided, and the jungle fell to a deafening silence.

Javed released his and was breathing heavier now. His heart raced mine. When he stood abruptly, I fell over with a squeak, startled due to shot nerves. He just looked down at me with a gaze both cool and heated, and said, *Hunt now. For food.*

Why couldn't you have done that earlier? I lamented and buried my red face in my arms again.

Javed left and I busied myself with building another green-wood grill. My mind replayed the last hour over and over again. I paused every time I recalled how he hastily jerked my dress over my head and laid me on the ground so he could remove my underwear. A wobbly whimper escaped my lips as I notched a piece of wood to fit into another piece. His hands were so big and so, so warm.

It was too much! My muscles remained tied in rigid knots as my brain mercilessly combined everything into one forbidden fantasy. In my new version, he looked at me with that burning intensity again and yanked my dress off, but I scrambled away and ran into the jungle to see if he thought I was worth pursuing. He decided that he couldn't live another second without me and hunted me down, pounced and then… well, I had a hard time imagining the sex, since I'd never done it. I had no idea what he looked like under that flap of leather he wore or how sex would feel, but I struggled to calm myself after those two shifters had collided. I wasn't sure my underwear would ever dry.

"It's just because it's all new, and he's gorgeous," I whispered, placing the last green stick. I kept repeating it while taking deep breaths. "It's new and therefore exciting. That's all."

I doubt that, Field mused. *I think he's special.*

Of course he's special. He's an enormous, muscular, protective, providing man. No one in the village has… Oh my gods, did anyone from our village have any of those traits? At all?

Mehr certainly hadn't protected you, Field said darkly.

The reminder punched me in the gut, and I bit back tears. His betrayal still stung. He'd promised… He'd promised he would help me avoid becoming a pure mother. He'd lied when he'd offered his protection. I wrapped my arms around my breasts again, still able to feel his touch. Nausea clawed at my belly like it wanted to scour my insides clean.

You don't think Javed would betray us like that? I asked, clenching my teeth, angry that my chin had started to wobble. No matter how strong I tried to stay, I always crumbled into tears.

Based on your fantasies, I can hardly picture you being unreceptive, she said dryly.

That wasn't what I m-meant! I replied defensively. *Betray us in general.*

I'm starting to think he'd sacrifice a lot for us, actually. She quieted in her pondering.

What do you mean, Field? I asked, and when she didn't reply, I prompted her again. *Field?*

I think he's ours, she blurted.

I froze in the process of stoking the campfire. *I don't understand. What do you mean by 'ours?'*

I have this instinct that recently... flared up? It's telling me that he's supposed to be our spouse or something. Field sounded a little shy about it, like she was expecting ridicule.

That sounds a little odd, don't you think? That was far too convenient considering my growing attraction to him. *I don't think you've ever lied to me, so I have to wonder if maybe you misinterpreted it? I've been struggling with arousal, so mayb—*

Look, I said what I said, and I stand by it, so think what you like. She was surprisingly unyielding, so I let it drop for now. It wasn't really something one could prove anyway. I'd only ever known arranged spousing. I had no idea how spousing was done outside the village. I especially didn't know how it was done for my kind. My kind—that was extremely weird to think.

Just remembering Mehr had sucked all the energy out of me, and by the time Javed returned with a small deer, I was feeling a little listless. I didn't like how memories of my betrayer made my body and mind react, and I just wanted to drift away on the night breeze. I wished there was a way to wipe my body clear of him. I left to be free of the village, but somehow a part of the village had left with me. I wasn't sure if a thousand baths would be enough.

After cooking and eating with minimal communication, I thanked Javed for the food and curled up into my blanket, hollow in body and mind. Though he looked concerned, he didn't ask any questions and retired across the campfire, facing away from me with his hood drawn tight. I craved a place by his side, but that feeling was easy to fight in my tired, numb state. It wasn't like he was going to let me in anyway. How could I possibly be spoused to someone who kept me at a distance? Field had to be wrong. Either that or she was pranking me again.

I woke to the sound of low chatter and the robust smell of a dead campfire. I gazed up through the canopy, realizing that it was a little later in the day than when I usually woke. Javed must have let me sleep in a bit. I needed it. After days of traveling, my body screamed for rest.

I rose and tried to tidy myself. The sky was still a sparkling blue wherever it managed to peek through the vines and leaves, but a smattering of grey had me worried that rain was coming. How did one find refuge in a deluge?

I finished freshening up with what was left of the boiled water and went to find Javed. I could smell him, so he had to be nearby. I followed it, realizing that my nose had sensitized quite a bit since last night. A lot of things felt different, actually. Aside from some changes in vision, hearing, and smelling, I felt more in tune with my body. Field was just under my skin, not just ready to shift at a moment's notice, but properly settled in to live life alongside me. Except for the small, empty part of me that craved Javed, I felt whole. Maybe if I got over my liking of him, I'd feel completely whole.

Something about that tasted bitter, though.

The village leader and several villagers had been the source of the talking I'd heard, and it seemed like Javed was wrapping up a conversation with them. I didn't approach, knowing that they wouldn't appreciate my presence. That still hurt. My nose stung, and I blinked away tears, already aching from the potential rejection.

Javed's head turned, spying me past his shoulder and taking note of my arrival. I immediately looked down at my feet and waited patiently for them to be done so we could leave. I really wanted to peek past the village gates to try to find any of my little friends, but I knew that'd be frowned upon as well. I peered back up to see Javed write one last message into the dirt and shake hands with the leader. A villager handed him a leather bag, and he made a gesture of gratitude.

I flinched when the leader's sharp eyes locked onto mine. Instead of sneering or scowling, she simply nodded and turned to leave with the others. I exhaled what remained in my lungs, not realizing that my legs had been shaking. Javed grabbed my arm, which made pleasurable tingles erupt wherever he touched.

"Ah!" I recoiled in surprise, startled by the sensation. It wasn't the first time it'd happened either. He jerked his hand away and raised both in apology. "What was that?" I asked. "I've felt that before!"

He continued past me, and I ran to catch up, staring at what I could see of his profile. His lips were drawn and rigid with tension. "Javed?" I asked in a whisper, not liking the frustration rolling off him.

We arrived at our little campsite, and he thrust the bag he'd received from the villagers at me.

Parting gifts. From orphans, he explained rigidly. His face hadn't changed, but I didn't give it another thought after what he'd just said. I snatched the bag and plopped onto the ground, eager to see its contents. I knew Jam had found a feather, but I wasn't sure what I'd do with Sam's dead lizard. I hadn't really paid attention to what the other orphans had shown me because I'd been preoccupied at the time, but it was sweet they'd chosen to give me their little treasures instead.

When I opened the flap and pried it wide, I gaped at the surprise. No, these definitely were not what they'd found on the trail. I bit my lip, touched by the obvious effort they'd put into this, and shuffled through the bag to see everything.

Cubs made. Adults helped, Javed said quietly as I sniffled like a weepy child. There were two very simple dresses that looked like what some of the village women had been wearing. It was an odd design, without sleeves or shoulder straps, but two braided straps appeared to be meant for tying around the neck.

Halters, Javed explained. *Easy removal. Shift quick.*

I nodded vacantly and rubbed the pretty fabric between my fingers. It was simple, but the azure dye was rich, and the pineapple-yellow stitching was striking. They'd be easier to clean than the one I wore too. I was a little embarrassed about the slits and how they'd fall mid-thigh, but I had to admit that it'd make moving easier. Maybe the world outside of the village didn't find this amount of leg scandalous. I supposed I shouldn't be picky in the middle of the jungle.

There was a cloak made from a heavier fabric and dyed a dark green that reminded me of basil.

Help blend. Jungle color, Javed commented as he packed up our camp. I knew it'd also help keep me dry, which was well timed considering the state of the sky. The last thing I needed was to catch a cold out here.

The rest of the gifts were individually wrapped loaves of bread and sweet-smelling baked items. I hummed when I breathed in the unfamiliar, rich aromata. I'd definitely try one tonight—I didn't have much of an appetite this morning.

Lastly, my fingers fell upon the hard edge of a note. Anxiety crept back into me as I opened it, hoping it wouldn't be an unkind message from the villagers. I knew not all of the children had learned to read and write yet.

"Huh?" I turned the note upside down, then sideways, but I still couldn't read it. I flipped it around and held it up to the sky to see through the paper. No, that didn't help either. Maybe they were drawings? Had the children drawn me little pictures? Some repeated, like letters that made words, but I didn't recognize any of them.

What's wrong? Javed asked, appearing over my shoulder. I started in surprise but then handed it to him.

"I don't know what this is. I found it in the bag," I said, wondering if he had any ideas.

What mean? This letter. You read. He held the note out for me to take.

"No, this isn't a letter. Those aren't words," I argued.

He frowned and tilted his head to adjust his hood. *Show me. Your book,* he ordered, pointing to the bag on my left. I pulled out my survival guide and handed it to him. His breath caught when he took a closer look, then he exhaled as scorn settled onto what I could see of his face—which wasn't much.

Fake language, he snarled and tossed the book onto my bag with an angry flick of his wrist. *You can't. Can't read. Can't write. Useless language.*

I shrank, suddenly feeling wooden and hollow like a tired, old tree. With an unsteady hand, I slipped the book back into my bag. "Oh," I whispered and rested my face in my hands.

Chapter 11

Javed

Niusha was as lethargic as she was last night. I was uneasy about her dark emotions, but I didn't have any way to offer counsel. I had no means of helping when I was limited to speaking like a barbarian. Also, the more we communicated, the harder it would be to let her go. I was already gutting myself with every aloof response I gave her.

Last night, she struggled with feelings of betrayal, violation, and emptiness. This morning, she felt shocked and humiliated, but at least I knew why. Her village had taught her a fake written language, still managing to sabotage her well-being even after she'd left. My guess was that the leader wanted them to be illiterate if they ran away, but then why teach them to read at all? Or if they were going to go that far, why not create an entirely new spoken language? That'd really fuck with anyone who left the confines of the village—cult, slave farm, whatever they were.

I glanced over at Niusha as we hiked through the jungle. She hadn't said anything since she'd returned her survival guide to her bag. She'd also put the note away before I could offer to read it. I sensed that she didn't want to talk at all, which somehow made it a thousand times harder to distance myself.

Her pain called like a signal fire. It tugged at the weak bond we shared, like her soul cried to get my attention. I could hardly speak, and touching her would only raise more questions and weaken my resolve. I didn't know how to comfort her, so I just kept quiet, and she did the same.

The early evening brought a misting to the canopy, which resulted in fat droplets trickling down to the undergrowth. The wildlife was unfazed by the rain, which was the drumbeat to the monkeys and birds who filled the sky with their feral calls. When I felt a change in the air pressure and the animals quieted, I knew it was past time to find shelter.

Uphill, I grunted, pointing off the trail to a hill. *Build shelter. Storm coming. Fast.* I'd misjudged the weather. I wanted to get this trip over with so badly that I'd rushed us, and I hadn't been paying attention. I should've stopped an hour ago, but no, I just had to squeeze in more distance today.

Fucking idiot, I swore at myself.

We scrambled to higher ground as the misting turned into a downpour, our feet occasionally slipping from the water sluicing downhill. When I noticed that Niusha was only pulling herself along with her fingers, I grabbed her attention and gestured for her to use her claws. She nodded fervently, released them, and had an easier time navigating the incline, pulling herself more securely over slippery sections with just a couple claws into nearby branches.

When I found a spot that wouldn't flood, I immediately started constructing a lean-to. Had it been just me, I would've shifted into Convict and let him find a dry spot to hunker down for the night. It wasn't just me, though, and even if we had no future together, I wasn't going to make my fated mate wander around with me until we found a spot our cats deemed acceptable. That could take hours.

Once Niusha understood what I was doing, she flew off to supply me with branches. The grimace I wore from the wind-driven rain turned into a reluctant smile. I was grateful for the help, but I was more proud than anything else. She was such a good female. I fought to hold that thought there before it slipped into something depressing.

I built the largest frame I could in the short amount of time I had to do it, filled in the sides, and rushed to cover it all with detritus and large leaves. When I began placing the last row of wood down to sandwich the insulation, I told her to get inside the lean-to, but she refused.

Niusha! I ordered again. *Get inside!* She shook her head and ran off to find more branches. I clenched my teeth in irritation and secured the last of the wood I had on hand. When lightning flashed, I counted the seconds until the thunder roared. Five miles away… I needed to get her into th—

Niusha's shriek was audible once the thunder had its say, and she came barreling out from behind a thicket with a white face and an armful of wood. I would have laughed had it been anyone else, but she looked so fucking terrified that I grabbed the branches from her, hauled her off the ground, and placed her in the shelter.

Stay, Niusha! I growled with a finger pointed down at the pile of leaves that'd act as the bed for the night. I'd covered smaller leaves with the largest, driest fronds I could find, but it'd still be a little damp here and there. If I hadn't waited so fucking long, we would've had a much better shelter to stay in tonight.

I finished stabilizing the lean-to but hesitated when I reached the entrance. I shouldn't go in there. I was too close to losing control, and it'd be close quarters. I cracked my knuckles anxiously and pulled my hood down as far as it could go.

"What are you waiting for?" Niusha yelled over the din of the storm. "Get inside!"

I'll guard. Outside tonight, I replied, knowing that I sounded like a complete idiot.

She looked at me like I was a complete idiot and hollered, “No, I don’t think so! Get in here!”

I bit my lip nervously when my canines began to itch. *Change first. You’re soaked,* I said and turned to give her privacy. When she was done, I crawled into the shelter and dragged several massive strips of bark across the opening to keep out the rest of the elements. I collapsed onto the slightly damp bed of leaves and heaved a colossal sigh. That had been exhausting.

I tugged my hood down and let my gaze slide up Niusha. She was running her fingers through her soaked tresses and flicking the water away from where we were laying. Her eyes were cast down but didn’t seem to be looking at anything. Thunder boomed over us, and this time we both were startled. I laughed soundlessly, but she covered her eyes and curled into a ball.

We’re safe, I reminded her. *Remember. I protect.*

She peered through her fingers at me, blinking her long, curled lashes before asking, “But why? I need you to give me a real answer this time.”

I held a groan back and closed my eyes. *Give minute,* I asked, trying not to lace it with the agony of indecision.

Convict, her cat should have recognized us by now, right? There’s no way she could shift without having that instinct awakened? I asked my tiger, running my hand over my face to swipe away the rest of the rainwater.

Yeah, she should know. To be honest, I’d completely forgotten about it since we were so focused on keeping our distance.

Right… I stared blankly at the top of the shelter and listened to the rain. Then I glanced over at Niusha, who had sunk back into depression.

Niusha, I said to get her attention. Her eyes flickered to meet mine and stayed there. *I help. Because care. Care what…* I closed my eyes, clenched my teeth, and pounded a fist down on the bedding. I couldn’t fucking communicate like this! *Hard talk. Can’t…*

A hand fell gently to rest on my fist, and the tingling, soothing touch of my fated mate calmed me. "It must be really frustrating to not be able to talk," she murmured. I nodded, keeping my eyes closed, and just focused all my other senses on her voice, her smell, and her touch. "I won't ask that question again, Javed. Living in the village made me into someone who doesn't trust easily. I've trusted you from the beginning. So far, it hasn't been misplaced, and I'll keep putting that trust in you. I don't want to seem ungrateful. I just get suspicious when something appears too good to be true."

I sensed her embarrassment after that last sentence. It was a bit revealing, and I fought to keep a smile from my face.

"N-not just when it's too good to be true; when it's good at all," she stammered out to possibly clarify that she absolutely did not have any feelings for me whatsoever. I moved my other hand over my mouth, pretending to scratch at something to hide my amused grin. So we were both going to pretend the mate bond didn't exist.

That was a sobering thought.

Speaking of which, I'd probably have to redo the partial mark soon. It'd been two nights already. I opened my eyes and crooked a finger at her to lean down a little. Her cheeks pinkened, and I slid my hand out from under hers to brush her hair away from her neck. I eyed my marking, which was still visible. If I kept redoing it, she'd eventually scar. That wouldn't bode well for her if the lions thought she was already marked.

My hand fell away, and a fresh wave of pain rolled over my heart. She needed to know what to expect before I continued making any more decisions for her.

Niusha... I said, rolling onto my back to stare at the branches above us. *When home. You won't. Have choices. The males. They decide. For you.* Even saying that much was so fucking hard that I was going to have a panic attack. I scrubbed my shaking hands over my face. Was I going to have a heart attack instead?

"Javed? Shhh," she murmured and dragged my hand from my face. I held on to my hood with my other hand out of sheer paranoia. "Don't talk if it makes you panic. Don't worry about me. Whatever you're concerned about, I'll figure it out. I did run away from an entire village with a handful of children and a newborn." She laughed lightly but squeezed my hand affectionately.

Great Sky Gods, her laugh and touch were a tonic for every ache and pain. I breathed in deeply and released it slowly, absorbing what I could through her tingling fingers. I couldn't imagine the luxury of having this for a lifetime.

"Do you think a third bite would help you communicate better?" she asked, and I tilted my head to stare over at her. She was trying to hide her blush by looking down at a strand of hair and playing with it, but there was no hiding anything from me.

Worried. You'll scar, I replied, nodding to her shoulder.

"Oh, I don't care about that," she said, instantly dismissing it. Of course she didn't care. She didn't know enough to care.

Will look. Like permanent. Mating mark, I explained the best I could, knowing this would likely open up a new bundle of questions. *Males won't. Like that.*

"I don't care what these males of yours say," she retorted.

You don't. Understand. I groaned. This was going nowhere. Would one more marking make her scar? I should have waited longer in between them, but I hadn't thought about the potential for scar tissue forming. Shifters healed well, but if I kept damaging the same spot over and over again, there was a good chance of that damage becoming permanent. I could mark her other shoulder, but I didn't want to risk scarring her elsewhere.

She lay down on her side and moved her hair to expose her neck. The rain continued to thrum on the shelter, nearly matching the pace of my heart. I swallowed as I struggled with my decision. She and I both knew that marking was also a pleasurable act for her, and I had no idea if my control could survive one more marking without mating. If I bit her now, it could fucking ruin everything.

When I took too long to reply, Niusha tried to hide her disappointment, but I could sense her utter humiliation. She thought she'd been rejected, but I still hadn't made up my mind. I wanted her to understand the seriousness of the situation, but I couldn't fucking communicate it properly. Lions did not take anything lightly, even with their own females. I'd go as far to say that they were the most controlling of all the shifters, including the dragons.

She ducked her head as she rummaged through the leather bag, trying to hide her flaming cheeks and pinched face. If she indeed felt the fated connection to me, I wasn't surprised by the intensity of her pain. My own chest ached in response, surprisingly, and I resisted the urge to massage the spot over my heart.

"I-it's a good thing we have bread," she said, forcing a nervous laugh to hide her wavering voice. "Can't really start a fire, can we?" She handed me a loaf and started taking large mouthfuls of hers.

It's fortunate, I agreed and ate mine rather quickly. *Leftover meat. In leaves,* I said, pointing to her backpack. She pulled them out, and we shared what was left. That would do for now. Storming or not, I'd make sure to obtain more food tomorrow. I really should have prepared better for this. I didn't want to let Niusha down again with conditions that were more uncomfortable than they needed to be. I was not being a very good mate.

I shook my head at that mistaken thought. I was not her mate. We were fated, that was all. Still… I could do better. My eyes roved over her again, unable to control their focus when it came to Niusha. Doing another partial might be able to prepare her for what was to come, and I'd be better able to answer the questions that were slowly piling on her shoulders. I just needed to do it slowly and make sure she didn't climax. If she cried out again… I might lose control.

Niusha, I called, and her eyes flickered nervously to mine. *Come here. I'll mark. Partial again. Lay down. We try.* I patted the spot next to me, hardly able to sit up in this shelter. I'd made sure it was long enough and wide enough, but I was still a little too tall, and I needed room to do this.

I didn't sense any relief from her. Perhaps she thought I was doing this out of guilt. I kept a straight face as she reclined again, and I gestured for her to turn away from me. I scooted up behind her and propped myself up on an elbow so I could move her hair and manipulate her shoulder into the position I needed.

Oh Sky Gods, I could sense the instant her arousal sparked. I felt it with every nerve in my fucking body. Her little hairs all stood on end, her heart and breathing accelerated, and all her muscles drew tight in anticipation. My hand twitched, wanting to slide down her round bottom, pull up her skirt, and dig between her legs until I could feel her wet heat. I knew she was weeping for my cock because I could not only smell it, I could fucking taste it in the air. The shelter didn't exactly allow for a breeze, and I was drowning in her erotic call to me.

I held back a groan and clenched my teeth when a wave of need splintered through my body and went straight for my cock, which was already fit to bursting. I kept my hips back a bit; I was so fucking hard that it was like my dick was reaching for her.

Get it the fuck together, I cursed at myself. *Partial mark, partial mark, partial mark!*

I cleared my throat and angled my mouth to fit over the fading mark. My canines had elongated the moment I scented her slick—fuck, everything had elongated. A shudder that I couldn't control rippled down my back. As soon as I was still again, I placed my teeth on her salty flesh and started pushing in. Suddenly, I experienced a massive spike in her anxiety and paused.

I pulled away from her, concerned. *Niusha, what's wrong?*

"C-can I face y-you?" she asked and tucked her arms to her breasts.

I furrowed my brows. *Why?*

The answer was given in the tiniest, mousiest voice. "S-so that I know i-it's y-you."

I'm only. One here, I said, confused by her sudden change in behavior. She was quiet for a long time, and the only sound around us was the pelting rain and the occasional roll of thunder.

Niusha? I prodded again. *Please explain...* She remained silent, clearly distressed. I placed a hand on her arm and rolled her on her back so I could see her face. *Niusha?* I shook her arm a little, then rubbed it gently. Maybe the mate touch could calm her enough to answer me.

"I had a f-friend who promised he w-wouldn't let me be turned into a p-p-pure mother. The d-day I ran away, he b-betrayed m-me to make me h-his p-pure mother. E-even worse, h-he followed me back to m-my hut and..." Niusha froze for almost a minute before continuing. "He groped m-my breast." She started crying, and it took all my self-control to let her keep talking when all I wanted to do was leave right now to rip her "friend" to shreds. I'd pull out the arm that touched her and shove its bloody stump into his mouth until he choked on his own blood and died.

"Now, I can st-still feel his h-hands on m-me. I f-feel dirty. When I can't s-see you, my mind replaces you w-with h-h-him." Her composure deteriorated more and more until she could hardly finish talking.

I pushed my outrage aside as much as possible so I could focus on her. When I was certain she was done explaining, I pulled her onto her side to face me this time. I raised my hood just a touch so she could see a little of my eyes and said, *It's me. Only me. Face me. Just make. Three promises.*

She blinked in surprise, and though her chin still wavered, her crying abated. I rubbed her arm fiercely, trying to warm and comfort her at the same time.

"What are they?" she asked in a voice husky from crying. Her fluttering blink loosened a droplet that fell to her cheek. I gently wiped it away with a thumb and answered her question.

Do not. Remove Hood. Do not. Touch back. Or look. Do not. Look at. My throat, I listed, feeling my own privacy violated by the situation and for even having to mention what I desperately wanted to stay hidden—what I wanted to stay forgotten. Saying it made it feel more real, and I didn't want that. I didn't fucking want that one bit. I felt like puking.

The only reason I'd make myself this vulnerable was because Niusha needed more of me. How ironic that I was now willing to go this far when all I'd done was try to push her away. How much more would I crumble before I got her home? If I fell completely, maybe it didn't matter. I wasn't certain I'd survive losing her anyway.

"I p-promise," Niusha said, eyes wide and tear polished.

Say it. Whole thing.

She took a deep breath and steeled herself. "Javed, I promise that I will not remove your hood. I promise that I will not look at your back or touch it. I promise I will not look at your throat."

She said the entire thing without a single stutter, and I slackened a little in relief. I believed her. She hadn't lied, and I saw the resolve in her jawline. Mistakes might occur, but at least she'd not do it intentionally.

And I. Promise you. Are safe. As long. As I'm. Around, I swore, though it took some time to say it. *Ready, Niusha?* I asked, reminding her what we were about to do. She wiped a new tear from an eyelash and pulled my hood down a bit, smiling a little. Ah fuck, that gesture went straight to my foolish heart.

"Ready," she said and waited as I adjusted her position. I would not groom her before biting because that'd arouse her more than necessary. I still needed to prevent her from climaxing. I placed my teeth over the old mark and slowly bit down until I punctured her skin. She stiffened and her hand flew to my shoulder, gripping hard. She mewled quietly while I dug in at an agonizingly slow speed. When I entered deep enough for a partial, I felt my venom release, and I cautiously withdrew my canines, lapping just a couple times to clear away the excess spit, venom, and blood.

She was panting heavily now and squeezing my shoulder with her eyes locked safely onto my lips. One of her legs had bent and lifted so she could rest her knee on my leg, which offered me a richer taste of her desire. My abdomen clenched, and I moved a palm down my stomach to my leather flap, needing to push my erection down before she noticed it. I angled to keep it pinned against the ground and out of trouble.

All ok? I asked, trying to maintain a serious face. My muscles screamed at me as I fought the shaking—the incessant need to catch and mate. Not knowing where else to place it, I casually rested my hand on her waist. She didn't seem to notice because she was just staring at me while rubbing her thighs together, obviously desperate for release.

I had to repeat my question before she nodded, and I got into a more comfortable position. It was too dangerous. *How much of this can you hear?* I asked.

"You said, 'How much of this you hear,'" she reported. "That seems like an improvement."

Not perfect, but better. How much of that did you hear?

"Not perfect better. How much of did you hear?" she parroted back, and I nodded thoughtfully.

We can work with that, I said with a sigh. *Should sleep now.*

I heard her whimper as she turned to sleep on her other side, squirming miserably. I winced because I loathed to leave her unsatisfied. We hadn't done that partial to experience pleasure, though, and I really did need to maintain control. Her climaxing would only make me think of her clenching channel.

My cock was still rock hard, so as I adjusted my position, I slung a wrist over it to force it into submission. Honestly, I wasn't sure if it'd go away until Niusha's arousal faded. Her body still called to me through scent alone.

I tried to get calm enough to rest, but after about twenty minutes, Niusha continued to suffer. Great Moon Goddess, how was this female still on the edge? After another five minutes, I could tell that she was trying to take care of it herself, but from her motions and frustrated sighs, she clearly had no idea what she was doing. I tried to ignore it because I was so close to losing my mind to lust, but she continued squirming for another twenty minutes.

I sent a prayer to all of the gods, propped myself up with a heated growl, and snarled, *Great fucking Sky Gods, do you need me to take care of that for you?* I had no idea how much of that she'd heard, but I was pretty fucking sure she'd get the idea.

Chapter 12

Niusha

I'd never been more embarrassed in my entire life. I'd tried to stay quiet, I really had, but the ache between my thighs was intolerable! When Javed had pulled his teeth from me before I could experience what the doctor had called an orgasm, it was like a vibration had started as deep as my bones and wouldn't stop. My clit continued to pulse hotly with the beat of my heart, and my sex ached mercilessly, feeling swollen and empty—except for what was leaking from it.

I felt like an eternity had passed before I became desperate enough to touch myself, to press on it so maybe it'd go away, like putting pressure on a bleeding wound. The pressure helped, kind of, but it wasn't nearly enough to free me from the torture. Something inside me, between Field and me, was a feral energy that told me I needed hard, hot flesh inside of me. My body screamed for a male, and the one next to me was the best possible choice. It was telling me to either get on all fours or rip his loincloth aside to let my needs be known.

The thought of approaching the man I liked like that—especially after he'd gone to sleep—was simply impossible. Instead, I'd chosen to ignore the instinct and massage the ache, praying my noises would be drowned out by the storm's assault on our shelter. I hadn't even known Javed was awake. Oh gods of the sky and earth, I couldn't believe he could hear me this whole time!

I slid my hand discreetly from my underwear and looked guiltily over my shoulder, my lips humbly sandwiched between my teeth. I had not, however, expected the expression on his face, and my inner muscles contracted viciously, nearly ripping my breath away. His sensual mouth was pulled back slightly to expose one of his canines, and he growled again when I didn't answer. I whimpered when the sound caused more moisture to seep onto my thighs, and I floundered for a response—any response!

"I-I'm sorry! I didn't mean to keep you up. I-I'll go to sleep!" I squeaked out, which made my body so incredibly angry at me. A rush of arousal made my breath catch, and I turned my head to face the slanted shelter wall again. I held my breath, flexed my thighs, and waited for the aggressive throbbing to pass.

A burning, rough hand landed on my hip, and Javed said, *If it hasn't away in forty-five minutes, do think it's likely to soon?* His fingers slightly flexed and shifted just the tiniest bit over my hip bone. I bit my lower lip and tried to stifle an aroused moan. The lioness inside, the origin and sum of Field and me, wanted to encourage that hand. She preferred this tiger's cock for his semen, but she'd accept relief by other means.

A couple words seemed to be missing, but I understood him just fine. I shook my head reluctantly and muttered, "I don't know…"

Do you want me to rid of it or not? His hand was tense on my hip; it felt like a hunter's grip.

"O-ok…" I mumbled under my breath, feeling not just my face blush, but my entire body go up in flames. My lioness roared so loudly, it nearly burst through my chest.

With a deep, rumbling grunt, he rolled me onto my back and propped himself up on an elbow. Before he could do it himself, I pulled his hood down a little, and his sensual mouth lost its sternness for just a moment. An appreciative smile tugged at his beautiful lips, and his overall irritation seemed to soften.

Ready? he asked as his large tan hand pinched the bottom of my dress. I nodded, and he pulled the fabric up to expose my underwear. I watched his face strain and a deep, growling groan squeezed through his parted lips. My heart flipped in exhilaration as his touch went from being demanding to reverent. Hooking his thumbs under the top of my underwear, he dragged it down until he nodded for me to lift my knees. I let him slide the underwear off the rest of the way, and he laid it out on one of the bags.

Let it dry overnight, he grunted. *Too wet.* I covered my face with my hands, not knowing how much more humiliation a woman could take. He pulled one of my hands away and said, *Don't be ashamed. Natural. You are lucky you lubricate well. With a future lion will be easier to tolerate.*

What was that last missing word? What with a future lion? He very nearly choked up in his attempt to get through that sentence. His mouth returned to a frown, but he continued to do what he promised. He slid his palm down my inner thigh and pressed against the inside of my knee to get me to spread for him. I felt like hiding my face again, but I settled for fisting them timidly under my chin.

Spread legs help you find better, he explained. *Can reach more spots.* His gaze followed his hand, which glided up the inside of my thigh, collecting moisture on the way. Shockingly, he held his slickened fingers up to his nose and took in a deep, shuddering breath. A groan echoed through his chest as he licked his fingers clean, and my toes curled in arousal and horror, nearly making me slap my thighs shut again.

He growled and shook his head sharply, like he was trying to fling away a thought, then his hand went straight to my sex, completely focused on my problem now. His rough fingers traveled down my folds, and I bucked in surprise. I knew his touch was coming, but this was the first time I'd ever been touched down there by anyone but me, and the sensations his touch commanded lit up my flesh like a lightning bolt. A short whimper burst through my parted lips, and his head swiveled to face mine. His head tilted slightly, studying me with a great deal of interest while he ran his fingers back up to graze my clit.

"Ah!" I cried and clamped my lips shut. The tingling from his touch, the only time I'd ever felt such a thing, made every single sensation a hundred times more sensitive! It had not felt like this when I was massaging myself!

Did you like that? he asked in a seductive voice, and I caught the slightest smirk tugging at his fuller, lower lip. I tried to open my mouth to reply, but he slid a thumb over my clit again to make a plaintive mewl spring out of my throat. *I didn't quite catch that. What did say?*

I gave up trying to talk because I was panting too hard, and my mind was unable to form words. I blinked feverishly, not wanting to close my eyes but finding it hard to keep them open with how pleasurable his touches were. His thumb started circling my clit, and I bit my lip, holding back a delighted scream—a scream fed by my roaring lioness. I was going somewhere now, the fires were growing hotter, and I begged for the rain to come after I'd been consumed.

An erotically masculine growl rumbled from Javed as he slid his fingers down my sex. *Remember. Remember that I was the first male to enter your pussy, Niusha. A tiger, not a lion.* His thick, calloused finger swirled around an opening, and he squeezed a finger into it. We both released wild noises at the same time. Mine was from unadulterated excitement, and his was laced with arousal, satisfaction, and yearning. Oh gods, oh gods, Javed had his finger in me! I slid my hands up to my hair and arched my back, releasing a tortured cry, but this time it was louder, deeper, hungrier and came directly from the beast within me.

Javed replied to my moan with a hungry snarl and started thrusting his finger in and out with ravenous abandon. *Sky Gods!* he cried to me. *Your pussy is perfection! I fucking hate who gets to you. I hate it! I want kill them!* His voice was full of hunger and venom. What I could see of his eyes held splinters of blind rage and jealousy.

I didn't care if some of his words made no sense to me, the possessiveness behind his message had me writhing, and his thrusting had me wailing. "Javed!" I nearly screamed, not knowing what to say but needing his name on my tongue. Maybe his name could be bait for his lips—oh his delectable, seductive lips. His lips were the only ones I could think of now.

Yes, Niusha? he asked and looked down at me while adding a second hand to simultaneously rub my clit. His voice held a desperate, feral note to it now.

I couldn't answer, couldn't think. I simply shrieked and tossed my head from how his fingertip scrubbed against a wall within me. My tresses fell across my eyes, and Javed immediately swept the hairs away before tilting my chin to keep my eyes on him.

Look at me. Watch me bring pleasure you'll never with another, he ordered in a superior tone, his growls growing louder as my body drew tight in agonizing anticipation. *Watch me. No one else can do what I can to you! No one can make you climax like I can!*

He rolled me onto my side and lifted my leg over his hip. With our faces inches away from each other, he worked his skillful hands between my legs until I froze, tilted my head back, and released a choked shriek. I jerked into his hard body, crying at the top of my lungs as the heat between my legs ignited into the hottest, most uncontrollable wildfire. Javed's fingers dragged and pumped at my flesh to make each feverish flare roar longer and burn brighter. His aroused, panting breath on my face and in my ears would have brought me to my knees had I been standing.

Yes. Enjoy it. Enjoy what only I give you, he rumbled in my mind with a voice that sounded like a hundred seductive licks.

Eventually, the mind-numbing pleasure eased into a gentle rainfall that soothed the devouring wildfire. The tingles from his touch had brought me ecstasy while the calming effect eased me into marrow-deep contentment. The incomparable pleasure and the flawless tranquility swaddled me in a blanket of complete happiness, and it was so satisfying. My body shuddered like it couldn't possibly contain so much of such a perfect feeling.

When I opened my eyes, I was hoping to open them to Javed's, but his were shut tight, lids half hidden by his deep hood. His face contorted like he was in pain, his teeth were bared, and his canine must have punctured his lip because there was blood on his lower one. What was wrong with him? I could definitely sense lust, but this was a very different reaction than mine. It was feral, wild, and seemed almost uncontrollable.

I looked down our bodies, and he had his hand pressed firmly against his leathers. "Are you erect, Javed?" I inquired. "The doctor said that men get erect when they're ready for se—"

I can't stay here, he blurted out and moved to get off the floor.

I clamped my leg higher over his hip to try to stop him. "You can't go out there! It's storming!" I protested, reaching to intercept the hand that was trying to pry my leg off him. I felt a little too relaxed to put up much of a fight, but I'd try.

Niusha, you don't understand! I cannot here! he snarled madly.

"Do you need release too? Just do it in here! You already helped me! You've... helped me a lot... You've ear-earned some pl-pleasure. I'm offering my... p-pussy to you," I stammered out, not knowing how to communicate my feelings.

I cannot believe things you are saying, he sputtered with wild eyes.

With his hand off his leathers, I felt his cock spring across the inside of my thigh. Seizing the opportunity, I moved my leg off him to sandwich his member and trap him... hopefully. Oh my gods, though, it felt colossal. Its throbbing purred to my sex, and arousal squeezed from me in response to its offer.

"I'm not letting you go out to get struck by lightning!" I snapped, but then swallowed hard when I saw the expression on his face. "Oh no, oh no, oh no. Did I hurt you?"

His face had drawn tight, and he grabbed my shoulder in a near-bruising grip. *On contrary.* He gasped and clenched his teeth. *I wish you hadn't... done....*

He tilted his head down to look between us and yanked aside the leather that had gotten trapped along with his cock. Javed hissed in a deep breath and tried to retract his cock, but I pressed my thighs tighter together in defiance. *Oh Sky Gods, female!*

"If you promise not to go, I'll release you!" I demanded, but he just laughed silently.

If you don't let me go, I'll find release in you, he threatened. *I cannot do that!* He released a bone-rattling roar of frustration, moved me off him like I was a kitten, and scrambled out of the shelter into the pouring rain. *Do not follow, female!* he snarled aggressively. *I'll return when calm! Stay!*

"Javed, no!" I stumbled out to chase him. I nearly stepped on his muddy cloak and leathers. He'd shifted and ran into the ravaging storm.

"Javed!" I screamed, trying to yell above the sound of the pelting rain. I was instantly drenched from the storm, and a gust of wind nearly pummeled me to the ground. "Javed!" I shrieked louder and sobbed as panic gripped my chest. Anxiety wasn't far behind, gripping my stomach and twisting it into impossibly tight knots.

Shift! Shift! I thought to myself and my lioness at the same time. I sank to my knees as I shoved my human form back while pulling out Field. She pushed through, panicking as much as me, and darted into the underbrush.

How do we find him! I cried to her, mad with worry and guilt.

We're made to hunt at night! We can hunt in the rain! We can find him! She panted, following the displaced mud made by Convict's paws. *I can't scent him, but I can follow his tracks!*

She certainly could. Her vision remained crisp despite the night and the rainfall. Flashes from the lightning were only brief distractions, though the booming thunder put me on edge. It rattled our ribs like Javed's roar had and worked as a miserable reminder of his suffering.

I was confused, and I was definitely going to get answers out of him—if not tonight, then tomorrow. Yes, I wanted him, and the rebel in me no longer cared about being touched or untouched anymore. If my lion family had a problem with it, I'd just deal with the repercussions. I was certain I could reason with my blood relatives! I couldn't imagine anyone as unreasonable as the pure elder.

What could his reason be for not taking my offer?

Maybe he's saving himself for someone else? Field asked, and that was like a punch to the gut. *Or maybe he's right about the lions. Maybe he thinks he's protecting us.*

It can't possibly be that bad! I snapped.

I do wish you'd listen to me more often! she growled as she pursued Convict's wild tracks, occasionally scraping painfully against a hidden stick or a jutting rock in her haste. *You're not this naive, Niusha! Or this stupid. We're realizing the world is more complex than we thought.*

I didn't want it to be. By the gods above and below, I wanted it to be simple! I thought that running away would be the hard part, not interacting with other people once I'd left.

A roar sounded from the right, and I felt relief. The relief, however, was short-lived when I realized it wasn't from Convict. It had come from the wrong direction. Another roar came from behind, and Field found herself pursued by a tiger and a panther.

No! No, no, no, no! Field cried, putting on a burst of speed in an attempt to outrun both of them. She slowly outran the tiger, but the panther shot forward and tackled her. She roared in pain as it raked its claws into her ribs and bit into her neck, trying to pull her onto her side. It almost matched us in weight, and Field put up a good fight, but we weren't experienced enough to know how to counter his attacks.

The tiger caught up to us and shifted into a man who quickly worked with the panther to roll Field onto her side. She snarled and growled in bone-throttling cries, trying to sink her claws and canines into anything she could reach. The rain pummeled everyone, and we were occasionally blinded whenever water pounded forcefully into Field's eyes. Mud sprayed like blood, and the only thing that gave us the slightest break was the other two slipping in the mud as much as Field was.

A third cat appeared, another panther, and we knew the fight was now impossible. Our movements slowed as we became pinned, and all Field could do was snarl and roar at their smug faces. They worked to press Field's feet together and threatened to cut her throat if I didn't shift back to my human form. Once the tiger dug his claw into Field's neck, piercing flesh, I immediately shifted, angling my head to get the bloody claw away from my skin.

Prying baby vines from a nearby tree, two of the males reached to tie my wrists and ankles. "Can't believe our fuckin' fortune. Who would've th—" The tiger never finished his thought because another tiger—one twice his size—exploded through the underbrush and wrapped his maw around his neck, breaking and tearing it halfway off his body.

Convict then unleashed a roar as unsettling as the booming thunder and jumped over me to latch his teeth onto one of the panther's arm so he could toss him into a tree. Lightning flashed when the second panther jumped onto his back, trying to get a grip on his neck, but Convict rolled him off, crushing him with his weight. I could barely hear the snapping of bones over the downpour and thunder, but I knew they'd cracked brutally loud.

The last injured panther tried to run, but Convict shifted into Javed who darted to catch him. I looked away before I could see Javed's back, like I'd promised, and heard a scream that was cut off with a horrible gargling noise. In my peripheral vision,

Javed paced a circle around me and roared multiple times into the flashing black of the jungle, his cries of rage joining the crashing of the storm.

Something happened in that moment that triggered my lioness, and everything simplified. A feral blanket drifted onto my mind, and I instinctively rolled onto my stomach and propped my body on all fours. My male had warned off others, announced his territory, and defeated his rivals. He'd secured his rights, and my lioness wouldn't deny him his reward. He continued to protect us, and we would make our offer whether he liked it or not.

I kept my eyes off his body as he approached, his feet slapping in the mud—the same tepid mud that swelled around my palms and knees. *Niusha…* he rasped as he stopped behind me. *You don't…*

My lioness destroyed whatever self-restraint the male had left. I lowered my chest and raised my rear, releasing my own short roar that ordered him to just mount me already. His bulky arms wrapped around my waist, and he put me down in the mud by a tree where the rain wasn't hitting as hard.

I keep my promises, he snarled, leaving me on my back while his hand went down to spread my legs. I widened them automatically, making him shudder violently and groan in approval. *Good female…* I heard a feral tone accompany every sound he made, making it clear that the tiger in him was as present as my lioness.

He dropped his body over me, one elbow slapping into the mud by my ear while the other slid down between us. I focused my eyes on his chest, keeping my promise to not look at his neck. I'd avoid his head too, as much as I desperately wanted to see what the rest of him looked like. I felt an urge to wrap my arms around his chest but resisted because his back was off-limits. I ended up leaving my hands on his pecs, whimpering at how hard they were under my fingers and palms.

The arm between us jerked several times before I felt a large domed tip press against the entrance to my sex. It prodded forward several times, rubbing into the threshold like it was asking permission to enter.

Remember, female, he rasped into my mind, *that I was the first to have you.*

I arched against him, crying and begging for his male sex. A low growl bubbled up in his chest, vibrating into my hands as it grew louder. When lightning flashed, I watched his abs stretch, his body tense as he seemed to wait for something. When the thunder shook through the trees around us, I started in surprise, and he made his move. His rippling abdomen contracted, and the head of his cock lurched forward, parting my threshold to force its way past the barrier. A sharp pain stabbed at my sex, and I gritted my teeth as tears sprang to my eyes.

The male froze with just the head of his cock imbedded in my flesh, and he wrapped an arm around my back, pulling me up to cradle my torso to his chest. His other arm pivoted, with his elbow still buried in the mud, to support the back of my head. He released a rolling huff into the crown of my head, nuzzling to comfort me.

Bite, female, he murmured and held me to the edge of his shoulder. I bit hesitantly, then sank my canines into his flesh to get through the pain, and he grunted again in approval. I felt his hips flex as he pushed in another inch. Despite my flowing arousal, I still winced at the burning stretch from his girth and sniffed as I remained clamped on his shoulder. Everywhere we touched generated pleasure and comfort, which I welcomed to combat the pain of his mounting.

Slow, he groaned, and I couldn't tell if the male was speaking to me or himself. His hip and buttocks flexed again, pushing himself in another inch. Lightning and thunder clashed again, making me buck during one of his measured pushes, and he moaned in pleasure before sinking in several more inches this time. I lost track of how many times he nudged in until he was fully seated within me, his sack hanging heavily against my sex and bottom.

His abdomen curled in excitement, and he released another moan. The sound of his reverence had my skin vibrating from a surge of pleasure, and it pulled a responding moan from me. I then removed my teeth from his shoulder, making sure to lap at the bleeding wound in apology. He breathed out a soft growl and huffed into my head again.

Sorry for pain, female. I am not sorry for being first, though. Remember this. The male's voice was wild, fierce, and feral. It was amazing this tiger could speak at all in his state. *Remember no lion will fill you like I do.*

I felt his anger flare, and I knew he spoke the truth. His hips grinded in a circle, then rolled to gift me with a spark of throbbing warmth. I was already wet, but his teasing unleashed more of my arousal, which streamed down a buttock upon his next rotation. The motion stretched my opening a little at a time as he worked to loosen me, but my flesh continued to clutch possessively, occasionally clenching and making him gasp.

He made me feel so full, almost unbearably so. His swollen length pulled slowly out, but my sex clutched desperately to keep him where he belonged—inside me. He growled, tugged back a tiny bit, before pushing back forward, driving back in until he filled me to the brim. I arched into his heaving chest, and his grip tightened hungrily. A thrilled mewl curled from my lips when he was properly buried again, and I wiggled my bottom to enjoy the weight of his sack resting against me.

He tilted his head away to unleash a lustful roar and moved on to the next stage of mating. He drew his hips back to remove most of his cock, then thrust forward to fill me, only to pull out and repeat the process. He laid me gently back into the mud and leaned back to kneel, grabbing my hips so I stayed connected to him.

I kept my eyes on everything below his shoulders and squirmed at the erotic scene before me. I dug my claws into the mud, panting as I watched his carved hips clap ripples across my thighs. His fingers dug into the soft sides of my hips to yank me into each of his thrusts. Water streamed down the both of us, but it looked especially sensual in the way it ran down his defined muscles and parted over the base of his erection. Lightning lit him from behind, and only the thunder was able to drown out his lustful grunts.

I writhed from all the pleasure he bestowed upon me. His cock filled me repeatedly in the most satisfying way, indulging me. His possessive grip validated my attractiveness as a female and my worthiness as a mate. My body, my feral mind, and my soul were wrapped in ecstasy, topped off by every pump into my sex.

He roared at my last writhing arch, and his erection swelled harder from sheer carnal arousal. Javed increased his speed, each fevered slap sending his head thumping into the back of my sex. I roared through my teeth, feeling both pain and pleasure, but mostly an overwhelming thrill that ignited the skin the rain fought so hard to douse.

I thrashed my head, lost to the deep connection between me and this powerful male. I scrabbled madly in the mud with my claws as we both added our feral snarls, growls, and roars to the swirling storm that raged above and between us. The male moved faster, harder, slapping into me with abandon, each movement lending itself to the wildfire that promised to burst through my skin. Then it became too much, too pleasurable, too arousing, too perfect.

The heat peaked into a broiling pool, burst, and overflowed into a colossal climax. I shrieked in euphoria. My sex squeezed his thrusting cock, and he choked on his own roar, speeding up until he couldn't resist my grip. He slammed in one final time to spill his seed, grunting, gasping, and panting as he joined me in ecstasy.

I bucked up with each flare of fire, awash in heat as I consumed this male's offering. Our hips rolled together as he filled me, completing the final act of mating as nature intended. His large hands dug into my buttocks, squeezing with his spurts until he emptied his last drop.

My waves of pleasure eased me into deep satisfaction, taking what he had to give and hoarding it like my own personal territory. My lioness was happy, deeply grateful for the seed he gave us and his eager reception of our gift. I groaned as the male pulled out of me, leaving me with a profound sense of emptiness that I loathed. I batted the water from my eyes and avoided looking at him while he rose tiredly to his feet. I wasn't expecting him to pick me up, as exhausted as he was, but he did and started walking us back to our temporary shelter.

My mind buzzed with pleasure, joy, and contentment. I was barely aware of the male's satisfaction and how it slowly became shadowed by dread.

Chapter 13

Javed

I cradled Niusha to my chest as I took her back toward the shelter, then settled her onto her feet for a moment so I could wipe the mud from her shivering body. She kept her eyes closed as I used the rain to rinse her, holding to her promise like the kind, good female she was. I nudged her thighs apart so I could rinse between her legs and blanched at the sight of blood and my seed dripping down them.

I'd tried to be careful with her. I'd tried so fucking hard. I should have spent longer loosening her up for me. She'd been way too tight. Oh gods, and I finished in her too. I shouldn't have done that.

I shouldn't have had sex with her.

I lifted her up one last time to rinse her feet and deposited her inside the shelter. I rinsed myself off and sighed at the sight of my soaked cloak and loincloth. Guess I was sleeping naked tonight. I shook off what water I could before joining Niusha in the lean-to, where she had dried herself with her old, ripped dress and was now tearing a long strip of cloth from the bottom.

Niusha... I warned before I slid in beside her. *Please don't turn around. My cloak i—*

"I got it sorted," she said quietly and wrapped the strip of cloth over her eyes, tying it behind her head. She held the dress out in my direction and murmured, "This is still a little dry. You can use it if you want."

I took it from her and ran it over my dripping skin. I was touched by the generous gesture and her mindfulness in handling what mattered most to me—my privacy.

Thank you, Niusha. I returned the dress to her, and she found a small branch at the back of the shelter to hang it from. She reached for the blanket at her feet, shivering, but dragged it over both of us this time.

"Share mine. It's cold, and you're without your cloak," she said as she lay down next to me.

So are you. You have another dress, and it should be dry, I noted. *You should put it on.*

She shook her head. "No, I want to put it on in the morning. It'll just get damp on the ground right now."

I stared guiltily at her blindfolded face. *Are you not anxious wearing that?*

"My eyes will be closed sleeping anyway. This'll just help prevent accidents until your cloak is dry. Besides, I can still smell that it's you. It should get me by."

Do... you want me to hold you? I asked hesitantly, almost hating myself for offering. It was one more act that would make it harder to let her go. My soul wanted me to warm her, though, and offer her closer access to my scent.

"Oh, o-ok." I nudged her to roll over so I could pull her back into my chest. I tucked an arm beneath her breasts to hold her to my heartbeat as the rest of her body molded perfectly to mine. She was tense for several seconds, but she relaxed and melted against me, lulled by the soothing fated mate sensations. I pulled up the blanket to tuck us both in, and we lay in silence for a while, listening to the storm rage on beyond our shelter of wood, leaves, and detritus.

I buried my nose into the top of her head and breathed in her scent of fresh figs and warm oud wood. An involuntary chuff rolled out of my chest. Perhaps I felt the need to comfort both of us.

"What's that sound mean?" she whispered.

It's called a chuff. Tigers do it to greet each other, comfort each other—especially cubs—and it's common communication in c-courtships. I stumbled across that last word like an idiot but didn't bother getting too worked up over it. We'd just had sex—granted, it was due to an incredibly feral mating frenzy.

All the right conditions had been met tonight to break my self-restraint. Males had threatened to take a female that, by all rights, should be mine. If I couldn't have her due to the lions, then they definitely couldn't. I'd killed them for taking and hurting her, which triggered my feral urge to breed. My fated mate's reaction to my territoriality by displaying her sex in lordosis had ultimately conquered me. It was almost like it was as ordained as our matching.

"It's calming. I like it," she murmured.

I'm glad.

Dawn arrived with no change in the weather, and we slept in, waiting to see if the storm would break. I left to forage for food in the early afternoon, raiding trees for bananas and other fruit to fill our bellies. If the storm didn't calm by the evening, I'd have Convict teach Field to hunt and eat raw kills.

Niusha and I stayed under the blanket while we waited, and she eventually brought up last night. "I need answers, Javed," she began softly and turned to face me, still blindfolded. "It confuses me when you seem to want me but then run from me."

I heaved a heavy sigh and tucked a hand under my head. *How much do you want to see your family, Niusha?*

"I definitely want to see them. I feel like I must. I have so many questions. And isn't family where one belongs?"

My heart sank. It shouldn't have disappointed me that she hadn't changed her mind. I knew it was coming, and I was letting myself get too vulnerable.

What's going to happen is that you will be taken into the lion-shifter's territory to meet your family, and you will never be allowed to leave. You will be placed in one of their many harems where you'll be used to breed and work until your dying day. Do you know what a harem is? It's a group of females used for breeding. You are given no choices. They obsessively cling to their old traditions, no matter who gets hurt.

"No…" she sputtered, appalled. "That cannot be true. You saw how the villagers treated their long-lost children. My family wouldn't do that to me. Those parents were sobbing with joy."

And even if you did manage to flee, which no lioness has done before, you'd be targeted everywhere you went. Every town, village, or city would sell you out for a reward or keep you as a hostage. Some might even kill you for just being a lioness. I paused and added, *You need to tell me if some of my sentences are missing too many words.*

"Some are missing, but I-I'm following you. Javed, that all can't possibly be true…"

You underestimate how much people hate lions, I replied, trying not to scold her too harshly.

"Why? What have they done to others that warrants such treatment?" she asked, her soft voice laced with desperation.

Lions believe in maintaining a kingdom while the other cats resist their imposed way of life. Many tigers, for example, live in sprawling territories that are not strictly governed. They have a chieftain to rule on disputes, but families mostly keep to themselves and don't need—or want—someone looking over their shoulder. Every species thrives differently, so you can see how their attempts to spread and control territory that doesn't belong to them comes across as theft. Many cats didn't even know what taxes were until their lands were invaded.

Niusha was silent after my long rant and seemed to crumble in on herself. I licked my lips and clenched my teeth, not liking what I was about to say next.

We... cannot have sex again. I should not have lost control. If you become pregnant with anything other than a lion, they will kill the cub. I can only pray to the Sky Gods that we didn't create a cub last night that's already sentenced to death.

"But I eventually... want a..." she whispered, then choked on a sob. "No, they wouldn't do that. They wouldn't do that to their family. I wouldn't let them! I'm certain my mother and father would intervene."

You wouldn't let them overpower you, hold you down while they poured poison down your throat? I asked, staring at her distraught, blindfolded face. It was the hard truth, and if I was to protect her, she had to know.

She rubbed her eyes through the blindfold, damp from her tears. "I have to see them, though. No, I'll figure it out. If I can escape the village, I can escape them."

Did your village have giant stone walls with guards everywhere? Her naivety was frustrating me. I needed her to understand, but I was afraid she didn't have the building blocks for that. She'd probably never seen a fence that was higher than five feet.

"It had no walls," she whispered vacantly.

So you still want to see your family? I asked one last time, knowing the answer hadn't changed.

"I have to..."

Then I will take you to them, but we must avoid being seen. I cannot be seen. Once I drop you off, that will be the last we see of each other, I forced out, each word ripping out a piece of my gut. My stomach cramped from distress, and I turned over to face the slanted wall of branches and sticks, staring at a small returning droplet that'd plip onto the leaf bedding every several seconds.

Niusha failed to suppress the tiniest whimper as she rolled away from me. "Even if we are... well suited?" she finally squeaked out. That seemed to have taken all her courage to say. Neither of us had brought up our fated connection, but it didn't matter anymore.

It won't be by my choice. Once you're in, there's no leaving. I was tired now. The rain and the emotional conversation drained me. I wanted to sleep for a week, but I could not. I wanted to run from reality, but there was no escape.

"No..." she said, locked stubbornly in denial. "I'll sort it out."

It's your life, I muttered. It came out more bitterly than intended, but she was too gracious to comment on it.

A long moment passed before she whispered, "I was so sure it'd all be simple, like the children's reunion."

Cubs, I corrected.

She gasped and I felt her roll over to face my back, which made me nervous, so I turned to face her as well. "Wait, the children are shifters?"

Was... that not clear? I asked.

"Not to me..." she murmured, deep in thought.

I listed off their species, and her mouth gaped wider with each name. *The newborn, which is a healthy, normal cub, is a tiger like me,* I said lastly, wistfulness creeping into my voice as I remembered holding the little thing.

"Oh... I didn't know newborns looked so... wrinkly," she remarked. "You sound like you miss her."

I do, I confessed. *It was nice to see a tiny tiger again.*

"Do you want children—I mean, cubs?" she asked, sounding more hopeful than I liked.

I do. I would have liked to have had a family someday. I only wanted one with my fated mate, though, so it will not be happening.

"Are you s-sure you don't want to m-make one with me?" she asked timidly. "I really want one too."

I will not father a doomed cub. I had to make my feelings on the matter crystal clear if there was any confusion about what I'd said earlier. *I hope I have not done so already.*

She signed in defeat and shivered. I watched goose bumps spread across her skin, and try as I might to fight it, I caved and pulled her against me to warm her with my body heat. It was too bad there was nothing around to warm my heart. It was starting to frost over from hopelessness.

As much as Javed's adamant rejections tore at my heart and soul, I was still pulled into a state of bliss when he brought me to his chest. Maybe he thought I was cold, but my shivering had nothing to do with the weather. If anything, I was starting to get too warm, and that wasn't Javed's fault. The heat was coming from within, and I was starting to worry that having sex out in a thunderstorm had been asking to catch a cold. My sex was aching too, but I just figured that was due to our rough joining—our mouth-watering, soul-shattering joining. I grew a little aroused just thinking about it.

I'm confused, Niusha, Field said abruptly to me.

What's wrong? I asked, but I was certain she was going to bring up what I was desperately trying to avoid.

I'm worried about the lions. I'm worried that Javed might be right, but I've taken some time to think about it, and I think there's more to why you're being so complacent about the risks.

I'm not being complacent, I snapped. *I'm being optimistic. You saw yourself how real parents react.*

Optimism regarding what we've heard is anything but wise, she scolded. Part of me knew she was right, but the other part was stubbornly adamant that everything would turn out ok. *I'm feeling a strange pull. Maybe we're a species that is not meant to be alone. We could simply be drawn to joining that harem, even if neither of us wants what might come with it. Lionesses just do not live solo. I think we'll crave being among our kind.*

I swallowed hard, nervous about the implications about my behavior. I didn't like the thought of instincts driving me to do something I wouldn't want to do.

I don't necessarily want to stay with them... I defended weakly.

But don't you want to meet your own kind? After decades of believing we had no family, aren't you even the slightest bit hopeful of how it'd feel to be welcomed back with warm arms? Like Nisha's and Raju's families?

Their families aren't lions. But... yes, of course I want to meet my own kind. I'm just trying to share something that worries me. I also don't want to be trapped forever to serve as a breeder.

I don't either, I whispered to her. I shuddered at the thought of another male like Mehr being completely free to do whatever he wanted to me. *So what do we do?*

I think we should head toward them but not decide yet. We should see with our own eyes what life is like out there and if it's as bad as Javed said. There must be things on the way that we'll witness to give us a better idea of what the lions are truly like. We'll just be careful to stay hidden, like Javed said.

Alright, Field... I think that's wise. I sighed, giving in to reason despite my heartache. I supposed I should be grateful that she was more self-aware than me. She'd been my guide when I lied too often and almost lost touch with reality. I was beginning to realize how poorly some things would have gone without her stabilizing presence.

I nuzzled closer to Javed, looking for comfort and wishing to bury myself in his body for just a little bit longer. I didn't know what was going to happen, but I also didn't want to lose him. I hated being torn between two desires. I wanted to know what my family was like and how I came to be orphaned in a jungle where I spent most of my life drugged into a stupor. I also knew I'd never find anyone else like Javed, and I was starting to believe what Field had said about him. I felt that he was mine, and the thought of him ending up with any other female filled me with such a rage.

Ah, ow! Niusha, what are y— Javed's voice popped into my head, and I felt him pry my claws out of his chest.

"Oh no! Oh no, oh no!" I cried in horror, blindly patting his chest and feeling some wetness. The faint coppery scent of blood seeped into the air. "I'm so sorry! I'm so sorry! I didn't notice!" I fumbled toward my ruined dress and lifted the cloth from my eyes for a second so I could tear a small piece off the skirt. I covered my eyes again and scrambled back to him, hastily trying to sop up whatever blood had smeared on his chest.

It's ok. I was just startled. It'll heal quickly, he consoled and took the fabric from me so he could do a better job. I was probably just making a mess.

I scooted back to give him room to clean, feeling just as useless now as I had with the baby… er, cub. My heart throbbed a moment at the sense of loss. She'd been a little tiger. I wondered if she'd been the reason why I wanted a cub so badly. My instincts might have known more before I did. I could have easily fantasized that Javed had given her to me with his seed. She was gone forever now.

Out of nowhere, my body flooded with heat, and a small moan got stuck in my throat.

Uh, what is this? Field asked, alarmed.

I knew very well what arousal felt like now, and what I was suddenly experiencing was exactly that. It was exactly that, except ten times worse. My entire body flushed with fire, especially my sex, which developed a churning ache. A groan of frustration finally found its way past my lips, and I wrapped my arms around my chest as subtly as I could, trying to ignore the discomfort in my breasts.

The sound of Javed swiping at his body paused, and his beautiful voice invaded my head again. *Niusha?*

I ignored his call out of embarrassment and turned my head to the side, shifting my position to crouch. I leaned forward a little and rocked in place to both comfort myself and ease the throbbing between my legs with a strategically placed lower leg. I squeezed my arms tighter over my breasts, like I was trying to keep all my heat and scent from exposing my state. He wasn't going to have sex with me again, and I didn't want to pressure him into releasing me.

You're not in heat, are? he asked warily, sounding unexpectedly frightened.

"I don't know what that is," I replied tersely through my teeth. "Just… finish cleaning yourself up. Ignore me."

Niusha, can't possibly be in heat. It hasn't a month! he argued, but I had no idea who he was arguing with. I wasn't exactly fighting his idea.

"Sorry," I growled, growing defensive. "I can't tell you what I know nothing about!"

Did you just growl at me? he asked warily.

That was a stupid question, but I restrained my retort. I also restrained the urge to bare my teeth, so I sandwiched my lips instead. A cool set of fingers then landed on my arm, and I sighed in relief.

You're burning up… he said. I leaned into his fingers, reveling in the chill and the soothing sensations his skin always gave me. I needed more of that.

Yes, get more of that, please, Field groaned. *Too hot.* A shudder raked over me, and I crawled to where Javed lay.

What are you doing? he inquired tentatively when I lifted a leg to straddle his hips. I patted around his chest to feel if the blood was all gone, and I discovered some stickiness. I frowned, not wanting to lie on that, especially if it'd get my new dress bloody.

Because—for some reason—it made all the sense in the world, I leaned over and started lapping his chest to clean it. His entire body went rigid beneath me, and I was suddenly straddling what felt like a pile of boulders. A slight trembling told me that

I was still on top of my preferred male, so I continued to drag my tongue over the sticky spots where I'd cut him. It was a way of apologizing too. I was cleaning up my mess.

Ni-Niusha, this entirely unnecessarily. He sounded more panicky now. *I'm fine. I'm totally fine. In fact, let me get up so I rinse off.* He gently placed his palms on my shoulders to pry me off, but I wasn't having it. I growled into his chest, showing the male my displeasure, and he froze.

You need to come back to. I think you're in heat; you need to rein in lioness. She's controlling you right... Don't let her do that. You're the one in.

I was certain that he was speaking nonsense. It was very simple. I was hot, he was cold. I wanted to lie on him to feel better. He was bloody, and I didn't want to lie on that. I was licking him clean. This was all very reasonable. If anything, he should thank me for washing him. I thought I was doing a pretty good job.

The male's groan when I dipped my tongue between his pecs validated my assessment of my performance. I was doing a fine job.

Ahhh... don't do that, he warned. *Alright, this needs to stop.*

My body lurched when my male's two large hands wrapped around my waist and lifted me off him. I bared my teeth, growled, and slapped at his chest, keeping my claws in this time. I kept batting at him until I was dragged along leaves and straight into a waterfall.

"Ahhh!" I shrieked and covered my head, running blind to find cover.

Oh, no you don't, the male snarled, and I was tugged back into a hard chest. My blindfold was ripped off, and I blinked rapidly to stare into the wind-wrecked, rain-soaked jungle. The cold water was a slap to my senses, and my clarity returned.

"Javed?" I asked, shaking my head. "What just happened?"

You're going into heat, but have no fucking idea why. It's way early for that. He grunted, sounding incredibly annoyed. He brushed my hair away from my face, his touch gentler than his tone, and he led me back into the shelter where I closed my eyes again. I heard some shuffling, and he said, *Open eyes now. The cloak and leathers still a little damp, but I don't want blindfolding yourself anymore.*

I opened my eyes and indeed he wore his cloak. I sighed and just stared at him from where I sat. "What's heat, Javed? What's wrong with me? Do I have a cold?"

He lifted an arm to rub his eyes, and I saw the corner of his lip curl like he'd surrendered to some amusement. *No, not a cold.* His chest bobbed up and down in silent laughter. I frowned as I pulled at my soaked dress, wishing it'd been removed before I was yanked outside for sobering.

He groaned, scrubbed at his face a couple times, and turned on his side to stare at me. *Heat is a recurring phase when female shifters are most receptive and ready breed. Female shifters go into heat month after they've met fated mate, but it's only been six days since I saw you. You've only known me two days,* he said very quietly, fixing a pensive stare on me. He was waiting for me to understand what he'd just said. There had been something meaningful in his words.

"It's been more than that," I said, squinting while trying to count the days. "Four days since you saved me from that toothy fish." I shuddered at the memory and rubbed at an ankle, reminding myself that my foot was still attached.

You met body, but you didn't know me. Not until shifted. His shaded eyes studied me, waiting for my reaction.

He's talking about what I told you, Niusha, Field reminded. I cast my eyes downward and fidgeted with the edge of the blanket. Javed heaved a sigh, but he didn't move. He was being very patient with me.

I was afraid, but I decided to go out on the terrifying, rickety branch. "My lioness said you're ours," I mumbled under my breath and wrapped my arms around my knees, partially covering my face. "If that's wrong, I completely understand. I mean, I thought it was crazy t—"

She's right, he said, interrupting my embarrassed rambling. *The Moon Goddess pairs all with a fated mate—someone we're meant be with. It's our beasts recognize the ones we're supposed to take as permanent mates. You're mine. It doesn't always end happily, though.* He rolled onto his back, tugging his hood down, and rested his head on his hands. Javed looked distant now—colder.

My stomach twisted and writhed in discomfort because I could sense him shutting down and distancing himself. I had a lot of questions, especially about this new goddess he mentioned, but I couldn't seem to be able to form a coherent thought.

He thinks you've chosen the lions over him. You can't blame him for protecting himself, Field said darkly.

"I n-need to meet my… I need to think about meeting m-my kind. I need… time. Everything is different out here. I'm not sure what I'm going to do y-yet. Can I really not have both?"

You can try. But as soon as walk into their territory, no one—not even me—expects see you again.

Chapter 14

Javed

I loathed being cold, but I absolute needed to accept that I was going to lose her forever. I didn't know how to do that without closing my heart.

If only we could sate her curiosity without her going into the pride. Convict spat that last word out with revulsion, then sighed mournfully.

I don't know how, I replied, feeling an urge to crack my knuckles. I needed to suppress it. I needed to suppress all urges, especially now that Niusha was beginning an impossible heat. *There are no living outsiders. They hunt down all the shameful. Well... the one we do know hadn't really lived there long enough.*

Maybe we could find a soldier in an occupied tribe she could talk to. Once she's done, we could make him disappear before he can arrest or report her... Convict offered.

I don't think talking to anyone other than her family is going to cut it.

I doubt we could lure her family from the pride. None of the females could meet her that way. Convict simply heaved a sigh.

After a minute, he mumbled, *I'm going to keep brainstorming, Javed. Unlike you, I'm willing to fight to keep her now.*

Would you have such an easy time fighting temptation if you'd never met another tiger? I spat, seething from his assessment of me, but Convict had gone silent. He tucked himself in the back of my mind to hibernate, clearly as overwhelmed as I was.

Without Convict acting as a distraction, I was bombarded by Niusha's despondence. I gritted my teeth, wanting to roar and tear down everything within a thousand feet of us. How were we supposed to travel like this? Only the Sky Gods knew how long it'd take to get to the lions' territory. Maybe I should go back to guiding her from a distance but remain extra vigilant. Or I could let the partial marking wear off and stay nearby—close the connection between us. It might make it easier to resist the call of her heat.

I hated both of those options.

"I hate myself for never asking this, Javed," Niusha said timidly, her small voice nearly drowned out by the thrumming of the rain on our wooden roof. "What do you want? You… seem to be an exile, and you don't need to tell me anything about that, but would you really return to exile after helping me escape the jungle? If you chose to l-leave me."

I really wanted to fight her on that last sentence, feeling like I absolutely had no say in the matter, but I let it drop. I had to exercise restraint. Instead, I focused on the question that took me off guard.

I hadn't really thought much about it, I said honestly. All I'd been able to think about was how dead I'd feel once she was gone from my life.

"Do you not have people you miss?"

I miss hundreds of people. I miss them every single day, but if I'm caught out of exile, I'd likely be executed. Should the lions find out I had sex with a lioness, not to mention took her virginity, I'd be tortured before my execution. And don't you dare say that it cannot be true. Ask any cat-shifter. They probably knew someone who was killed for much smaller infractions.

After a minute of silence, she asked, "What about if the lions weren't a problem. What would you do? J-just humor me."

I bit back a retort that I wasn't here to humor her, but I knew my sour mood was making me unreasonable. Nothing had ever provoked me like the thought of her disappearing—like the thought of her choosing those loathsome lions over me.

Any place I'd be welcome, preferably in tiger territory. If I had the luxury, I'd return to past... projects, I muttered. I privately added that if I had a mate, I'd fill her every night until she was round with cubs. I wanted a large family and a pleased female, but that could only be Niusha.

I could feel her curiosity, but she was kind enough not to ask. I didn't want to talk about this anymore, so I offered a distraction. *Do you wish for me to read that letter to you, Niusha?* I offered, and her pretty eyes lit up in recollection. She scrambled for her bag, and I twisted my lips, feeling guilty about her soaked dress. My eyes roved down her curves where the dress clung and deep yearning knocked the air from my lungs. It'd be so easy to have her again.

Restraint! I snapped at myself and ripped my eyes away when she handed the note to me. *Dear Nini,* I read aloud, *we wanted to thank you for saving us. We don't hate you. It's funner here. Did you know we are cats? We want to shift, but we have to wait ages, which is so dumb. We already miss you bunches. Like bananas. The biggest bananas! Say hi to Volcano, Rooster, Ginger Muscles, Mountain, Cloak for us.*

I stumbled over the next section of the note, incredibly uncomfortable saying it. *If you get mated, we want to visit. Mated is a weird word. Just don't kiss in front of us. Kissing is gross. They do it a lot here. We love you, Nini! Love, Nisha, Tahmina, Raju, Sam, Jam, Gerhard and Chirasmi. P.S. Nisha's parents helped write this, so we might sound smarter than we actually are. P.P.S. Jam gave up picking his nose in honor of you. P.P.P.S. Chirasmi cries a lot. We think she misses you and Volcano, Rooster, Ginger Muscles, Mountain, Cloak.*

I finished reading and handed the note back to a weeping Niusha. *Don't cry...* I begged, unable to be terse with her now. *They are happy. You gave them an incredible gift. You gave them a future... a happy one.*

She nodded, grimacing as tears trickled into the corners of her mouth, and covered her face with her hands. She tried to suppress her noises, but her shoulders shook from her sobs. Before I knew it, I drew her to me and covered us both with the blanket. My body was revolting against my mind, and that terrified me.

With her face buried in my chest again, I felt my embrace soothe her, and her crying quickly trickled away into silence. I realized that she'd fallen asleep, and I groaned in agony. Every time I swore to hold firm, I crumbled. Should I risk her hating me if I fought to keep her? I didn't know. I'd give anything to look into the future and see if I needed to shut my heart down or not. With that depressing thought, I closed my eyes and tried to fall asleep with the object of my ultimate desire nestled against me.

We slept on and off until the next day. The rain continued, but the bulk of the storm seemed to have finally passed. I insisted that we returned to our traveling, not trusting myself to be stuck in the shelter for one more day. If her heat had truly begun, I had a chance of surviving it with the rain wiping her scent from the air.

We gathered our belongings and took to the trail in our cloaks. It would have been convenient to travel as Convict and Field, but our cat bodies weren't built for carrying bags. We simply trudged on through the underbrush, occasionally having to navigate around parts where the trail had drowned.

I'd occasionally spot an exile stalking from a distance, but I kept their numbers in mind, needing them to come closer before I'd risk attacking them. They were likely trying to draw me away from Niusha, who was their golden opportunity to escape their exile. Like fuck they were getting her.

If some of them knew me, they wouldn't recognize me by sight with the cloak on, and they wouldn't be able to scent me as a warning, so they might get a little bold. I was perfectly fine with leaving a trail of bodies in our wake if that served as a reminder of whom they were stalking. Convict had never been squeamish about executing criminals, and he wouldn't hesitate for a single heartbeat if they put their sights on Niusha.

"If prisoners are exiled here," Niusha said after a day of silent traveling, "there must be something that will keep us from leaving this jungle. I remember one of my… a-abductors… mentioning getting on a ferry. What's that? An animal?"

No, it's a boat, I said, slashing aside a thorny bramble so Niusha didn't have to deal with it. *There's a large river that prevents criminals from crossing. An illegal ferry gives rides to those who can pay, but the price is steep. The waters are full of predators, and it has a heavy current.*

"So how are we to cross?" she asked. I heard a thud, a splat, and a curse, and I turned to see a scowling Niusha regaining her balance.

There is a narrow, shallow section that spans across most of it. We will cross there.

"That's convenient. You'd think the exiles would take that instead of the ferry."

I laughed silently. *It's a breeding ground for some of the largest crocodiles in the world. They were introduced to the region by lions to keep us in. They really fucked up the ecosystem.*

I heard Niusha's steps falter, and she stammered, "W-won't that be d-dangerous, Javed?"

For anyone else, yes. Tigers prey on crocodiles. They may be too large for other cats to take on, but Convict is the largest tiger around. I'm more worried about the food going to waste, I said, faking ruefulness.

"If it's so easy, why haven't you left before?"

Never wanted to, I answered dispassionately.

"You'll still be outnumbered... won't you?" she asked.

You let me worry about that.

She muttered, "How will you worry about that when you are eaten?"

I shook my head, suffering a burst of anger and jealousy. *You put so much faith in the lions and none in your fated. Surprising,* I spat bitterly. I instantly regretted the words.

Niusha fell silent. She wasn't angry, though, but I wished she would be. I deserved a thrashing for that. I only caught hurt, irritation, and regret. She was in turmoil too.

I'm sorry, I apologized after I calmed myself. *That was unkind.* She merely hummed in response, and I scrubbed a hand over my face. I shouldn't be tired, but I was exhausted.

The cloudy sky darkened further, signaling the end of another day, but at least the rain had turned into a light misting. Fat droplets landed obnoxiously on my head and shoulders, and I decided it was time to retire for the night. I guided us up to higher ground again and started building another shelter. It was swiftly made now that Niusha knew exactly what to bring, and after I foraged for food, we crawled inside to dry off and get comfortable.

She rummaged through her bag and brought out two wrapped pastries. She held one out to me with her eyes averted. I could sense her discomfort and figured this was a peace offering.

I held up a hand and said, *The cubs made those for you, Niusha. You should enjoy them.*

Her frown verged into pout territory, and she shook her head stubbornly. "I will enjoy them by sharing them."

I hid a smile because I sensed a small spark of pride in her. She was probably smug as fuck for thinking of a loophole.

I suppose I shouldn't ruin your fun then, I replied, unable to hide my smirk. I took a bite of the chocolate scone and took in a deep breath. I hadn't eaten something this fine in a long, long time.

I stared at Niusha as she took a bite, watching her soft lips part as she bit into the crumbly sweet. She slapped a hand to her face and stared at me like she'd just solved the meaning of life. After swallowing, she pointed excitedly at a chocolate chip.

"What is this brown stuff?" she whisper-shrieked.

So that was what was happening. I broke into a grin and nodded to her scone. *Chocolate. You can find the cocoa bean here. I'm surprised you've never encountered it.*

"Are you saying I could have been eating this my entire life?" She gasped and grabbed my arm without thinking. I kept my composure and nodded, taking another bite of mine. She stared at it and said, "I regret giving that to you."

I grinned and slowly took a large bite, teasing her. I could tell she was at least half joking.

You've discovered orgasms and chocolate since you left the village. The jungle can't possibly seem that bad now, I said with a silent laugh.

When she released a heavy growl of warning, I wondered how dangerous it was to tease a lioness.

"It seems to me that giving you that pastry has made you cocky," I remarked with an accusatory finger pointed at his grinning face.

He took another slow bite of the pastry and said, *And it seems to me that you're just looking for an excuse to take back what you've freely given.* He shook his head sadly. *And here I thought you were better than that, lioness.*

I gasped, in too good of a mood to be offended, and playfully lunged for the treat. I made sure I didn't land on him, not wanting to make him uncomfortable, even though all I wanted to do right now was grind against him. He was such an attractive male.

I rolled, nearly kicking the top of the shelter with my swinging feet, and tried to grab at the pastry he kept just out of reach.

He took another quick bite of it, grinning like a rogue, and I redoubled my fake efforts into committing theft. I released my most harmless growl, twisted myself into a bizarre position next to him with my head on his arm, and flailed hopelessly at the distant prize.

I was warm, but momentarily happy. It was nice to just forget about everything and harass my male over food. I squirmed and wiped sweat from my brow as I panted joyfully. My foggy mind didn't see anything but him and the prize.

Alright, I suppose you've earned it with that outrageous display, the male said, and he held the piece over my mouth. *I'm very concerned about your future as a huntress, though.*

I snatched it from him and held it over my mouth teasingly before placing it on his lips. He coughed on a crumb, quickly ate it, and gave me a bewildered look.

"You've passed the test! You are a very good male."

And you have a very low bar, he remarked wryly.

"Not when you've passed everything else," I announced but then squirmed uncomfortably. I was getting hotter and everything ached once more. If only my tiger would tend to my needs. I squeezed my thighs together, groaning as arousal began to seep from me. "No…" I groaned and rolled over to curl into a ball.

Shit. Niusha, go cool off outside, Javed ordered, apprehensive. I glanced over at him with a sad frown and whimpered in frustration. He smelled so good, he looked so good, and I knew he felt so good when he was inside me, but he wouldn't let me have him.

I untied my dress and wiggled out of it, making my male's eyes grow ten times larger. "What?" I growled defensively. "I'm not going to get more clothes soaked just because my male doesn't want me." The lioness in me was growing cranky, hating that we had to get wet again when being mounted would solve the problem.

I crawled out, ignoring my male's responding, angry growl. I'd meant what I said! I sat out in the rain, miserable and pathetic, letting it soak me from head to tail. Goose bumps spread across my skin, and I shivered, but I couldn't tell if it was from the cold or my heat.

My mind had returned to me by the time my hair was plastered to my head, and I crawled miserably into the shelter. I was handed my destroyed clothing to dry myself, so I wiped off the water before crawling under the blanket next to a suddenly anxious Javed.

Are you not... going to dress?

I shook my head belligerently. "No," I grumped. "Not if I have to keep going out in the rain."

Maybe it won't come back...

"You'd be so lucky." I snorted and closed my eyes, forcing myself to go to sleep.

I'd dreamed that I'd escaped the village again, but this time Mehr had actually managed to follow me into the jungle, which had nearly driven me mad with terror. He touched me everywhere when he pinned me down, making me gag and cry from distress. Somehow, I already knew about Javed living in the jungle, and I screamed for his help.

That was when I woke to a dark space, surrounded by Javed's scent and skin. I was on fire, and the air was thick with the aroma of desire. It was mostly mine, but I detected a muskiness that had to be from him.

Niusha... female... he purred, easing me awake with a nudge of his nose into my hair. He was being unusually attentive. Was he reacting to my heat?

I realized he was braced over me with a hand rubbing my left arm soothingly. My skin burned, and my soaked sex throbbed weakly like I'd just had a small orgasm, which dismayed me. I hadn't wanted to climax to such a horrific dream.

"Make him go away," I croaked and tossed my head with a grimace, trying not to cry.

I think I may have. You called to me. Bad nightmare? he crooned, nuzzling the side of my head. I spread my legs, and he slipped between them, adjusting himself more comfortably over me.

"Repeating nightmare, but this time he followed me after I escaped the village," I explained hoarsely. "He… did things. Male, help me forget him…" I leaned into his nuzzles as the subtle rocking I'd woken up to became more noticeable. He grunted and tilted his head to lap at my neck, making a gasp of pleasure burst through my pursed lips. His abdomen lowered, and I felt his hard erection through the leather of his loincloth.

Why can't I stay away? he groaned as he rocked breathlessly over me, grinding his cock into my thigh. *I try, and I try, and I try...* His hand went between us, and he removed his leathers, letting his heavy cock rest like a colossal fallen tower on my hip. It radiated heat, and its pulse called to the one between my legs. I felt it leave a substance in its wake, and I wondered if males had their own arousal fluid.

My hips twitched as I suffered another hot wave of lust, the sensation ripping a deep, feline moan from my throat. Javed wrapped his arms tight around me and shifted down a bit to nestle the head of his cock between my folds. In additional preparation, he tilted his head to clamp his teeth around my neck, like he was expecting me to run or fight him. He finally flexed his hips and buttocks, slowly pushing his member through my threshold, squeezing his cock in until he was just inside me. He released my neck so he could start pushing up.

We both exhaled sharply, panting in the darkness as we grew accustomed to our intimate embrace. He tensed as he thrust several more times to fully sheath himself and growled loudly when we were properly joined. The vibrations of his ardor rattled through my rib cage to sing to my heart.

Female, he whispered thickly and lapped apologetically at my neck where he'd held on with his teeth. When he rotated his hips to grind against mine, I nearly sobbed from the pleasure and raised my hips to meet his movements in an erotic, slow dance. *Yes, lioness. Enjoy our forbidden union while it lasts,* he murmured in a feral, gravelly tone. *I face death for a dip within you.*

He made wider motions now, like he was continuing in his efforts to stretch me. I hissed in pain when he rubbed against a sore spot, and he licked my neck once more in apology. *I am trying to make it easier, female. You are so tight. I don't want to hurt you.*

"Thoughtful tiger," I breathed out, hearing my words thicken with feline wildness. My lioness was out, a proud observer of our unexpected joining. "You are a good male..."

He grunted in reply and slowly started retracting his pulsing cock, sliding in retreat along the shape of my channel—perhaps leaving his own arousal behind in a trail. He shuddered, growled, and pushed back in, then withdrew to repeat his thrust. I arched my back to press into his hard, tight chest, and he tightened his embrace, squeezing me with his arm muscles like a hungry python while he plunged in and out of my heat.

Arousal displaced with every pump of his hips and streamed down my buttocks to slicken the natural makeshift bed beneath me. It quickened his movements and further eased his passage. It was an aphrodisiac as well, as the slick, slapping noises spurred both him and me into rougher thrusting. The wet sounds were a reminder of what we did to each other, a reaction that occurred whether we intended it or not. It was the sound of nature calling us together.

He shuddered powerfully, and a long, thundering groan burst into another booming growl, like he was announcing me as his territory once more. I desired looking at his face, but I had to settle for the male's cloaked shoulder while he was braced over me like this. I could see him, though, and knew him to not be the bad male who'd tormented me in my nightmare.

Don't think of anyone but me, he growled, knowing where my moment of fear had come from. *I am your first, and I will be the one you'll never forget. No one else will fuck you like me, lioness. No one can massage your soul the way I can.*

I knew that to be true. Even now, it felt like our souls were pressed together, desperately groping at the other for fear of being parted again. I reached down as far as I could and gripped his hips and upper buttocks, squeezing and pulling him down with each thrust to encourage him. I loved the feeling of his muscles contracting under my hands the moment he surged forward, like every part of him was determined to dig deeper into me—to get as close as two can get.

I mewled in arousal and panted beneath his large rocking frame. "So big… so strong… so protective." I was barely aware I'd spoken the simple words aloud. He growled, and his next thrust was brutal, possessive. It made my stomach twist in carnal arousal, and I was left breathless before releasing a keening moan. "Male, I need all of you…" I lamented. "I want all of you."

I felt a flash of anger from the tiger, but he just buried his face in my hair, growling low while his pace increased. I spread my legs wider and arched as far up into him as I could, wishing we could melt together just once. I felt him in every part of my sex, stretching every space until there were no more secrets between us.

I rubbed my chest along his a little, massaging my achingly swollen breasts between us, and his carnal arousal hit an all-time high. His cock started hammering into the back of my sex with every thrust, and his sack rose and tightened, like he was on the edge. He released a roar away from my ears and began slamming his hips into mine with abandon, like he was in a mad race for survival.

The sudden, brutal pounding yanked me into a giant firepit and lit me on fire. I released a surprised, screaming roar as I climaxed around the male's engorged cock. I gripped his shoulders as I pulsed under him, nearly blinded by the suddenness. Exquisite pleasure radiated from my sex, and I bucked into the male who was still panting and pummeling into me.

He grunted and gasped with every contraction of my sex, squeezing him aggressively as it sought his seed. *Need... pull... out... fe—Niusha...* he cried in turmoil.

"I-I unders-stand." I gasped and hissed through my teeth, deeply disappointed that he was still going to avoid filling me with his cubs… if he hadn't already.

F-fuck... he bemoaned. Arousal, pleasure, and indecision whirled within him. *Fuck, you're s-so unfulfilled. Shit! Fuck!*

I couldn't focus on talking anymore, my bursts of pleasure were too euphoric, and I wanted to bask in him. When a contraction gripped him, I could feel every subtle curve of his cock, and it nearly drove me mad. "So beautiful." I sobbed quietly and scratched at his chest.

Fuck! Lioness! he cried. He lowered me, slid his hands down and around to squeeze my buttocks, then slammed his hips one last time, burying his cock to plant a kiss deep into the back of my channel. His abdomen contracted powerfully, and he roared through his teeth, sealing his eyes into tight slits like he was in agony. His jerking hips and throbbing cock told me he was spending his seed, and I drifted lazily down from my climax to accept his gift. My lioness moaned in glorious satisfaction, pleased that my tiger had changed his mind.

"Tiger, my tiger," I groaned out, stretching under him while he lurched, grunting in rhythm with his ejaculations. Around his panting, he growled one last time before gasping and collapsing to his elbows over me, hanging his head near mine. I closed my eyes and savored the moment. Lazily, my mind cleared, and I knew it was only a matter of time before he returned to his aloofness.

I thumbed his trembling arm and stroked it gently. When he caught his breath, he slumped a little, weakening from a wave of misery. I didn't need to ask why.

"I'm making a fourth promise to you," I whispered and continued to caress him. He tensed, waiting for my next words.

“If I get with cub, I will protect them the way you protected me. I know you don’t believe I can handle the lions, but that’s a different matter. If someone tries to kill them, I’ll fight to the bitter end. Maybe I’ll fail, but I’ll draw blood long before that occurs. I’ll kill for them.”

All I got from him was a wet sniffle as he tried not to break down.

Chapter 15

Javed

I choked on my emotions while I remained propped over Niusha's sweaty body, still embedded in her after giving her my seed. Why had I done that? I'd tried so hard to resist, but when I'd awoken to her cries, found her lightly orgasming, and gotten a lungful of her pheromones, I'd descended into feral lust. I'd been worried about it, and it'd finally happened.

Why'd I been paired to a lioness? It was the cruelest joke, and for a moment, I loathed the Moon Goddess for putting me through this. Hadn't I suffered enough? Hadn't I paid the price already? I held tears of despair back and tried to get myself together.

She was especially fertile right now from her heat, and it was likely she was already pregnant with a tiger or lion. I hoped to all the gods that it would be a lion. If my cub was killed… Losing Niusha would likely kill me, but losing a cub would guarantee it—not that I'd even find out about it. Whatever happened in the pride rarely became known outside of it. I'd spend the rest of my life not knowing if my offspring lived. It had a fifty percent chance of surviving, and a zero percent chance of surviving if…

I took a sharp breath in and willed my thoughts to stop there. I hadn't gathered the courage to share that with her yet. I'd have to, though. Maybe it'd be enough to change her mind.

Please, Niusha... Please don't return to the pride, I begged her, abandoning my own pride.

"What's a pride?" she asked, stroking my arms to soothe me with the mate touch. I was too agitated to be soothed so easily, but I appreciated the sweet gesture.

Just what you call a group of lions with a harem. There's only one pride now. They've all combined. It's... where your family would be, I explained. She was silent after that, and my heart clenched, knowing I'd tried. I'd let my desires be known.

This was a mistake... I'm sorry I allowed the heat to sway me, I said, going numb again. The agony was too much. *I shouldn't have taken advantage of your altered state, and I definitely shouldn't have finished in you.*

I pulled slowly from her channel, grimacing at the exquisite pleasure of our tingling flesh sliding together. I'd likely be hard again in an hour or so if her heat spiked. Tigers can mate up to sixty-two times a day, which encouraged their shifters to mate much more often than usual with a female in heat. If the rain stopped, I'd have to stay upwind of her or I'd spend the entire fucking day with tented leathers and a short temper.

When I pulled my wet dick out, Niusha lifted her hips and placed a hand over her sex, like she was trying to keep my seed from leaking out of her. It was the most arousing thing I'd ever seen in my life, but it simultaneously stabbed brutally at my cracking heart. We had such conflicting opinions right now. She wanted my cub so badly, and though I wanted one just as fiercely, I also desperately didn't want to give her one—not if it'd just end up dying at the hands of lion's poison.

She released a satisfied sigh, one that echoed most of her emotions, and she clamped her thighs together as she rolled onto her side to face me. "I feel better," she whispered. "My skin isn't on fire anymore. Does sex do that for a woman in heat?"

Yes. A female, yes. You're not a human woman. You're a female. It's what we call she-shifters. We are males, not referred to as men.

"Oh… sorry," she said quietly. "I suppose I have been saying male… my instincts go against memories sometimes. It's confusing."

I'm sure it is, I replied, a little more coolly than intended. Whatever was left of my heart had to be hardened. I'd never known myself to be this fragile—not even close.

Something changed instantly within her; she'd gone from satisfied to horrified in a heartbeat. "Why do I feel like I r-raped you?" she asked all of a sudden, starting to bawl into her hands.

Her words slapped me in the face and shattered my defenses. *Gods, you didn't.* I instinctively pulled her to my chest again, melting like sugar on a humid day. *Heat is powerful. It's not your fault. I don't know why it hit you so early, though.*

"I'm sorry. I'm so sorry!" she sobbed, making my sweat-dampened chest wetter from her tears. "Javed, I'm so sorry. I should try to rinse you out or something. M-maybe stop it if… before it develops more," she whimpered and scrabbled to her feet to see if it was still misting outside the shelter. "Didn't… didn't want to use… you. I didn't..."

I pulled her back down into my arms. *Too late. Can't rinse out what made it into your womb. What's done is done. We need to move on.*

"I'm sorry… I'm sorry…" she kept repeating, no matter how many times I tried shushing her. Nothing seemed to stop her grief. It was likely she'd felt the coldness within me because neither of us could suppress our true emotions right now. In my mind, I knew I was going to lose her. In her mind, she thought she had enough power, like how she'd escaped the village. The pride was not the village, though—far from it.

If I looked at it from a distance, this whole situation was stupid, pointless, and needlessly cruel. It displayed how incredibly different two minds could see the world. Maybe the only reason

I was fated to her was to get her to her pride. Sometimes even the goddess wasn't strong enough to deter Fate's plan. Perhaps I'd reject her later and hope for a second-chance mate.

That thought made me want to vomit.

Sleep, I urged, palming the back of her head to keep her close. She curled up into a ball, tucking her knees to her belly with her little toes grazing my thighs. I tried to clear my mind of all joys and sorrows, finding the whiplash too nauseating and provoking to tolerate.

We woke earlier than normal, and since the rain had abated enough to track, I decided to teach Niusha how to hunt. Her lioness probably already knew most of it by instinct alone, but it never hurt to share some tricks I'd learned over the years.

Not sure if this is a good idea, Convict said nervously as I stored our bags under a tree. He wasn't exactly wanting to be around Niusha's lioness at the moment.

Of course it's not a good idea, but we need to hunt. We haven't had enough meat, and we need all our strength. We'll arrive at the river by tonight or tomorrow, and we'll have to take down some crocodiles.

Convict just grunted in frustration, and I stripped down to shift into him, giving him full control. We watched Niusha timidly disrobe and shift into Field, releasing her lioness in all her glory. Convict groaned as soon as he caught sight of her and her scent. Her heat hadn't spiked, but we could definitely scent her fertility.

I hate you, Convict told me bitterly. *You bastard.*

Just focus on the hunt.

I'd rather focus on her sweet ass, you furless piece of shit.

I'll shift back if you lose control, thistle-dick.

Bigger than a thistle. Bigger than yours.

And yet who leaves their females not bleeding to death? I wonder.

Fuck you.

Thank the gods you can't.

After we'd politely vented some of our arousal-induced, pent-up crankiness, Convict led Field around until he'd caught sight of some small deer. I wasn't sure how much Field used her sense of smell, but if she'd scented them before Convict, she hadn't said anything. Then again... I just realized that Niusha hadn't marked us; of course Field couldn't speak to us.

She crouched as low as she could in the underbrush and approached the herd slowly.

Flank on the left and drive one under me, Convict grunted, crawling silently onto a solid, lower branch to the right of the herd.

Field approached a deer that was facing Convict's hiding place, aiming to scare it in the direction that it was grazing. My tiger was momentarily distracted by her wiggling lion haunches and had a delayed reaction when she finally lunged at the grazing deer. It spooked as planned, but Convict wasn't completely ready, and he missed its haunches by a hair.

Son of a bitch! he roared and chased after the smaller mammal who'd gotten past him.

Get it before it speeds up too much! I snapped, angry at his embarrassing fumble.

What do you think I'm trying to do, fuck it?

That'd be another way to kill it!

He snarled furiously, both at me and the deer that was slowly starting to outrun us. He started and swung to the side when Field darted past him, going at least ten miles an hour faster. She sidled up to the deer, swung a paw over it while biting into its neck, and dragged it down to its death.

Convict slid to a stop and held it down as she broke its neck. He panted and stared at her blood-soaked maw as she removed her teeth from it.

I've never been so turned on and so pissed in my life. I hate you, I hate heat, I hate her beautiful ass, I hate my penis, I hate this fucking deer, I hat— Convict continued to ramble at me about everything that was wrong in the world until he noticed that Field had backed up and settled to lay in the damp soil. He froze with a mouthful of haunch and stared at her.

What are you doing? Eat, he said, too weirded out to be angry.

She laid her head on her paws, waiting.

Come eat. I'm not an asshole lion. We don't do that whole males-eats-first shit. You did the work. If anything, you should eat first.

She eyed Convict suspiciously.

Come eat, Field! For fuck's sake, enjoy this 'luxury' before you sacrifice your self-worth to those lions you so covet, he spat.

Convict! I hissed at him. *That's shit you say in your own head, not to her!*

Field, more dignified than my idiot tiger, simply got up to feed from the carcass, but we could practically taste her seething. The damage had been done, and Convict must now be a fine piece of asshole in her mind.

To my surprise, Convict forced himself past his hormone-induced crankiness and apologized. *I'm sorry, Field. I am horny, and it makes me angry and stupid, just like Javed.*

What the fu— I began to protest.

I shouldn't have said that. I don't like lions taking what's mine, he grumped, as tense as a coiled snake. For him, each word of apology felt like swallowing poison, but he trudged through it admirably.

She ate, but did so with obvious irritation. The awkwardness of her not being able to talk and Convict blowing it was absolutely killing me. I was determined to stay out of it, though.

Convict glared at the deer's butt and ripped out another piece of flank. I knew what he was thinking, and I really wanted him to keep that shit to himself right now.

Convict... I warned.

Make sure you leave the sex stuff to Niusha. You wouldn't like it anyway, he huffed.

The lioness gave him an uncertain look, silently asking a question with a tilt of her head.

Tigers and lions have barbs on their cocks, he informed petulantly, and Field froze mid bite.

She's eating... I groaned to him. *Why would you bring this up now?*

Because I'm an idiot.

And there I was, eating my victory meal, when he just had to bring up penises, Field vented again as we returned to our belongings. *And barbed? Barbed? My vagina is no longer open for visitors! That rude, slow, arrogan—*

I know... I was there, I said for the third time. *He's hurting too. He's just showing it in a... different way*, I counseled. It was interesting how we found ourselves switching roles whenever we shifted. Whoever was tucked away just seemed to, somehow, have a broader perspective.

We arrived where Javed had stashed our things, and he immediately shifted back from Convict, looking incredibly tense. Field averted her eyes, keeping our promise to give him his privacy until he was dressed in his leathers and cloak. She then bound up and wrapped her lioness arms around him in a burly hug, nearly knocking him off balance.

He laughed silently, but when she didn't let go, I shouted, *Field, don't you dare! No, no, no, no, n—*

She shifted into me so fast that I was hanging haphazardly from Javed's shoulders, screeching like a monkey. "Field! Quit it with the pranks! Oh, you rascal! I can't believe..." I fumed, feeling Javed's laughs deepen. He was holding me up with one arm and was pinching his hood down with the other, quaking with silent mirth.

She's incredibly fast shifting. Almost didn't catch in time, he said, then his demeanor changed when his laughter abated. He grunted and lowered me, making sure to hold me away from his body so I didn't slide down it. It... was a good call. I ignored his slowly bulging leathers and dressed hastily.

"R-ready!" I declared, hopping around with my foot halfway into a slipper, and he started walking away without another word.

You need to stop doing that! I snapped at Field, who simply pretended that she hadn't heard me.

After about a half hour of awkward silence, Javed said, *Field did well hunting that deer by herself. You should be proud of.*

"I am..." I replied quietly. "Didn't know she could move that fast."

Only cat faster than a lioness is cheetah, or so been told. Been a long time since anyone saw lioness, but cheetahs always outrace any cat in bursts.

I swallowed nervously, stepping over a raised root that threatened to sabotage my stride. I knew he didn't want me to go, and he could easily be making up scary stories to prevent me from seeing my family, but I didn't think he was. The more he spoke of the lions, the more frightened of them I became, but that fear seemed only to stoke the coals of my burning questions.

If I was to go into the lions' den, I needed to start thinking of escape plans. When Field killed that deer without a heartbeat's hesitation, I felt incredibly incompetent and fragile when I returned to my human form. I needed to get stronger, but I was discouraged by my own build. I wasn't nearly as tall as Javed or naturally bulky. Even if I developed some muscles before arriving, I'd be no match for anyone... I didn't think. If I shifted into Field, how much stronger were the male lions? If they were anything remotely like Convict, I'd be completely overpowered.

"Javed?" I asked, eyeing his position off the trail, trying to stay from my scent. "How would a female protect herself against a male who outweighed her?"

He glanced over at me, his lips pressed firm under the shadow of his hood. *If he stronger, she'd have to either take him by surprise or use his weight against.*

"Are you… familiar with any techniques?"

Of course am. I've taught a number females self-defense, he answered, slashing angrily through a poor fern.

Jealousy rose in my gut for absolutely no good reason, and I couldn't bring myself to inquire further. If anything, I shut my jaw so tight that my face hurt. All I could think about was a group of giggling females surrounding him while he wrestled with one at a time. I fumed and clenched my fists, trying to regain my sanity. Good gods, what was wrong with me? I was so angry!

Though my heat nearly spiked multiple times that day, which made me physically and mentally miserable, I was grateful for Javed pushing us hard to reach the river by late evening. It was nice to feel like we'd reached some kind of destination. The sight of the same jungle, day after day, was starting to make me feel like I was getting nowhere.

He brought me to a small cliff and pointed to a trail that we'd take tomorrow. A large expanse of water was just beyond that, twinkling under the moonlight and roaring like cats in the night.

We'll down. Here tonight, he said, and I shook my head, feeling like I had gone deaf for a second.

"Can you repeat that?" I asked with a frown.

Go down. Stay here, he tried again, then tilted his head in a silent inquiry.

"I'm hardly getting any words from you," I told him and parroted back what he'd said. He scowled and turned away from me.

Temporary bond. Fading, he said shortly, then went about to making a campfire. I followed timidly, gathering kindling along the way.

"Shouldn't we r-renew it? So we can t-talk?"

We probably without it, he answered stiffly.

"What?" I asked, squinting like that'd help me hear better.

He heaved a sigh. *Bad idea,* he said. *Your heat. I might. Make permanent. On accident.* It took him a while to communicate, and though I waited patiently, my heart sank after his first two words.

"What happens if a mark is permanent?" I asked, still not fully understanding the subject.

Like marriage. Like spousing. I will. Not be. Able to. Mark another. Unless you. Died. Permanent, Niusha.

So if he accidentally fully marks us, and he loses us to the lions, he'll never have a spouse for the rest of his life, Field said, completely on the alert for this topic.

I wanted to fight him on the whole 'losing me' scenario, but I settled for solving the other issue at hand. I looked around with my hands on my hips and strayed from the campfire's glow to find what I needed. I strode back into camp with a solid branch in my hands—not much thinner than my wrists—probably looking like I was about to beat him with it.

He eyed the branch but didn't otherwise react. I held it out and said, "Use this to keep your teeth from going in deeper than they should. That should help prevent a full marking, yes?"

I had no idea if it was nonsense, but it was all I had. He took it from me and looked thoughtfully at it. I also wasn't sure if he could snap it with his jaw. Convict had frightening power behind his maw, and I didn't know if Javed benefitted from that strength.

As if he was reading my thoughts, he brought the much narrower end to his mouth and clamped down on it with his molars. I winced when the wood snapped, and the small section fell to the ground. He tossed it into the campfire and moved his teeth farther up the stick to where it was closer to its thickest. A sharp crack then nearly made me jump, but the wood didn't break in half. It suffered a split from his assault, but its volume held. He looked speculatively at it and shrugged.

Could work. Good idea. Still difficult. He stared at the branch in his hands. He tried to hide it, but I could feel his stifling anxiety. He was taking a huge risk for me just to be able to communicate. Maybe he was right. Maybe it was too dangerous. I blew out a heavy breath, not sure if that had come from my lungs or my heart, and plopped down by the fire.

If only he could talk. I wanted to know what had happened to him. I rested my arms on my knees and buried my face. It was overwhelming me again. How had I come to be camping with a man—a male, I mean—whom I'd given the most private parts of my body to, and yet still knew nothing about him? I didn't even know what his entire face looked like. He had also committed a crime big enough to face the sentence of exile. Shouldn't all this terrify me? I had a feeling that if the fated mate bond wasn't involved, I'd be a lot less agreeable. Then again… I wouldn't be suffering from this torturous heat.

I tilted my head enough to peer at him from over my arms. He was idly carving a piece of wood with his claw, looking lost in thought as well. He was risking too much. He was always risking too much for me.

"If you accidentally mark me—permanently, I mean—I won't go back to the lions," I said, blurting it out before I got too nervous to say it. He froze in his carving and gave me a penetrating look.

How know. I won't. Take advantage? he asked, sounding more confused than anything else. He didn't seem to believe that I was capable of making this offer. He and I both knew he could very easily make an intentional marking look like a mistake.

"Because I trust you," I mumbled into my knee, studying him. The orange fire flickered off the edge of his eye, and I wondered if I'd ever get an opportunity to find out their color. "You're taking a risk, so I must face one as well. I'm giving up ever knowing my family, much less my own species." Saying the sacrifice out loud made me angry, so I took a deep breath and buried my head again.

Admirable… he said quietly and scrubbed a hand over his face. *Come. We try.*

I dragged my sore body to my feet and kneeled in front of him, tilting my head to the side to give him better access. His grunt was frustrated, and I could see him shake his head in the corner of my eyes.

Turn. Back to me, he ordered, knowing I was uncomfortable with it, but if he didn't think he could get a good angle, I'd tolerate it. I jumped slightly when he rubbed my arms soothingly, trying to comfort me. I cringed and hung on to his smell of mangoes and bamboo, hoping that Mehr's hands would stay away while he did this.

Just me. Only me, he reminded, leaning forward to lightly chuff into the back of my head. I nodded and simply waited for him to do it, too nervous to talk. My heat was making me uncomfortable, my sex ached, my breasts ached, my mind was whirling with stress, and I was either going to be able to continue this strange camaraderie with Javed or become his spouse… his mate… overnight and never see my family or species. Bile rose in my throat from the unmanageable stress, and I just cringed until I felt him place the wood and lower his canines to pierce my skin.

I couldn't hold back the moan that was made from fear and desire. It was tentative but ended on a note of pleasure, one that Javed echoed in his chest with a responding groan. When he was just about to finish and my sex was trembling with anticipation, there was a rustling in the jungle that startled the both of us. Though we'd both jerked, the wood saved us, and he quickly finished his partial marking.

He jumped up and strode to the edge of the fireplace, alert, wild, and definitely not caring about his massively tented leathers. I was wobbling on the ground for just a second, startled away from a much-needed climax. I shakily rose to my feet and looked into the night with Field's assistance. There were some plants bobbing a good distance away… maybe eighty or a hundred feet?

Javed growled, bristled and released a quaking roar that had me freezing in place. I couldn't move a finger for the life of me. He darted out in a blur, and I heard the sound of a person encountering a very sudden death. It had been a stomach-churning scream that'd gurgled and cut off suddenly, and I didn't need any guesses to figure out why.

Javed returned, wiping blood from his hands with a wet leaf while scanning the rest of the jungle. He was breathing heavily and baring his canines, looking extremely agitated.

We cannot expect to be alone tonight. Whoever's left that's aware of us knows this is likely their last chance to steal you, he grunted, his eyes never leaving the darkness around us. It will be stupid exiles who don't know about me, or ones who do that don't recognize me. I'm going to cover some trees in my scent as a warning; do not go anywhere. I am keeping you in my sights the entire time. I'll come back to do you next.

Wait, what? Field asked about that last part, but before I could even form the question, Javed strode off to go… do something to some trees.

Chapter 16

Javed

After I was done rubbing my back against some trees like a fucking bear—and pissing on one of them because I had to go, and my erection had finally died a slow, painful death—I returned to our campsite to find Niusha peering out into the dark. She was, unfortunately, bending over a little, and I could see partway up her halter dress. The firelight bounced off the half-dry stream of arousal on her inner thighs, and just like that, my erection returned with a vengeance. I was about a minute away from cutting my cock off and being done with this torture.

What are you looking at? I asked tersely, forcing myself to move my eyes from her inviting rump. How I was able to do that, I'd never know.

Her claws had dug into the branch she was leaning over, and she whispered, "I see a floating thing with people on it. Is that the ferry?"

What?

I crept to the edge and spied a ferry that had dropped anchor near the crocodiles' shallow strip of land. Niusha joined me at my side, assaulting me with her incredible scent. Her heady smell of figs and oud was blending seamlessly into her pheromones and her arousal. Her heat made her smell better every fucking day. My mouth flooded with saliva, and I fought off the distraction because the activity on the river was beyond unusual.

This is not the ferry that transports paying exiles, I said in disbelief. *It looks different, and it's too far upriver... on the wrong side of the breeding ground. I've never seen it before. I've never heard of it before!*

Niusha gasped when a body was rolled out the side and into the crocodile-infested waters. The river exploded with thrashing jaws that made quick work of the corpse. Several more bodies were rolled out, and the lioness next to me released a choked cry, planting her hands over her mouth while she stared ahead in horror. I looked back, and a dead female was tossed overboard, discarded back to the gods with equal disrespect.

"S-Sarita!" she whispered with tears flowing down her cheeks.

Who is that? I asked, unable to keep myself from pulling her in front of me and caging her in my arms so I knew she was safe.

"She disappeared from my village a couple weeks before I left. She was just about to turn eighteen but wasn't spoused... and those who don't get spoused..." She didn't finish the sentence due to dissolving into quiet, frantic sobs, but it wasn't necessary.

They disappear. Clearly, they either used her to exhaustion or no longer had a need for her, I said, trying to figure out what I was seeing. We were too far to catch any scents, and I couldn't hear anything over the roar of the river.

I could feel that she was absolutely crushed by this discovery, and I pulled her back into my chest, wrapping my arms under her breasts to let her know I was her support. I chuffed gently into her hair as I studied the boat. When it seemed like they were done with their illegal activity, they, surprisingly, continued forward to dock on our side of the river.

What the fuck are... are they waiting for someone? Convict asked, completely baffled.

I don't know, I replied, transfixed. How long has this been going on, and why hadn't the news spread like wildfire among the exiles? Traveling merchants couldn't keep their mouths shut and were the source of news from the outside world. Certainly, something like this would have garnered their attention. Were people being paid off or were any witnesses killed? Exiles disappeared all the time, so they definitely wouldn't be missed.

Niusha, I can't let this opportunity go. I must go down there to scent and get a better look. You'll follow, but do so quietly. Can you handle that? I asked, unable to keep myself from nuzzling and chuffing. My body was fighting my mind, intent on initiating our emotional courtship. By the Sky Gods, I needed to fight harder.

"Yes," she whispered, and I grabbed her hand, leading her down the path to the riverbank. I felt that she'd fallen into shock, but I fought the urge to carry her. Despite her pained state, she navigated the ground beautifully and didn't make a sound that would travel.

We found cover by a swell on the upper riverbank that hosted a thicket. I leaned around the prickly branches and prayed for the wind to shift. There were several shifters on the deck, and based on their build, I could hazard a guess on their species, but I needed to make sure.

A half hour had passed, and I grew anxious, not certain how long they'd stay there before either meeting someone or leaving for the other side of the river. I squatted to the ground and looked for some damp soil. Scooping up what I'd found under the thicket, I went up to Niusha and started rubbing it into her upper chest and neck.

Stay here. I'm going to hide your scent the best I can, but you must remain hidden. I will be back in five minutes or less, I said, and she nodded, flushing from what I'd just done. I tried not to think about how much I wanted to dip my hands under the neck line, but I ordered her to crouch and snuck closer to the boat. If I was right, the shifters on deck didn't have night vision better than a human's, so I wasn't particularly worried about being spotted. I nearly laughed at the unintentional joke and found a spot downwind of them.

I took a deep inhale and nodded, saddened like usual, then retreated to get Niusha. I guided her back up the path where we could watch from our campsite. I didn't need to discover anything more than what I'd uncovered.

I sat her down on the ground and rubbed my fingers over my eyes. She was not going to like this, but like everything else so far, I knew it still wouldn't change her mind.

Niusha... I began, trying to find the right words, *those are cheetah, and their story is a very, very sad one.* Niusha's face turned from the boat to me, her face expressionless but her eyes red and puffy from crying.

They are the fastest of us, but also the weakest of the big cats. It made it easy for the lions to take their territory first. They were easily chased away because they didn't have the strength to fight back. The lions allowed any who wished to stay if they remained loyal to their new king. About three-quarters of the cheetahs abandoned their homeland, but the rest decided to stay and were put to use by the crown.

Officially, they worked in positions that benefited from speed, like messengers or outpost servants. Unofficially, they were mostly used for trafficking and working slaves because anyone who'd run would be caught in seconds, and the slaves were too weak to fight back.

I studied Niusha's face as I told her all this, but she continued to look more detached by the second. *I guarantee you that those cheetahs down there are working for the lions. I guarantee you that your friend was taken, used for some purpose by the lions, and dumped in the river when she was no longer useful or was worked until she expired.*

The last sentence broke her composure, and she crumbled, placing her arms over her head. She was heartbroken, lost, and confused.

"Is this a part of me?" she whispered in a voice that was so small, so quiet that I almost missed her trembling words. "Will

I turn into something like that? Will I crave power and slaves now that my lioness is awake?"

That wasn't what I'd wanted her to get out of the story, and it broke my heart to see her question her own soul. I placed a hand on her arm, knowing that the truth would continue to hurt her. I hadn't even gotten to the worst part, and that definitely had to be saved for another day. *I don't know how much of lion behavior is learned or inherent from birth, but I know that you are far too sweet and self-sacrificial to ever be at risk of that. It is a fact. I don't say it just because we're fated—were fated, I mean. I've felt inside of you— er, I'm not talking about sex, I mean your emotions.* Oh gods, I was becoming stupid again, and it was out of nowhere.

"I know what you mean," she assured me quietly, muffled from her position.

I glanced back at the boat and noted that a short line was boarding now. *Do you recognize any of those people?* I asked, nudging her quickly. She popped up and stared down at the small, tired-looking crowd.

"Sushila… and her pure father… Niraj. Javed, I've never, ever heard of spoused disappearing. Something must have happened back at the village. She'd lost her baby recently… stolen without her knowing it… of course…" The last was said with deep bitterness. "I'm so glad I saved Chirasmi," she choked out, wiping several new tears from her face.

Me too. I'm so proud of you. And that's why you'll never want for power or slaves, I reminded her. Yes, she saved the little tiger. The reminder just made me want Niusha all the more—mind, soul, and body. I tried to clear my mind, but for some reason Niusha's heat had spiked. What the fuck had caused that?

She shifted uncomfortably, and her heart rate accelerated, though she looked so sad. It was incredibly confusing to me. *What was the last thing you thought of?* I asked, unable to resist the burning question. The mystery was too great to ignore.

"Just about how I miss the orphans. Chirasmi was a lot of work, but I really miss her," she said quietly, staring at the last person boarding the ferry. "They're leaving, Javed," she said, nodding to the departing vessel.

I didn't want to suggest it, but we could potentially attempt to follow the trafficked villagers once we crossed tomorrow. It'd be dangerous and might detour us from our destination. It'd give me more time with her, but I'd let her decide. I didn't want to put her in danger for the sake of my feelings.

On the other hand, her heat would draw attention. She was definitely easy to scent from a distance, which was probably why there were so many exiles skulking around tonight. I bristled at the thought of other males scenting was what intended for me and fought off the urge to bend Niusha over a low branch. Right… I remembered what I was going to do.

I stood and held a hand out to Niusha. We went down to the river to fetch some water to boil, and I navigated up a nearby palm to collect some sweet water from a flower stalk.

You need to hydrate, I said. *You've cried a lot, and I'm sure losing all the fluid from your heat isn't helping.*

Her face turned red, and she choked on a swallow. I cringed and squatted to pat her back while she coughed and sputtered. I probably shouldn't have mentioned arousal fluid while she was in the middle of drinking.

See? Convict pointed out gleefully. *Idiot like you. Just like I said.*

Fuck off, I growled at him.

Idiot.

Once Niusha had caught her breath, she drank a little more from the canteen and returned it to me. "Delicious… though it tasted better on my tongue than in my lungs," she said, chuckling weakly.

I definitely would like you to swallow next time, I said, then nearly palmed my face at the accidental innuendo. Thank all the fucking gods that she wouldn't understand that one. Her heat was going to be the end of my brain.

Her scent is getting stronger, Convict murmured as I went through Niusha's bag to find her soap. *She's going to draw more attention tonight. We already have exiles sniffing around despite your scent marking.*

It deterred some, I claimed indifferently, grabbing the soap and a small cloth I'd seen her use. I turned to the beautiful, libidinous lioness in heat, the absolute death of me, and handed her the cleaning items. *Wash off by that tree. I'll make sure you're undisturbed,* I said to her, nodding to the nearby trunk.

"Thank you. I've been needing a wash, and this mud is itchy," she said, picking off a crusted flake on her chest. She wrinkled her nose and frowned, then placed the water on the flattest part of the tree's wild, sprawling roots. I slung her old dress over a branch to act as a curtain, then stood with my back to her on the other side, crossing my arms and glaring into the jungle. No one else was allowed to look upon her, and if more exiles became bold or stupid enough to approach, I'd probably end up killing again before dawn.

Let them come, Convict hissed.

I addressed Niusha when I heard the sound of her disrobing. *Make sure you're thorough in removing all your oils. I will cover you in my scent again when you're done. Wash that dress too,* I added gruffly, shifting uncomfortably from the slick scrubbing noises. I'd rather be the one massaging her breasts with soap.

I tried to keep my emotions together, but it didn't help when my words encouraged a spark of excitement in her. Her developing heat had made it harder to ignore her amorous reactions over our brittle bond, and her soul was very nearly singing for me right now. I could smell her natural lubricant even as she washed, and I was starting to doubt the effectiveness of my plan. I groaned internally and rubbed a temple, willing myself to think chaste thoughts.

Sunsets. Cubs' laughter. Grandmother's uneven doilies. Picking flowers. Deflowering. Gods, I can't believe I had sex with her twice, I thought miserably to myself, failing the exercise. I turned to my tiger out of desperation. *Convict, are you able to hold me back at all tonight?*

At this point, why would I want to?

Why do I have to keep answering that question? I snarled, gritting my teeth in annoyance. *We're getting too attached.*

It's too late, you know that. Just enjoy it while it lasts, he snapped back at me, cranky.

It's not too late. We could still reject her and get a second—

If you can honestly tell me that you're not falling in love with our fated mate, I'll try to hold you back, but don't make me laugh, Javed. You don't want a second chance. It's her or nothing. I'm perfectly fine with withering away and dying with you when this is all over. Our lioness has ruined everyone else for me. Now if I could convince Field that I'm not a complete asshole before they leave us, that'd be great. I'd die as a slightly less miserable tiger.

I bristled, angry at Convict for poking at such a raw, sensitive spot. Try as I might, I couldn't deny his accusation, and it made me furious. I dug my claws into my crossed arms, seething while I waited for Niusha to finish her bathing.

I could picture every trickling noise as a line of liquid falling down the slopes of her breasts to bead and drip from her nipples. After all we'd done, I still haven't tasted them ye— I shut my eyes and shook my head in an attempt to clear it. Restraint! By the Sky Gods! Restraint, you idiot!

I finally heard her drying herself and hanging her dress to dry. "Ready…" she said timidly, and I raised my arm to encourage her to duck under my cloak with me. She glued herself to my side as I took everything that scented strongly of her and shoved it into the bags.

"Am I-I not getting dressed?" she asked, watching me store her blanket as well. She was breathing heavier, and her skin remained quite warm.

No, not tonight. Too many exiles in the area. There could be more passing through from delivering those ex-villagers and the other captives. Your heat is going to going to announce your presence like a smoke signal if we don't try to hide it. We need to lie low since tonight will be the last night they can strike.

"No." She cringed in disbelief. "That can't be t—"

It's pretty potent to males who haven't scented a female in ages, I reminded her. She peeked into the jungle with a look of distaste, her heart rate accelerating from either fear or desire.

"Gross…" she mumbled. "Seems pretty excessive if I'm only supposed to be enticing you." I felt her cringe of embarrassment after the words had left her mouth.

Don't be embarrassed. You make a good point, I said gruffly and helped her sit down in front of me, keeping her obsessively hidden with my cloak extended around her. My possessiveness and territoriality were climbing to an all-time high with her spike in heat, and I was becoming agitated. By the Sky Gods, I wanted her somewhere safe, not in the middle of the fucking jungle, surrounded by lecherous criminals!

After instructing her to hold on to the cloak for me, I repeated what I'd done for her days and days ago. I rubbed my hands against my chest, neck, and jaw, then slid my hands over her skin to transfer my scent to her. I couldn't keep her from producing her pheromones, but it might help to make her smell strongly of me and then keep her under my cloak tonight.

I ran my hands methodically from the top of her body and worked my way downwards. I was planning on doing this quickly, not allowing an extra second for any stroke to turn sensual. *I will not touch what you do not wish me to touch,* I said. *This is not intended for my pleasure; do you understand?*

"I understand…" she said, biting her soft lower lip. I clenched my teeth and continued to work, realizing quite quickly when I grazed her armpits that she was extremely ticklish, and her automatic reflexes were very fast and quite painful. I avoided her breasts and leaned forward to scrub my scent into her back.

My asshole mind told me another way I could get my scent on her back, but I snorted quietly in irritation and just focused on what was going to help keep her hidden.

"You seem to be ready…" Niusha murmured quietly, and I knew she was talking about the erection that wasn't so well-hidden under my leathers—my cursed, throbbing, aching, pulsing, angry erection that felt like it was two feet long and made of steel. It was close enough to being a weapon, which was just as well because it was going to be the cause of my impending heart attack.

Just like you don't have control over your heat, I don't have control over its response to you. Ignore it, I ordered, almost growling. *It'll go away.* I could almost hear my dick yelling at me.

She merely whimpered, head rolling limply to the side as I finished covering her in my scent. I wasn't pleased with how hot her skin had become, and she sighed when I placed a wrist on her forehead.

"Too hot, too achy," she murmured, and I leaned over to grab the canteen for her.

Drink. Replenish, I said and made sure she finished every last drop.

I frowned when I felt her skin become tacky with sweat. My plan wasn't going to work, was it? The longer she suffered, the hotter she'd get, the more she'd sweat, the more she'd… everything. We didn't have the rain to hide it. I looked around, checking for any males near our site.

I growled lowly, not liking any of my options. My inner tiger, the ultimate sum of Convict and me, was getting pretty pissed off too. It wanted to protect and hide our mate, thinking the answer was pretty fucking simple—mount her immediately, quell her heat, and stay low until dawn.

I pulled her panting body against my chest, trying to decide the right course of action, and her quiet pleading wasn't helping me think. I shook her shoulder with urgency to get her attention, and she looked up at me with pleading, dilated eyes.

What do you want? I give up. This won't work, I asked, cupping the back of her head.

"Need…" she breathed, pawing at the edge of my leathers. "Need my male," she panted, with flushed cheeks as bright as coffee cherries.

Then you'll get him. I grabbed her other dress from her bag. *Put this on. I'll have no other lay eyes on your skin,* I growled, and she slowly wriggled into it. I didn't know what it was about her heat, but whenever she moved, it was like she was performing a sensual dance. Even time seemed to slow as her hands slid the fabric over her hips. I bit my lip at the sight and wrapped a hand around my overly engorged member, squeezing it in anticipation.

Hands and knees this time. Sorry, I ordered next and kneeled behind her. I didn't feel any fear or discomfort from her, which was good. Perhaps her lioness was blocking out everything but her instincts now. She was simply ready. She needed me to put out the fire in her.

The feral tiger in me responded quite aggressively to that knowledge, and I shuddered, feeling my stomach and groin tighten when she leaned forward to get on all fours. I quickly scanned the jungle and then flipped up her skirt to bare her rump to me. Oh, my female had a beautiful ass. I moved some of the fabric down a little because I only needed access to her pussy. I stared at the plump curves where her hips swelled while I untied my loincloth and let it drop to the ground. My dick lurched free, unhindered, and throbbed so hard I was robbed of a breath.

A rumble that threatened to turn into a roar boiled in my chest as my blood grew hot and restless. When I felt between my female's legs, I blinked feverishly to overcome a rush of lust that rolled through my abdomen like thunder. A warm, glossy fluid met my fingers, and I rubbed it between my thumb and forefinger to feel its fresh slickness. Her sex was excessively weeping, and when I slid a finger between her folds, she grinded mindlessly against it, huffing and moaning in need. It was too much, and that was when my restraint shattered.

Chapter 17

Javed

I leaned forward to clamp my jaw around the back of her neck and pushed my lioness down so her breasts were pressed into the jungle floor. I let a growl vibrate down her spine and clamped a little harder with my teeth, warning her to stay there until I was done breeding with her. I needed to be alert and keep her low at the same time.

I leaned back and forced her sweating thighs apart, tilting her hips upward to display her swollen pink pussy to me. I stared into the jungle, flaring my nostrils as I fought to scent anything through the concentrated arousal of my needy female. I didn't hear, see, or smell anyone yet, but it didn't mean they weren't lingering beyond my senses.

Keeping my female as covered as possible with my cloak and her dress, I lined my pulsing dick up with her snug slit. Once I was notched in place, I pushed my hips forward while pulling her back by the handles of her pelvis. My eyes narrowed, and my arms shook as I fought to go slow, pushing my crown in with the help of her arousal seeping out and around it.

I grunted when my crown popped in, then moaned as I slid slowly into her superheated channel, stretching her entrance wide. She was so snug, and I could feel every soft ridge along her slippery walls. Pleasure exploded hot and wild into my abdomen and bloomed up into my chest when I became fully buried up to my sack. A groan was pulled from my throat, and it burst into a lustful, carnal growl.

I tilted my head back and closed my eyes in bliss. She felt perfect wrapped around my dick. It was like stepping into a hot spring after a run in the snow—that perfect temperature right before it got almost too hot to touch. I absorbed her heat as I stayed embedded for one more sky-blessed moment, pulsing slowly against her sweet rump as I prepared to meet my female's needs.

I planted my fingers firmly into her hips and pulled mine back, gritting my teeth as she fought to keep me inside her. My female was tight… so tight, so perfect. Perhaps this wouldn't take long after all. I pulled out and immediately plunged back in, making her mewl in pleasure. My erection was soaked in her slick, and I had an easier time fighting her clenching muscles. She arched her back to tilt her hips up, offering her enthusiasm to me, and I answered by starting a regular pace. After a minute of warming her up, I started thrusting faster and turned my attention to the jungle now that I'd set a preferable speed for her.

I narrowed my eyes and snorted as I caught some movement. There were two males stalking about one hundred and fifty feet to the left and another to the upper right, but much farther away from us. I pushed my lioness's torso down as much as possible while I fucked her moaning little body. I knew exactly what the cats were doing, and I'd be ready. Oh, I'd be ready before they were.

I massaged her right buttock idly as I slid in and out of her, displacing her fluid with each push in and making her squirm into the ground in utter ecstasy. Her claws raked thick, severe lines into the soil with every other wild pant that escaped her feral lips.

That's right, female. Take my length and accept your pleasure, I purred to her. *You take it so, so well. Your pussy was meant for my dick, sweet lioness.* I kept an eye on our pathetic voyeurs while I courted my female, trying to work my way into her heart as I rocked pleasurably between her legs.

When four more males crept into sight, I yanked my hood back to expose my face and curled my lips back to show off my extended canines. Most of their faces turned ashen when they recognized me, and the virtueless gibs fell over themselves to escape my territory. The two other males, who watched the departing cowards with uneasiness, were not even worth being called competitors and did not have many breaths left to enjoy.

I sped up, staring them down as I slapped into my female's wet heat, dipping my long dick into her repeatedly for her enjoyment. They did not know me, and it was laughable that they thought they could take me down while I was distracted by my ripe mate. I growled quietly, feeling the brutal power deep within me that gave me my confidence on the battlefield.

Beautiful, beautiful female, I purred to my mate. *Just feel me in you. Focus on how I spread your swollen, silken pussy. Feed on what I offer.* I thrusted forcefully into her with each word, driving my length in as I drove my plea. I wanted to keep her distracted from the approaching cats, who'd sunken to the ground behind a tall root and a mess of vines, waiting for me to exhaust myself.

I extended my claws, careful not to scratch a single invisible hair on her smooth skin and sped up like I was about to finish. I slammed in once more and held myself there, buried to the hilt while I drooped over, stroking her bottom.

Let your male take care of some business, my queen, I crooned to her as I pulled out and intercepted both attacking cats before they could even step into the firelight.

I lunged, wrapped a hand around each neck, and cracked their skulls together, roaring in an unnecessary show of dominance. I shoved their brained, lifeless bodies to the ground and fell into a roll when a third attempted to ambush me. I tripped him by swinging out a leg, caught his head in my arm, then broke his neck in a single yank. I tossed the body to the other side of my territory, then rushed back to my female, who was writhing in a ball from being interrupted.

She was so lost to her heat that she hadn't even noticed the encounter. My captivating lioness was mewling and pulling her dress up, unsticking it from her sweaty, blushing skin. I repositioned my hood, rolled her onto her back so she could look at me if she wanted to and slipped easily into her again. I returned to the pace I'd been at before and brushed her blond tresses from her drawn brows and fevered eyes. I could give her my full attention now. I was certain we'd no longer be interrupted, especially with those corpses decorating the edge of my territory like a morbid wreath.

There we are, I groaned, back in her snug, dripping heat. *Back home. Did you miss me, my queen?* I asked, leaning forward to bury my sensitive nose in her neck, taking deep inhales of my new favorite drug. *Oh, your scent makes me so hard.* I bit into her soft, salty flesh as I fucked her, making her buck and wrap her legs around my hips. I felt myself grow harder from a rush of lust, bottoming out against the threshold of her womb.

"Ah! I did, I did, I did," she breathed, tilting her head back and showing me her own canines as she gaped in satisfaction. "Missed you." She sighed and tossed her head, panting with flushed cheeks and parted lips. I lapped at her neck and bit again, loving the control I had over her right now. She couldn't run from me in this moment. She couldn't leave me for the pride this very second. She was pinned, and it was exactly where she wanted to be—exactly where I wanted her.

In this moment, lioness, you're mine, I growled, panting as I rocked over her, dripping my own hot sweat to mingle with hers the way our arousals did. *Not the lions. Mine.* I leaned into her ear, my puffs of breath forcing a shudder through her as I lapped at her earlobe. *I will find a way to change your mind. This is your first warning of my intentions,* I murmured.

I leaned back, gripped her hips, and started fucking her as hard as I could, driving mercilessly in at her favorite angle to make her mad with pleasure. I blinked away sweat that trickled down my brows and grinned ferally when I saw her tighten up from head to toe. I delighted in using the mate touch to please her. Being able to give that one perfect partner something no one else could was an addictive feeling. I relished it. Her heat gripped me tighter as I built up her pleasure, letting it grow until she could show me how good I made her feel.

"Male… my male…" she panted, mouth wide as she gaped and gasped for air. Her claws were buried fast in the ground, and her breasts heaved, just barely covered by the dress that'd ridden up her waist.

Come, female, I groaned, gritting my teeth as I fought to fight off my own orgasm. *Come on my dick so I can fill you. I want you to suck me dry.*

My hips landed wetly against her skin, which was flushed red from the constant slapping. "Ah…" she moaned, thrusting her chest up to the canopy. A low groan bled from her lips and grew louder until her legs shook from sustained tension. When her sex clenched down viciously on my length, nearly halting my thrusts, I knew she'd gotten there.

She released a roaring cry of pleasure and climaxed, undulating under me as I forced my thrusts along to the rhythm of her orgasm. She dragged her fingers through her hair, moaning with each wave that rocked her senseless. With my teeth bared in a grin and a grimace of pleasure, I rocked into her until I'd ridden her ecstasy out and then focused on my release.

I adjusted my grip and moved faster, grunting from the aftershocks of her climax as her sex squeezed me. My hips moved in a frenzy to wrap my erection in euphoria until I slammed in and came, tilting my head back to roar my victory.

I pulled out of her and released the rest of my seed onto her belly, covering her abdomen in ropes of my essence. I growled through gritted teeth, hissing with each ejaculation that made my nerves sizzle with pleasure. When the last spurt landed on her soft skin, I released a quiet sigh of supreme satisfaction and collapsed to her side, pulling her over to lay on my bicep.

Her eyes fluttered open, looking up at me with sleepy contentment. The feral edge was gone from both of us, and now it was just Javed and Niusha. The beasts in our hearts and souls were sated, as well as Niusha's heat.

Are you feeling better? I asked, finally slowing my breathing to a normal rate.

She blinked and stared shyly at my chest, tracing a line along a tiny scar on my left pec—one of many scars. Her cheeks, already flushed from sex, bloomed in a deeper blush.

"I am… thank you," she whispered, and I replied with a low, quiet chuff. I slid a hand to her belly and dipped a finger in my seed, then I dabbed it onto her upper chest and rubbed it into her skin. "Is that…?" she asked, trailing off as she tried to look down at where my finger was.

My seed… I like our scents combined, I replied softly. *It may be my favorite scent, next to just your pure one.* I dipped my finger in again and spread more of it, trailing a finger up her neck. Some might not like it, but I found it highly erotic. I couldn't read Niusha's mind, but I knew that she was currently in a state of bliss. I smiled at having been the one to do that.

"I barely remember, but did you mean what you said? About trying to change my mind?" she murmured drowsily, not seeming to be angry or sad in her recollection.

Yes, I said. *If I don't, I'm not being true to myself. It's a fine line to walk, putting your happiness, safety, and quality of life at the top of my priorities.*

"So you won't take me back to the lions anymore?" she asked with a deepening frown.

I don't go back on my word, Niusha. If it's where you wish to go, I'll take you, but I won't stop trying to change your mind, I answered firmly, tracing my thumb along her collarbone.

"That's fair, I guess." She closed her eyes and relaxed once more.

I obsessively continued to cover her chest and neck in the seed I'd spilled on her belly, needing to scent us together. I needed the comfort of having claimed her. It was like a strange security blanket. In this moment, I could pretend she was completely mine.

"Javed?" she murmured drowsily into my arm.

Yes?

"Did someone try to kill us in the middle of you… helping me?"

Yes.

"Did you kill them?"

Yes.

"Oh… thanks."

You're welcome.

Niusha

The more time I spent with Javed, the more I had no idea what a normal relationship was supposed to look like, but what I did know was that waking up next to him was quickly becoming the best part of my day. Making sure his hood was properly in place, I stared at his sleeping lower face. I could barely make out the warm mahogany color of his eyelashes as they rested on his tan cheeks.

He had the most subtle smattering of freckles across his nose and cheekbones that I hadn't noticed before, and for some reason, they made me smile. Perhaps they softened the stern—but handsome—edge to his face. I let my eyes drift down the slope of his nose; narrow at the top, a touch wider in the middle and turned up ever so slightly at the tip, with the tiniest indent just under that.

I longed to trace my fingers over his mouth. I wanted to brush my nails along the stubble that framed an upper lip neither too thin nor too plump. His fuller lower lip had a beautiful curve;

it was sensual even in his sleep and rested over a strong chin that had a small dimple. I followed the mahogany shadow of his facial hair up his jaw to the smallest lock that escaped the cover of his hood. It was a deep, rich orange—very much the color of Convict's shiny coat. Once again, I wished I could see his whole face—his whole head. He was a mystery to me, and as much as I respected his privacy, I had so many burning questions.

I scooted closer to rest my head on his broad chest so I could be lulled by his heartbeat in the early morning light. My gaze drifted down his body, but my brows shot up when I noticed his erection. He was asleep… how could he possibly be ready? Maybe he was having a nice dream. I knew that sometimes I…

I squeezed my eyes shut, trying to wipe my mind of the nightmares, the horrible males that made me wake up wet. There was no explaining them, and I clung to Javed in my near panic. He was my log in the river—along for the bumpy ride and something to both hold me up and block all the dangers.

What were we, though? I still didn't know how to think of us. We were fated by a goddess, and I had a hard time denying that because I felt it for myself, but how different was that from an arranged spousing? Was I supposed to have loved him at first sight? I knew about love, but I'd never seen it, at least I didn't think I had. I heard that there'd occasionally be a pure mother and father who had feelings for each other. I supposed I loved the orphans, but that was different… wasn't it?

So how did one know if they were in love? Was love required for a permanent marking, or was it expected to grow over time? I had too many questions, and I didn't really feel like Javed was the best person to ask. I needed to see more of the real world. The village of shifters had been an eye-opener, but I needed a closer look at more relationships to know what I was even feeling.

All I could say was that I really, really liked Javed. I'd never been attracted to a male before, but there'd never been anyone as handsome as him. Oh, how I sorely wished I had a mother I could talk to about all of this—or even a sister. As much as I was growing afraid of the lions, I had such a deep need for familial female guidance. I hated being forced to pick between him and my family. I felt like I needed one before the other. I was so lost…

Your emotions are busy this morning, Javed said, then stretched his arms with a large yawn.

I sat up and smiled weakly, not really capable of sharing the mess my mind was in right now. "Just trying to sort things out. It's been a long journey through this jungle. At least we're leaving it today." To get the focus off myself, I pointed at his tented leathers and asked, "Are you ok?"

It's a morning thing. Ignore it, he grumbled, standing up quickly.

I gasped when his movement disturbed a venomous snake that'd been coiled under his cloak for warmth, then I darted forward with my claws outstretched. I lopped off its head and found myself sprawled out on the dirt, breathing hard with snake blood on my hands. Javed was frozen.

"Oh my unnamed gods," I squeaked, nearly choking on my heart, which had somehow lodged itself in my throat.

You just saved me, Javed sputtered. *Shit... that was close. I didn't even scent it.*

I just stared blankly at the venomous snake until Javed picked me up and stood me in front of him. *You busted your chin open,* he noted in dismay, licking his thumb to swipe off some dirt and blood. *It'll heal today, though. I'm so sorry you got hurt!* He tidied up my face and hair, chuffing a couple times as he fussed over me while I stared at the dead snake. *Thank you, Niusha. And look,* he said, reaching down to pick up the body, *you caught breakfast!*

"Isn't it poisonous?" I asked, finally able to speak.

He chuckled silently and shook his head. Jerking his thumb to the remainder of the snake, he said, *You already separated the poisonous bit. The meat's just fine. Let's eat!*

After my first experience with cooked snake—which tasted ok, a bit like the fowl we'd kept at the village but tough to chew—we gathered our belongings and left for the river. Javed had wanted to wait until noon to cross because the crocodiles would be more active at dawn. When we reached the river bed, I stared bitterly at the spot where the bodies had been dumped. My chin wobbled as I thought of how heartlessly she had been rolled off the boat. No one deserved a send-off like that.

Javed seemed to know what I was thinking and stood at my side to hold my hand. *The Sky Gods already have her. Their starlight will preserve her soul until she returns to these lands again.*

"Who are these gods you speak of, Javed? I've known only the false ones the pure elder spoke of." Then I decided to share my own deviation. "I started believing in my own to fill the void. The ones that live in the moon, the skies, the sun, and beneath our feet… It seemed to bring me more comfort. They made more sense to me…" I said blankly, unable to take my eyes from where she'd been torn apart.

The Sky Gods must have been guiding you. Those are the ones who watch over us. The Moon Goddess gave birth to the wolves and lycans. She's also the one who blesses us with our fated mate. The Sun God gave rise to the dragons… He's fierce but protective. The Earth Gods birthed the Moon Goddess. They also gave rise to men and women. Our gods, Niusha—the ones who birthed cats like you and me—are the Sky Gods. They are innumerable but act as one. They are the watchers…

I shuddered. That was too many eyes. What were all those other creatures? Dragons? Lycans? So odd how my mind had sought the true gods for comfort in my darkest days. My soul must have known where it had come from and could no longer deny the truth.

"Their starlight preserves her…" I murmured quietly to myself, and Javed squeezed my hand.

Wait here while I get a sense of how many crocodiles are around, he said and strode confidently down the shallow path. I snapped out of my fog and watched nervously. My gaze then shot ahead to see if I could make out any crocodiles lurking under the water, but the surface was too reflective, too busy to expose them.

Don't look, Niusha. Javed started undressing, so I was forced to stare at the ground, feeling like this was the worst possible thing that could be asked of me. Above the hammering in my ears, I waited to hear Javed's screams of pain. I fought to swallow and backed away from the water until I heard Convict's growl.

I glanced up again to watch Convict bound down the shallows toward a crocodile that was slowly lumbering out, hissing. I covered my mouth now that I was able to compare their sizes. The crocodile was massive, bigger than anything Field would want to go near, but Convict was about half its length from nose to tail. Minus the tails, they seemed to be equal.

I screamed into my hands when a crocodile splashed out of nowhere on Convict's right, but he hopped around its clapping maw and dug his teeth into its neck, keeping the growling crocodile between him and the one he'd originally targeted. His prey tried to turn to get to Convict, but he placed a paw on its back and leaned into his bite until the reptile died.

He dragged the dead predator off to the deeper side and trotted around the other crocodile to flank it. The monstrous creature hissed and swung its head to strike at Convict, but he dashed around again and went for its neck. This time the crocodile scuttled forward and turned sharply, lashing its tail so the colossal tiger had to splash away and try again.

Convict raced back in, chasing the tail while the crocodile turned. He got ahead of its rotation and finally claimed the back of its neck, biting hard to secure his victory. The tiger's tail thrashed as he anchored the reptile, straddling until it succumbed to crushing jaws. As before, the tiger dragged the body to deeper water and trotted out, panting and surveying the immediate area.

To my disbelief, he settled and took a break on the shallow stretch. I fisted my hands and shouted at him to come back and rest in safety, but he ignored me, which further stoked my anger.

"Convict, you get back here right now, or so help me!" I yelled.

Tell him that I'm mad at him! Field snapped.

"Field is getting mad at you!"

The tiger visibly flinched and quickly returned. After chuffing and rubbing against my hip, he collapsed to take a breather. I grumbled nonsense and glared at him.

"One could have snuck up on you!" I snapped. He turned his head away, and only the gods knew what he was thinking.

After a minute of grooming his face, he butted his head against me in another loving rub. I squealed when I nearly fell over and had to wrap my arms around his neck to stay upright. He nuzzled and chuffed so intensely that I started cackling at the sight of this terrifying crocodile-killer cuddling me.

T-tell him to stop with the cute act... Field stuttered.

Nah. I grinned as I scratched behind his ears, then told Convict, "Field says you're cute." It wasn't lying... not really.

Niusha! That's not what I meant!

Maybe you should cool it with the pranks then, I replied as I cooed over Convict's affection. *Shall I tell him that you think he has a nice butt? What do cats find attractive? Does he have handsome ears? Should I tell him he has nice testicles for a tiger? I don't know what makes for good testicles, but surely he'd appreciate the sentiment.*

No! Absolutely not! Don't you dare! Her high pitch was totally unlike her, panicking like it was the worst thing that could possibly happen. I chuckled and petted Convict's rumbling side before he got up to continue clearing out the path. Suddenly, I was in quite a good mood.

Chapter 18

Niusha

Convict gradually chipped away at the crocodile breeding ground, and it wasn't until his tenth kill that my nerves truly strained. Unless it was my imagination, he was slowing down and had been grazed by a smaller crocodile who could turn a little tighter than the others. After that, Convict picked up Javed's discarded clothes and returned to my side, clearly needing another break.

"You're such a strong warrior, sweet Convict," I said, crouching to pet him. He chuffed in greeting again and leaned into my strokes, grunting and groaning his happiness in the tiger language. "Poor thing." I sighed, looking at the cut on his side. "That looks painful."

Convict raised his chin, stubbornly showing that he was above crying over such injuries. When he started shifting back into Javed, I closed my eyes and listened to him slip on his clothes. I'd probably be safe looking at his hips and below, kind of wanting a peek at his butt or cock, but I held firm against the temptation.

Dressed, he announced. *I think it should be safe to cross now. With the number of crocodiles Convict killed, it should keep the others busy. They can be a bit... cannibalistic.*

He didn't mention how the bodies discarded last night also probably gave some of the reptiles their fill, but I think it went without saying. When he turned, he winced and carefully pushed his cloak back just enough to look at his side. The cut was still there, but it was a wide gash now.

Ah shit. He cringed. *Shifting made it worse.*

"Oh no. Will you be ok? Does it ever make it better?" I asked, mindfully placing my fingers near the gash on my chin.

Very, very rarely. Since so many things move around, the skin can tear if you have a cut. Internal injuries are extremely dangerous. Shifters usually don't take the chance. I thought I'd risk it to shift back. Convict tried to mind-link you, but apparently the partial marking is unreliable for him. I didn't want to guide you through the shallows without being able to talk.

"I suppose that's wise," I said. Even with him, the thought of crossing that river rattled my nerves.

We'll get through it, he said with a handsome, encouraging smile.

"R-right!"

Javed picked up one of the bags, and I grabbed the other. *We should still run across. They're slow when they have to walk, but they can lunge out and surprise you. Are you ready?* he asked.

No, Field said flatly, reflecting my sentiments exactly.

"Yes," I asserted and girded my loins.

He strode toward the shallows, gave me one last look, and started splashing forward, sprinting across the silty, algae-covered path. I ran after him, noting that the ground was a little slippery, and grimaced, praying to all the gods Javed had mentioned that I'd make it across in one piece.

On both sides, I could see the dead crocodiles being tugged at by the other reptiles. One would occasionally sink and pop back up, missing a limb or a chunk of its body. I nearly tripped on a slippery rock about halfway through but stumbled upright while trying not to have a heart attack. A frightened whimper would occasionally burst past my lips whenever thrashing water would startle me. I could make out some crocodiles that were lurking in the murky depths past the shallows, but they all ignored me; maybe they were full from last night's meal…

We were ninety percent across the shallows when I was starting to reach exhaustion and had developed a cramp in my ribs. Javed pointed off to the right in warning, but when I turned my head to look, I stepped awkwardly on a rock and went down hard. After some loud splashing, the next thing I knew was white-hot pain.

I felt the exact moment the bottom of my right lower leg got crushed, and the most excruciating pain I'd ever known took hold of it. I screamed louder than a mother giving birth, barely noticing Javed splashing next to me, roaring.

Niusha! It's rolling! Roll with it! he shouted, sounding more panicked than I'd ever heard. I thrashed, unable to do anything but scream and keep my mouth above the silty water. A blinding pain tortured me as I felt my limb shred, then get released.

I was swept up and carried, but all Field and I could do was scream. I shrieked past the point of a raw throat, unable to tolerate the agony in silence. I didn't know how I stayed awake through it, but I desperately prayed for unconsciousness.

Niusha, oh gods! Niusha, hang in there! Javed's voice cried.

I writhed in his hold, moaning and screaming with every additional jostle from his gait. Tears soaked my face, and my teeth threatened to crack, gritting through this torturous nightmare. I was placed down on hard ground, heard a ripping, then felt something being tied around my leg. I was picked up again and carried faster this time.

I had no idea how much time had passed, but it felt like three years. Three years of horror.

"Oh gods!" I wailed when I was finally laid down in cool grass. Someone was shouting and footsteps came running toward me.

Niusha, I got help! Stay awake! Stay with me! The voice palmed my cheek. I sobbed.

Something felt wrong with my foot, and I couldn't bring myself to look at it. Fear, pain, and horror utterly trapped me. When I felt someone move it, I screeched at the top of my lungs, then fell unconscious.

I bobbed in and out of sleep for ages. Every time I woke, I'd stay awake a fraction of a second longer before succumbing back to the black. I didn't dream. I was just gone. I occasionally heard a soothing voice, felt a soothing touch, and smelled a soothing scent. Sometimes I felt hot, sometimes I felt cold, and sometimes I felt numb. Pain was almost always a constant. It was bad at first—I'd notice a great deal of it for the split second I'd be awake—but then it faded to a deep throb.

Eventually, I was able to stay awake, and I tilted my head into warm skin smelling of mangoes and bamboo. I groaned and licked my lips, trying to find saliva to speak. My ankle hurt, but it wasn't as bad as it had been.

I lifted my hand to poke the arm slung over me and blinked as I slowly adjusted my eyes to the evening light. I heard a deep intake of breath, then the body next to me jerked upright, and Javed's cloaked head appeared in my line of sight. He looked terrible; what little I could see of his eyes was red, and his nose seemed to be irritated, like he'd shed tears.

"Why're you crying?" I croaked out, brushing his arm tiredly.

Oh gods, you're finally awake, he said with a wet sniff and leaned over to hug me, tucking his head under my chin and burying his face in my chest.

"Finally?" I asked. I tried to wake up more, to shrug off the foggy confusion.

You've been out for four days. Tsisana kept you asleep for three, but you just stayed unconscious...

"Do I know a Tsisana?" I murmured, furrowing my brows as I struggled to remember.

"You do now," a flat voice said. I tilted my head toward the sound, and a woman kneeled in the grass next to me. She was young, pretty, with her dark brown hair tied up in a ponytail. Some braids had little beads, claws, feathers, and other trinkets woven into them. Crescent earrings swayed from her ears with every movement, and her eyes trailed down to my feet where she leaned over to look at something. "You seem to be nearly there. I'm just treating a small infection, but that should be gone by tomorrow."

"Infection?" I asked, blinking rapidly as I tried to sit upright.

Woah! Slow, Niusha! Slow down, Javed said, grabbing my shoulder. The other hand reached to catch the blanket that had begun to slide off me. That was when I realized I was naked. It was a little weird to be lying nude around an extra person, but since it was a woman, I wasn't too embarrassed.

"What happened?" I asked, propping myself up on my elbows.

Do you remember the crocodiles? Javed asked the same time the witch spoke, saying something different, but I hadn't caught it. I shook my head and looked between the two, not sure who was going to speak next.

"I remember the crocodiles..." It was a distant memory, though. "What happened after that?"

The woman gestured to Javed who said, *You nearly lost your foot... I'm so sorry. I should have had us run across as cats. I was so stupid! I was overconfident, and it nearly cost you! I'm so sorry. I'm so sorry!* He wrapped his arms around me again, burying his face in my neck. I couldn't hear him, but I definitely felt his tears land on my shoulder.

"I almost lost my foot?" I asked, not processing it. That couldn't be right. I sat up a little more and pulled up the blanket, then turned green at the sight of my foot. It was a little swollen, especially around the ankle, and stitches had been sewn all the way around it. The bruising and discoloration was… simply atrocious. I grimaced, nausea churning my stomach.

"Yes, fortunately it hung on by your back tendon. I reattached everything with some tools and a lot of magic. To be honest, I wasn't completely certain I could save it," Tsisana explained. "And to be blunt, it was really fucked up. That croc got you good. You lost a lot of blood."

Well, that's a lot to take in… Field uttered.

"Your male ran you miles inland and found me outside a town in bobcat country. The nosey bastard smelled herbs on me and almost ran me over," she said in a deadpan voice, but her cheek lifted and a tiny smirk formed a dimple.

Figured she was a nomad witch, Javed said, not at all bothered by her way of speaking.

"What's a nomad witch?" I asked, looking at him, then at Tsisana.

Her eyes darkened, and her lips drew into a flat, tense line before she spoke. "What cave have you been living in, lioness?" Her voice came out harsh, and I shrunk in on myself. Javed glared at her, but the woman snorted. "Your kind invaded our coven years ago. We were either taken as prisoners or managed to escape. Those of us who escaped turned into nomads, seeking jobs where we could find them. If we stay in one place too long, the lions find us. They always do."

I couldn't say anything to that. It was another horror story to add to the overwhelming stack. All I wanted to do was crawl back into the cave she'd mentioned.

"I'm sorry," I whispered, not knowing what else to say.

"Sorry won't bring my sister back," she snapped. "That's why I'm way the fuck out here. I don't suppose you know where they take the witches they steal? I don't even know what the fuck a lioness is doing out of the pride."

"I don't know. I didn't even know I was a shifter until…" I tried to count on my fingers, but it was hard to add with my muddled memory. "I only found out… maybe a little over a week ago? I grew up in a village south of here, in the jungle. Thought I was a human. They drugged us."

"That's fucking weird," the witch said, squinting one eye in bewilderment. "I guess I'm sorry for being an ass. You are completely out of the loop."

I relaxed, glad to be around another person who might not hate me after all.

I told her about the traffickers we saw, so she's going to try to track them, Javed said, idly untangling my hair and brushing it with his fingers. *Glad she had a paper and quill. Tired of drawing in the dirt.*

"How… can I repay you for saving my foot?" I asked and worried at my hands.

The witch waved in dismissal. "Your male already paid. He hunted some beasts for me. The food is good eating, and I can sell the pelts. We're even." She stood and wiped the dirt from her knees. "I left you some ointment for your injury and some pills. I gave your male written instructions for the next couple of days. You can remove the stitches tomorrow."

"Thank you. I…" I choked up, too overwhelmed to speak.

"One more thing since you probably know nothing about your sweet and caring people," she said impassively, lifting her large bag that tinkled and clanked with dangling bottles and jars. "Make sure you don't go near the lions. Once they find out about those cubs you're developing, they're dead."

She waved as she strolled away and left me reeling from shock.

I stared at where the witch had disappeared, completely astonished, until I felt Javed's broad hand settle on my shoulder. I swung my head to look up at him, and I had no idea what I should be feeling. The tiger next to me was wearing a surprised but pained expression. The emotions swirling within him were as complex as mine; it was hard to pick out any from the tangle.

"I'm sorry," I blurted out, forcing the words past the lump in my throat.

His lips parted, and he sighed, tilting his head to give me a penetrating look. His eyes flickered between mine as he studied me, then he raised a hand to tuck a strand of my hair behind my ear. Without a word, he cupped the back of my head, pulled me forward, and placed a soft kiss above my brow.

I was thunderstruck and speechless. The temporary shock vanished, replaced by delight. He kissed me! Aside from Mehr's assault, no one had ever kissed me! I decided that I... very much liked it—at least I did when it was from Javed. My soul warmed, glowing from his sweet gesture as much as his grooming—maybe more. My heart fluttered, and though I was somehow aroused through my physical pain, my lack of an extreme sexual reaction had me realizing that my heat was gone. I didn't know whether to be happy or sad about that. Now I didn't have an excuse to be close to him.

Niusha, don't be sorry, he said softly, resting his head on top of mine. *If I didn't have to worry about you going to the lions, I'd be roaring at the sky in celebration. A part of me is in mourning for them already. I'm not going to stop trying to change your mind.*

"I already made you that promise, Javed. I told you I wouldn't let anyone hurt them if I got with cub. I'd draw blood for them," I insisted, too tired to get riled up and defensive. "I-I'm not even sure I will go to the lions. I'm... struggling."

You're going to make me crazy, you know that? he said, placing a palm on my lower abdomen. He kissed the top of my head again and left his face there, taking deep inhales and relaxing. *It's not like I'm clueless. I feel your torment.*

"I have so many questions. Now that I'm pregnant, I wish I could see my mother even more," I whimpered pathetically, wiping a tear from a cheek. I then took a deep, steadying breath, balled my fists, and willed myself to stop crying before I broke down completely.

The reality is different from that fantasy. You'd be trading your cubs for a conversation about them. But I understand... and that really fucking sucks. I'm sorry.

My shoulders fell. "It does. It really does."

How does your foot feel? he asked, scooting down to check my ankle.

"Definitely not as bad as it looks," I said with a weak laugh and managed to wiggle my toes, though they were a bit stiff. "Throbs and itches a little. There's a swell of pain every now and then, but it's very, very mild."

Gods. I'm so sorry. I wouldn't be able to forgive myself if you'd lost it. I was so stupid. He leaned down to lay a soft kiss on my swollen ankle, then chuckled silently at the sight of my toes curling. My face heated. That was the third time he'd kissed me!

"It's ok, Javed," I said, clearing my throat and trying to move past my embarrassment. "You got me help. Everything will be fine. I can't believe you ran miles for me!"

I'd run around the world for you, he said, averted his gaze, and picked at a random blade of grass.

I very nearly choked on my heart, unable to speak once again. It made me feel something, but I didn't have a name for it. Whatever it was, it had me struggling not to drown.

When I didn't say anything, he went over to my bag and pulled out my clean dress. I raised my arms when he held it open and allowed him to slide it on so I could cover myself. He rolled up the blanket and packed up the rest of our belongings.

As much as I'd love to stay here and hold a naked female, I want to get us into town, get you in a real bed at an inn. I won't be having my pregnant fated mate sleeping on the ground if I can help it, he said, slinging both bags over a shoulder. I scooted my butt to my ankles and moved to try to stand, but Javed scooped me up instead. *No walking until that infection's all gone.*

"Alright, I guess I don't want it to get worse. Thanks..." I said, feeling down about him carrying everything. I was taking too much, and I didn't know how to give back to him. I honestly loved the attention, but the guilt was as overwhelming as everything else.

A thought occurred to me. "Javed, I won't be welcome in town..." I said nervously, looking up at him. His eyes flickered down to me as he walked, and he tucked his cloak around me.

I covered you in my scent again since you're not in heat anymore. They'll assume you're a different cat I got territorial over.

I tilted my head to take a cursory sniff. I was already surrounded by his scent, so I had a hard time telling how much of me smelled like him. Then I caught a whiff of...

"Did you...?" I asked, looking down at my chest then up at his face, which was blushing.

Only a little, he defended, turning a brighter shade of red. *I-I didn't want to risk anything.*

I fought the hardest I'd ever fought to hold back a smile, incredibly amused by his flustered reaction to getting caught. Had he hoped I wouldn't notice? I decided to take it as a compliment and turned to lean my face against his chest. I actually did like his territoriality. It made me feel special—something I'd never felt before leaving the village. At least it wasn't pee. Oh, we'd definitely have words if that was the case. I chuckled lightly, still sensing his embarrassment, but he just squeezed me a little closer and kept on walking.

The sounds of his feet striding through grass were slowly replaced by the noises of town life. I turned my head to see homes that were more developed, like the ones the pure mothers and fathers had. There were also other buildings that appeared to be open to anyone, and I pointed to one.

"What are those houses?" I asked, noticing the big windows in the front that had items placed in them, like they were showing off trophies or something.

Those are shops. He grinned down at me. *You have a lot to catch up on. People make things and sell them in their own buildings to make money. Money is used to buy the necessities of life, like food, clothes, and items of comfort.*

"Like merchants? I've seen a couple merchants come to our village every once in a while. The pure fathers and elder hand them bits of metal for our supplies."

Exactly. Merchants. These ones don't travel. People come to them, and it allows them to sell more things. You can put a lot of goods in a building.

"You certainly can," I breathed, eyeing a shop that had soft leather boots. Those looked comfortable... Another shop had dresses—the simplest of which was nicer than anything I'd ever seen. "Wow!" I couldn't keep my eyes on any one thing, and Javed's chest bobbed with his silent laughter. A swell of happiness in him made me smile as well.

"Bloody, shite-stealin', son-of-a-monkey's-ass!" a voice hissed out from between two shops, and Javed's steps faltered before he speed-walked to the next gap and turned into it. An older, stocky male was peering around the corner behind the shop, eyes wide like he'd spied demons.

The hair on his head was a greying brown, tied back at the nape with a piece of leather. His sideburns extended down into well-groomed mutton chops that framed his face in silver. His brows rested thickly over deep-set eyes, and the nostrils on his small nose flared, like he couldn't believe what he was scenting.

His wide mouth parted, but he appeared lost for words. Then his eyes flickered to me and back to Javed. "I'll be a bald, parrot-eating, snake puncher..." he whispered. "That you, Javed?"

I felt Javed nod, and I squirmed to get down so he could try to communicate with his friend, but he tightened his grip on me.

The male gaped and ran a hand through his hair, loosening some strands. "But how? How?"

Javed looked down at me for help, and I responded enthusiastically. "Oh! Oh. Ok!" I tried turning and sitting up a little more to better face the male. "I ran away from my village in the southern part of the jungle with a bunch of orphans because the elder was going to sell them. Javed found us and escorted them to a village where they were safely adopted. I discovered that I was a shifter and not a human, so he promised to… uh… return me to civilization. He helped me escape the jungle… and now I'm… trying to figure out what to do with my life." I pointed to my foot. "This is what happened when we crossed the river… but I couldn't have crossed at all without Javed's help." I laughed nervously at my own misfortune.

"Starlight preserve my battered, old cat noggin." He slid his palm to the back of his head, held out his other rough, calloused hand, and said, "Quennel. I'm, ah… an old friend of Javed's."

I took his hand and shook it, grateful that greetings here were the same. "Niusha. Wandering orphan."

Tell Quennel you're my fated mate and that you're carrying my cubs, Javed prompted, burying his nose in my hair and squeezing me again. I felt a swell of pride in him that I hadn't felt before, and I wondered if this male was considered family. He certainly seemed important to Javed.

"He wants me to tell you that I'm h-his fated mate and that I'm carrying his cubs," I said much more shyly and looked down at my fingers. I never thought I'd ever say such a thing. Javed just chuffed into my hair, pleased.

"Shite's be shittin' me!" Quennel gasped, his reaction pulling a bark of laughter out of me. "Why're we standin' in this dank old alleyway? Let's get you warm and have that foot propped up, yes?"

Tell him we can stay at an inn… Javed said. *I don't want to put him in danger.*

I repeated his request to Quennel, but the older male just waved him off. "Bah! I've been at risk since the day I was born."

So I've heard a thousand times. Javed chuckled. *Alright, we'll accept his offer. I'll follow him. He's as trustworthy as his mouth is foul.*

I smiled weakly and asked Quennel to lead the way. The journey was short, and soon enough, he brought us to a rather nice cottage on the edge of the village. It was hard to imagine a male like Quennel living here. With an expansive flower garden, it had a distinctly soft touch. When I noticed toys propped up against the side of the house, I realized he must have a family.

Ask him how Vail and Oriel are. They're his mate and daughter, Javed requested. I repeated it as Quennel opened the front door for us, and his shoulders fell. I could hear his hand shaking as he closed the door behind us.

"Set her here, Javed," he said with a heavy-hearted sigh, patting the couch. We'd arrived in a sitting room with several leather chairs and a quaint white fireplace. It was a little dusty, but otherwise tidy.

I was lowered gently onto the couch, and Quennel propped a pillow under my foot, making the throbbing subside a little. Javed sat in a chair across from Quennel, who interlocked his fingers, rested his elbows on his knees, and stared at the floor.

"They didn't make it out in time, Javed. After our attempt… well, they found some of our families. I know Vail's not dead," he said, thumping his chest miserably. "I would have felt it, but I don't know where she and Oriel are being held."

"Who's they?" I asked, confused. "What attempt?"

Quennel sent Javed a pointed look, who tilted his head and glared back. I didn't know what transpired between them just now, but Quennel only answered one question. "They? Why, our people, the lions of course." He smiled wryly at me, tapped his nose, and said, "No amount of Javed's scent and"—he paused and sent a teasing glance over to the blushing tiger with the flat lips—"possessiveness can keep a lion from recognizing another."

Chapter 19

Niusha

"You're a lion?" I whisper-shrieked, unable to contain myself. "I have so many questions for you!" I leaned forward so far that I nearly fell off the couch. Then, as something occurred to me, I whipped my gaze to Javed, alarmed. "Did you know? Wait, was he supposed to know? Do we need to make a run for i—"

I jumped up to one foot and made to hop for the door, but I was scooped off my feet again by a chuffing tiger-shifter. *Niusha, calm,* he soothed. *Your heart is beating like a rabbit's. I wouldn't bring you somewhere you're not safe. Calm, my queen.*

"I take it that it's been an educational overload for her?" Quennel asked, scratching at his mutton chops while Javed returned me to the couch. The tiger sighed and nodded, sitting back down to accept a pen and notepad from the lion. I scratched at my ankle and slightly adjusted the pillow. Quennel placed another pillow behind me to prop my back up, and I smiled gratefully, a little sheepish about my outburst now.

"I was hoping that'd fade," Quennel said to Javed, gesturing to his own throat. The tiger shook his head sharply and glanced at me for just a second. "How's th—" Quennel began asking but was cut off by another sharp headshake. "Oh… so that's what's going on with the whole…" The older male gestured to his cloak, and Javed grunted. He wrote something down and showed it to Quennel, who simply nodded and crossed an ankle over his knee.

I was starting to wish that Quennel didn't have paper at all, because I was dying to be let in on all of these secrets.

Javed wrote something else and stared somberly at his old friend, who looked so unbearably sad. "Thank you. Yes, I'm sure they would have loved to see you. Vail would've put you right to work on the back shed." The lion's eyes became unfocused, looking somewhere far away from here. "I wonder how much Oriel's grown. She'd be ten by now…"

Javed clasped him on his shoulder in sympathy and wrote something else. Quennel leaned over and said, "Ah… I'd be grateful. More than you know. Any help finding them… I couldn't turn it down. But what do you mean by dropped off? Where you dropping her off?"

Javed sent me a look, and I supposed I should tell him myself. "I… asked Javed to bring me to the pride so I could find and meet my f-family…" I said timidly, not knowing how he'd react to that. What was he doing outside of the pride anyway? This wasn't a lion outpost… or something.

Quennel barked out a laugh and gave me a sharp look of warning. With a darker expression, he shook his head and said, "No, I don't think you'll be wanting to do that, little miss."

"So I've been told," I replied in a smaller voice and dropped my gaze to my hands. It was brutal to hear it from a lion.

"Does she know about the cullings?" Quennel asked, and Javed shook his head. He wrote something down, and the lion snorted. "I don't blame you. I don't even want to talk about it." Quennel tilted his head as he regarded me. "You know they'll kill Javed's cubs if you go and they find out about them."

"I… I told him I wouldn't let them!" I argued. "I'm not planning on staying… I just wanted to visit and meet… my family."

"Ah, gods. Great blathering frog gobblers. You don't get a choice!" Quennel shouted, startling me, and Javed gave him a warning growl. The lion turned back to him in bewilderment. "Since when can your tiger talk and you can't?" Javed gestured for that to be discussed later, looking irritated.

Quennel brought his attention back to me, scooted his chair closer, and leaned forward to give me a serious stare. "Do you know why I'm not in the pride, Niusha?"

I shook my head, too intimidated to talk.

"When I was a cub of only nine, our king was killed after another lion challenged his place on the throne. Now, do you know what happens to the king's offspring when he's overthrown and killed?" he asked, his left eye twitching a little. I repeated my headshake. "No, of course you don't. Well, the new king gets to order a culling. That means that every cub sired by the previous king that's under the age of thirteen is 'put down.' With how many years the king has access to his harem, I think you can imagine that it's a great number of cubs that get slaughtered."

"No… that can't be…" It was the same denial I'd been saying for over a week. Tears blurred my vision, and I slapped a hand to my gaping mouth.

"Now to be fair, which is hysterical," Quennel stated, holding up a shaking finger. "Historically, many cats have killed a competitor's cubs when they take a female away from another male. Tigers have been guilty of this as well. The problem is that every single one of the cats has evolved past that behavior except for our people."

"But why?" I asked with a sob. I couldn't stop imagining it. Horrifying.

"No king wants to put resources into raising the cubs of the one he conquered. Plus losing offspring forces the lioness into heat. All he has to do is start replacing the lost young with his… and keep the throne for as long as possible so they can actually grow up."

"And the lionesses just… allow this?" I all but shrieked, placing my hands to the sides of my head.

Quennel scowled and prodded my forehead with a thick digit. "Get it through your thick skull, lioness. Your gender doesn't have a choice! Don't make me repeat it a third time! My mother didn't have a choice when she dropped me from the castle wall, praying I'd survive the forty-foot drop instead of handing me over to be slaughtered." Quennel snorted as he stared intensely into my eyes, which were locked on his in horror. "Ninety-nine percent of cubs thrown off the wall don't survive. Guess who that one percent was?" He jerked a thumb back at himself. "Me!" He raised his right pant leg, showing off a limb made of wood.

I withdrew into myself, shrinking and tucking my arms from a sudden chill. Quennel sat back, pity in his eyes. "Now, I'd carved a life out for myself," he continued quietly while Javed came around to scoop my shaking body onto his lap. "I met my lovely Vail, and we found a quiet place to settle in bobcat territory. At least until…" His hung his head and scratched the back of his head. "You can find a life worth living, little miss, but it means staying away from the lions. It'd be a dark day for me if I found out that Javed's cubs were killed over something entirely preventable."

Tell him that's enough, Javed demanded, and I repeated it in a much weaker tone.

Quennel stood and cracked his knuckles. "You know someone had to say it to her, Javed. Can't be soft about such a tough topic. Tea anyone? I have green and suma."

Niusha was in bad shape after learning about the cub cullings. She shut down and wouldn't even drink the tea Quennel brought, so he showed us to our guest room where she could rest. I had plenty of time to catch up with him, but she came first to me, and he knew that. He felt the same about his Vail.

I carried Niusha in, pulled the quilt back on the large bed, and laid her down, mindful of her injured foot. I tucked her in and reclined by her for a little bit, stroking her dark blond hair. All I could feel through our partial bond was numbness. Her pulse throbbed slow and steady. At least her heart had calmed for now… on the outside.

"I feel so lost," she eventually whispered, staring unblinkingly up at the painted white ceiling.

I know, I murmured and ran the back of a finger over her soft, tear-stained cheek. I licked my thumb and cleaned her up a bit, unable to resist grooming her.

Her face remained blank, and her emotions stagnated as she spoke. "I spent most of my life fighting someone else's reality only to find myself struggling to accept the truth. At what point had I turned into another purity drinker?"

Some things are just too much to accept at once, I replied, sensing that her mind was in turmoil.

"Denial is unacceptable…"

Denial happens when a mind needs to rest and heal before it takes on new things, I insisted and slid my hands around to embrace her. I scooted closer, tucked her head under my chin, and kissed the top of her head. I couldn't resist the call of her body. Heat or no heat, I was having a harder time keeping my lips away from her. Maybe I'd give her a kiss on a day where she hadn't just found out she was pregnant… on top of waking up from her severe injury… on top of meeting her first lion who told her that her kind kills cubs by the dozens. Fuck… I should have stopped him sooner. That could have waited until tomorrow at the very least.

Take a nap and think of happy things, Niusha, I said, pulling back to leave the bed. *If you need inspiration, you can think of that time when you saved my ass from a sleepy snake.* I smiled at my pathetic attempt to make her laugh and tried to catch her gaze.

Her blank expression twisted my heart, but at least she nodded to acknowledge me before closing her eyes. I tugged the quilt up to her chin, kissed her on the head again like a lovesick fool, and left to find Quennel.

My old right-hand male was reclined in his rocking chair with a boot resting on a wooden stool. He'd removed his false leg and was nursing his cup of green tea. The lion raised a brow at my approach and gestured for me to pull up a chair. I plopped down on a free seat and regarded him with a nostalgic smile. Fondly, he patted my knee and took a sip of his now-cold drink.

"How's she faring?" he asked, staring out the window into the dark garden. I returned with the notepad and showed him my answer. "Ah… yeah. She'll be in shock, for sure. You can't drag these things out or she'll think you'll always be keeping things from her."

I sighed and nodded, scratching just under my nose. I wrote a question and showed it to Quennel.

"I have some of your rainy-day coin here. Haven't touched it. It's in my study. Upper right desk drawer. You should be fine going into the shops, but leave Niusha here. Cover her scent all you like, but she still has that lioness look. Most people wouldn't know since no one actually sees lionesses, but I think you should play it safe."

I frowned. I'd been afraid of that.

"What madness. Why the Moon Goddess would give you—of all people—a lioness… I'd laugh if it wasn't such a dark joke."

I grunted in agreement and scrubbed a hand over my chin. The concept itself was dark indeed, but Niusha shined like gold. We'd be perfect if we lived in a different world.

"So when's the next one?" Quennel asked. I shook my head, gave him a bleak look, and held up my notepad. He frowned at my answer. "Oh no, you're quite wrong about that, tiger." He held up three fingers, and I balked, which made him laugh.

"What? You think that being exiled instead of killed would prevent you from becoming a martyr? You can't silence a symbol," he said with a snort. I sighed and rested my head against the soft leather, staring out into the starlit garden. They'd certainly tried… and in a way, they had. After what happened last time, I didn't have anything left in me to give.

The next morning brought a great deal of unease as I approached the market in the bobcat town, Blaye Tanka. I'd been greatly distracted carrying Niusha, then overjoyed to find Quennel, but now that it was only Convict and me, I was letting old fears sink their gnarled roots under my skin.

When were we here last? I asked Convict, brushing a long, aromatic eucalyptus leaf off my cloak.

I'm not even sure how many years we've been gone. We guessed—what—four years?

In exile? I believe so, I replied with a sigh. I turned onto the main market street, hoping that the clothing store was open. I'd left as early as possible in an attempt to run some errands before the streets crowded.

And then… those other years w—

Just one… though it felt like three, I interrupted, not wanting to think about what was making me so on edge. *So around five. No one should recognize us… right?*

I don't know, Javed… we've bulked up, but you might want to keep your cloak wrapped tight. We're too tall to not draw attention.

They should have forgotten our scent, though, right?

Quennel certainly hadn't. Convict laughed.

Quennel knew us for too long to forget it, I argued. *The last thing I can handle right now is feeling like an outcast, Convict. Sky Gods know what our people think of us now.*

Just put one paw in front of the other. We have things to buy. Shake a tail.

Right…

I peeked into a shop that was open to find that there weren't any other customers, then entered, making the little bells attached to the door jingle merrily. A tiny bobcat-shifter bustled out from the back room, a broad grin stretching her freckled cheeks. If her keen brown eyes recognized me, she didn't let it show.

"Good morning! How can I help you?" she inquired, putting on her best mercantile face. I jotted a note down on the pad of paper and held it up for her to read. She grinned greedily at the long list and ran off to procure the items. If I hadn't been so anxious about being recognized, I would have been amused by the eager gleam in her eyes. It was still good to be back among regular folk.

I know I'm not the one wearing them, but I can't wait for you to put on fresh clothes and burn that sky-forsaken loincloth! Convict grunted while we waited for the shopkeeper. I glanced down at my hips and nodded. As much as I loathed how it'd been acquired, it had been convenient for quickly shifting in the jungle. Those days were over, though. If I lost the fight to sway Niusha, I would disappear somewhere else. I was never returning to that place.

I wasn't even sure if my own people would take me back now. Had I gone too far?

"Here we go!" the she-bobcat sang melodically, yanking me from my gloom.

She offered what I'd asked for, including shirts and pants, and held them up so I could check the fit. The pants didn't reach my ankles, and she chuckled at my frown. "That's the longest we have in town, big tiger. Sorry. The boots'll cover the rest!"

I snorted, bought my clothes, and dressed quickly so I could move on to the next shop. As soon as my fingers landed on the cold metal doorknob, a male's voice came from behind me.

"We're less proud than we ever were."

Dread crept up my spine. Who'd recognized me?

An older bobcat in green overalls and thick glasses stood in the doorway behind the counter, staring meaningfully. Two bobcat kittens, no older than five, gawked from behind him, their little fingers clutching his clothes. I didn't recognize any of them, but that wasn't surprising.

Sweat slicked down my back under the shirt I wasn't used to wearing. My skin couldn't breathe. My lungs didn't have room to expand.

I would have been left speechless had I been capable of speaking. I wasn't expecting such a message, but what was he trying to say anyway? Those days were over, and I needed to leave. I grunted and departed the store, walking quicker to get to a place where I could calm myself. I slumped against a wall in an alley and placed a hand over my lungs.

Breathe, Convict urged. *Breathe, Javed.*

Breathe, I echoed to myself.

Ok, Convict stated slowly and clearly, knowing my mind wasn't able to focus. *It's very simple. Get Niusha's things, find the apothecary, and head back. We know what we need, so we'll make it snappy. That was probably a one-off anyway.*

One-off. My heart thumped away in my ears, muting my sense of hearing, which stressed me out even more. I rubbed my eyes, took a deep breath, and rushed to the dress shop. Upon arrival, I had to mime Niusha's approximate size for the dressmaker, who went through their inventory to find a match. I bought everything that seemed about right and escaped the shop, feeling all the hairs on my body stand on end. I glanced down at the receipt and spooked at the word freshly written at the very bottom—'proudless.'

I paled and grew panicky but pushed myself toward the last shop. Almost done. I was almost done. I entered the apothecary, making sure my hood was pulled down as far as it would go. The bobcat behind the counter regarded me impassively while he stuck a pen behind his ear, nestled under his curly black cloud of hair.

I slapped my note down on the table, needing only one thing. The chemist leaned over, scrunched his nose as he read, then shook his head.

"You're asking for something that's been illegal for years," he said, straightening. "But then again, you wouldn't have known that, would you?" A fresh wave of anxiety surged into me, but before I could turn to leave, he shoved a bottle onto the counter and fixed me under a stare. There was absolutely no emotion in his expression as our eyes locked. He waited me out while my lungs threatened to hyperventilate.

After a moment, he nudged the bottle closer. "Just take it. You don't want to cause an uproar, do you?"

The stealthy use of the old nickname was another shock to my system, and I swiped the bottle off the table, then shoved it into a pocket. I slapped some coins down onto the counter, though he'd asked for none, and stormed out of the shop. I'd been recognized every single fucking time.

We need to leave, Convict rumbled.

I know.

I rushed back to Quennel's house in a black mood, and the lion-shifter stopped me, calling from his chair before I got to the guest room.

"What happened? You look like death."

Too many recognized me, I wrote to him. My hands shook, and my handwriting suffered for it. *Niusha and I need to go.*

"What? You think the bobcats are going to do… what? Turn you in to the lions?" he asked, his nostrils flaring before he burst into husky laughter. I scowled at him, in no mood to tolerate his ridicule. He stopped laughing only to give me a wry look. "I meant what I said. The numbers increased threefold, Javed. Are you really going to run from it?"

Was he seriously lecturing me after all this time?

Does he not understand what we went through? Convict asked, but I barely heard him through all the blood rushing in my ears.

Numbers don't fucking matter. They didn't matter last time, I wrote furiously and nigh illegibly. *Sorry if I don't feel like being tortured for another year and then exiled for four!* I crumpled up the note, threw it at his forehead and escaped into the guest room, slamming the door behind me. I dropped the bags on the floor and scrubbed my shaking hands over my face, at a breaking point.

"J-Javed?" Niusha's sweet voice trickled into my ears, and I slumped in response. She disarmed me so. "Are you ok? What happened?"

I uncovered my eyes and started to see her hunched naked behind a towel. Her hair was dripping wet, and her clothes were laid out on the bed. I must have caught her after a bath. I stared silently at her for just a moment, letting my gaze fall from the swells of the sides of her smooth breasts to the healthy curve of her hips. I could just barely detect the blond curls of my favorite paradise between her legs. I'd give anything to lose myself in her right now, my nude, heart-stoppingly gorgeous pregnant female.

I sighed, rubbed my eyes with my knuckles, and rummaged through the bags instead of bending her over the dresser. Before she could dress, I displayed the clothes I bought for her, spreading the options out on the bed. *Just stressed from going into town,* I said. *I brought back some new clothes. See if they fit.*

"Oh," she said in mild surprise and reached for the items. "I see you bought some clothes too… You look… handsome," she complimented quietly. I kicked my new boots off and reclined on the bed with my hands under my head. She eyed my too-short pants, obviously holding back a laugh.

Bobcats are short, I defended, too stressed to enjoy the humor but feeling more relaxed than when I'd entered the room. *And don't laugh too much until you try yours on. I didn't have your measurements.*

She smiled faintly, slipped the dress over her head, and dropped the towel when she was covered. The dresses were the nicest ones I could find that were still convenient for shifting—trimmed with pretty lace and had a thick ribbon around the waist to tighten with instead of the complicated strings of a bodice. I could sense that she was pleased, to my relief, and it fit well enough. She then looked at the lace panties as if they were scandalous, but I shrugged, not really having anything to add. Her ass would look nice in lace was all. She didn't have to wear them.

When she slipped them on under her dress, I hummed silently in victory.

I was reminded that it was time to remove her stitches, so I patted the bed next to me after I grabbed the ointment, pills, and a cup of water. She hobbled onto the bed and scooted up, sending me a questioning look.

Time to remove your stitches, my queen, I said while grabbing her leg and placing it on my lap.

"Why do you keep calling me that? Queen?" she asked as I hooked a claw under the first string.

It's just a term of endearment for adult she-cats. I sliced through a stitch and pulled the string out to remove it. She twitched from discomfort, but since she didn't utter any pained sounds, I cut them quickly, just to get it over with. I worked around her injury, eventually having to lift her leg to reach the other side. To preserve her modesty, she placed her hands on her skirt, which almost made me laugh.

Oh Niusha, I've seen it all, I thought to myself, smirking.

I scented and felt her excitement grow until I was done removing the last stitch. It wasn't as overwhelming as her heat, but it didn't fail to make my new pants tighter. Lastly, I rubbed the ointment into her sealed wound and gave her the medication to swallow. The color and swelling had improved. Perhaps I'd allow her to walk on it tomorrow.

I heard a knock on the other side of the house, then muffled voices murmured after the front door had been opened. I groaned as I heard Quennel's telltale gait approach the guestroom door. Before I could get to the doorknob, he knocked and said, "Javed, there're people at the door looking for The Great Convicto—"

I yanked the door open, nearly ripping it off its hinges, and seethed at him with bared canines for announcing it so loudly. He knew I couldn't silence him with a gesture through the door and had just said it outright. I didn't want Niusha to learn about any of this, for fuck's sake! I was livid.

Quennel might have had a small smile on his face, but his eyes were dead serious. He wasn't going to let me disappear so easily, and it was another reason why Niusha and I had to leave immediately.

Niusha, I said, not letting my gaze wander from Quennel's, *pack your things now. We're going.*

Chapter 20

Niusha

Something had happened between Javed and Quennel. As I rushed to shove everything into our bags, I kept glancing over to find them standing chest to… well… not quite chest to chest, considering Quennel's stature. Javed was absolutely furious, and whatever I could see of his lower face had flushed crimson with anger.

I limped over, ready to go but felt a great deal of trepidation as I approached. I didn't know what was being silently communicated, but it felt like we were standing at some kind of tipping point. The air was heavy with Javed's disquiet, and I nearly held my breath when I got to his side.

With both bags slung over my shoulder, I gave into the compulsion and reached for his large, warm hand. I squeezed it to offer comfort, but if he relaxed at all, it wasn't noticeable. With a gentle tug, Javed pulled me closer to lift me into his arms. He shoved past an unbothered Quennel and strode toward the back of the house, bursting out the door and into the fresh morning air. Birds sang in the tall, swaying trees with joy, oblivious to the dark cloud below them.

"You've always had to have the final say," Quennel called out from the doorway, leaning against it to take the weight off his false leg. It wasn't said aggressively, but he did heavily emphasize the last three words.

Javed froze and spun around to look at him. *Don't...* I heard him warn, but I knew that the word wouldn't reach his friend's ears.

"He says don't!" I snapped at Quennel, deeply protective of Javed. As much as I was curious about what was happening, he'd suffered enough. I'd learn in due time if he felt like sharing. I'd been betrayed before, and the last thing I wanted to do was betray Javed's trust in me. I wouldn't pry into his precious privacy.

Quennel's eyes flickered to mine, and I was surprised to see a great deal of sympathy there. His behavior continuously confused me. The middle-aged lion was almost as much of a mystery to me as Javed, but as hard as it was to admit, I'd benefitted from the hard truths he'd spat. It'd been brutal, but I'd gladly take a dose of honesty in almost any form. I'd left my old village in search of the truth, and he'd been one to dole it out in giant scoops.

"Niusha, little miss, remember that you have the last word," he reminded me, and Javed bristled at the last three stressed words. Quennel was obviously trying to convey something that Javed wanted to remain hidden. "Lives rest on your shoulders—the cubs and Javed." He gave me a pointed look. "Please don't kill my friend. The Proudle—"

I was startled by Javed's interrupting, explosive roar of outrage. The thunderous sound froze me and appeared to have frozen Quennel as well. My muscles locked in fear, and I found myself paralyzed. Javed snorted, growled, and ran into the eucalyptus forest with me limp in his arms.

He ran north for a long time, holding me tight like I was a cub, which made a thought occur to me. When I could finally move again, I glanced up at Javed, wanting to share it. His face was flushed from exertion, and his eyes had turned ruddy and glassy, like he was holding back tears. I couldn't sort through his tumultuous emotions; they were far too chaotic to follow. I'd tell him my idea later...

When his breathing became labored, I grew worried and placed a hand on his chest. "Javed, stop. Set me down and take a break. Please!" My words seemed to wake him out of a trance, and he slowed to a walk, gasping for air. He then trudged to a pile of eucalyptus leaves and fell to his knees. With a keening moan that came straight from his tiger, he bent over and clung to me like I was a lifeline, desperate for comfort.

"Oh Javed." I sighed and hooked my arms under his, resting my hands on his shoulders in an attempt to avoid touching his back through his dark cloak. "I'm so confused, but I wish I could help."

Don't go to the lions, he whispered.

"It's not quite looking like I will, but I haven't decided yet," I said, not wanting to lie. If I had to lie, I'd lie to anyone but him, even if it was painful. "Quennel did put a massive dent in my trust of them, so don't think I haven't been listening. I like them less by the day... which hurts me deeply. I can't express how much it hurts to hate my own kind, Javed. It makes me hate myself to some extent."

You're not like them. He buried his face into my neck and took a deep breath. After releasing a bone-weary sigh, he leaned away, reached into his pocket, and gestured for me to stand. I hobbled to one foot with his help, and he opened a small bottle with a nozzle.

This will hide your scent, Niusha, he said tiredly. *Apparently, it's illegal now. I was lucky to find someone supplying it.* He sprayed a fine mist over me, thoroughly coating my skin and dress in the chemical. He slowly touched my arms when he finished and rubbed it into my skin. I stared at him while he worked to hide who I was. Would this be my life if I stayed with him? Would I be forever in hiding, living in the wilderness and buying illegal products to stay safe—to keep our cubs safe?

I didn't like how the lions—and the thousands willing to turn me in—loomed over my head like that. I felt like I was in the village all over again, living a life full of lies and chemicals. That thought made me deeply unhappy. I deserved better than that. Javed did too.

"Javed?" I asked as I stared at his anxious, taut mouth and jaw. "What would happen if we left cat-shifter territory? Would we be welcomed elsewhere?"

He hesitated in his grooming of me for just a moment, then continued to massage, squatting to rub the scent remover into my legs. I bit my inner cheek to hold back a pleased groan and stay focused. Oh gods, I loved his touch.

The cats haven't quite nurtured positive relationships with the other kingdoms... I honestly don't know what it's like these days. I've been gone for a long time, and news wasn't always regular or reliable.

"How long?" I asked, but then backpedaled nervously. "D-don't answer that… I didn't mean to pry."

Four... well... five years, I guess.

"I'm sorry… that sounds like it was difficult," I said hesitantly, hoping he didn't take it the wrong way. The last word I'd ever use to describe him was 'weak.'

He merely grunted and lifted me up again. He wandered around until he found a thicket where he tucked me out of sight. *Stay, Niusha. I'll hunt.*

He disappeared for a while and returned with several pheasants that he cooked over a small campfire. We ate lunch, wrapped the rest, and he carried me north again. I leaned my head against his chest, lulled by the comforting consistency of his heartbeat, and eventually drifted into sleep.

I snapped out of the recurring nightmare with a pounding heart, my shivering body soaked miserably with ice-cold sweat.

I patted around the sheets, confused about where I was and why Javed wasn't here. I dreaded moving when I woke like this, knowing I'd freeze when the cold sweat hit the cool air. Still, I had to find Javed. I stretched my violently trembling legs and sat up. The movement made my head throb, and a desperate thirst struck me. I was out of sorts, and that only worsened my confusion.

Glancing about in the dark, I found myself in a small room with wooden floorboards and two doors. There was a wood-burning stove, but it hadn't been fed yet. My bags were on a chair by a little wooden table decorated only with an unlit candle. Low murmurs hummed through the walls and floor, telling me that a lot of people were nearby. My nose said that food was also just as close and identified the savory scent of stew and freshly baked bread.

Where's Javed? Field asked, as groggy as me.

"I smell him, but it's old…" I mumbled, rubbing an eye as I slid off the damp bed. I didn't feel like I was in immediate danger, but I was quick about changing into a clean dress. I loved the new ones that Javed had bought me. I'd never seen such lovely clothes in my life. My face flushed in pleasure as I recalled his thoughtful, beautiful gifts.

I slipped my shoes on, opened one door, and found that it led to a small bathroom. I patted some water onto my sweatiest parts, hating the sour smell that always came with the nightmares. When I felt slightly more put together, I peeked out the next door and discovered a dim hallway with stairs at the very end. Should I wait for him? Was he ok? I cautiously followed Javed's scent to the stairs and peered around the corner, then looked down to find the first floor of a very, very busy room.

It was like the dining area inside the temple, except all the tables were round and spaced almost at random. People were eating but mostly drinking, and a great many of them were socializing, though it was a little rougher than any socializing I'd witnessed prior to this place.

A huge crowd of people gathered at the other end of the floor, near a long table where a man was busily handing out beverages. I licked my dry lips, still thirsty and craving something that didn't come from a dubious sink pipe.

I finally spied Javed at the center of the crowd, sitting at a table with three other males. I frowned when I noticed a number of females surrounding his end of the table. They'd occasionally paw at his shoulder or play with his hood, and though he'd nudge them away, the sight still bothered me, making my stomach twist with jealousy. What was he doing? Who were all those people? The crowd all seemed pretty invested in whatever was being discussed.

Javed was gesturing and holding up scraps of paper, so I assumed he was involved in an important conversation. I wished I could hear what the others were saying, but it was too noisy—too drowned out by the clattering plates, guffaws, belches, and heated conversations. I didn't know if my pain grew from all the females trying to get his attention or from me feeling unwell, but I was starting to get additionally bruised by not being a part of whatever this was.

Suddenly, I wasn't feeling so special anymore. I knew Javed had secrets that I'd respect, but that didn't make this hurt any less. Why did those females get to listen to what I couldn't?

Get those females off him, Niusha! Field snapped.

Her reaction pulled me out of my insecurity, able to look at myself through her behavior. I took a mindful breath and shook my head. *No, he's not encouraging them. He's probably sorting out something important and will tell me when he gets back to the room. We must be staying here tonight.*

It took all my effort to be reasonable, but my stomach lurched with pain. I wasn't feeling too well either, physically; I never did after drenching the bed from nightmare-fueled sweating. Discomfort and thirst did nothing for my emotional resilience.

When I turned to retire, a number of things happened simultaneously. First, as though he'd felt my presence or emotions,

Javed swung his head to look directly at me. His teeth clenched, and he subtly swiped his hand in the direction of our room. At the same time, a handful of people stood, knocked their chairs over and yelled that they scented a lion.

Niusha! Get back in there! Javed hissed. *I can smell you!*

I paled and stumbled back before running straight into a large male. In a blink, he picked me up and wrapped his arm around my neck, his muscles flexing like a snake and threatening to choke the air out of me.

His furious roar nearly shattered my hearing. "What the fuck is a lioness doing here? Who sent you?"

I wasn't locked in his hold for long. Javed's more explosive roar froze the room. The tiger-shifter barreled his way through the crowd and yanked the male's arm off me so violently that it dislocated with a sickening pop. My captor screamed as I collapsed into Javed's arms, paralyzed.

He ran up the stairs with me, grabbed our bags, and forced his way through the stirring, confused mass of cat-shifters to escape the building. Javed strolled out onto wet grass, growling and occasionally burying his face in my hair, chuffing as though he was calming himself as well as me. I was in slack-jawed shock from what had just happened but quickly snapped out of it when I heard the crowd following us into the town's streets.

Instead of sounding like a violent mob, there was a plethora of questions and cries for Javed to stay.

"Convictor, why are you protecting a lioness?"

"Uproar, don't leave! Explain!"

"Tell us what's going on! You have the final say!"

"Is she important? We didn't know!"

"Are you a lion sympathizer now, Last Word?"

"Who is she?"

"Don't leave us!"

"What's going on, Great Convictor?"

"Come back! We'll listen!"

"Javed, wait!"

Javed's body shook more as the crowd pursued him, begging for answers. I felt his anger, frustration, and marrow-deep despair swirl through our bond. There was shame buried in there too, and tears welled into my eyes when I sensed how overwhelmed he was. The stress was crushing him.

"Hand over that rag-puss and let us have our justice!"

That last one nearly drove Javed's tiger right out into the starlight, and he whirled on them, booming another petrifying roar that halted their advance. Javed immediately released another furious, bellowing roar that forced them all to their knees in fear. I was not doing well myself. His noises had melted all my muscles and joints, and I was a limp corpse in his arms. I heaved a weak sob, and his face snapped down to look at me, stricken.

Niusha, I'm so sorry!

A gangly male stumbled weakly out of the large building, which I was beginning to suspect was the inn that Javed had mentioned wanting to find. He forced his way through the crowd until he stood before us, panting and shaking.

"Still as p-potent as ever," the male said, brown skin wan under his mop of sandy hair. When he looked up, I was startled to find him missing an eye. It'd been scarred over from a hideous cut that must have been excruciating. The male then held out a notepad and pen and gestured timidly, encouraging Javed to take it.

Javed stared at the writing tools for a long moment, visibly torn. I sensed that he wanted to run away, and I placed a hand on his arm so he could feel my skin. Maybe if he calmed he could make the best decision for his well-being. He ultimately exhaled and resigned himself to address these people.

Can you stand, my queen? he asked, brows knotted in worry. I nodded, though I wasn't entirely positive that I could. Javed crouched as he set me on the ground and started massaging my legs to wake up my stiff joints and weak muscles. *I'm sorry, Niusha. I wasn't thinking.*

"It's ok," I whispered, and the lanky male looked sharply at me. He must suspect that we could mind-link. Apparently, that could only mean one thing to him. Javed's attention to my body got the crowd murmuring a variety of reactions, but they were otherwise quiet with their observations, too frightened to trigger my tiger again.

Once he was done stabilizing me, he nuzzled the side of my head, making the crowd more uneasy, and snatched the notepad and pen from the male next to us. *This is Mas'ud, Niusha. He is... a reliable individual from my younger days,* Javed introduced reluctantly. I felt his fear now, and it tasted bitter.

"Do you want me to go?" I asked, and he shook his head unhappily.

He put the pen to the paper and gave it to Mas'ud to read.

In a raised voice, Mas'ud shared the message and sounded more shocked by the word. "This is Niusha, a lioness without association to the pride. Being who you are, I will be generous with punishments. To speak ill of her will earn you a broken bone. To show her disrespect will cost you a finger or limb. To hurt her will result in your execution. This is because she is my fated mate and is carrying my... cubs."

I swallowed and licked my dry lips, now wishing I had risked the tap water. I was growing increasingly more lightheaded, and the stress was making me nauseous. I eyed a male taking a hesitant step forward to address Javed, who reacted with a threatening growl. The male retreated at the warning, shaky, and asked, "So... what is your plan? Are you still going to abandon us?"

Javed wrote his answer and handed it to Mas'ud to read aloud once more. "I have an obligation to fulfill. Regardless of how it turns out, I plan on leaving. I have no intention of returning to oversee a futile project..." Mas'ud trailed off at the end, crestfallen.

"You don't need to have a voice to be our voice, Convictor," a cat I couldn't see shouted from the crowd. There was murmuring after that, but the overall mood was bleak. I shuffled a little closer to Javed and reached subtly for his hand, offering comfort in a way that didn't have to be visible. Javed clasped his large, rough hands around mine and brought it to his lips, kissing my knuckles for all to see.

"We don't blame you for the three anymore..." someone added quietly, fearfully. I couldn't imagine I would've been able to hear it before Field gifted me with improved hearing. Javed stiffened further at those words and wrote another message for Mas'ud to impart.

"You do not speak for everyone," he read, then frowned over at Javed. My tiger-shifter cut his hand through the air like he was firmly dismissing that topic. Mas'ud read another message. "There is nothing more to discuss here. We are leaving now."

As Javed turned, the cats protested again. One voice cut above the others, saying, "We... we'll accept the... lioness!" It was grudgingly stated, and the reluctant compromise stung. It almost hurt as much as rejection. The concession didn't faze Javed, though, who just snorted derisively in response. I leaned into him as he took another step, then stumbled dizzily into his arm.

"Sorry," I mumbled tiredly.

Someone—likely the owner—shouted, "At least stay at my inn for the night! Look how tired your female is. W-we'll treat her like a queen, Convictor! Come eat warm food! Let her sleep in a warm bed! I'll prepare our biggest room!"

Javed hesitated and looked down at me. I waved dismissively and whispered, "We can leave. Don't worry about me. We'll do what you need to do." He frowned and looked over his shoulder at the owner, who'd stepped forward to make his plea. "Javed, it's fine, really," I insisted, rubbing his tense, veined arm.

Javed scooped me up without a word and marched back to the inn, grunting at the owner as he passed. There was a large reaction among the cat-shifters; some were aghast, some were relieved, some looked pleased, and some looked beyond addle-pated by the whole scene. I was a bit addlepated myself.

The owner rushed past us and shouted orders to his inn workers. He led us up the stairs and unlocked a different room, which was larger and had a lovely fireplace instead of a stove.

A female rushed in to replace the sheets on the large bed and fluff the pillows. It felt strange to have all this handed to us after surviving our long trek through the jungle.

Javed settled me into a cushioned chair by a small dining table, and another female came scurrying in to deliver several large plates of food. I smiled tiredly at her, but she didn't meet my gaze. My heart sank, and I wondered if it was even possible to make friends now. I had an unhappy revelation that the one time I did have friends was in my old village. Even though everything was built on lies, I had people to keep me company.

When I looked up to find Javed staring emptily at his stew, my self-pity evaporated. I waited until everyone left before speaking to him. I reached across the table and placed my hand over his. "Javed," I said, "I wish I knew what was going on… but…" I sighed, not sure how to proceed. "Just promise me you'll ask me for whatever you need."

He pushed his stew aside and leaned forward to bury his face in his arms. *I didn't know, Niusha. When I got to this town... I hid your scent and got a room. I didn't know that they'd taken over this town. I wouldn't have come here if I'd known. They saw me and... they had so many questions, and you were asleep and...*

He was drowning before me, overwhelmed. All I could do was move closer and squeeze his hand. I took a piece of beef from the stew and simply sat by his side, rubbing his hand while listening to the popping of the fireplace.

Eventually, words came to me. "Whatever it was, it was an accident. I was just confused. I… could have been patient and waited for you to return. I think my sweat killed the effectiveness of that spray, and I rinsed some of it off too without thinking. I should have realized; I was just so out of it."

I was just going down to get food... once someone recognize me, I was accosted with questions. I must have lost track of time... Shit, I'm so sorry.

His emotions grew darker by the minute. After a while of this, I started really worrying. He'd withdrawn and stopped responding to my little touches.

Now wasn't the time to think about my emotions, but the rejection still hurt. He jerked slightly and pulled my hand closer to him, squeezing it firmly. I guess he'd felt that…

When I was fifteen, he began, finally breaking his long bout of silence, *I started joining protests against the lions' encroachment into territory that wasn't theirs. There wasn't any organization to the protesting. People just kind of gathered at a listed time and day.*

Shortly after I turned eighteen, Convict and I talked about forming a group, and we spearheaded what turned into a movement... a revolution. Nothing happened to Convict and me personally to start this movement, but we witnessed a lot of suffering and felt compelled to do something about it. Everyone was fearful, and no one wanted to take charge of anything serious, which had frustrated me. Convict and I never felt afraid of speaking our mind, and we always had something to say.

We interrupted assaults on critical locations, we intercepted supply shipments, and we freed as many slaves as we could over the years. We did much more but... I think you get the picture. We gave the lions nightmares for a good three years before I was captured. Since they'd gotten their claws on the 'great revolutionary leader,' they threw me in their arena and forced me to fight. It was a sick joke. Said they'd generously given me something else to fight for during my imprisonment. To make an example of me, and to further my humiliation, they muzzled me.

I ended up fighting in their arena because my opponents never gave me a choice, but I refused to kill them once I defeated them. As punishment, they'd take me to the scarmaster to be tortured every single time. I never caved, though... and that had only been the beginning.

I was crying at this point, inconsolable, horrified by what he'd been forced to endure. I wanted to rip the entire pride to shreds. A rage I'd never known mixed with my grief, but a wave of dizziness had my head spinning. It was too much. What he'd gone through was too much. How could he even look at me?

I don't know how you could even look at me now. Javed stood and turned his back to me. He dropped his cloak, then removed his shirt to show me what he'd kept hidden this entire time.

My crying turned into grief-stricken, sorrowful sobbing.

Chapter 21

Niusha

Suddenly, the tiger-shifter looked a lot bigger without his cloak, and I tried to swallow past the lump in my throat. The battleground was a lot larger than I imagined… At first glance, I thought that Javed's broad back was covered in flesh-colored layers of clay, but I knew better.

Help me, F-Field. I needed her. I needed to stand. I needed to get my legs working so I could go to him.

Y-yes... She gave me some of her strength to get me to my feet. I was weak from so many things, but the sorrow nigh crippled me. I steadied myself on the edge of the table and limped toward Javed, barely able to hear my own sobbing.

When I stepped within reach of him, I hesitated. "May… I touch you now?" I asked in the tiniest voice. He'd already destroyed several of the promises I'd adhered to, but I didn't want to assume…

Why would you want to? he asked bitterly, and I cringed, which sent fresh tears down my cheeks.

"Because… I just do." I wasn't sure how to put my feelings into words. "Do you not… want my touch? I can't see how you'd want to be touched by any lion or lioness again…" I choked on those words, feeling sorrow for the both of us. I didn't know how to approach this at all. Was I already making mistakes?

Only if you can stomach it, he answered roughly, and I felt his emotions waft away, replaced by the deep freeze one feels right before they become numb.

My right forefinger landed on a striated, raised line—a scar left long ago by some sharp object. Perhaps it had been a razor, or maybe a knife. It could have easily been a claw as well. I ran my finger along it and asked quietly, "Are these words?"

Yes, he said, his tone strained. *I will not repeat them. They are bad words.*

"Don't then. That's ok…" I ran my fingers across what must have been dozens of words carved into his back. The raised scars were uneven, as though some words had been recut more times than others. Anywhere there wasn't a word, there were older slashes that seemed more random, and I had to assume they were merely done to cause pain.

Ultimately, his back was in ruins, and the words were brutal, lumpy insults to his magnificent body. How long had it taken for all his nerves to be severed? Could he even feel anything?

I reached behind me and untied my dress, wanting to make my opinion clear with actions instead of words. He stiffened when he heard me slip the garment over my head and drop it to the floor. I stepped forward to lean my body flush against his back and slid my arms around his waist to hold him. I could feel every indent, every insult, come between us in body as thoroughly as it had in his mind.

He was a rock-hard statue of pure tension now, but I just breathed into him and rested my forehead against the lumps. The scars pressed against my nude breasts and belly as I squeezed him. I curled my fingers to dig into his abdominal muscles, possessive of this male who'd just shown me his biggest vulnerability.

I breathed deeply and let his scent caress my senses. It curled into my nose and played with my tongue. He smelled so good. The scars didn't change who he was, especially not to me.

"I can't believe how strong you are," I murmured into his spine, tilting my head to leave a gentle kiss on a scar.

Javed's left arm twitched. *I was not expecting those words,* he said, but not as coldly this time.

I kissed another scar and nuzzled into him. "I think you know very well how I feel, Javed," I replied quietly, letting my lips brush his skin as I spoke. "I think you know that I'm not so easily swayed. You're going to have to try harder to disgust me. All I see are scars of a hard-won victory. Look how your skin protected you. Look how many times it grew back to spite them."

I was not so victorious... He hunched a little, which only made me tighten my grip.

"Had you not been exiled, we wouldn't have met… not that I'd wish exile on anyone for such a selfish reason…" I said sadly, groping in the dark for the silver lining.

Do you remember... one of the cats mentioning the... three? The three they supposedly don't blame me for anymore? he asked, and I felt a swell of grief bloom inside him like a toxic flower. I nodded, vaguely remembering something like that.

He fell quiet for a long time before he spoke again, and his fear was stronger than ever. *Niusha... I can't express how... torn I am with the memories. It's enough to drive me mad. It almost did.*

"Then don't share them," I whispered. "I don't want you to force it."

I... can't keep these things a secret anymore. You need to know if it changes... how you see me, he said hesitantly.

I could feel his fear spike, and I clutched him as tightly as possible. "Breathe," I murmured into his back, kissing it again. "Breathe. Don't let the fear win."

His body wanted to fight my words, twitching and tensing as his breathing accelerated, but he eventually let out a colossal exhale that moved against my face and breasts.

I nuzzled into his skin. “Javed, you can tell me about the three another day. You’ve shared a lot, and it’s time to heal now. Whatever you’ve done… we’ll sort it out soon. I’m not unreasonable… I’ll listen. You know that.”

He sighed and pulled from me, scrubbing his hands across his face as he moved to sit on the floor before the fireplace. I followed suit, settling where he hunched in distress with his hands covering his face. His fingers shook, and I decided it was time for me to take over now.

His breath caught when I crawled over his legs to straddle his lap. When he didn’t move his hands, I lifted mine to let my fingers run through his thick tiger-orange hair. It was a delight to finally see it, and I thought it suited him quite well, even though it was haphazardly cut from—I assumed—years of blind trimming. I smiled whenever I’d find a particularly long lock he’d missed, but it all mostly fell to his cheeks and jaw in messy, layered waves.

“Perhaps we should get a professional to see if this nest is salvageable,” I said softly, trying to drag a chuckle out of him. “Otherwise, we might have to donate it to a bird.” I played aimlessly with his locks and smiled when I felt a tiny flare of amusement from him. It was very small, but I considered it a victory.

I hesitated for a moment, but then raised myself up to plant a kiss on the top of his head, like he’d done for me the other day. It’d taken all of my courage to do that, but I thought he needed it. He took in a deep breath, then froze. I detected the smallest tremor, like a buzz, humming throughout his body. His anxiety was petrifying him, and I dug deep to comfort however I could.

I grabbed his shoulders and rubbed them firmly, like I was warming him up, even though there was a fireplace right behind me. The lioness within brought out something new, a soothing, purr-like noise on an exhale. My lioness couldn’t actually purr, but it had a similar comforting effect. I closed my eyes and buried my face in his shoulder, releasing the throaty, growling purr until I felt his hands land hesitantly on my back.

His fingers slid up my shoulder blades and traced my neck until they cautiously cupped the back of my head. He pulled my face from him, and I sat upright with my eyes closed, respecting his privacy until he was ready. I felt his eyes on me, but I just gave him a small smile and released another growl-purr.

You... can look now, Javed said, his thumb caressing my chin. I blinked my eyes open, and had I been standing, I would have found a way to trip over myself.

Yes, I was shocked. I was shocked because I was positive that I was sitting on the lap of the most attractive male ever born. I immediately wanted to scramble off of him but didn't want him to misunderstand, so I ended up slapping a hand over my mouth, failing to hide the embarrassing squeak that slipped past my lips.

His straight mahogany brows slanted over a pair of eyes so sharp they struck me senseless. Long, dark lashes fluttered with each blink as his lush eyes searched mine. I couldn't find any words to save my life. They took me back to the rainy jungle, his irises flooded with streaks of blue and green. Next to his vibrant orange hair, his gaze was as arresting as his roar. There was a clever, predatory gleam in it, which was what I found the most arousing. His keen eyes spoke of his quick mind and thoughtfulness, and it was my turn to quiver.

I brought my hands to my chest and worried at them, incredibly shy all of a sudden. Why did this feel like meeting him for the first time all over again? His scars hadn't struck me nearly as intensely as his eyes had. If his voice used to be as compelling as his gaze, I could see why he had thousands of followers—perhaps more. I could also see why those females had surrounded him too… My lioness definitely wasn't happy about that thought.

Niusha... you're missing what... He sighed and pointed to his forehead, then brushed his locks back so I could see what he wanted to show me. A large symbol had been branded into his forehead, and I scrunched my face up, trying not to fall back into tears. I traced it with a finger and sniffed. Oh gods, how could my people do this? That must have been utterly agonizing to endure!

I fought it with all my might, but I couldn't keep my chin from wobbling as I looked at Javed. I couldn't say anything. Mucus trickled embarrassingly out of a nostril, and I quickly wiped it away, sniffling hard. My upper lip twitched as I tried to open my mouth to talk… to say anything, but words just wouldn't come forth. My voice was a coward.

I pulled away and glanced down at his neck, still frowning, shaking, and sniffling. There was a line of symbols encircling his throat, but they didn't look like the same symbols that were on the rest of his body. This was a different style of letters.

Just before my exile, they forced one of their captured witches to mute me. She took advantage of a loophole and only muted my voice, not Convict. That's how I can still roar and make other sounds... That ended up being... kind of a lifesaver...

I knew I was supposed to be strong for him right now, but I felt like a wilted plant. I trailed my finger along his neck in misery. How could I be of any comfort when my species did this to him?

"I'm sorry," I tried to say, but it was so hoarse that it wasn't very understandable.

Am I hideous? he asked with lowered eyes.

Oh gods, had I given him that impression? "No!" I said quickly, then mumbled, "Your handsome face almost gave me a heart attack. You're far too attractive for the likes of me…"

He snorted and burst into silent laughter, leaning forward to thunk his head into my shoulder. *Now you know how I felt when I first saw you. Niusha, what are y—*

"Showing you how not hideous you are," I said seriously as I started unbuckling his pants.

When I'd brought the sleeping lioness to this inn, I hadn't expected the night to end like this—not with me exposing my shadows in a town full of Proudless. It was both surreal and freeing to be around Niusha without my cloak. I'd fought with myself a great deal before taking it off, wanting to show her what'd been done to me, and enough was enough.

I didn't like hiding my truth from her. It'd been doing as much damage to her as it had to me. Just before I'd scented her on the stairs earlier, I'd felt her jealousy, her hurt, and insignificance. After my fear and rage had died down, I'd wondered how much of my past was worth it. She'd find out eventually if she stayed with me. If she chose not to… well, perhaps it would be enough to make her stay—nothing would matter if she didn't.

I wasn't quite sure how I'd expected her to react to my scars, but I hadn't expected admiration to be mixed in with her sorrow. I viewed those disgusting cuts as the lions' victory over me. Niusha saw them as my body rejecting what'd been done. I supposed it was like an uprising in a way; when oppressors encroached, all one could do was fight back, heal, and regrow forces until something changed.

I'd have to think about that more when Niusha wasn't in the middle of removing my pants.

My veins thumped against my skin at the sight of the topless female tugging at my hips to get me to lift my ass off the floor for a second. I complied, and she pulled the fabric down, eyeing how my already erect dick jutted against the material. Her cheeks flushed a pretty pink as she mindfully pulled my pants down and over, letting it spring free and startle her. I held back my smile, mostly because I felt like it was too soon to feel amusement after reliving my nightmarish memories. I wasn't sure if I'd ever feel free until she knew about the three.

Until then… Niusha had a point to make.

I promise it won't pounce, I said to her as she finished undressing me. She was observing my length like it was a terrifying predator.

"I just… haven't really seen it that much up close without feeling… that wildness," she said shyly, getting to her feet and limping slightly to go behind me. I grew nervous but didn't move. I wanted her to know I trusted her; she'd earned that much.

Females in heat are susceptible to going feral... to losing control to their inner beasts. It usually triggers their ma—Ah... I was interrupted by a soft, smooth, and wet object running up my back. My breath caught whenever I could feel it and quickly realized that Niusha was licking me. Oh gods… what…

I stiffened when she placed a hand on my shoulder to balance herself while she groomed my back, licking up in smooth strokes like she was caring for fresh injuries. I wasn't quite sure how to feel about it at first. I was definitely numb in a great many spots, but when I could feel her, it made me shiver in pleasure, and I couldn't resist fisting my hardened cock while she worked.

I wasn't sure why she was doing it. Maybe she was apologizing for what her kind had done, but that was pointless. She wasn't the one who did it. She wasn't the scarmaster or the nobility who were allowed to play with my skin. Maybe she was simply showing her affection by caring for old wounds, or maybe she was simply just showing me that I wasn't hideous, like she'd said. I had no idea, but it was pleasurable.

I tilted my head back and moaned silently, rubbing the tip of my throbbing crown with my thumb to spread around the precum. When she completed her grooming, she lingered on the back of my neck, lapping lazily. Each slow lave sent a throb straight to my groin, and I found myself leaning against her grooming mouth. The tingling from the mate touch alone was almost enough to make me come. I knew how her sweet pussy felt, but I wondered how those lips would feel wrapped around me. I gritted my teeth as my canines lengthened, incredibly aroused by the mental picture.

She moved around to return to my lap, and my breath caught again, wondering what she was up to now. Niusha palmed the sides of my head and raised herself to kiss the brand on my forehead. It felt like she was offering her compassion, but I closed my eyes and tried not to think. I wasn't comfortable with this one. I hated the brand with my entire being; it reminded me of what had hurt me the most—something that made me mad with grief if I thought too hard about it. I didn't want her lips on something so horrific.

Niusha must have sensed my discomfort because she stopped abruptly and put her forehead to mine, whispering an apology. She leaned down to lap at the front of my neck, and I tilted my chin back to give her room to work. I sighed and shuddered under her ministrations, and my abdomen contracted with desire. I could so easily move her underwear aside and part her flesh with my slavering erection. I could reward her for treating me with such kindness.

She seemed to have other plans, though, as she started kissing down my chest. A rumbling groan broke through my lips as she traced her tongue down my abdomen, between the grooves of packed muscles that tensed more the lower she went. I sensed how pleased she was by my noise, which only seemed to encourage her.

I stared at her, breathing hard as she finally stroked a finger down my cock. She was glorious as she sat by the firelight. The flickering glow danced along the swells of her hip and the lovely curves of her breasts. Her blond hair tumbled around her sweet face in wild waves, and the charged emotions in her blue-grey eyes, tucked under long lashes, flickered with greater intensity under the flames.

She studied and stroked my cock thoughtfully, unaware of how she was torturing me. I wanted to tilt my head back and savor every touch, but I also wanted to watch her. There was no way any of this could be real, could it? Perhaps I was still asleep in the jungle, about to wake up to another lonely day of idle surviving. It was not possible that I was reclining by a fireplace, being touched by a fated mate—especially one as beautiful as Niusha.

She appeared fascinated by how I hardened for her and continued to explore my length with her caresses. I released a tortured moan and clenched my jaw, barely able to stand not being inside her. I flexed against her hand, silently begging for more, and her eyes slid up to lock on mine.

It could be... I groaned, *that my cock might benefit... from a grooming as well.*

I would gladly admit that this was my low point.

I sensed that she was mildly alarmed for just a moment, but then it turned into curiosity. She propped herself up with a palm on the floor, carefully positioned my cock, and opened her mouth to take an experimental lick up the swollen crown. I released a long, tight moan as I felt her wet tongue slide around my tip. The tingling from her touch made me silently beg to the gods to not let me explode in her face.

Oh Sky Gods, I exalted, tilting my head back to blow out a disbelieving exhale. Niusha was pleasantly surprised by my reaction and started lapping up my erection in languid strokes. Her smooth tongue molded around the veined, throbbing surface as she spread her saliva up to the crown, unintentionally coaxing out precum. I stared heatedly at her as she regarded its path down my cock, then tilted her head and curled her tongue to lick the trail clean. I hissed and moaned again, bucking my hips in an aroused twitch. The sight of her tasting my cock was almost too much—too much!

Your mouth might... I grunted and braced myself better on my elbows. *Be more effective. If you wanted to be more thorough. You know... more saliva.* I'd never acted so fucking shameless. What was she doing to me? *It's possible... I'm quite dirty.* Great gods, what was I saying? What in the everlasting fuck was I saying?

Niusha gave me a serious, penetrating stare that was belied by her concealed amusement and simply lowered her head to suck in as much of my erection as she could. I bared my teeth and balled my fists, barely able to contain myself within the velvet heat of her mouth. She lifted her head, dragging her soft stretched lips as she removed me from her mouth and glanced up at me.

"Like that?" she asked, eyes hopeful.

I feel cleaner already, b-but I think it just needs a bit more attention... It was clear that I no longer had control over my idiot brain. Niusha seemed to be thrilled, though, which was the only reason why I wasn't completely mortified.

When she sucked me back into her mouth, I scented her arousal, which made me buck my hips involuntarily. Oh gods, was this exciting her? I reached forward with a hand and pulled her hair from her face, wanting to get a better view. She hummed and subtly wiggled her own hips. Was that unintentional? I didn't know. I didn't know anything but the pleasure of her soft, wet inner cheeks and tongue massaging my length.

Fuck... Niusha... Go faster, I directed, breathless. She hummed excitedly and started bobbing her head up and down to please me. I felt something drip onto my leg and quickly realized that it was from her sex. I tilted my head back, crying without sound. I wished I had my human voice back just so she could hear what she did to me.

Better remove your mouth and get a napkin... I'm about to come, I cautioned and released her hair from my grip. I leaned back onto both my elbows again and was surprised to find she'd switched to using her hand. Who was I to keep her from doing what she wanted to do?

Certainly not my idiot brain.

I placed my fist around hers and showed her my preferred speed and pressure, which she got the hang of immediately. A surge of arousal splintered from my chest to my groin as she pumped away at my length, which was unbearably hard at this point. It needed release so badly. I wanted to release everything—wash out all my stress and bad feelings along with my seed. I just wanted a moment of pleasing peace—just a moment. It'd be even better gifted by my fated match.

My breathing accelerated until I was panting and begging for air. My muscles contracted and my sack tightened as my blood came to a boil within my ears. The small, encouraging noise from Niusha was what tossed me over the peak.

I hissed as euphoria shot through me, then tilted my back in a silent cry, only hearing the tiger roar through our combined shouts of ecstasy. My claws scoured the wood floor as I bucked my hips to my release, coming repeatedly in blissful spurts. I groaned and lifted my chin, clenching my itchy teeth as I once again felt the all-consuming desire to be gum-deep in Niusha's waiting neck.

I licked my lips, almost able to taste her as I spent the last of my seed. I brushed a hand over my damp brow and slowly gathered my senses. Then, I dragged my gaze up to find a red-faced lioness still straddling my thighs.

"Well… you got me," she said quietly, looking down at her chest, which was glazed from my release. I probably should have been embarrassed by the result of my idiot brain, but I was only turned on by the sight. I pulled her to my lap so I could bury my nose in her neck. I was addicted to her sweet scent of fig and how it mixed with the spices of oud. I also deeply loved the smell of myself on her and wondered if I could detect her pregnancy later when there weren't so many heavy aromas in the air.

I nuzzled into her neck and replied to her comment with a sensual promise. *Not yet, Niusha... not yet.*

Chapter 22

Niusha

The male with the tiger-orange hair brushed his nose along my neck as his cock relaxed under my buttocks. He seemed much more at peace, which ultimately brought me relief as well. I hoped he understood now how desirable he really was. He could never disgust me.

Tell him that, Field prodded.

I placed my hands on his warm, slow-breathing chest, then slid them up and over his shoulders. "Was that proof enough?" I asked quietly. "You are so attractive that I almost can't handle it, Javed. I almost had to run away when I saw your eyes." I bit my lip and waited for his response.

I felt his flush of pleasure, and he chuckled silently. *Yes, Niusha. You've offered more proof than I'd ever ask for.* He then sobered as he stroked his hands up and down the sides of my waist, making goose bumps prickle in their wake. *Thank you... I don't know if I'll ever truly feel attractive again, but... thank you. You've helped me a great deal, my queen.*

He sat up and stared at me with his hunter's gaze for a long while, like he was memorizing my face. I stared back, feeling like I was waiting for something, and his expression slowly grew tender. His brows drew in, and he tilted his head ever so slightly. He took in a deep breath and let out what was on his mind.

May I kiss you? he asked quietly, his cheeks flushing from his inquiry. His fingers flexed tentatively in their grip on my waist.

I couldn't help my automatic reaction. Thinking of Mehr, of his violation, I flinched and closed my eyes. A shudder swept through me, brutally, and I wrapped my arms around my breasts, as though I could prevent the memories from manifesting into those awful sensations. His lips had been so cold, and his laugh had been so dismissive. The way he'd spoken to me, it was like he was trying to get me to question my reality again—like there was no way we wouldn't turn out happy together.

—sha? Niusha? Javed's urgent calls snapped me out of my bad memories and confusion. I blinked rapidly and fell back into his blue-green gaze. *After all that, I can't believe asking you for a kiss was what turned you off,* he joked half-heartedly.

I placed a hand to my temple and shook my head, trying to clear it. "No… no… I was just remembering something," I said tightly. I felt an urge to wash my lips again.

Him? he inquired, going rigid. A tic in his jaw accompanied his burst of anger.

"Yes…" I whispered. "He forced that on me too. So cold. So arrogant."

Oh Niusha… he groaned and looked up at the ceiling. *If only I could have given you all your firsts. You deserved a beautiful first kiss under starlight.* He tangled his fingers in my hair, then fisted the locks possessively. The territorial move pulled a soft mewl from my lips—the lips that never strayed from his gaze. I watched the ball in his throat bob, his swallow thick as he stared at me with hungry jungle eyes.

"I wish you could have too," I said, still held fast by his grip on my hair.

I wish I could permanently mark you, he confessed with a strained expression on his face. *Make sure no one else can claim you.*

"Why don't you?" I asked, not really needing to think about it too hard. There were two things I desperately wanted in my life. One was to meet my parents, and the other was to be by Javed's side. I had no idea if the first one could ever come true, but I knew that the second one was possible…

Why not indeed... He was fighting some kind of new, internal battle—I could see it in his tortured eyes. *Maybe I don't want to waste another second with you. If I can't convince you to avoid the lions, maybe I'd be lucky to have what I can of you until then. I don't know if I can take it anymore. If I have to be a shell of a shifter for the rest of my life, it'd be worth the small amount of time I'd have with you.*

"We remain in disagreement," I murmured. "My head is a mess about them now. I still have much to think about, but if I ever went to them, I'd find a way out with our cubs safe and sound. I know this, but I won't argue it again. I do not like arguing." I rarely felt my lioness react during conversations, but she added her voice to my words. She did not like to be questioned. When she was confident, she was resolute, and her resolve gave me courage.

Javed growled and squeezed his eyes shut for a moment. *You've been heard. You and your lioness.*

"Thank you."

You will be the death of me. He sighed and brought our foreheads together. I nuzzled his nose affectionately, and the gesture eased his tension. *If you stayed with me, I'd build us a beautiful home. I'd hunt for you and our offspring every day—I'd even cook too. I'd give you as many cubs as you want. I'd please you as often as you want. I'd make love to you as often as you want... I'd do anything, Niusha, if it meant keeping you.*

"Make love?" I asked, not sure if the term meant what I thought it did.

Sex.

"Don't I have to be feral… or in heat?" My first encounter with sex was a bit fuzzy in my memory, and the doctor hadn't really been specific on a couple things. Had that been a warning at the time that my heat was coming? Maybe… Maybe not… I had so much left to learn about my body. So many blessed questions…

No. A small, wry smile spread across his face. *We could easily do it this very moment.*

"Oh," I whispered, my face erupting into a heat that could rival what was coming from the fireplace. Come to think of it, his erection had been pressing against my butt for a little while now. Arousal fluttered in my belly, and I resisted the urged to squirm on his lap.

Despite the excitement his words had instigated, it was a lot more flustering to be facing that level of intimacy with a clear mind. I was a lot more self-aware, which made me really shy about certain things.

"Well… I… er… haven't really bathed, and I'm covered with sweat from my earlier nap…" I muttered in embarrassment, starting to climb off him, but he pulled me onto his lap again and leaned me back so he could bury his nose in my collarbone.

I love the scent of your sweat, he murmured. *It reminds me of when I work your body.*

"Oh dear," I whimpered, almost as quietly as a mouse squeak.

It would be very hard to repulse me, not when your body sings to me so sweetly. I desire every part of you. I wouldn't waste good seed to mark my territory on just anyone's skin, he said in a lower, more seductive tone.

"Oh dear gods."

His fingers slid across my chest to rub his seed into my skin, and I bit my lower lip to hold back another small noise. A shudder raked down my spine, making my skin flutter under his fingertips. I wanted his hands to go lower, but I simultaneously didn't, and it made me incredibly frustrated.

Someday, Niusha, when you are comfortable. I will worship every part of your body the way it deserves to be celebrated, he comforted, then laid a soft kiss over the mark on my shoulder, making me gasp in pleasure. The skin there was so sensitive! *You will never know pleasure in the way I can give it. No lion could even come close to making you feel as good as I can.*

I had no doubts about that…

I've decided, he said while opening his mouth to show off one of his extended canines, *that I am going to make you scream tonight. I'm going to make you feel so good that everyone in town, all the Proudless, will know how much I worship my lioness.*

"Oh my dear gods."

His hands palmed my hips and slid down to the back to slip into my underwear, cupping a butt cheek in each hand. I jolted in surprise, my heart leaping into a run without any signs of slowing. He groaned as his large, rugged hands dug into my flesh and began massaging in large circles. His erection was very nearly wedged along my backside and much larger. Another deep groan rumbled from his chest, vibrating a shiver right out of me.

You are so fucking hot, attractive, desirable, beautiful, he moaned and scraped his sharp teeth along his old mark.

I arched sharply and nearly shrieked at the bolt of pleasure that shot straight down to my clit. It settled into a warm throb that heated up my entire sex. My panties had stopped being dry ages ago. They must be in ruins by now.

Please, can I have you? he begged into my neck, creating a whirl of pleasure with every brush of his kissing lips against the mark. *May I take you? Make love to you? Fill you? Bury myself so deep in you that you'll beg me never to leave?*

"Oh my dear sweet gods."

He slid his right hand farther down the curve of my butt cheek, exploring under me until he found my sensitive, swollen folds. His thick finger dug between them and sank into my waiting sex. I leaned back and released a desperate, lustful cry. Yes, that was exactly where I wanted him to be. I didn't care if he ripped me with his size, I needed all of him… desperately.

"Yes, fill me," I breathed out, butterflies of excitement fluttering under my skin.

Oh fuck. You make me so gods-blessed fucking hard. He growled quietly as he slipped his hands from my underwear. *Kneeling's not high enough. I need you to stand,* he commanded, and the order sent a thrill through me. I got to my feet, took my underwear off, and let him guide my hips down toward the top of his erection.

Angle me at your entrance, he ordered, and I reached between my legs to grasp his… fifth limb.

"Oh my dear sweet giddy gods," I whimpered under my breath.

I felt so exposed doing this outside of a feral mind, but his compliments made me feel more comfortable, oddly enough. I lined him up, or at least I was pretty sure I did, and he guided me down to part my folds with the rounded head of his cock.

Mmm, you're glazing me beautifully, he said with an erotic, carnal edge to his tone. I glanced down and whimpered. I was not afraid of heights, but my eyes followed a trail of my desire down him, and there was a long way to go. He leaned forward to kiss my stomach. *Relax, we've done this several times. You can take me, my queen. The Moon Goddess made us a perfect fit. No one can take you like me. No one can take me like you.*

"Oh my dear sweet giddy Moon Goddess," I squeaked, his words setting me ablaze.

I watched him as he lowered me, then I felt his wide cock stretch the skin of my threshold. Javed let gravity do most of the work, and with some anxious rubbing on my part, my slick allowed his head to pop past my entrance. He pushed me down slowly, squeezing his girth into me while I gritted my teeth. Ah, the stretch was nearly unbearable.

Keep those claws in if they help. They don't bother me.

I glanced down and gasped when I saw that I'd dug my claws into Javed's shoulders and hastily retracted them, drawing a startling amount of blood. "I'm sorry, I'm sorry! I'm s—" I apologized, then my breath was taken away when I finally hit the tops of his thighs. He groaned in bone-deep satisfaction, tilted his head back, ecstasy dropping his jaw.

I nearly fainted against him in relief, then nuzzled into his chest, moaning at the incredible sense of fullness. I mindlessly lapped at him as I focused on all my inner sensations. He plugged up the empty space that was meant for him—a part of him that my body missed so often. Joining like this spoke of so many things. It spoke of a future family, it spoke of our attraction to each other, and it spoke of our feelings—that we entered this with free hearts. It spoke of a need to be as close as possible for as long as possible.

I'm going to make you mine tonight. Ok?

"O-ok." Oh my dear sweet giddy Moon Goddess on rice.

So we're really going to do this? Convict asked, both relieved and nervous. It almost felt like he was pacing in my head.

Yes, Convict, I said as I wrapped my arms around Niusha, savoring a moment of just being inside her warm heat. *I don't want to mark anyone else. I want to enjoy having a mate as long as possible. If we lose her to the lions, at least I won't lie awake at night being tortured by the thought of someone else marking her. This way, they'll never truly have her, and I'll never truly have lost her... I guess...*

At least I'll get to apologize to Field, Convict replied. *That's been weighing on me.*

I nodded, stroking a hand through Niusha's wavy milk-and-coffee hair. I swallowed and wrapped an arm around her waist, placing my other hand on the floor to brace myself. *Grab onto me,* I ordered, and she complied, taking a firm hold of my shoulders.

I moved to a crouch, then stood, and she immediately wrapped her legs around my hips. I chuffed in contentment and walked her toward the large bed, laying her down on the edge so I could stay standing. Her hair splayed around her, more lustrous than any lion's mane could ever hope to be.

She shyly rested her hands on the comforter near her chin. Her breasts, just a touch paler than her arms, legs, and face, rose with every breath she took, and I could only hope to taste them someday—show her the pleasures she could get from them instead of feeling violation and disgust. I wanted to bury myself in the smooth, round surface of the fatty, swollen globes, suckle on her darkened, blushing nipples, and listen to the thrumming of her amorous heart.

I held her hips as I slowly pulled my heavy, throbbing dick from her clasping channel, enjoying the sound of her slick guiding our intimate flesh along each other. When only my crown was left inside, I slid back in just as lazily, wanting to warm up my lioness a bit more. She'd pleased me of her own volition—when I was at my most vulnerable—which made me want to return it tenfold.

I enjoyed my vantage from this position because I could see her body's every response. I held back a smile when her shy face reddened under my gentle surveying. She wasn't used to being this clear-headed during a mating, and she was even more unused to seeing my entire body. Her blue-grey eyes often flickered away when our gazes met, but since it always coincided with a spike in her arousal, I took it as a huge compliment.

Look at me, I urged as my heavy sex slid wetly in and out of her warm pussy. *It's just me. We've done this before. I'm not a different person.* I suppressed another smile when her eyes glanced back up at mine. *I love looking at your pretty eyes, especially when I'm inside you.* I tilted my head as I studied her blushing form, rolling my hips to grind against her clit.

"I know…" she murmured on an exhale and made an obvious effort to relax. She spread her arms out a little more and took a deep, steadying breath. Her full lips parted in a silent moan as she tried to keep her eyes on me. I smirked slightly and slid a finger slowly down from her belly button to play with one of the short, beautiful curls of blond hair between her legs, then moved my finger past it to graze the top of her petal-soft folds.

We can go a little louder than that, I said, and pulled my wet dick out to steal some lubrication off it. I plunged back into her with a slap and startled a pleased cry out of her. My smirk spread a little wider, and I rubbed my slicked thumb around her clit. Her cry quickly turned into a moan, and I murmured, *There we go. Good lioness…*

The more aroused she got, the more her body bloomed for me. She was always beautiful, but the way the blood flooded her body when she was turned on was impossible to ignore. Her red cheeks, pinkened lips, swollen breasts and blushing folds were like a buffet laid out for me and only me. My seed splattered on her chest made for an arousing garnish, and I shuddered in satisfaction at the scene.

I held her firmly and increased the speed of my penetrations, slipping in a little harder and a little faster while my other hand meandered teasingly around her clit. My loping heart quickened, excited from the carnal pleasures of sex and the sight of Niusha's rocking breasts. A light sheen of sweat broke across her flushed skin, making her figure shiny and oh-so-sensual.

Sky Gods, you feel so good, I groaned and arched to roll my groin into her, grinding into her sex while I ran my thumb around the apex of it.

"Javed! Ah… ah… ah!" Niusha stretched and arched before me, unknowingly spurring my lust to new heights. My dick swelled more at the sight of her writhing form and jutting breasts, and I felt myself press into all the limits of Niusha's beautiful, sopping channel. Despite my hardness, her muscles fought to clench, and the resulting friction sent bursts of pleasure up my cock. Excitement sizzled in my chest and skittered down my spine in little electrical currents. She, my gorgeous lioness, was pure ecstasy—my favorite paradise.

When I felt her body tense up after yelling, I removed my thumb from her clit. *That was good, but I think we can still go a little louder,* I speculated and slowed my thrusting down to an easy rocking. Her building orgasm calmed for a moment while I gave her a breather.

She was gloriously flustered—an absolute, moaning mess. I noticed, with some curiosity, that her hands had wandered to caress her own belly and the bottom of her breasts; I took that as a good sign. She needed to get comfortable with herself first, and I felt a small blooming of affection for her. She'd be safe in her healing with me.

That was when it dawned on me.

Ah… fuck. I love her. I love Niusha, I confessed to my idiot heart.

The finality of it was accepted by said idiot heart. I knew it could happen, and it did. It'd been part of the worst-case scenario, but never had something so tragic felt so fulfilling. Looking down at her panting face—rosy-cheeked and clear-eyed—I melted for her.

Wrap your arms around me, sweet lioness, I said, leaning down with a hand to scoop under her hips. I dragged us both fully onto the bed and settled comfortably between her legs. She cupped my face with her hands and brought our foreheads together, making my soul flutter against hers.

"Thank you, ah…" she whispered, moaning when I slowly drew out and pushed back into her.

For what? I asked, kissing slowly up her neck.

"For finding me… th-the cubs and me, I mean." She sighed blissfully and arched against me, rubbing her nipples deliciously against my pecs. "For helping me… saving me… c-caring about me," she listed across three slow breaths as we held each other.

It was never an option, I declared quietly and licked a line up her earlobe, causing her to shudder and groan. *I never stood a chance against Fate.*

"Wh-why does that feel good?" She gasped when I dipped my tongue to follow the inner curve of her ear. I smiled, then nibbled her earlobe.

The body has many erogenous zones... pleasure spots, I explained as I made her writhe beneath me. *I guess I found another one that you like...*

I licked my thumb, slid my hand down between us, and began massaging her clit again. "Ah! J-Javed!" she cried out as I worked both her sex and nibbled on her ear. Her fingers dug into my back, and I momentarily tensed, but she showed no signs of disgust, thank the gods. I relaxed and allowed myself to let go so I could build her climax again.

I spread my knees a little and began bucking into her. Each pulse of my hips thrust the crown of my cock into her back wall, forcing generous kisses against the threshold of her womb. Her cries fluttered at each deep invasion and grew louder with every slap of my sack against her ass.

"Please!" she sobbed and wrapped her legs around my slamming hips. "M-m-mark me!"

Soon, I promised, and kissed a trail from her ear to her rosy cheek. *Just needs to get louder in here.*

I accelerated my thrusting, groaning at the sound of our flesh slapping and sliding together. I laid fresh kisses across her face, from one cheek to the next, avoiding her lips to maintain her sense of safety. Her gasps and panting joined my rhythmic grunting as I felt her tighten once more. She became a thrashing, yowling mess when I rubbed aggressively into her clit and lapped sensually at the shell of her ear.

Oh, you are so... I groaned and released a primal, guttural growl into her neck, which made her shriek. I felt her arousal flood out between us when I pulled out and slammed back into her tight channel. I shuddered from the insanely intense pleasure. It was nearly making me feral, but I held on tight.

"Javed! Javed, please! I need you!" she shouted, arching into me and grinding against my busy hand. "Mark me!" she cried, tilting her head back and exposing her smooth, pulsing throat. "Take me!"

You wish to be one with me, Niusha? I asked, panting and dripping with sweat. I slapped my hips forward and increased to a bruising speed. Her sex clutched tighter as her climax approached, and I had to work harder to pull in and out of her.

"Yes!" she yelled, echoed by her lioness, clawing at my back like she was about to throw a feral fit. Her legs fell off me, and she planted them on the bed to raise her hips.

Louder, I grunted, then released a roar away from her head. I focused on fucking her as fast as possible now and rubbed furiously at her clit.

"Yes, Javed! Yes!" she shrieked.

Roar for me, lioness. Join me! I yelled and released another roar, plunging my cock in three more times before she reached her peak. I rapidly flicked my thumb across her clit, and she finally screamed.

Niusha climaxed, arched against me, and released an ear-piercing, roaring scream. I sped up, and it only took a heartbeat for the clenching waves of her orgasm to rub my seed out of me. I roared one last time and bottomed out to empty myself in her.

Nigh delirious with the pleasure of spending my seed, I tilted her head and buried my canines into her marking spot. She screamed again, and the grip of her fingers on my shoulders was only outmatched by the vice of her heat wrapped around my spurting dick. My venom ejected past our fragile, tenuous mark and hurtled toward her very soul to deliver a piece of mine. It latched itself onto her eternal being to protect and warn off all others. It inscribed my name inside her and shone like a guiding star so I'd never lose her trail. The gods and goddesses had blessed our joining, and I swore I could almost sense their approval.

I pulled my canines from her and was about to lick her wounds clean, but a savage bite into my marking spot wrenched me senseless. I roared into the sheets, feeling every muscle in my body bunch as Niusha marked me. I white-knuckled the sheets, shredding cloth and my palms as I was blindsided by another climax. My hips thrust uncontrollably as I came hard, but I could barely pay attention to that because I was under the assault of Niusha's venom.

It flooded my soul with obsessive territoriality and stationed itself there like a feral guardian. It changed my biology, fully intending on keeping all the other females away and identifying me solely as her male—her forever mate. She'd always know where I was now. She could stalk me, hunt me, and I'd never be able to escape. I'd never want to escape… I was hers. I always would be. That was my fate even before marking her. That was simply what it meant to love Niusha.

Chapter 23

I slowly released my canines from Javed's shoulder, startled by the instinct to mark that'd come out of nowhere. Once he'd claimed me permanently, I was unable to resist reciprocating. I licked away the blood, saliva, and venom I'd left behind on him while I nursed my own stunned haze. Javed did the same to me and pushed himself up to meet my eyes.

For once, I didn't feel the need to look away in shyness. I relished the sight of his handsome, breath-stealing visage. I was overwhelmed by our new connection, though… from that brief moment of burying ourselves in each other that'd tied us forever. A flurry of strong emotions rose like chatter in my heart and soul, and I realized that some of them were his. He was lost to wonder, joy, and disbelief. My own disbelief was from being seen as something so precious to him.

"I can feel you," I whispered, staring up at the male hovering over me, his tangle of orange locks framing his flushed cheeks and teal eyes. His parted lips were slightly red and swollen from all the kisses he'd peppered across my skin. I could still hear his heart thumping away, though it was slowing from our surreal lovemaking—our mating. I placed a palm on his burning cheek, almost unable to believe that this moment was real.

I feel you, he echoed and lowered his head to softly kiss my cheek. He left his lips there for a moment and took a deep breath, scenting my skin. He released his mouth from my face with a soft pecking sound, then nuzzled his nose where his lips had been. He released a satisfied chuff every several seconds, which eventually made me smile. He felt so happy, and I returned his happy noise with a growl-purr. The noise seemed to elate him, and his happiness blossomed into bliss. He always did react strongly to my lioness's noises.

I want to clean and groom you, he murmured and slowly eased his cock from me. My eyes widened at the pool of semen he'd left between my legs and on the comforter, and I became a little embarrassed—well, maybe a lot embarrassed. The maids would not enjoy cleaning that…

Javed brought me to the next room to run us a bath, and we cleaned each other in comfortable silence—aside from the occasional sighs and contented chuffs. This time there wasn't any charged, erotic tension. We were both still lost in wonder at what we'd just done, and all our movements with the soapy sponges were reverent and sweet. He'd left the cleaning of my breasts to me as well, showing his sensitivity. I'd never been taken care of like this—not even close. I had no idea that I'd been so starved for affection. He must have been too… considering his long, lonely exile.

We dried, and he carried me back to the bed, apparently unwilling to be more than a few inches away from me at any given time. After Javed spot-cleaned the comforter with a wet cloth, he blew out the lamps and joined me in bed. He nuzzled into my neck and sighed. I was surprised to feel a pang of disappointment from him.

The only thing I hate about baths is now my scent is mostly gone from you, he complained, dragging me flush against him as he ran his hands all over my skin. He lapped at my neck, making me shiver in pleasure, but then he sighed in discontent after taking another breath. He grabbed the towel he'd used to wipe his seed from the bed, and I felt him dab a small amount of something onto my neck, then rubbed it into my skin.

When I identified it, I nearly erupted into laughter. It was a strange obsession, and I didn't mind it, but I hoped it didn't come from a place of insecurity. He had nothing to worry about with other males—I had claws now and wouldn't tolerate another's approach again.

He scented me one last time, groaned quietly in approval, and pulled me to lay my head on his chest. His hand rested on the arm I'd slung over him, and his thumb stroked in lazy circles. I held him tight, too moved by everything to speak. I was too happy with him to put any of it into words.

So… A voice popped into my head—a deep, powerful, and virile voice I'd only heard several times before—and it startled the wits out of me. A responding shudder straight from Field vibrated down my spine. Despite the tiger's dominant tone, his words came out fast and a little frantic. *I just wanted to apologize to Field for my poorly timed comment about tiger… and lion… penises… with… bar— Is now not the right time?*

Whatever excitement Field had been feeling went right out the window. I witnessed Javed's hand move up, then heard it scrub across his face. I didn't know what to say at first, but since Javed was at a loss for words, I fumbled for ideas. "H-hi, Convict?"

Hi… Did Field go hibernate?

"What does that mean?"

Did she tuck herself away? I don't sense her well anymore…

I searched inward, and it seemed like she was sulking. It was the best way I could word it. "I guess so," I verified.

Fuck. Good night. Sorry, mate.

"Good night…"

Good night, idiot, Javed muttered.

"That was… interesting," I mumbled sleepily, scooting closer to my mate. Great Sky Gods, I'd have to get used to that.

Javed's exasperated emotions turned into unease, and he asked, *What is the plan for tomorrow?*

I sighed, wishing it hadn't been brought up tonight. I wanted to enjoy the moment and not stress out over the future. "I wish to continue in the direction of the pride," I answered and winced when I felt his heart sink. He was scared, and I wished there was a way to comfort him. He wouldn't understand why I still needed time to think on everything I'd learned.

My initial feelings about the lions had gone from excitement, to dislike, to horror and now… an overwhelming compulsion. I didn't know what it was, but it definitely wasn't a compulsion to join the pride. I felt like I couldn't breathe as long as their weight hung over my head, but I didn't know what to do about it. I continued to feel lost.

I'm sorry. I feel your torment. He wrapped both arms around me and turned on his side. Tilting my chin up to face his gaze, he asked, *Do you wish for forever with me? Despite everything, do you truly wish to be mine until the day we return to the Sky Gods? I'm not just something to pass the time with... right?*

"Oh gods, you're so much more than that! I do want forever, Javed," I said, blinking back tears, hurting from his worries. "I want you. I desperately do. I'd have no other. I want you to father all my cubs."

Then we will figure this out together. Will you fight alongside me? Fight for us? I could almost taste his insecurity, and it would have broken my heart had I not also felt his newfound determination.

"I will fight for us. I always will," I promised. I gathered my courage, propped myself up, and laid a soft kiss on his cheek. I tried to fill it with all the affection I could, then snuggled back into his arms.

Then that's all I can ask for. He pulled me into a near crushing embrace, and I surrendered happily to it until I fell asleep.

Javed was ravenous come breakfast, and I put a rather sizeable dent into what they'd sent up as well. There was an excess of pastries with chocolate, and I suspected Javed had something to do with that. I gorged on them with abandon, still obsessed with the novelty of the brown confection. Javed seemed very pleased with himself, laughing at the crumbly mess I'd created on the table.

He stood after eating, came to my side and licked what must have been a tiny smudge of chocolate off the corner of my mouth, eliciting a silly cackle from me. *My female looks beautiful this morning,* he said, stroking a finger down my blushing cheek as he knelt to treat my ankle, then went to pack up our things.

We've been spoused! Field commented in awe.

Better than spoused! The bond is incredible, I said as I changed. *No going back.*

No going back... she said thoughtfully. I wondered what was going to happen between her and Convict. All I knew was that I didn't want to miss a second of it, and I was disappointed that she didn't volunteer any additional thoughts. Perhaps he'd annoyed her more than I thought.

When we left our room, I clung fearfully to Javed, not wanting to look at anyone. I hated being stared at with loathing, and even if Javed had threatened them, I was too afraid to free my gaze. After failing to meet the maid's eyes last night, being ignored felt almost as bad. I'd never experienced anything so intolerable as the rejection of my very existence.

My mate, my tiger, drew his cloak around me as we walked down the stairs. There were more people on the bottom floor than I was comfortable with, and I leaned into Javed when my anxiety finally spiked.

"What does rag-puss mean anyway?" I whispered, remembering what I'd been called last night and when I'd been abducted. "I've been called that twice already."

Don't think about it. It's vulgar, and only stupid gibs use it, he said shortly, and I sighed in frustration. I didn't like being called something I didn't understand. Also, what was a gib?

The inn owner intercepted us on our way out and performed an apologetic bow. "I hope we were able to make your female comfortable. Please regard this as a safe place for you both if you ever pass by again."

I appreciated the sentiment, but I still couldn't look him in the eye. "Th-thank you," I said on behalf of us both, and Javed whisked me out of the inn and into the crisp morning air.

"Javed!" Mas'ud came running from the side of the inn. Had he been waiting for us? My tiger released an aggravated growl, angry over being delayed. He didn't seem to want anything more to do with these people. "We hadn't gotten to it last night, bu—" Javed cut him off with a snarl and moved past him, but Mas'ud was not to be ignored. "The Proudless have been approached by new shifters!"

That got my mate's attention. He turned his head to the lanky male and raised his brows.

"It's pretty recent," he said, waving his hands in supplication. "They claimed they moved into their ancestral lands north of cat territory. They've been investigating and trying to shut down the beginnings of what looks like illegal blood trading."

Blood trading? What the fuck has been happening while I've been gone? Javed asked, and I echoed his question. Mas'ud hesitated, so I showed him my fresh mating mark. I didn't know if he needed proof, but it seemed to settle him somewhat. Javed could always make a gesture if I wasn't relaying his words properly.

"They apparently are trying to establish a regular import of donated blood, but it's strictly regulated by them and some of the other kingdoms. They met with us because the lions have been ignoring their attempts to initiate discussions. Anyway, they've tracked a lot of activity between the jungle and the pride… I just wanted to warn you if you're going in that direction," he said and scratched at the back of his head. I had a feeling that he'd also brought it up in hopes of getting Javed to lead the Proudless again.

Your warning has been heeded... What manner of shifter are these? my mate asked, and once again, I relayed the question.

"Ah… bat, apparently. Rather odd, but… it is what it is. None of us have ever heard of them."

Odd indeed, Javed murmured thoughtfully, then grabbed my hand and turned to leave.

"Thank you, Mas'ud," I called back to him and followed my mate out of town. "Why does everything go back to the lions?" I wrinkled my nose, frustrated. "Why couldn't I have been born a tiger?" Javed squeezed my hand to soothe me, and I wrapped my arm around his, leaning in to absorb all the comfort I could from my new forever mate. I had no doubt that he was doing the same.

Javed

I was watchful over Niusha as we continued our trek north toward the wretched lion pride. I figured her ankle was mostly healed, but I wanted to make sure she didn't overburden it. Her decision to continue toward the pride unnerved me, but I wouldn't go back on my word. The only way to find out what would happen would be to see this task through to the end. Niusha was acutely aware of my unsettled emotions and would occasionally fall into nervous small talk. We took turns soothing and calming each other, knowing that we were both struggling beneath unique burdens.

"I think I figured out why I went into heat so early," she said as we moved through the creaking eucalyptus trees.

Oh? What did you come up with?

"I lost my cubs," she said, looking up at me with a faltering smile. "The orphans… the newborn… I lost them all at once. It wasn't a culling because they're alive and well, thank the gods, but I lost them all the same." Her smile was wobbly as she struggled to maintain it, and her eyes swam with tears.

Ah shit, that totally made sense. I stopped in my tracks and opened my arms for her. *That does sound like the reason...* I murmured as she leaned in and dissolved into tears. *Oh, my sweet queen. I should have realized that myself. Those orphans imprinted on you, and when they all disappeared, your body just reacted to replace them.*

"It's h-hard to think that I'll never see them again," she wept, sniffling wetly.

Who knows, my female. A clawed tree doesn't always fall, I replied, stroking the back of her head. *And you'll have several to care for in less than a year... should they make it.* I reached down and stroked her belly meaningfully. She recoiled heatedly from me, and for the first time, I could see Field in her eyes—golden, wild, and furious.

"They'll make it!" Niusha snarled aggressively, bristling. I froze and thought it wise not to push further on the subject. Convict was spooked himself.

Back off... Back off, back off, back off, he whispered to me, like she'd turned into a deadly frog.

I could tell that her inner lioness was getting extremely fed up with me on that topic. She started breathing rapidly and pressed a hand to her chest, so I pulled her back to me and worked to soothe her anxiety.

Shh, Niusha, calm, I murmured, chuffing and stroking her back until her shaking subsided. I really, really didn't want to laugh, but a silent, nervous chuckle ended up escaping me. I was going to have to warn everyone once the cubs came that my mate was a mother not to be trifled with.

She pressed into me for a minute, then rubbed her hands over her face. "Let's keep walking."

Do you want me to carry you? I inquired, always looking for a reason to have her in my arms, but she shook her head. I settled for grabbing her hand, then got our feet moving again through the long, rustling, fallen leaves.

Her lioness was surprisingly… unyielding. Field had always appeared confident, but I believed I'd been unintentionally deceived when it'd come to her self-reliance and conviction. She was stronger than I'd discerned—definitely forceful enough to fight Niusha for shifting control, which I'd witnessed several times now. I also wasn't sure if I'd seen anyone as fast at shifting as her. I wondered if any of it had to do with growing up outside the lions' territory.

I stared down at my mate, who seemed busy with her own inner reflections, and felt an ironic sense of pride.

When night fell, we set up camp in a clearing behind a hill, and it was nice to be under the stars again. I hadn't been able to get a good view of them for years. It occurred to me that my exile had even isolated me from my own gods.

It's been a while, Sky Gods, I murmured up to the twinkling stars as I digested dinner. *Are you still watching over me? Do you remember me? Can you hear me when almost no one can?*

Niusha came to lay next to me after washing her hands, apologizing quietly for snapping earlier. I ran my fingers through her milk-and-coffee hair as she settled, then pulled her over so she was laying on top of me. My lips found their home on her warm neck, and as I kissed slowly up her throat, I made it very obvious to her that there were no problems anywhere near this campfire.

We will probably arrive at the pride by tomorrow night, I murmured, licking up the shell of her ear while my hands hiked up the skirt of her dress.

"Oh!" she exclaimed quietly in surprise. "Oh…"

I had no idea if that was a response to my words or my actions, but I pursued my courtship of Niusha. We were mated, but until the issue with the lions was resolved, I wouldn't truly feel like she was safely mine. It was ridiculous, certainly, but every minute was a battle with my insecurity. It was a miracle that I hadn't stopped every couple of hours today to mount her.

I groaned in deep pleasure as I slid my hands down to scoop her bottom out of her underwear. "Oh, Javed…" She mewled sweetly into my neck as I massaged her cheeks downward, grinding her core against my thick erection. My blood heated up when my fingers brushed against the soft folds of her sex.

A throat being cleared startled us both from our foreplay, and I jumped up with a roar. I released my claws and stood obsessively by Niusha as she fumbled with her clothes. My entire body was extremely on edge guarding my pregnant female in our temporary territory, and it wouldn't take much for me or Convict to lash out violently at other travelers. I roared again, louder and lower, to make fucking sure I scared the piss out of whoever was there.

As I reached out with my senses, my nose encountered something I'd never scented before, and I narrowed my eyes at a figure on the outskirts of the firelight. I sniffed again and realized there were three other individuals.

I hope they're not thinking they can overpower us, Convict sneered. *If these are the new shifters, they're not immune to our roar either.*

Convict was right. Whoever had tried to approach us was frozen, like every other cat who'd run into our potent infrasound. I stalked up to them and studied the intruders while they shivered. Two of them had no scent, but based on their features and postures I'd hazard that one was a cat and the other was a dragon.

Scent remover… I murmured as I studied the tall one I suspected was a dragon. He was the only one who didn't look completely shaken, and he managed to flash a weak grin, showing off gleaming white teeth and fangs that contrasted sharply with his obsidian skin. This one was a charmer.

A shorter female, catlike with dark curls, stood pressed against him in fear. I saw recognition in her eyes when she stared up at me. I didn't know her, but she obviously recognized me. I sighed internally.

Maybe we should dye our hair, Convict muttered.

Tempting. I snorted, irritated by my lack of privacy.

These last two must be bats, Convict surmised, and I grunted in agreement. The male looked around my age and was similar in build, though a touch leaner. I had a feeling that I could overpower him, but I suspected he was much faster, and though he was very pale, he didn't look unhealthy. His red-brown eyes reminded me of drying blood, and his hair was a strange mix of dark brown and striking streaks of white.

Maybe we should go for that look.

I laughed silently at my tiger's suggestion, then turned to face the female who stood ahead of everyone. This was the person in charge here. She was pale as well, with thick, dark brown hair that fell to her shoulders. Like the male, she appeared strong, but leaner—almost spring-loaded.

I did a double take when I saw the bats' pointed ears, so I narrowed my eyes and backed up to Niusha. I'd never seen a shifter with pointy ears before now. There was something a little unearthly about their human forms.

The female cleared her throat again, albeit weakly. "G-good evening. We're sorry to have interrupted."

Who are you? I asked the flustered female. I stood protectively in front of Niusha while she parroted my words. It pleased me how fast my mate caught on when I needed her to speak. We didn't require words to work well together.

"Ah, yes. My name is Luzia. I'm a… er… I'm from the bat-shifter territory. We're looking for a tiger… Javed? Also known as th—"

I swiped my hand through the air with a growl to interrupt her. There was no need to go through all that nonsense. *What do you want with him?* I asked. They knew they'd found him.

"We're trying to meet with a representative for the cats. The lions are not responding to our requests, and this Javed is apparently the closest thing this territory has to a leader," Luzia said, shifting her weight uncomfortably.

I am not anyone's leader, I grunted in irritation. *Leave us. The cat territories are independent.*

Luzia did not look happy with that answer.

The dragon spoke up next. "So who do we need to speak with to get permission to hunt slavers that've migrated into cat territory? We'd like to liberate their 'stock' before they get too far."

"Slavers...? Stock?" Niusha murmured from behind me.

The stock being people. Humans and shifters, I clarified.

"I thought it was the lions that were kidnapping people?" she asked, confused.

The dragon burst into handsome laughter, and I regarded him warily. "Well, if that's the case, no wonder they won't meet with us," he said, then strode forward with a hand out in greeting. I narrowed my eyes as he approached. His body was relaxed, but any trained warrior could attack out of nowhere. "Leofwine. Master spy. Sent by King Keyon."

I cautiously accepted his greeting and clasped arms. *King Uhtric?* I inquired. The last king of the dragons was old, but I didn't think he was that old.

"Murdered," he answered flatly. "Very recently."

What else has changed since our exile? Convict asked. *Fish start walking?*

"That's a lioness," the female with the black curls whispered to Leofwine. "What's she doing here?" She looked at my mate like all the others did, and I released a low warning growl directed at the pair. I would not tolerate disrespect of my mate.

"I-I'm his fated mate... Niusha. I only found out I was a shifter recently. I have nothing to do with the pride here," Niusha said quietly, moving closer to me. She was hurt by the mild hostility per usual.

"Now, let's not make the sweet lady Niusha feel uncomfortable, my dear Adelais," Leofwine said, comforting the cat-shifter while maintaining his disarming smile.

Smart dragon, Convict muttered.

So what does any of this have to do with the bats? I asked, gesturing to Luzia and the male behind her. *Why are you both involved?*

"We've been approached by third parties looking to sell blood that we believe has been illegally obtained. After speaking with the dragons, we fear that some slavers are trafficking for blood farms now," Luzia said, crossing her arms over her chest.

"We've been raiding dens and rescuing slaves, but the slavers who've gotten away from us may have found a new way to make money with those they've managed to keep," Leofwine added in disgust, scowling like he'd just tasted something rancid.

"Javed," Niusha murmured, tugging on my arm. I looked down and found her eyes wide with terror. "Mas'ud mentioned the activity was between the jungle and the pride… Is this what happened to Sarita? Did they drain her for blood?" Her fear curled into deep, panicky dread. "What about Sushila? What about Niraj? Will they be drained?" I clutched her with both arms as she began to hyperventilate. "That would have happened to the cubs! Javed…"

I plucked her off the ground and cradled her obsessively to my chest. Warily, I kept the visitors in my line of sight while I tried to comfort my distressed mate.

She asks good questions, Javed, Convict rumbled.

Yes… yes, she does.

Chapter 24

Javed

Our 'guests' chatted among themselves as I comforted Niusha, stroking her wavy hair in long, affectionate sweeps. Her panicky breathing finally slowed as I chuffed into the top of her head.

That's my queen, I said softly when she finally calmed.

"It's still so hard to accept," she said, looking up at me through her damp, clumped eyelashes. "It's always one more thing. How do I come to terms with this?"

We'll leave this region if you stay with me, I said, not feeling any less anxious myself. *We'll go where we'll just be two cat-shifters starting a family.*

"Shouldn't we… help?" she asked, drawing her brows in and looking doubtful.

There's nothing we can do, I stated resolutely. I'd already paid my dues, and I wasn't going to put lives in my hands ever again.

"But what about Sushila and Niraj?" she pushed back, nervously fidgeting with a strand of her hair. "What about Quennel's family? What about Tsisana's sister?"

These people—I gestured to the shifters—*will find them, I'm sure.*

"But they can't even get an audience with the lions... They could be dead tomorrow."

I bit back an aggressive noise and removed Niusha from my lap. I paced by the fire, intensely agitated, and all my old injuries came flooding back to me. She was pushing too hard on wounds that were reopening, and I couldn't even begin to imagine joining this fight again.

The dragons have an entire kingdom. I'm sure they have the resources to sort this out, I replied, getting wound too tight. The nightmares would return tonight.

"I just thought..." she started saying, but I interrupted her with a hand gesture.

No, I asserted and met her eyes so she'd know I was completely unmovable on this. Her posture slumped, and she nodded, staring down at her feet.

"I should have known better than to ask. I'm sorry. I know you've been through too much already," she whispered, and I heaved a sigh of relief. She understood. Not meeting my gaze again, she asked, "Should I give them Quennel's name?"

"No need," Luzia said from the outskirt of the campsite. "We already spoke with him."

"We're just getting the runaround," Leofwine murmured to her, turning his back to us like he was preparing to leave. I bristled at the way he worded my declination. I was not the fucking leader, and I didn't have the authority to speak for that many territories.

Niusha, please inform them that if they want to hunt in cat territory, they will need to get permission from whatever subspecies owns the individual territories. That person is not me, I directed and stared angrily at my claws while she relayed the message. I needed them to go. *Tell them if that's everything, I'd like for them to leave.*

"That sounds a lot like what a leader would say," Leofwine mused after Niusha finished speaking. It didn't look like he was leaving.

"I guess nothing's changed," Adelais said with a sigh. "This was how it was when some of my family immigrated to your kingdom. Whatever territories maintained their independence from the lions didn't have a shared representative."

"That's probably how the lions expanded so fast. There wasn't a united front from all parties. It's weird because the other kingdoms recognize this region as a kingdom, though that form of government seems only utilized by the lions. And back to what you said about immigration to the dragons' territory, I think you mean our kingdom, sex kitty," Leofwine corrected, tugging the cat-shifter possessively to his side.

"Our kingdom…" she echoed, flushing.

Luzia was staring thoughtfully into the fire while the other bat glared jealously at the pair. They also didn't look like they were leaving. "This is messy, Ferrer. Queen Hekla won't like this."

"I wish we had better news to report," Ferrer muttered.

Who is Queen Hekla? Is that the bats' queen? I asked Niusha, who repeated it aloud.

"She's… not really our queen, but it feels like she is," Ferrer replied, crossing his arms and shifting his weight. "She liberated us from our court prison in the Realm of the Fae."

Realm of the Fae? I've only heard several stories. I didn't know if they were true or not, I said to Convict.

That's solitary cat life for you. Not much news gets around between the territories.

Yeah…

"She is the new queen of the Summer Court, though. So she's a queen in the Realm of the Fae, even though she's a wolf-shifter. I guess she considers herself more our guardian than queen," Ferrer corrected himself.

"I see her as my queen," Luzia murmured.

"We don't really have a solidified... system in place yet. We're just a colony."

I rubbed my temples with both forefingers. Why did I care? No, I didn't care. None of this had anything to do with me. I didn't care who the bats called queen. I didn't care about the fae.

"Well," Luzia said, stretching while cracking several bones in her spine, "I know your king is anxious, Leofwine, but we have time. If they're collecting blood, they won't be killing anyone, unless it's on accident. Blood comes back."

"They killed Sarita," Niusha muttered darkly with her hands wrapped around her, "and a bunch of others that they dumped into that crocodile-infested river. I wonder who'll be next?"

"Where are you from?" Adelais asked her suddenly in a tone that was neither aggressive or friendly.

"A village south of that giant river, somewhat between the mountains and the jungle..." Niusha answered evenly, but I could sense her stress rising. She quickly explained her story, graciously leaving details of me out of it.

"We should send people up to that village," the dragon said. "Sounds like they're breeding slaves. Very remote. A very easy location to keep your stock under control, especially if they're drugged."

"I don't know what they are..." Niusha said with a frown. "The pure elder isn't exactly the most lucid person I've met. The belief system there is... weird. I see that more than ever now that I've left."

"They don't need geniuses to run these locations. They only need willing people. Only the numbers matter. We'll be subtle about it, and if we need to extricate any victims, we will."

"Tell Gerlind that her newborn is alive..." Niusha whispered.

"Gerlind? Got it."

Why is blood such a hot commodity now? I asked before I remembered that I didn't care.

Luzia's lips puckered, her expressing souring. "We're what King Belenus refers to as hematophages," she stated reservedly.

"We've been cursed this way. Blood is the only food that can sustain us." She didn't seem to enjoy sharing that information.

"And as much as they try to establish strict regulations, there's a new illegal market now. The bat-shifters don't have the numbers to crack down on them like the dragons can," Leofwine said with a shrug, seeming unbothered by the nature of the bats. "But at least we have a large enough prison for slavers now," he added with a wicked grin.

Oh, Convict said in realization.

I don't get it, I replied to my tiger.

Give it time. We just ate.

Luzia turned to Ferrer. "Can you bring this information back to the colony? I'll sniff around here," she directed, then looked to Leofwine and Adelais for verification, "while you two investigate the southern village?"

"Agreed." The dragon nodded. He gave a graceful bow to us and departed, holding hands with the cat-shifter, who took one last speculative look at Niusha before they disappeared. In a matter of minutes, a black dragon burst into the night sky on silent wings.

Just as quietly, Ferrer left to shift in the woods. I stared impatiently at Luzia, who lingered for a moment. She glanced at us both and said, "I will probably see you again."

Assuredly not, I replied sharply, but she shrugged all the same after Niusha's parroting.

She turned to leave, then paused and looked over her shoulder at us. "I've never tried tiger or lion. I don't suppose you'd mind a little bite, would you?"

I snarled at her and sent her away with a rude gesture. She ran off laughing nervously and disappeared just like the others. Once I was certain they were all gone, I collapsed tiredly by the fire. I felt a thousand years old with the weight that everyone was trying to put on my shoulders. I'd paid my dues. I'd suffered for it, and I'd gotten people killed. They didn't need me. I'd made decisions I still…

"Javed…" Niusha cooed softly and crouched in front of me to offer a hug. I leaned to rest my forehead on her shoulder and squeezed my eyes shut. "I'm so sorry you're feeling so overwhelmed. I wish I could help…"

I didn't know how she could help. I was being asked to do something that had led to becoming a pariah while I was still under the scarmaster's claws. They said they'd forgiven me, but I still didn't know if what I'd done had been wrong, and that was what hurt the most. How could they ask me to return after that? I didn't understand. Why couldn't they find someone else?

"Do you want to talk about it?" my lioness asked, stroking the back of my head like I did so often for her.

Do we? Convict asked me.

I don't know. I'd planned on telling her, but I feel like my resolve is weakening. I sighed.

She'll find out eventually. Do you want her to learn about it from us or someone else? Convict had a good point, but…

"It's ok. Not tonight, I understand. Maybe tomorrow?" Niusha kissed the top of my head while waiting for my answer.

Maybe… I replied reluctantly.

"Should we just turn in for the night?" she inquired, and I nodded weakly. She patted my back and set up a place for us to sleep. The night had started so well, and now I just felt drained. This wasn't how I'd wanted to spend tonight. I'd planned on being balls-deep in my mate by now.

As if she'd read my mind, Niusha was naked when I joined her under the blanket. I groaned, torn about mounting her when I was in such a distracted headspace. If I did, it'd be rougher than I'd originally intended, and I liked savoring Niusha.

"Would it help to take your pleasure from me?" she asked over her shoulder.

That's not how I like to do things, I replied with a chuff into the back of her head and wrapped an arm around her waist, stroking her lower belly. *I want the energy to please you, and I just don't have it.*

"I think I'm adult enough to offer what I want to offer," she replied dryly, and I chuckled, pulling her flush against me.

You're very sweet, my queen, I replied, nuzzling and chuffing my love song to her. I was already feeling better just holding her. *Go to sleep, my Niusha. Tomorrow will be a long day.*

I smiled and held back a laugh at the cranky disappointment I felt across our bond.

Like so many days before, I woke to the scent of Javed mixed with a dead campfire. I'd hardly slept at all, and the smoke wasn't doing any favors for my tired, bleary eyes. I'd wanted a distraction before bed as much as Javed seemed to need one, but he hadn't felt up to sex, so I'd fallen into nightmares like I'd feared.

This time, I'd dreamed that I had to escape the village, but every section of the village was represented by our journey thus far. I snuck from house to house, then had to crawl through someone's overgrown, jungle-like garden, and barely managed to cross a stream that had tiny crocodiles waddling around in it. I was approached by cheetahs who started throwing people into the stream. Though I'd never met them, I'd dreamed that Quennel's mate and cub were tossed into the water along with Tsisana's sister. They were still alive, and I struggled to drag them out before the crocodiles could get to them. Every time I pulled one person to safety, one of the others would slide down a muddy slope to roll back into the water, and my frantic dilemma repeated until I'd woken, fraught with panic.

I'm starting to feel haunted by all these victims, Field said vacantly, as exhausted as me. *I know it's not our fault, but part of me still feels responsible. I think it's from all the loathing I see in people's eyes. I hate that.*

I know what you mean, Field, I replied and reluctantly crawled out from under the blanket to get dressed. I was too awake and distressed to be still, and I didn't want to wake my mate. Our true heritage has been a slap in the face. We'd inherited darkness.

Will they remain in our nightmares? the lioness wondered anxiously. I didn't have that answer. I wasn't sure if I could handle a lifetime of nightmares where I was trying to save victims from crocodile-infested puddles. They were bad enough to begin with, especially when Mehr appeared in them.

Javed sat up suddenly, scaring the blessed starlight right out of me. He patted around where I'd been sleeping but relaxed when he saw me by my bag. His tiger-orange hair was sticking up in funny angles, and I chuckled quietly at his half-awake state. When I felt his distress, I realized that maybe he'd had a bad night too, and I rushed over to him.

Javed wouldn't speak about his nightmares and wasn't talkative in general, so we ate breakfast in a melancholy state, then left for the pride. I held his hand, but he never opened up throughout the entire day. I wondered how long we could go on like this, struggling to support each other in a time of great suffering. I understood that he wanted to run far away from here, and I wanted to give him that, but I didn't know if I could live with the guilt that I'd placed on myself. I didn't know how to get rid of it. No matter how many times I told myself the victims weren't my fault, the shame continued to seep relentlessly under my skin. I felt like innocent lives were slipping through my claws, like I could catch them if only I tried.

Javed's pace slowed considerably toward the late afternoon, and when the sun began to set, it was clear that he didn't want to walk any farther north. The last hill we climbed to the rhythm of the tall, creaking trees exposed our destination—the pride's expansive castle. It sat a handful of miles away on a low hill devoid of trees, and a premonitory, wind-blown chill blew past us.

The walls stood at a height I couldn't have imagined, as tall as Javed and Quennel had warned, and made from faded orange bricks. Towers kept watch in every corner with overlapping scales of a lackluster blue-grey. It nearly met the height and the appeal of a looming thundercloud. And as far as the entrance went, there was only one gate I could see, and it was guarded by four individuals.

There is your pride—Edeletrots, Javed said in a tight voice. *What is your plan, Niusha?* He looked down at the ground, and I could see his face twitching as he tried not to cry. He'd fallen completely to fear and dread. He was so scared—more terrified than I'd ever seen him.

"We'll camp here tonight," I said quietly, not wanting to lie to him about my own state of turmoil. Maybe I could talk to him about the source of my distress?

Niusha, please, he begged and fell down to his knees before me. *Don't go. Don't go to them. I'm going mad.*

I tried not to fall into tears myself from his plea, hating the water brimming in his eyes. I didn't feel like I had the right to cry.

"Javed." I sighed and joined him on the ground. "My reasons have changed now, and I'm very confused. Please just give me one more night to try to get my mind straight…"

He pushed his hood back and looked over at the pride's castle. The setting sun lit his messy hair on fire, and his teal eyes violently caught the contrasting light. He looked pained, exhausted, and I was afraid to even touch him. Would he be so mad, so disappointed, and so devastated that he'd push me away like he'd done in the jungle?

I'll give you anything you want, he said sadly, then stood and helped me up so we could find a campsite. Convict ran off to bring back a fresh kill for Field so we could eat without a fire tonight. It was too risky if anyone from the castle was able to spy or scent the smoke from a distance.

Convict spoke up once Field began eating and said, *I also do not wish for you to leave. I know that I am an idiot, but I would make a good idiot mate, Field. I would provide… protect. You know I could.* Somehow, he managed to not mention penises, and I found that a rather impressive accomplishment.

I know all of those things already. That is why we marked you and Javed, Field replied calmly and firmly. *I would prefer an idiot over a male lion.* She said that last bit a little playfully but still maintained her dignified tone.

I am technically the biggest idiot you could find... as far as cats go, Convict muttered and was astonished when Field started laughing. He didn't say anything else, likely afraid of ruining her mirth.

When she calmed, she stated, *Niusha and I are suffering more than you realize, Convict, but I would not allow her to enter an impossible situation. If we go to the pride, we will return whether you believe me or not. I strongly advise you to not underestimate me. Niusha is also a lot more clever than she lets on. Niusha and I must decide our next course of action. You and Javed need to decide how much you are willing to torture yourself unnecessarily. We are coming back for what belongs to us.*

Then we are at a standstill, female, Convict replied with a lash of his tail.

I've said what I've said, she retorted, completely resolute.

When we returned to our human bodies, Javed jerked me toward him, making my naked body slap against his. The hulking male loomed over me, arched my back, and gently bit my ear.

I need you tonight, my female. I need all of you many, many times. I can't stop thinking about the other males who'll be near you if you go. I can't... I can't stop... he said gruffly, sliding his large, warm fingers down my back to grip my buttocks. *It's either this or cry all night. I'm going mad, do you understand?*

"I understand very well, Javed, my male, my mate," I replied calmly, though my pulse was wreaking havoc in my chest. As though responding to the blood rushing fiercely through my veins, I felt his cock throb between us, desperate for me through Javed's obsessive possessiveness and deep insecurity. The latter sent a pang through my heart, and I wanted to give him all of me—everything he wanted to take. I didn't want my own pleasure tonight. In so many ways, I felt like I didn't deserve it. I didn't deserve it simply for being a lioness, and I definitely didn't deserve receiving it from a male who was suffering because of me.

You will be completely mine tonight, he growled. *Though I must be quiet, I can't promise to be gentle. My tiger is roaring at me, and I can barely hear anything else.*

"Honestly… I don't want you to be gentle," I said quietly, truthfully. "Take what you need."

You're mine tonight! he repeated, growing wilder. He hadn't exaggerated when he told me his tiger was extremely active. I could hear it bolstering his messages in my mind. *Your mind, your heart, your body!*

"I'm yours forever," I argued half-heartedly, knowing he wouldn't believe me.

He yanked my blanket from the bag and threw it angrily on the ground. I quickly lay down on it and waited for him to assail me the way I wanted him to—and hoped he would. Before Field left me to our privacy, I felt her excitement at the prospect of dominance and pain, which surprised me—she'd been developing a larger sense of dominion for a while now. I hadn't expected her to relinquish control so easily.

Javed, however, did not approach me in the manner I'd expected. He fell to his stomach and spread my legs for him. I tried to squirm away, appalled by how close his face was to my sex.

"What are you doing?" I hissed in horror. "Get your face out of there!"

Are you mine tonight? he asked, looking up at me with bared teeth. I swallowed and nodded. *Then you will let me do this. Scratch me if I go feral.*

I knew I'd done it on accident before, but I wasn't sure if I could do it on purpose. Despite my uncertainty, I simply nodded again.

He growled angrily and leaned down to lick up my folds. "Oh my!" I gasped, feeling his smooth tongue travel hungrily over my sensitive skin. I propped myself up on my elbows to watch him, needing to tell my brain that this was Javed and not the male who'd hurt me at the village. Like always, Javed knew where my mind had gone and chuffed, nuzzling his nose into the blond curls between my legs.

I'm the tiger-shifter who had you first. I'm the tiger who took you first. I'm the tiger who was within you first—who gave you your first orgasm. I'm the tiger who has been finger-deep and balls-deep inside your tight, hungry pussy. I'm the tiger who was gum-deep in your neck, who invaded you with my venom the way I filled you with my seed. I'm the tiger who's tangled with your soul in ecstasy.

"Oh gods," I moaned, immensely turned on by his impassioned speech. His words blazed as fiercely as his hair in the setting sunlight.

I'm the tiger who came on you and massaged my essence into your skin to make you smell like my territory. I'm the tiger who impregnated you, who put cubs into you by fucking you so thoroughly so many times. I'm the tiger who did my duty as your fated mate—protected you, guided you, pleased you, and bred with you.

"Yes, you did," I breathed, and he brought his mouth to my clit to lick it in short strokes. "Ah!" I cried out, then reached for my dress to gag myself with some of its fabric. We couldn't risk being heard despite our distance to the castle. I knew very well how loud we could get.

His licks sent fire through my nerves, and I felt my sex weep embarrassingly close to his face. When he lowered his mouth to lap up the trail of my arousal, I was simultaneously horrified and turned on to the point of releasing more. He groaned and his delight relaxed me a little. My male was strange, but he made me feel so good. I didn't deserve this...

"I haven't earn— Ah! Ahhh! Earned p-pleasure, J-Javed!" I protested as he licked a long line up a buttock to my core, rumbling in satisfaction. I felt his enjoyment, his carnal hunger, but it baffled me. He always took his pleasure with his cock.

I believe I've earned more than a taste of you, female. I've earned a regale. Are you disliking this? he responded vehemently, lightly biting the inside of a thigh. I bucked up with my hips, not expecting the sensitive sensation that shot straight to my core. My channel clenched, and I moaned from my body's euphoric reactions.

That's what I thought.

Chapter 25

Javed

Niusha tasted superior, finer, and more entrancing than any wine you'd find in the wealthiest male's cellar. Her unique flavors were a combination of what she'd eaten and her natural scent, and I basked in the saltiness, finding it mixing so well with the sweet fig and spicy oud. I'd wanted to taste her for ages, and tonight might be my last chance to do so.

The thought of our time being finite put me in such a feral rage. It wasn't enough that she was pregnant already; I wanted to empty myself in her all night long until I fell unconscious from exhaustion. Only then would I be able to sleep.

I spread her legs farther apart, opening her folds a little to display the entrance to my own personal paradise. It continued to cry for me, and I slanted my head to bury my tongue inside it, taking her juices before they spilled wastefully. They were for my mouth and dick only. To allow any of it to touch the ground would be a shame.

I drank from her sex, swirling my tongue around to stroke her inner walls, and my female shivered violently as a result. I relished the creaminess as it hit my tongue and didn't think I could wait much longer to coat my straining, veined dick with it. I knew I was going feral, and I wasn't sure if I was willing to lose some of my clarity to it.

That was when I started massaging around her clit with my fingers. I wanted to enter her when she was at her tightest, so her orgasm could massage my dick as it welcomed me home. I rolled my thumb across her raised flesh while I dug as deep as I could with my tongue. I could barely hear her cries through the fabric she'd stuffed into her mouth, and I pretended that my member was muting her instead. Pleasure shot through me at the imagery, making my abdomen clench in excitement, and I released a deep, lustful groan into her channel.

When I felt her entire body tighten like a pulled bow, I got back up to my knees, rubbing more feverishly into the apex of her sex while I pumped my own dick, preparing both of us for my descent into her private heat. I stared at her smooth breasts and parted lips while she arched, and I tried to come to terms with the fact that I might never taste either. It hurt, and I clenched my teeth from the pain that blossomed in my chest. The fucking lions would take the only thing I cared about from me. I just wanted my mate by my side. Was that too much to ask? It made me furious.

Niusha sensed my torture, and her orgasm faltered when my distress became hers. I snarled and redoubled my efforts, knowing I might need to talk her into a climax. I explored her with both hands, moving around to chase the elusive bastard. I plunged two fingers into her channel to work her inner pleasure spot, and it made her buck like I was pulling on a marionette's string of desire.

You will come for me, female. You will tighten and release so I can plunge into your throbbing tunnel, I commanded with a deep growl. *Take your pleasure so I can find mine. Give in so I can take what I need. I need to mount you, fuck you, and seed you.*

She tossed her beautiful milk-and-coffee hair, panting and mewling with abandon. She stared hungrily at me as I glared up at her. I wasn't mad at her, but I was furious in general, and she knew it. She was taking what I doled out for the both of us.

Gods, he's too gorgeous, she moaned loudly in my head, unaware that she'd just mind-linked me for the first time on accident. *I can't handle it. I can't...* A rumbling growl escaped my chest, pleased beyond words by her accidental compliment.

She closed her eyes and tilted her head back slowly. I felt her anticipation and the buzz of her approaching climax. She gaped and furrowed her brows in concentration as she gradually arched her back. Here it was...

She shouted into the fabric, and she bucked into her climax, tightening her curved back with each pulse that rocked through her core. I notched my cock against her threshold, gripped her hips, and slammed past her threshold, immediately bottoming out to kiss her back wall. I bit my cheek to hold back a roar, and my abdomen clenched from the pain and pleasure. My sack immediately threatened to unload into her, but I wasn't ready to let go yet.

Niusha's shriek was muffled, likely not expecting me to plow forward in one thrust. I grunted and growled through my teeth, contorting my face to ride out the exquisite agony and ecstasy of burying myself during her tight contractions. I could feel everything inside of her—every ridge, every curve, and every throb.

I'm home. Tell me you missed me, I grunted through clenched teeth. *No one makes my dick as hard as you do.*

"No one else should make your dick hard at all!" she snarled angrily through the rhythm of her euphoria. "Uh... Ah... No one!" she moaned and writhed beneath me when I began to pull back out of her channel.

They might have to if you leave me, I growled to provoke her with an empty threat. I immediately regretted the cruel words that hurt her and spurred her anger. Her nostrils flared, and she pulled away from me unexpectedly, freeing herself from my cock.

"You will wait for me if I visit the pride!" she hissed and wrestled me to the ground. I sensed Field's strength behind her push, and I allowed her to have her way. She crawled over me, her blue-grey eyes flashing with rage before she growled into my ear. "You will wait because I am not weak. You will wait because I am clever. You will wait because you're not allowed to have another," she seethed and bit my neck as she raised her hips high, aligning my cock with her entrance, and sat down, driving my length into her. With several shoves, she completely buried me and started her merciless riding.

I bit the back of my hand to mute a roar, drawing blood with my canines. Her sex and ass slapped wetly against my groin as she left her arousal on my skin. I couldn't tear my eyes away from her bouncing form, enthralled by her erotic show. I fixed my gaze on her breasts and felt saliva pool in my mouth. Fuck, she was glorious!

It took hardly any time at all before my climax shattered me. I gasped for air when my sack tightened, and my dick released its seed into my female. I jerked up into her, reaching out to dig my fingers into her hips as I roared into Niusha's swiftly placed palms. I unloaded ropes of cum into her channel, and she released satisfied growl-purrs, grinding against me in gratification. Her soul warmed; she was pleased.

The lioness jumped off of me when my orgasm faded into quiet contentment, and she stalked over to lie down on the blanket. Her sharp eyes fixed on me, and I could tell she was still alert—as angry as I was. I grunted and crawled the several feet to lay by her side, then wrapped an arm around her to jerk her back against my abdomen. My lioness growled softly and pressed her lovely ass against my sated cock, inviting me again as soon as I was ready. I chuffed into her hair, continuing our courtship despite the strained emotional collision that'd been building to this peak since the day we met.

I slid my palms along her ribs and belly, then reached down to hover over her lower abdomen where her womb was nurturing our offspring. *I want to see them,* I said quietly. *I want to be there when you give birth.*

"You will be," she said heatedly. "You will be there when I birth your tiny, wrinkly tiger cub."

Cubs, I corrected. *Tsisana said cubs. And I better be there.* I grunted and raised her leg because my erection had finally returned. Remaining where we were lying on the ground, I gripped her hips and notched myself in place, then thrust into her with a thrilled groan. Pleasure wrapped deliciously around my cock and spread throughout my tense body. She hissed and mewled, then tilted her hips back to make the angle easier for my immediate thrusting. I plunged in and out of her sex from behind, displacing the mixture that was her arousal and my seed.

We moaned in chorus as I rocked my hips, dragging my entire engorged length in and out of her gripping, sopping channel. I moved my lips down to her shoulder and kissed it while we mated, making her shudder from head to toe. Arousal curled in my sweating, working abdomen, making agonizingly perfect pleasure shoot down to my sex. Every response I pulled from my fated mate felt as good as each thrust into her heat.

So hard, so full, so good. She sighed, still unaware that I could hear her.

Only for you, I growled, but she didn't seem to catch on that I was replying. I bit down onto her shoulder, more out of possessiveness than a need to keep her still. My canines itched to mark her again, knowing that it'd both satisfy me and bring her a great deal of pleasure.

I started bucking wildly to find my release, eager to surprise an orgasm out of my mate. When I felt myself tighten, I abruptly positioned my lioness to receive both my venom and my seed. I climaxed and muffled my roar with her shoulder, then bit down into her hypersensitive mating mark. She started and shrieked into the blanket as she was thrown into euphoria. Her hips danced with mine as she joined my orgasm, spasming against me as pleasure wrapped us both in ecstasy.

I pumped excitedly against her as I came to prolong our pleasures, groaning in response to every moan she made. We panted as though we shared one breath, and I clutched her fiercely, unloading the last of my seed into her waiting body. I finally removed my teeth from her salty skin, lapping sensually to clean the punctures I'd made. A shudder of satisfaction trickled up my spine and curled into my heart at the sight of our mixture. Every piece of evidence that remained from our joining was an aphrodisiac in and of itself. The mark on her was a reminder that our souls were joined even tighter than we were at the hip.

"I d-didn't deserve that," she breathed out after her trembling subsided.

You deserve everything, I murmured into her neck, kissing it softly to make her whimper in delight. I didn't remove my cock from her heat, choosing to let it either slip out on its own or return to its erect state within her. *You are all that you say you are—strong and clever. Most of all, your heart is full of selfless love. Even though it results in my torture, I wouldn't change it.* I frowned when I felt her guilt flare up, and I cursed myself for wording it the way I did. For the thousandth time, I wished things were not the way they were. The lions have taken everything and have come between my Niusha and me. We were both emotional wrecks tonight, and I blamed them with all the loathing I had within me.

I didn't know how to protect my heart and enjoy what could be my last night with Niusha. The warring between fury and despair had me strung tighter than ever. The only release I had from my constant state of anxiety was losing myself in Niusha.

I slid my fingers down over her hip and reached for the curls between her legs, gently stroking her. She was probably too sore or sensitive after several rides and orgasms, but I still wanted to touch her. I found some of my seed trickling down her inner thigh and rubbed it obsessively into her upper chest, careful to avoid her breasts. I leaned into her neck, closed my eyes, and took deep breaths to memorize every nuance of our combined scent. I wanted to remember this moment, this night, until the day I returned to the Sky Gods.

Niusha became aroused again for some unknown reason and reached back to tug on my hip. I growled into her neck because I didn't think my member was recovered enough to respond, but her urging and her sensually stroking fingers—enhanced by the pleasures of the mate touch—made my cock twitch to life inside her. I released a rumbling groan and grinded my hips against her soft ass, eager to answer her needy call.

I lost track of the number of times I joined with Niusha. I mounted her from behind, I lay between her legs, I let her ride my lap once more and repeated everything else we'd ever done. The night was a blur of gentle sex, wild fucking, and long moments of drowsy embraces. It was a mix of anger, sadness, and feral madness directed at our situation rather than each other.

It felt too much like our last night. Each intimate act brought more desperation between us, and we fought to stay quiet, but we were both drawn to rage at the stars that blinked at us from the darkness—the stars… the skies… the watchers in the night that were our silent gods. I wanted to blame the Sky Gods for putting us through all this—for not helping contain Their destructive children. Were They proud of the lions? Perhaps They valued shows of strength above all else.

It wasn't until Niusha and I collapsed against each other, panting and laying on our sweaty and seed-dampened blanket, that we eventually fell asleep. The last thing I saw before my eyes gave up was the predawn light basking my mate in a hazy indigo glow. I gratefully let oblivion whisk me away; it swaddled me in a beautiful, false sense of safety for a time of precious reprieve.

Waking in the late afternoon had brought a calm sense of clarity. Somehow, last night let me obtain the gleam of an ugly truth. Javed's utter terror of losing me had made me realize that he might never stop feeling that way. No matter where we went, he might always fear me changing my mind, especially because he knew how torn I was.

I crawled carefully out of his large, rock-hard arms and stared down at him for a couple minutes. Even in his sleep, he looked worried. I hated it. I hated seeing him cry. I wanted to make him happy. I wanted him to be truly relaxed so he could enjoy the rest of his life by my side. As it was now, the lions would always be hanging over our heads, and I would always suffer the prickling fear of wondering who their next victim would be. Would Gerlind die before she had a chance to be free? Was she still in the village or was she on that slaver boat now, crossing the river where the crocodiles had nearly absconded with my foot?

The world was so much bigger and so much more dangerous than I'd realized. I hadn't expected it to take as many days as it had to get to the pride. The territories were massive, and I came to the conclusion that those blood farms could be anywhere.

I got to my feet and tiptoed to the bag to grab my soap and a dress. We'd camped near a small stream, and I needed to get all of Javed's scent off of me. My mind was encumbered with ideas as I washed. Scenario after scenario played out in my mind as I thought of the most extreme events possible. I filed each instance away into my mind with at least three different solutions, and the ideas continued to flood my thoughts. I was certain I'd washed my entire body three times over before I realized how long I'd been sitting there, absorbed in my planning.

I needed to get answers, and there was no other way to do it. I had to enter the pride. I had to live the lie again, but not just for my survival this time. If they were accidentally killing people by drawing too much blood at a time, who was to say that Quennel's mate or daughter wasn't next? Who's to say that Tsisana's sister wasn't already dead? I was confident I could keep my cubs alive, but I also believed that there were too many lives at risk to play it safe when I was the only one who could help. Three lives was not greater than hundreds or thousands. I couldn't rely on the dragons fumbling for permission to search the territories. There just wasn't enough time. I had to get in, and I had to get out as soon as possible.

You've made your decision, haven't you? Javed's voice flowed smoothly into my head. *Your mood seems... different.*

I blinked repeatedly as I was parted from my ruminations. Javed was walking toward me, naked and appearing very much like a wild god. His teal gaze was now hooded only by his untamed tiger-orange hair, and it locked onto me with dark, heavy-hearted acceptance.

I wordlessly handed him the soap, and he stared blankly at it. *You've completely removed my scent. You're going to them, aren't you?*

"I am going. I am also returning in less than two weeks with the location of the blood farms and Quennel's family," I stated calmly. I knew he wouldn't believe me, so I had to accept his grief and rage. I had to let him vent what he thought was the end. "All I ask is that you do not take another female during that time."

I'd rather abstain for the rest of my life, he replied quietly and placed the soap on a rock.

"That won't be the case," I said crisply. "Field and I will return, and we will hand the information over to the dragons or whoever is the most appropriate."

Whatever you say, he muttered numbly and bent over to rest his elbows on his knees. I dried myself with the old, torn dress and put on a newer one.

"I have three separate, solid plans for keeping the cubs safe," I informed. "I will deliver them when they're due months from now, and you will be there. They will not be taken from us."

He didn't reply, and I hadn't really expected a response. I was saying what I needed to say. What I would not say was my final goal before leaving the pride. It would stress him out unnecessarily. I believed there was a chance I could fail at everything. Field and I have made many perilous mistakes since we decided to leave the village, but we'd take what we learned and utilize it like any other tool.

Quennel had told me that I could live a life worth living, but it wasn't in running away from the lions like he'd said—it was in going to them, deceiving them. Field believed we could, and her confidence bolstered mine.

I fixed Javed with my most unshakable expression while I stood, fully dressed and ready to leave. I did all I could to minimize my terror, so I thought about everything good I'd ever accomplished to keep me composed. I wore my memories like a protective layer, needing to fool Javed as much as myself into thinking I was steeled and unflappable.

I grabbed my bag but decided I wouldn't be bringing it. It scented too much like my mate.

I'll hide your things, he said flatly, eyeing me as my gaze roved over the campsite. He threw on a pair of pants but nothing else.

"Thank you..." I stared at him as I took the first step toward the castle. His brows drew in a fraction, and he took the next step with me. The walk to the pride was done in agonizing silence, and it seemed like it took forever for us to arrive. I wanted to get this over with so I could return to him and make him smile again... laugh again. When I was done with the lions, I'd give him everything I had to give. I'd work for the rest of my life to make up for the stress that was put upon us both, especially him. He'd suffered through so much, but I knew this pain would be worth enduring a million times over in the long run.

We stood facing each other at the tree line, and I worked to memorize his face. It would be all I had until I made my escape. He was beautiful, so beautiful... far too beautiful for the likes of me. Tears beaded on my eyelashes and dripped onto my cheeks. I let them fall. It'd make my story that much more believable when I went to announce myself. They were born from true pain. When I saw Javed's mouth twitch, I knew he was holding himself back, despite the numbness I felt over the bond.

"I will mind-link you in three nights to check in," I said with a raised chin, which probably looked stupid considering how much I was crying. "I'll get close to the eastern side of the castle, so you can probably hear me from those trees." I pointed to where I believed was an appropriate spot, and he merely nodded to acknowledge I'd been heard. "I've never mind-linked you before. I don't think s—"

You did last night, he replied, interrupting me. *Multiple times. You didn't realize it.*

"Oh…" I replied, at a loss for words. What had I said? Gods, I hoped it hadn't been something embarrassing… I mind-linked him now to test it. *Can you hear this?* I aimed it at him, but it felt a little wobbly.

Push it through the bond instead of directly at me. That will come across more clearly over a longer distance, he answered impassively.

Like this? I asked, letting it slide along the tether that fed me his emotions and linked me to his shining, superior soul.

Like that... Yes.

"Ok. That seems to work. I will link you at midnight—not tonight, not tomorrow night, but the night after that. I will call out until you answer."

He said nothing, and I wiped the tears from my eyes. He was pushing me away like I'd expected. I had a lot to make up for when my tasks were complete. I'd work for his forgiveness.

We knew they'd shut down. We warned them, Field said, nursing her own hurting heart. *We must cope, and it's up to us to return to them... should they find us worth forgiving.*

I gazed up at Javed's face, and my eyes lingered on lips that I'd never gotten a chance to kiss. I hadn't been ready. I hadn't been ready for a lot of things. I would be… soon. I wished we had more to say to each other before I left, but he had completely locked me out of him. I was standing at the doorstep to his heart, but all was silent.

"A-all right, then," I stuttered, trying to accept our insubstantial farewell. "I will speak to you soon, and I plan to be out in less than several weeks—one week, preferably." I gave him a weak smile, losing a degree of confidence from how cold he was now, and rubbed at the ache in my chest. I scuffed the dirt with a shoe and said, "See you soon, Javed."

Goodbye, Niusha, he replied blankly, not moving a single muscle as he stared at me.

Bye, Convict said darkly and offered nothing more.

Field remained quiet, annoyed at their reaction. She found it childish, but I found it understandable. I deserved the chilly dismissal.

I looked down, kicked another small pebble, and met Javed's eyes one last time. "I will see you soon," I repeated, then turned and walked down the hill toward the castle guards, sobbing. I didn't need to act this time. The tears were very much real.

I stared at the gate where my fated mate had disappeared. I could have watched it for hours, hoping to see her run out in a daring escape once she'd realized her mistake, but I didn't linger because I had things to do. I hid our bags and let Convict run to the nearest town with only a pair of pants gripped in his maw.

When Convict and I arrived in Gantsara, I strode into town without my cloak, no longer caring who saw me. I ignored all the gasps and murmurs that doggedly followed my every footstep. I would have found their whispers haunting before, but nothing scared me anymore—the worst had already come to pass. Let them think what they wanted. If they found me a barbarian, so be it. If they thought me a savior, so be it. I only had one thought in my mind, and it was the only thing that gave me the energy to put one foot in front of the other.

I had a medium-sized following of shifters by the time I reached Aaron's home. I hoped he was still alive so I wouldn't have to look for another reliable assistant. I rapped my knuckles on his front door, noting that his scent still lingered here.

The door opened, revealing the shocked, disbelieving face of a snow leopard-shifter. His frosty-blond hair was cut short now, but his crystal-blue eyes were as wary as I remembered. He rubbed feverishly at them, like he thought I was a phantom he could simply wipe from his vision.

"Javed?" he hissed under his breath and looked behind me at the gathering crowd. "By all the stars, what are you… How did…"

I brushed past him and looked for something to write on, feeling a dull pang and wishing Niusha was here to help me communicate. He followed me, pestering me with questions I couldn't physically answer, until I found his desk and took a pen to some paper.

I wrote, *Pull whatever strings you can and get your fastest cheetahs to gather The Proudless. We're not going to fail this time.* I slammed the note down in front of him where he quickly read it, bowed humbly, and ran out of his home to do what he did best—no questions asked.

Chapter 26

Niusha

By the time I approached the castle guards, I was covered in tears and snot. My eyes ached from swelling, and I knew it wouldn't be long before my voice was little more than a croak. Leaving Javed's side when he'd turned stone cold was the hardest thing I'd ever done in my entire life. Leaving without his touch was brutal, and I'd desperately wanted to embrace him, but I couldn't risk getting his tiger scent on me. I'd washed between my legs as much as I could, but there was still a risk of some seed seeping out from last night, and I prayed that it wouldn't be scented. In hindsight, I wished I had sprayed some scent remover there.

I had no idea what cats the guards were, and though I hadn't encountered the scent before now, I had to imagine they were cheetahs. They all looked genuinely shocked at my appearance and quickly ushered me in without a word while I begged for sanctuary. It was my intention to keep my face tear-soaked and covered in mucus. The last thing I wanted to do was attract any sexual interest, so I aimed for appearing slightly revolting—someone they'd pass along fairly quickly.

I was taken immediately to a colossal room that shocked me with its opulence. I'd never seen so many colorful ornaments and shiny metals. The carpet that ran down the middle was woven with beautiful, ornate patterns and dyed with vibrant shades of orange and blue.

The feet that formed a line down the rug all belonged to males of the same species. *I think these are lions,* Field remarked as I took in a deep breath, trying to sort through the smells. *They seem more familiar than the ones escorting us. I'm reminded of Quennel.*

Thank you for verifying, Field. Help me maintain my act. Think about Mehr; I need my discomfort provoked, I requested, hating the fact that I had to pull on real traumas to get through this introduction. I had to live the lie again. It was something I'd practiced for almost half of my life, and I considered myself an expert.

Done, she agreed flatly, on the same strategic page as me.

As she pulled up imagery, nausea rose in my belly, and I wrapped my arms around my breasts. A grimace plastered itself onto my face, and I embraced it. *I'm running to sanctuary. I'm in shock from my journey. I was abused but escaped. I need my lion family. I'd do anything to stay. My loyalty is completely out of relief and gratitude,* I chanted on repeat. I knew I could rely on Field to keep me from brainwashing myself, but I had to fall into the disgusting lie. This would be the true test of my capabilities. All this was for my survival, for my cubs' survival, and for those at risk—families, sisters, slaves, and previous fellow villagers.

I was a complete mess by the time I was pulled before the person I assumed was the king. The male was probably in his thirties and was garbed in a black jacket with gold embroidery. More tassels than necessary donned his shoulders, and a blood-red sash fell over his large chest, a morbid waterfall. He wore his brown hair long, where it tumbled down to his shoulder in loose waves. As expected, he seemed brutally strong but wasn't as large or as muscular as my Javed, and that gave me a small, childish spike of gleeful pride. My mate was definitely stronger than him. Field repeated that thought in a sing-song voice that was out of character, and I loved it.

The guards quickly spoke up while the king eyed my appearance, subtly wrinkling his nose. "Sire, this lioness approached us from outside Edeletrots's walls. As this is unprecedente—"

"Throw her in the Jong Harem," the king interrupted scornfully, gesturing me away from him. I opened my mouth to thank him in tearful shock, but the guards herded me out as swiftly as possible and escorted me down a number of corridors to the aforementioned harem. This meant there was more than one place where the lionesses were being kept.

In an attempt to memorize the way back to the room where the king had been, Field focused on making a song out of the route. *The right way to right the problem is what's left of our plan. We left behind the rightest of the males we left,* Field repeated in deep focus. We'd have to reverse it on our way back, though—a necessary headache.

I sniffed and wiped my mucus on my arm, continuing with my disgusting display. I almost laughed at how gross I was being. At least it'd been effective so far.

We finally reached a huge entrance with two doors instead of one, split in the middle so each could open individually. My escort brought me to a rather unassuming guard who was posted just inside what I had to assume was the harem. Past him, my attention utterly snapped to the room's numerous inhabitants. Great gods, there were so many females in here! I didn't have time to get good look because I was immediately introduced to the male by the door.

"New lioness we found outside the gate. Weirdly unprecedented, but His Majesty wished her placed here," one of my escorts said in a more casual tone.

The somewhat short, skinny male in chainmail that seemed a little too big for him tilted his head and looked at me with confusion. “Huh. Alright? I guess… I’ll register her like we do with the newborns?” He walked to a large ornate desk, one beautifully carved, and pulled out some paperwork. He gave them a dubious look, then waved away my escorts and gestured for me to approach.

“Th-thank you for taking me in,” I said, thinking of Javed. My nose stung, tears welled in my eyes, and I cleared my throat, making a subtle but noticeable attempt to pull myself together. I had a fine line to walk here. I had to be believable.

“You seem to have a great many stories to tell,” he replied flatly, but there was the tiniest hint of compassion in his eyes when he shuffled through the documentation. “We’ll register you like this for now, but if you were born within the pride, we’ll have to figure out your sire. We can’t have you breeding with relatives.”

Gross, Field muttered, and I suppressed a disgusted shudder.

“I… am grateful,” I mumbled, looking down at my hands. “I just don’t want to go back out there…”

The guard cleared his throat. “Name?”

“Niusha. I don’t know my last name,” I supplied and dried my eyes with a thumb. “All I remember was being raised in a village.”

“I don’t suppose you know your own age?” he asked, raising pale blond brows.

“I think I’m twenty-three?” I estimated based on what the village records had said.

“That helps,” the guard said, rubbing his chin thoughtfully. “We’ll cross-reference with our birth records.” His lips pressed in a flat line, and he avoided looking at me for the next question. “Are you untouched? I assume not. Show me your neck.”

I held my hair up and cast my gaze down in shame. “I don’t know what you mean but…” I thought of Javed again and let tears drop to the floor. “Someone bit me and…” I forced my distress back, letting my face twitch uncontrollably into a grimace.

"Do you have their description?" he asked, revulsion distorting his features as he retrieved a new piece of paper.

I stayed quiet for a while, slightly adjusting a male from my wretched memories. I let myself drift off and muted my emotions. "I was captured by three… but they gave me something. I can't remember what it was called. Acpoa? Acama?"

"Acpoama?" he supplied but didn't wait for me to nod to make a note.

"Y-yes? I don't remember who bit me… I was… it was like the world had become a nightmare. I'd r-rather not talk about wh-what they d-d-did. One was a dark brown, one was a medium brown but had a yellower hue to his skin? The last one was pink… freckled. Dash! I remember his name now." I hugged myself, feeling my face turn a bit green at the thought of them ripping my dress for their pleasure.

"Stars above," the male muttered, writing all this down.

"Is there a d-doctor?" I whispered under my breath. My first step at protecting my cubs terrified me, and I let it show. I prayed that one of my three strategies would work. I just needed to buy time. I was an expert at buying time, but the risks had never been fatal.

"I'll escort you there myself," he replied, softening despite his attempt to remain strict and emotionless.

"Thank you…" I mumbled.

"Well, that's all I can really fill out here. When you're more settled, I have more questions, but I think you could do with a rest so you can answer them more thoroughly," he said, tapping the pages before him in thought. I could tell he was doing it out of kindness, but he didn't want it to show.

Odd how restricted their behavior is. It's like he's suppressing his personality, Field observed with interest. *Intriguing.*

"Shall I show you to your bed or do you want to see the doctor?" he inquired, putting his hands behind his back.

"All I can think about… d-doctor, please," I murmured under my breath as quietly as possible, sending furtive glances to the nearby lionesses, who were trying to be subtle about their staring. "P-please."

The male nodded, tucked the papers into a folder, and opened the colossal door for me. Field created a new song for our trip to the doctor, and I loved her for it. When we arrived at an office, the guard handed my folder to a female behind a clean desk made of heavy stone.

"Please make a duplicate for the doctor," he ordered, and the female accepted it, immediately pulling out materials to do just that. The guard turned to me and nodded. "I will wait here."

I murmured a thank-you and seated myself, waiting to be seen. A female walked out of an adjacent room, limping with a pained expression. She held her head high, though, and didn't meet anyone's eyes. I wondered if she was feeling pride or shame. I couldn't tell for the life of me.

The guard opened the door for her, and she curtly said, "Thank you, Jameson." I barely caught her shoulders sagging right before the guard closed the door—definitely shame.

A male, perhaps in his late forties, walked out of the room, grabbed my file from the female at the desk, and gestured for me to enter. I swallowed hard and followed him in, realizing that my hands were suddenly sweating a great deal.

"Very strange," the doctor said, tightening the gold ribbon that held back his brown-blond hair. "Strange indeed. Unprecedented. Never seen this before." He gestured for me to sit on an examination table and read through my very short file. He tossed it onto an old wooden desk with a stone surface and said, "Clothes off, please."

I blanched, not really wanting to do that, but slipped out of my garments and wrapped my arms around my breasts. I was taken back to that night when the three males abducted me and didn't fight the discomfort. I had to use my trauma to be believable. It manifested as sickening electricity, cold, jittery, snapping, making me shake uncontrollably. My stomach threatened to empty itself, roiling and churning.

"You've survived an unwilling marking and mating?" he surmised as he started examining me, looking in my eyes, ears, and spots below my jaw and armpits. I managed to squeak out a 'yes' but didn't volunteer any additional information. "That is unfortunate," he muttered and left the room to call out for someone named 'Keid.'

"Yes, doctor?" a female's voice was heard responding to him.

"Please do a full pelvic examination. Provide an abortive if there is a non-lion offspring. I doubt she'll fight you on that considering her medical history and the fact she came straight to us," the doctor ordered. I took in a deep breath. It was one thing to expect the words but another thing to hear them spoken aloud. This was my first trial, and I prayed to the gods above and below that one of my plans would work.

An extraordinarily beautiful woman walked into the examination room with the demeanor of an abused stray. Her appearance was unlike any I'd ever seen before, and I tried not to stare out of politeness, but I could hardly tear away my eyes. Her skin was a frosty pale pink, but every hair on her body was whiter than the parchment in my folder, including her eyelashes and eyebrows. I couldn't tell if her irises were a light shade of purple or blue because the hue seemed to depend on the lighting, but I supposed I'd call them periwinkle. I held back a frown when my eyes fell to her wrists. Though she was clean, there were impressions that suggested she was regularly shackled. I didn't like that… I suspected it was due to her being human, as Field had guessed by her smell. Perhaps this was a witch.

I stared at the woman, who instructed me to lay down on my back. I flushed with embarrassment when she washed her hands then spread my legs to examine me. "You have irritations from last night," she stated and wrote down her observations. My face ruddied deeper, and I allowed it to stay that way. Little did she know that whatever swelling or bruising was down there had not been from an unwanted activity. I thought of my mate sobbing and allowed myself to cry a little. Living the lie here was going to be brutal. There was a lot I did not need to fabricate.

"I cannot tell what your offspring is, so you are ordered to take this abortive," Keid stated, pouring a clear liquid into a glass, then recorded something new in my file. "I will leave you to your privacy if you wish a moment to grieve," she offered dispassionately, then looked left to regard a small rubber tree in a clay pot. "That needs to be watered. I am forgetful." She glanced back at me one final time. With eyes that verged on being lifeless, she added one last thing. "Please do not misbehave under my care. Two more infractions, and I will lose my left hand. It was a pleasure to meet you."

Keid left the room, closing the door behind her. I was completely dumbfounded by her mixed messages, but I couldn't waste a moment with the time she'd given me. I chose not to dig beneath the dirt to hide my 'watering' of the plant, which had been one of my adjusted original plans.

I filled my mouth with the abortive and tugged the rope over the sink to let water pour out in a steady flow. I soaped my hands up, then carefully let the large mouthful of liquid pour into my hands. I mixed it with the soap, needing to make sure the doctor wouldn't scent any of the chemical from the drain. It was unlikely, but I needed to be overcautious. I quietly spat as much saliva as I could into my hands to get more of the chemical out, then slumped, grateful I'd gotten past this first hurdle. Considering how much she'd poured out for me, the small amount in my mouth would likely be harmless. I didn't want to rinse it out in case they scented my mouth before I left. I began to sob in bone-deep relief and grew slightly weak in the knees. The hardest part of my plan seemed to be going ok for now.

Before I could open the door, I heard Keid tell the doctor that I'd taken the medication, and she let me have a moment because I was in a high emotional state. I had so many strategies ready for multiple scenarios, but I hadn't expected anyone like this witch. I didn't know what to make of her.

I left the examination room with swollen eyes and nodded to Jameson. "I'm tired," I croaked out, and he opened the door for me.

"Let's get you to your bed then," he said, a hint of sympathy returning to his face. I sighed and trudged along behind him.

Great fucking job, Field complimented, both tired and proud of me.

When we arrived back at the Jong Harem, I was finally able to get a good look at the room and noted that it was at least four times larger than the huge chamber where the king had been. A number of doors led off into other hallways, but this main room was lined with dozens of wide beds. Each bed was covered with a comforter of a fine red material that shimmered with the slightest change in angle, and heavy curtains looked like they could be pulled completely around the bed for privacy. The center of the room had tables that the lionesses were using for one purpose or another. Some were reading, some were painting their faces, and others were bent over clothing with a needle and thread.

There was also what looked like a hot bathtub built into the stone floor, and several females were being washed by others, as though they were being pampered before some kind of event—perhaps a ceremony? I needed to learn more so I could better lie.

Jameson escorted me around the large bath, keeping his eyes firmly averted from the naked lionesses. Javed told me that nudity was considered natural, so why did Jameson act so nervously? He must see this all day from where he worked, and he had to be used to it. I watched a muscle in his jaw tic, but he drew my attention away from his face when he pointed toward a bed in the back right corner of the room.

Drat, I said to Field as I approached my assigned bed, which seemed to be made already with fresh sheets. *I was hoping for a bed closer to the exit. More bodies to have to sneak past...*

We'll work with it, she replied, sounding unbothered, just sleepy.

"Here is where you'll rest during the night," Jameson said, standing in what seemed to be his usual stance, with his hands tucked behind his back. "The doctor ordered two days of rest before you're to be added to the breeding and work schedule. Before that happens, though, I will verify your parentage to avoid inbreeding. I'll get back to you when that information is properly documented." He sighed and tapped a finger against his chin, like he was making sure he hadn't forgotten anything. "We'll continue our interview tomorrow, but you can rely on any lioness to help answer your questions. More will arrive after their work shifts," he said, gesturing to the excessive number of females that were already here.

I stared numbly at the scenery, not bothering to hide how overwhelmed I was. I nodded vacantly to Jameson and sat down on the edge of my bed rather suddenly, a touch weak in the knees. Jameson turned to move, but hesitated and lowered his voice. "With the rise of our new king, His Majesty King Leudbal, there was a culling recently, so… keep in mind that the lionesses will be in mourning for some time. Best not to mention cubs around them."

That was horribly depressing.

I simply watched as he bowed and walked back toward his desk, probably starting his investigation into my parentage. I moved my waning attention to the lionesses, letting it sink it that I was finally among other females of my kind. I didn't feel a blessed thing. They all seemed so foreign to me. Perhaps it was because I'd only recently found out I was a lioness. Leaving a conservative village to end up in a giant room full of naked females who were half beast was a surreal change in lifestyle.

There was also not a great deal of variety among these females. Some were a fair peach, but the darkest tone among these lionesses wasn't much darker than my own skin color, and hair color only ranged from medium brown to light blonde. I held back a frown as my brain tiredly considered the implications. Only the gods knew how many cubs were already killed for their next generation of adults, and I wondered if there was a slow decline in their overall population because of that. Perhaps inbreeding was eventually going to become a concern.

Well, that won't do at all, Field murmured sluggishly. *They're killing themselves with their needlessly brutal, outdated traditions.*

That they are... I agreed. My anxiety grew as more lionesses noticed my arrival and my aimless staring, so I crawled under my comforter and allowed myself to enjoy the luxurious bed while I was here. Seconds before I was about to fall asleep, a woman climbed onto her bed, which was next to mine, and faced me.

I bit back an exhausted groan as she stared at me in curiosity. Her skin was a slightly darker beige than mine, and her dusky blue eyes held only a small degree of life under her thick, cedar-brown hair. She seemed relatively healthy, but it was clear that she was fighting the same gloomy cloud that hovered over the other lionesses.

"My name is Oudine," she greeted in a warm, rich voice. "I heard you came from beyond the walls." She rested her head on her arm as she studied me. "You're going to be sleeping by my bed, so I thought I'd introduce myself. You must be overwhelmed. I can't even imagine."

"My name is Niusha," I mumbled, yawning despite all my attempts to suppress it. "At least, I think it is. Several of the orphans from my village were renamed."

"Interesting." She was pretty, like all the other lionesses, but I had a hard time placing her age. Based on the tiny smile and worry lines, I guessed she might be around forty, but she seemed to still be in her prime, aging rather gracefully. "Where did you grow up?" she asked. Part of me suspected that our conversation was acting as a distraction for her. I wondered if she'd lost a cub to the culling, and I decided to humor her despite my extreme fatigue.

I told her about my village and how I eventually escaped north, making sure I only shared what I needed to in order to keep all my lies intact. Oudine absorbed every single detail with the rapt attention of a cub at story time, and she was constantly interrupting to ask questions. When she inquired about the puncture marks on my neck, I stared at her in bewilderment.

"That's a marking. Males and females mark each other when they decide to become mates..." I explained slowly. I couldn't believe I was explaining this. "They bite each other and inject a special venom. It joins their souls. You've never... heard of this?"

She shook her head. "What's a mate?"

Oh my what? Field asked, certain our ears were broken.

"A mate is a male you choose to stay with forever..." I said, confusion waking me. I must be more tired than I thought. Was she really that uneducated about that? This was a massive colony of shifters, surely there were fated mates among them. I knew my village rejected all knowledge of shifters, but it didn't make sense for that information to be unavailable here. "Or," I added, "you are paired with a special bond determined by the Moon Goddess."

She frowned. "So you are dedicated to one male? You will not like how we do things here. You'll be assigned a breeding partner until you become pregnant, and by assigned, I mean the males get to pick who they want to put cubs in."

"Yes, I'd heard you weren't given a choice." I rubbed a bleary, swollen eye. A headache was blooming from all the crying and stress.

"It is all we know. It is sometimes enjoyable if the partner is pleasing." She made a face and mumbled, "Sometimes they are not so pleasing, but we must do our duty to the pride..." Oudine sent me a sympathetic look. "The king always takes the new ones. I hope for your sake that he is gentle, but our doctors are good."

I had several plans for avoiding just that, but nothing was foolproof. I made sure to not let my disgust show on my face, which was easy because I was too tired to express much of anything. So far, this place was turning out mostly how I'd envisioned it. What a sad truth that was.

Chapter 27

Niusha

My recurring nightmare returned, but with some unsurprising changes. Instead of Mehr chasing me after I escaped the village, it was King Leudbal, who was completely naked. I screamed for Javed, but he was mad and wouldn't come help me. I rolled in mud, put sticks in my hair, and did everything I could to become uglier, but the king kept chasing until I woke.

That was hilarious, Field mumbled before I could open my eyes.

Now that I'm awake, I can see the humor, I replied.

Your brain gave him the tiniest penis. It was flopping about like a baby eel.

Well, let's stop thinking about weird king penises, ok? I snorted, then opened my eyes to see if I accidentally slept through the night.

I started when I saw three females watching me by Oudine's bed. My waking had startled them, and they fumbled to run away from me. The one in the middle smacked into the one on the right. I wasn't sure where she thought she was going; she'd been headed straight for the wall.

Oudine chuckled as they fled and regarded me from her bed. "They were asking questions. Everyone is too concerned about upsetting you since you arrived in such a traumatized state."

"That's… rather sweet," I murmured, eyeing the awkward one as she pretended to read a book at one of the middle tables. The literature she was holding, however, seemed to be upside down.

"Juliote's brain is often at odds with her body," Oudine whispered with a grin. "But she's smart."

My eyes flickered to one of the doorways opening to a balcony. A dim orange glow illuminated the stone outside, and I was momentarily disoriented, not sure if it was sunrise or sunset. I didn't hear any birds, so I guessed it was the evening.

"Have I missed dinner?" I inquired and noticed there were a lot more lionesses in the colossal harem chamber now. Most of them had gathered in small groups, gossiping while taking surreptitious peeks at me.

"No, I was about to wake you. We'll leave soon," Oudine answered, then stood and held a hand out for me. I frowned at it in confusion but took it and crawled out of bed. "You must be groomed before leaving. You cannot wear what you arrived in, Niusha."

I sighed internally, trying to think about how I wanted to proceed. If I tried not to go, citing that I was still too traumatized, they'd likely push me to get out of my depression. Oudine seemed understanding, but she also seemed to have become invested in my adaptation into the pride. I wasn't certain that I wanted to risk butting heads with her quite yet.

I could feign illness, but I needed to save those instances for larger problems—emergencies. I couldn't be sick all the time unless I came down with something chronic. With a doctor here, I wouldn't be able to keep that lie going.

If I went to dinner, there could be males there, and I needed to remain unappealing for as long as possible. I had to minimize the amount of pestering while I searched for answers, and I still needed to familiarize myself with the castle. I had no idea where anything else was yet.

Going to dinner will show us more of the castle, Field said, *if we don't want to wait for a guide or if the guide won't go in that direction. I have no idea. So many possibilities. We should go, but keep the crying act going. Swollen eyes can't be that pretty. Maybe add a dash of panic attack here and there, but don't draw attention.*

That will be an elaborate dance. Alright.

"How is your lioness handling the change?" Oudine asked as she guided me to the bathing pool.

I pulled up thoughts of Javed and let tears come naturally. I missed him so much. "She's scared," I whispered as quietly as possible. "We're afraid. We've been running for so long."

"You are safe here," Oudine cooed and handed me off to three lionesses who began undressing me and guided me into the hot bath. A euphoric sigh escaped my lips. Not only was the water the perfect temperature, there was some herb in it that released a soothing aroma. My calm was short-lived when the three females began washing me, including a fourth who was already bathing in the water.

Nope, nope, nope, nope, Field hissed.

I've helped little girls bathe, but hardly anyone but Javed has seen me naked, not to mention touched me while naked! I exclaimed, pressing my lips together and suppressing a freaked-out scream.

They must have noticed my tension because their demeanor changed, going from silent deference to gentle cooing and comforting murmurs. When a sponge found its way to my breasts or between my legs, I nearly kicked the person guiding it out of pure reflex. All I could do was try to calm my thrumming heart and accept that shifters were just freer with their bodies. This was normal for them.

But, by all the gods, it's embarrassing. Not to mention it makes me feel like we're a toddler, Field remarked uncomfortably.

I was relieved when I was finally rinsed off and released… right into the care of another group of lionesses who helped apply some kind of cream to my skin. It smelled good but…

Stop touching us! Field hollered.

Gotta get used to it, I grumbled to her. *It's… it's probably what it's like to have sisters and a mother. The community we grew up in was… the weird one, at least for shifters.*

I'd rather be licked by Convict while he talks about barbed penises, she muttered truculently, and I almost burst into laughter. That was saying a lot.

When the lionesses pulled some heavy fabric over my head, I nearly panicked. What now? After they did some adjusting, my head popped out of an opening, and I found myself wearing a tent.

"That's a good color," Oudine said, watching me while leaning against the wall. She was also wearing a tent… well… kind of. Like what I'd been stuffed into, the neckline went straight across the chest, exposing her shoulders and collarbone. The sleeves were short but puffy and ended in a bloom of lace, like her arms were being eaten by a pair of flowers. The waist had been cinched tight, and the fuzzy dark blue skirts flared out, making it appear as if she had an extraordinarily large bottom and a generous pair of hips. She looked simultaneously pretty, elegant, and utterly ridiculous. I had to assume I appeared the same.

How does one sit with two bottoms? Field asked as the lionesses tightened the waist on my dress.

Very… ugh! Carefully.

"That's a little tight," I wheezed, looking back at the lioness who was determined to cut off my air.

"It helps to stand up straight and definitely don't exert yourself," Oudine said, replying for the other lioness.

Maybe panic attacks are out of the question, Field cautioned.

We'll loosen it when they're not looking… or I'll try to.

This will make sneaking around impossible.

She was right about that. I looked down at the heavy material, dyed a dark red. I glanced up at Oudine as I was led to a table covered in... things—lots and lots of things. "Do you do this every night?" I croaked, genuinely about to cry because this was a new kind of torture.

"Only if we're not working the evening shift," she replied.

"Shift?" I inquired, not sure which meaning of the word she meant.

"We do labor at the castle. Some of us perform chores in the morning and stop in the evening. Others perform their chores at night and stop in the morning."

"Oh..." I replied and reached up to rub my eyes, allowing the tears to start flowing again. I might as well get an early start on the swollen eyes and headache.

"Ahhh," a lioness chided gently, "don't cry. It'll ruin your makeup!" The female next to me had a brush pointed at my face, and I immediately jerked back like it was a snake.

Cry! Cry like you'll never see Javed again! Field panicked.

Well, that did it. I began sobbing from a very real place, reminded of the dull ache in my chest that told me he was so very far away now, both physically and emotionally.

"Ah, no, no, no!" the lioness cried frantically, blotting my cheeks and chin with a piece of cloth.

"Might have to leave it off, Jehanne. Better she goes without paint than ends up with inky tear trails down her face halfway through dinner," Oudine advised with a sad glance at me.

Stop crying! Stop! We'll get to talk to Javed soon! How awesome is that? Field said, trying to calm me down so we could have an opportunity to look worse later. *We have such a handsome mate! Convict is... er... great!*

Damn her for making me laugh.

I forced calm upon myself, and Jehanne blew out a relieved breath. Despite Oudine's warning, she proceeded to paint my face. It took an eternity for her to do whatever she was doing, and I grew particularly nervous when she started drawing something around my eyes; I was certain they'd be poked out with the slightest mistake.

After they played with my hair, Oudine led me to another room packed with females in front of mirrors. They were all dressed up like me, but these preened at their appearances.

Are we certain these are not bird-shifters? Field asked.

It was a good question. Oudine turned me to face a mirror, and a stranger stared back. How odd it was to come here, to not just live the lie but to also transform into it. I didn't have any opinions on the creature in the mirror with her darkened eyes and rouged cheeks. It was a fine, flamboyant costume for this charade. So far, nothing here provoked any familiarity. Perhaps part of that was due to not knowing who my family was. Perhaps one of my sisters was in this very room, but I wasn't here for them. They were only a nice bonus if they existed… sadly enough.

"You look like you're in shock," the lioness behind me said quietly and rubbed my upper back to comfort. "You're safe here. Lionesses run together."

"Do we outnumber the males?" I whispered hoarsely. "I'm scared of males."

"Yes, but we can only do so much… We protect the best we can within the… rules," she mumbled falteringly.

I frowned. "Why do we outnumber them?"

She snorted and whispered, "The idiots among them will kill each other fighting over a single female. Don't know why they can't just wait until the breeding cycle restarts…"

"You mean there are non-idiots here?" I mumbled, unable to help myself. Oudine burst into raucous laughter and dragged me out of the room.

"I like you, Niusha. Let's be friends," she announced, breathless from her mirth.

I didn't reply as she tugged me along to a line forming by the door. I glanced around, finding the formation a little odd, like we were sacrifices about to be marched to our ceremonial deaths.

I shuddered as my nerves piled and made sure I stayed behind Oudine so she wouldn't catch me working on ruining my makeup.

Jameson looked at something on his desk, then stood to open the doors for the lionesses. His eyes flickered to me, and he frowned, then gestured subtly like I had something on my face.

Oh, we're working on it. Field guffawed.

I simply chose to look terrified and stared straight ahead while we walked to dinner. It wasn't much of an act. I sniffled as quietly as I could and would occasionally rub my eyes. Judging by the amount of rouge and black smudges on my hand, I must be an absolute disaster.

Field memorized the route to the dining area with a new song, and I continued to be amazed by her. I would have been completely out of my depth as a human, I was certain. When the guards opened the doors to let us in, Oudine glanced behind, and her eyes widened in dismay.

"Shit! Oh shit! Niusha… Oh no… What have you done?"

I chose to stare at her in tearful fear, like I didn't know what she was talking about, but Field simply fell into victorious cackling.

Though sabotaging my face had been a necessity, I did feel bad about upsetting Oudine. She gaped and muttered what must have been a curse. "Scraps!" Looking torn, she realized she had to keep walking into the room because she was holding up the rest of the line. "Wipe under your eyes!" she hissed under her breath, then turned to face the direction the line had gone.

I did not, which made Field burst into uncharacteristic, frantic giggles.

The cream-colored dining room opened into a larger space than the harem's room, which I would have thought to be impossible. Large columns, with candles ensconced on all sides, supported the vast space. Upon the ceiling were morbid paintings depicting lions slaughtering other cats, and my stomach turned at its brutality. I might have to burn this room down before I left.

Long, finely crafted tables and chairs packed the room, and decorations like colorful flowers and candles littered the surfaces. Places had already been set, and some tables were already occupied by females. I wondered if all the castle was gathering here. It certainly seemed big enough… How many harems were there?

Part of me wondered if I could scent out a sibling or one of my parents, but even if I could, there were too many smells in here to sort through. I was still highly tempted to wander by each table, sniffing everyone. Something about my family potentially being in this room gave me the jitters.

What a delightful first impression of a daughter we would be. Field laughed. *Face covered in smudges while we went about sniffing strangers.*

Don't make me laugh, Field, I warned her, feeling my lip twitch. *I'm supposed to look overwhelmed and intimidated by the smallest soup spoon.*

Right.

My line stopped in front of a table, and we all took our seats while the rest of the harem went to the adjacent table. The chairs across from us were empty, and I was just about to ask about them when the males finally started pouring into the room. Seemed like it was customary for them to sit across from the females even though we outnumbered them.

I was startled when I felt a wet thumb press against my cheek, but it was only Oudine trying to groom my face. "What am I going to do with you?" she mumbled. The male who settled across from me gave me a wary look, but after a second of absorbing this scene, his cheeks reddened and his shoulders bobbed with suppressed mirth. Primly, Oudine snapped at him. "Don't start, Roul. She's had a very tough journey back to her people."

"I would never." Roul chuckled and scratched at his short salt-and-pepper beard. He sobered fairly quickly after that and leaned forward in his chair to speak to her in a lower voice. "I'm sorry, Oudine. I know now's not the time for joking around…"

He left his hand on the table between them, possibly as a gesture of peace, but it went ignored.

She simply gave a curt nod and continued dabbing stealthily at my face when she felt like she could get away with it. My gaze traveled around the room, and it seemed like there were two very different prevailing moods. The females were all sullen, but one would occasionally respond in a hostile manner to a male. The lions all looked uncomfortable, like they wanted to be anywhere but here.

I have to imagine this has to do with the culling, Field surmised.

She had to be right. I wanted to ask questions, but it seemed like the wrong time for that—if there was even a right time. I wondered how the males felt about the culling. Certainly, they were just as upset?

Only the old king's cubs got executed, Field reminded me. *These males still have their own cubs... at least that's based off of what Quennel told us.*

Oh, you're right. I'd forgotten. But still, it must be horrifying to see cubs you've known for years get... I trailed off, unable to finish that sentence. Field hummed her dark acknowledgement, and I dropped my gaze to the plate before me. It was best I stopped thinking about that.

"What's her name?" Roul asked, nodding to me. It was probably because I wasn't looking particularly talkative. I jumped a little in my seat, wanting to come across as skittish.

"Niusha," she said shortly and leaned back to check her work on my face. "That's better..."

I held back a scowl. She'd ruined my perfectly good ugliness. Roul nodded slowly and muttered, "Maybe situate yourself a little closer to her so the king doesn't get a good look."

Interesting. I hadn't expected a male to suggest protection against another, Field noted thoughtfully.

"Good idea, though I'm afraid it'll only prolong the inevitable," Oudine responded and scooted her chair a little closer to block my view of what I assumed was the king's chair. It was an overly gilded piece of furniture tucked behind an equally ornate table. It all sat smugly on top of a dais lest one forgot how important the seated individual was.

"And the brave cub-killer has arrived," Roul whispered into his glass of water, eliciting a pained hiss from the lionesses around us. Foot stomping and roaring came from the majority of the males while others clapped more conservatively. None of the females made a noise, and Oudine looked over at me with an approving nod. I supposed we females stayed silent. How very pure motherly. Roul was conveniently too busy drinking his water to clap, and I studied him for a minute, wondering what his story was. Some of these lions were not what I'd imagined, but first impressions were sometimes as helpful as a roofless hut in a rainstorm.

I embraced the pang in my heart from that thought. I wondered what Tahmina was doing this very minute. If it hurt to remember the orphans, I couldn't imagine losing my own cub that I'd been raising for years. It gave me a little hope that maybe some females were discontent enough to consider helping me… as grim as the initiative might be.

I didn't bother trying to get a look at the king, especially with Oudine working to hide me from his sight. Let him remember my snot-covered, tearful face. I was sure that'd make for a tasty appetizer.

There was no speech before the meal, and someone must have given a signal because a procession of females dressed in simple dresses and aprons walked in carrying plates of food. They were set in front of all the males, but the only thing that was placed in front of me was a goblet filled with a dark red liquid. I stared at it with a great deal of suspicion. The lionesses here didn't seem like they were on netacaria, but I didn't trust anything that wasn't water.

"Have you had wine before?" Oudine asked, and I shook my head, not letting my eyes stray from the beverage. I'd have to find a way to get rid of it.

"Go slow," Roul said. "If you haven't had alcohol before, you'll get drunk pretty fast and end up with a nasty hangover tomorrow morning."

"Hangover? Drunk?" I asked. That didn't sound appealing in the slightest. Why would I want something that'd make me sick?

"Best not, Niusha," Oudine decided, taking the cup from me. I breathed a sigh of relief but gaped when she emptied my cup into hers. "I need this more than you do."

Roul flinched at that and turned his attention to his roast, starting to eat with the rest of the males. I remembered Field mentioning something about males eating first, and I placed a hand over my belly, hoping it wouldn't growl embarrassingly. The aroma of roasted meat had me salivating, and I'd missed lunch.

"When do we eat?" I whispered to Oudine.

"After the males do," she answered.

"Why?" I'd never gotten the answer to that question. Field just mentioned it was an instinct.

"Because it's an old tradition. It's a tribute to the males being stronger," she replied. "They've earned that right."

"How?" I asked, and Roul choked on his food. He was coughing so hard that the male next to him had to repeatedly slam his palm onto his back.

When he caught his breath, he wheezed, "Funniest shit I've heard in my life... Careful. Best ask those kinds of questions in private. Other males will find that disrespectful."

So sensitive, Field drawled.

Roul cut a small piece of his roast and slipped it into his unused napkin. He leaned forward and swapped his napkin with Oudine's. "Got a bit of cork from that wine on your lips, Oudine. Best clean yourself up."

I didn't understand what just happened, but Oudine's eyes widened in shock. The male next to Roul punched him under the table. "You're gonna get caught one of these days!" he hissed in concern, but Roul just shrugged.

"No idea what you're going on about."

Oudine took the napkin and pressed it to her lips like she was dabbing at a stain, but I saw her slip the food into her mouth. Roul focused on his food once more, but Oudine was blushing furiously—her beige cheeks glowing an apple red. Had I just witnessed something meaningful? It was just one more question on top of other questions—well, below the other questions. This was not more important than finding the kidnapped and enslaved cats.

Speaking of which, what's our plan at this point? Field inquired, checking in with me.

Not having anything else to do but sit until the lions were done eating, I said, *Obviously, we need to get shown around. We'll keep an eye out for any offices and meeting rooms. We'll have to start with the low risk searching first. If we get desperate, we might have to eavesdrop outside some rooms. No, wait, before that, we need to create our escape route. I think we'll have to find a way over the wall. We just need a better sense of what's available to work with. We have a lot of exploring we'll have to do as quickly as possible without raising suspicion.*

I suggest we use our trauma to explain away odd behavior, Field recommended. *If we're found in odd places, we can pretend to space out and claim we don't feel safe—that we'll always be running from the male who marked us.*

Right... Do you think they have a place they hold prisoners here? I wonder if they have slave records... I blanched when I realized that Javed's records would be here if they did.

I think we should explore all the above, starting with the least risky.

Got it... I replied. *Hopefully we'll have something to tell Javed when he...* I sniffed and rubbed an eye, this time trying not to cry. *Do you think he'll come?*

I don't know, she answered and went silent, leaving me alone with my torturous question.

A hand on my shoulder made me jump for real this time, and I turned to face a large lion sporting a chastising scowl. "New lioness, I am Advisor Eudes, royal advisor to His Majesty King

Leudbal. We were hoping to introduce you this evening, but you are in an inappropriate state for such a magnanimous honor. Please be presentable tomorrow evening or there will be consequences for your disobedience and disrespect."

The advisor tossed his blond hair over his shoulder and marched back to his own place near the king's table, not giving me an opportunity to reply, not that I was going to anyway. There seemed to be no desire to hear the lionesses speak at all. Oudine shifted uncomfortably in her chair and didn't meet my gaze. I wondered if maybe my plan to appear undesirable had brought more attention to me.

It was going to happen anyway, I said to myself. *My first impression must have deterred some males, right? I will be known as the snotty lioness... I hope.*

I had to think things through more carefully now that I'd seen the king and his advisor. I went back to considering my options, trying to distract myself from my hunger. It seemed to take forever for the males to finish eating, but they finally did, and our plates were served. I devoured mine after giving it a vigilant sniff. I never wanted to be dosed with netacaria or acpoama again.

I can do this, I chanted in my head while I shoved the last morsel of food into my salivating mouth. *I can do this. I can find them, and I can get out of this.*

Chapter 28

Niusha

Oudine was what Roul called ‘drunk’ by the end of the evening. He’d tried to take her cup away from her at some point, but she did not respond well to that. He’d ended up with a bevy of curses dropped on him like a pile of bricks and swiftly returned her wine. From this little exchange, though Roul was the “stronger” one, it certainly seemed like Oudine was in control.

When we were dismissed from dinner, Roul caught my attention and said, “Please make sure she gets to her bed and drinks a lot of water. Don’t let her keep drinking wine when she gets with cub again.” It was a request, but his eyes were pleading. It reminded me of the look in Javed’s eyes, and I wondered if that was what males looked like when they were in love. I still had much to learn about that.

That last sentence immediately concerned me though, and I inquired, “Why would she have to stop drinking it? Aside from the fact that it seems to be… making her happy in a very weird way.” I glanced over at Oudine who’d put her head on another lioness's shoulder, and she was laughing so hard that her face was a worrisome shade of the very beverage she'd imbibed.

"She could miscarry," he explained with a grimace. "Or the cub could come early… or it could be damaged…" Roul took a measured breath and murmured, "I know it helps her cope with losing five cubs, but she'll be even more hurt if she loses the next one."

Oh my gods… Five. Five cubs! Gone all at once?

All of a sudden, cold invaded my skin and bones, and I wrapped my arms around myself. My nose gave that little telltale sting that warned me the tears were on their way.

"She was one of the last two king's favorites and has… gone through this before. They all try to act like they're used to it…" he disclosed, his face now void of emotion. He must not have liked that at all, and I was simply stricken with the thought of her having lost more than five cubs in her lifetime. Roul's nostrils flared, and he grunted, like he was trying to get himself together. "Anyway, it would please me if you made sure she drank water and slept."

"I'll make sure," I answered quietly, and he marched straight out of the dining room.

I walked up to Oudine and fidgeted, not sure how to remove her from her circle of drunken lionesses. When I saw her lift another glass of wine, I shuffled toward her to tug on her sleeve. Her head rolled in an exaggerated arc, and she immediately pulled me into a smothering hug. Oh gods, she was stronger than she looked.

"This is my new cub," Oudine giggled and ruffled my hair. "Everyone say hi to Niusha!" There was a chorus of hellos from the drunk lionesses, followed by a smattering of random laughter. Wait, was that why she was so invested in me? That was incredibly depressing… for both of us. "She's such a lost thing, so I'm going to take care of her! As much as I can, that is." That last sentence came out with a pout.

"Can we go back?" I whispered, trying to escape her python-like grip.

"You don't want to meet your fellow lionesses?" she asked with a playful growl, mussing my hair again.

"I-I-I do, I j-just…" I turned on the tears, and it immediately killed their party. It unfortunately turned into a different type of event as the lionesses converged on me, trying to calm and coo me into a sense of safety.

Field! I need your guidance! I screamed out at her in frustration. Her presence emerged, and after catching up on my memories, she started laughing again. Well, I was glad she was having such a good time.

Just start bawling. Make enough of a scene, and they'll rush you back in no time. The males are all gone anyway.

She was right. They'd all mostly escaped in a hurry, one of the exceptions being Roul. I did as she bade and started wailing at the top of my lungs, feeling utterly ridiculous, but it'd worked because Oudine drunkenly rushed me out and brought me back to the harem. When she placed a cup of water at my bedside, I shook my head belligerently.

"You drink some too." I pouted through my tears. I wasn't sure if she was immune to pouts, having raised cubs, but it seemed to work. She sighed and wobbled over to grab another glass.

"There. We'll drink water together, ok?"

I nodded timidly and poured the cool liquid down my parched throat. When she finished hers, I mumbled, "Roul said you needed to drink more water. You should get more water…"

She bristled, then melted and leaned against my shoulder. "Stupid males. Stupid males, all of them," she slurred.

"Roul seems nice." I was hoping to pry more information out of her. It was on my risky list, but I wondered if Roul would make a potential ally.

"He is!" she moaned and slapped the comforter with a fist. "He is. He's always the first to put a bid on me, but the king supersedes claims. I'm tired of kings. I'm tired of losing cubs."

Her emotional agony squeezed fresh tears from her eyes. Oh no, I hadn't meant to make her cry.

"Roul doesn't seem to like the new king," I said, trying a new topic.

"Roul doesn't like cullings. Kings are not required to do cullings, but they always choose to. Some of us see our kings as traitors to our population, some do not. They cling to tradition, but we're not the only ones. The other cats cull too, and they're much more brutal about it."

Uh-oh. Field winced. *Big lie number one. Perhaps this place isn't so different from our old village.*

"Um... Oudine, can you drink more water?" I asked, prodding her while I took a second to think. She grumbled and rolled gracelessly off the bed with a thunk, making me wince. She wobbled to her feet and went to fill our cups. When she finished drinking, I said, "Oudine, you know I've been out of the pride for as long as I can recall, right?"

"Yes." She sighed, placing the empty cup next to her. "You poor cub."

I ignored being called a cub. She'd get a permanent pass for that. "I don't know quite how to tell you this..."

"What?" Oudine rolled her head to stare at me. She seemed a little less drunk now, so I just went for it.

"The lions are the only ones who cull. The other cats stopped doing that ages ago..."

Her face became expressionless for a long moment, but then she shook her head. "No... no... you must be mistaken. Our kings have always told u—"

"Lies?" I supplied, interrupting her with a grimace. Was this how Javed had felt when he tried to convince me of the lions' crimes? I hoped Oudine wouldn't be as difficult as I'd been with him.

"No... no..." she whispered, shaking her head. "Can't be true... They say it's an uncontrollable instinct... They say it's the unchanging nature of cats..."

"I can't prove it," I said, scratching at a thumbnail. "You'd have to leave the pride to believe me, but I know you can't. I just don't have a reason to lie…"

Oudine's distress slowly broke through her shock. She was now biting her lower lip so hard that it turned white. I saw an opportunity and went for it, feeling like it'd only be believable in this exact moment with this exact topic.

"Do you think there'd be any documents here that could prove it?" I asked.

"Maybe," she replied vacantly. "I… I'm going to sleep now. I…" She crawled off my bed, and I helped her undress. The gowns were ridiculously complicated, and I idly wondered if they were designed like that to limit the lioness's ability to shift. The corset would be as dangerous as the vines those three males had tied around my neck.

Oudine simply crawled naked into bed and fell silent. My heart hurt for her, but it'd been a necessary conversation. I wished I could make things better for all the lionesses… maybe even a couple of the lions. Clearly, these were not evil people. It was obvious that there'd been horrific leadership and carefully crafted beliefs that kept everyone… complacent.

This was the Pride of Pure Lies.

With that unsettling thought, I found the nearest lioness to help me out of my gown. She showed me the collection of clothes that'd been delivered into the drawers below my wooden bedframe. I pulled out an exquisite lace nightgown made from a shimmery gold material, then crawled into bed. I needed to think. I knew things would be different than anticipated, and I had to make adjustments.

I had three people I needed to learn more about, and those were Oudine, Roul and Keid—a lioness, a lion, and a witch. It was an interesting variety, to be sure, and if I found them to be of some use, it could significantly increase my chance of success. If they proved to be false, though, it could ruin everything. Lives were on the line.

Gotta go fast slowly. Field sighed.

At least we have two days before we need to implement our strategy against the breeding schedule, I replied, trying to hold on to some optimism.

Have we given a thought to enticing males, and if they fight over us it could buy more time?

It wouldn't work if the king made the claim, I answered, almost gagging at the thought.

I miss our mate. Field sighed again, heavier this time.

I thought you didn't like Convict? I inquired, provoking her out of sheer curiosity.

He may be an idiot with a barbed penis, but he's my idiot with a barbed penis, she grunted. I held back my laughter but was momentarily distracted when a brunet male walked into the room and addressed Jameson. The shorter lion pulled paperwork out, wrote something down, and gestured for him to continue.

A female sat up in her bed, rubbing her eyes, then closed the curtains that surrounded her sleeping area. The male passed through them, and it was immediately clear why the beds had curtains.

Oh my goddess on green beans! I cried, plugging my ears after I jerked my curtains shut. It didn't buffer the noise of their mating, but it gave me some… mental distance.

Is there no privacy? Field asked in horror. I swallowed heavily, turned to face the wall, and smooshed a pillow over my ear. This was worse than listening to the shifter couple mating in the jungle. She didn't sound like she was hating it, but she didn't sound like she was loving it either. The complacency was… weird to me. Javed had definitely spoiled me.

It felt like they'd been at it for ages by the time several more males arrived to do their 'duty.' How did females get any sleep around here with all the ruckus? I groaned into the mattress and did my best to pass out, but I didn't even get close to falling asleep until they'd all left.

Niusha, can you hear me? Javed's voice came out of nowhere. I shot straight up, nearly startled out of my skin. Thank the gods for the closed curtains!

Yes! Yes, I can! I yelled, probably a little too loudly. He wasn't as easy to hear as usual, but it wasn't so bad that I had to strain to make out his words.

I am... checking in.

I jerked my head back in surprise. *Our check-in is the night after tomorrow night...* I reminded him. Had he forgotten?

I could not... wait. His voice was terse. It was like he was trying to sound emotionless, but I could feel some of his anxiety trickle through our stretched bond.

Ok... I took a deep breath and tried to sort out my fluttery brain, which had somehow switched places with my heart. I was all agog and flustered beyond measure. *Short summary is I fooled the doctors into thinking I took the abortive; the cubs are safe. I have three individuals who may or may not be allies, but I'm cautiously going to learn more, and I'm safe from the breeding list for two more days. I have plans to avoid it after that. I may have an idea of where to find important documentation, but I'm waiting on someone who is... likely going to be hungover tomorrow. This place... I need to find out if there's a holding area. They may have a list of slaves hidden somewhere. Maybe it'll note where people are taken...*

Javed was quiet for a while, and it seemed like my report had triggered an avalanche of emotions in him. *There's a prison,* he said in a rigid tone. *That's where I was being kept.*

Oh, that's excellent news! Where is it? I asked. He went silent again, and I felt him warring with himself. The fear dominated him now, try as he might to not let it show.

After several minutes I caved. *Maybe you can tell me next time,* I murmured and fidgeted with the tassel on one of my pillows. *How are you doing?*

Busy, he replied immediately, like he'd snapped out of a daydream. *Goodbye, Niusha.*

Good night... I said, correcting his dark assumption once more.

Field groaned in misery. *My idiot didn't even say anything. Idiot. I hate that I miss that stupid idiot. That big, ol' stripey idiot!*

I woke groggily with a face full of cedar-brown hair and coughed quietly. I picked a strand out of my mouth and rubbed an eye, vaguely remembering crawling onto Oudine's bed in the middle of the night because of her crying. I'd stayed on top of the sheets because I still wasn't used to nudity around anyone else but Javed. My heart cringed when I recalled his coldness last night, but I'd known the repercussions for coming here. I just had to hold strong.

I slid out of Oudine's bed, desiring another bath but not necessarily in the huge pool, especially since it was in plain view of Jameson's desk. He was a good lion—I believed—but he was still a male. I looked into various side rooms but didn't find any other place to wash, so I steeled myself and took the fastest bath I'd ever taken in my life. There were a handful of other lionesses in the pool, and they all sent me odd looks when I scrambled out of the water to immediately snap a towel around myself. I felt stupid for being so shy, but it was hard to shake old discomforts. My little show probably looked ridiculous.

You could let me take the bath next time, Field offered, and I snorted while I sorted through my drawers, looking for a something comfortable to wear.

Good luck handling the soap. That won't go poorly at all.

I pulled on the simplest dress I could find, but I still needed help with the laces. No matter how I turned and twisted, I couldn't tighten it myself. I needed another pair of elbows to succeed.

"I can help, Ni... Niusha?" someone offered from behind, interrupting my frustrated growling, and I turned to find the willowy lioness who'd experienced some difficulty with her sense of... orientation yesterday.

"Juliote? I think… is it?" I inquired of the female with the honey-blond hair and deep-set light-brown eyes. Her fair fingers worked just fine now as she tied the back of my dress. She hummed a 'yes' as she tightened the last section.

"Thanks… these aren't easy to get into," I confessed, flattening the skirts with sweaty palms. I needed to think about my next step today. I only had two free days, so I had to make the most of them.

"I'm off to work... bye." She sandwiched her lips in a shy manner and rushed out of the chamber.

Alright… what now? Field asked. I was about to reply when the chamber door opened, and a lioness around Oudine's age walked in to speak to Jameson. Her clover-green gown and robes flowed elegantly to the rhythmic swishing of her matching slippers.

"Now, Jameson," she began in a voice a little huskier than mine, "you know I have five other harems of mourning lionesses to help care for at the moment. Can we please make this quick so I can g—" The female who looked just like an older version of me sniffed the air and searched the large room in shock. "Jameson, why am… I..." she mumbled, not finishing her question as her grey-blue eyes scanned the room… for me.

"I know. I apologize for taking your time. I believe that the lioness we brought in may be one of yours, though I'm not sure how that's possible. I need you to verify th—" Jameson stood at his desk and handed her a folder.

She immediately dropped it on the desk and shook her head. "No. Don't do this to me, Jameson." She spun on shaking legs, and I couldn't control my throat.

"Mother?" I called out to her. I knew it. I just knew that was my mother. I didn't recognize anything about her—not her face, her scent, or her voice, but she looked just like me. I held my dark blond hair to my heart and stopped breathing the moment she froze. "Are you…?"

She turned her head and spun to face me with a strained expression. Her features were a little more severe than mine, like she'd spent much of her life fighting or weeping. She had the face of a female who took on too much because of others who didn't or couldn't contribute.

"How old are you?" she asked in voice so tormented it pinched my heart. Her hand blindly groped for the folder until Jameson moved it toward her searching fingers.

"Twenty-three… maybe. That's what I was told," I answered, slowly approaching her because I didn't want to have this conversation across the room. It was early morning and some of the lionesses were still asleep. I willed my slamming heart to be quiet because I didn't want to miss a single word she said.

"She can't be mine," she said flatly, turning to Jameson. "That was the year of the culling. I lost all of them."

"Did you see all the bodies before they were laid to rest?" Jameson asked, trying to maintain a professional voice, but he also seemed a touch scared for his life.

"No… No… I couldn't. I left that to others… I couldn't…" she mumbled, wringing her hands and pacing by the short guard.

"Perhaps the doctor's witch can verify," Jameson said and opened the door, gesturing for both of us to follow him. She seemed torn, but with one last look at me, she swept out of the Jong Harem. I followed behind, certain that I was drenching my skirts with my sweaty hands.

Is this Mother? Field whispered during the moment of silence while we followed Jameson. *She looks like us. I wonder if her lioness looks like us.*

I imagine she must, Field, I said in a haze. *Oh my giddy gods, I didn't even catch her name. Did someone say her name?*

Not yet. Ask.

When we arrived at the doctor's office, the older male was standing at the front desk, making some notes. "Oh, you're back, new lioness. And hi, Tumidia. Who am I seeing first?"

"Both of us," Tumidia said briskly and walked straight into an examination room. "And bring Keid."

I followed my potential mother into the room and stood by the chair, positively drenched in sweat now. *Field, help,* I moaned to her, worried I was about to have a heart attack.

Relax, relax! Use this nervousness? We're still supposed to seem anxious and traumatized, so just... focus it on acting? I don't know. I can't think!

That helped for about a second, but when I started to feel lightheaded on top of a bout of cold sweat, Tumidia noticed, grabbed my hand, and urged me to sit in the chair.

Oh my gods, she touched us. Our maybe-mother touched us. Our maybe-mother held our hand! Field blubbered. We were falling apart pretty hard.

"We'll get this sorted out," Tumidia said quietly to me, softening her tone while she stared at the door. I thought an entire week had passed by the time the doctor walked in with the witch. Keid raised an eyebrow when she saw me and nodded in deference to Tumidia. I then placed a palm to my cold and clammy forehead, sick from stress and anticipation.

Wow, our body is all out of sorts! Field babbled. *Just listen. Listen to what they're saying. Don't get stuck in your head. We gotta pay attention—*

They're talking. Shhh!

"—ut it can't be possible. Is Keid able to tell if we're related?" Tumidia inquired, getting down to business while my lioness had a nervous breakdown. I was close to having one myself.

"I will check," Keid replied, and the doctor departed, leaving the witch to open a cabinet and pull out a slip of paper and a bottle of ink. She dipped a quill after sterilizing it and drew an image on the parchment. I wanted to go watch, but I was afraid I'd pass out as soon as I left the chair. She poured another liquid over the illustration and let it drip dry for several seconds. "Is this to verify parentage? I will not be able to tell you who her sire is."

"Yes, and the latter does not matter," Tumidia replied, sounding tired all of a sudden. Her shoulders pulled in a little, and she grabbed her arm with her other hand. She was growing anxious too.

Keid nodded to acknowledge her and brought the damp paper over to Tumidia. "Wrist up, please," the witch directed, and the lioness followed her instruction, lifting her arm like a sacrifice. Keid placed the illustration—image side down—over the lioness's wrist and pressed into it with a palm. She focused on it, and there was a small sizzling sound, but I didn't notice any visible changes.

When she pulled the paper away, the image had transferred to Tumidia's wrist. Keid grabbed both our wrists now and held them together. She focused once more, and I winced when a small shock ran up my arm. Sky Gods, that hurt!

"Ah!" I hissed, pulling my aching arm away once Keid released me.

"Let me see, Niusha," the witch said, reaching for my arm again. I looked up into her sharp periwinkle gaze as she studied the mirrored image that had transferred to my wrist. She compared it to the image on Tumidia's wrist and nodded slowly in understanding. "You see all these other symbols that are not on Niusha's image?" she asked Tumidia, who nodded. "There is only one that transferred over, that one identifies her as your daughter. Niusha is your daughter."

A loud gasping sob escaped my mother's mouth, and she fell to her knees by my chair, pulling me forward into her embrace. I stared into my mother's neck in shock as she cried, wailing with an occasional laugh that suggested a pinch of madness. It took a while, but moisture eventually found its way to my eyes, and when I finally blinked, it streamed freely down my cheeks.

"I will get the doctor," Keid said quietly and left. There was some pain in Keid's voice. She probably had her own mother she sorely missed. I wonder how long she'd been here? It snapped me back to reality, and I tried to clear my head. I was lost in a fog having found my mother, but I couldn't forget the reason why I came.

Just enjoy us having our mother for one minute, please! Field begged.

Of... O-of course... I said and hesitantly returned my mother's hug. She couldn't talk through all her tears, but she tried to calm herself once the doctor returned. Not wanting to move from me, she stayed crouched by my side and swiveled to look up at the lion holding my folder.

"So, it seems like one did survive..." He frowned and scratched the back of his head. "Unprecedented. Very unusual... Tumidia, what do you recall from that year?"

My mother furrowed her brows and subtly shook her head, like she was trying to break free of her astonishment. Her dark blond hair, with just a touch of grey in a couple spots, waved about her shoulders.

"What do you mean, Doctor Gris?"

"We obviously missed a cub at the culling," he replied, looking down at the notes, which forced a double chin to mirror his frown. She hissed at how he'd worded it. Even though I knew nothing about her, that protective gesture had me leaning into her embrace. "Do you recall anything strange occurring before then?"

"No..." she said, stretching the word out as she thought about it. "Nothing much changed that year. We moved the culling age down from... was it sixteen? We did move some lionesses around because some items started going missing... We stopped allowing anyone but lionesses into the crèche too."

"Was that before or after the culling?" he asked, and I winced. Now that I knew I was supposed to be dead, I couldn't stand hearing that word. I shuddered in extreme discomfort, and goose bumps rose on my arms, making my tiny little body hairs stand at attention.

"I... don't remember. I could check my journals..." my mother answered uncertainly.

"Alright, well, I'll add all this to my report. I'll send for the scarmaster too," the doctor said.

No! What? What did he say? Field yowled.

Isn't that who mutilated Javed? I asked in horror, feeling something akin to ice burrowing through my veins. I was cold. I was so cold right now. Chilled, lost nerves had me fall into shivers, and the lioness clamped a warm hand down on my forearm.

"Certainly, that's not necessary," my mother protested. "She's an adult now. It's a little late for that, don't you think? A little unnecessary? She's old enough to kno—"

"You know how it is, Tumidia," Doctor Gris replied, opening the door for us. "I'm not the king. I can't change tradition."

Chapter 29

Niusha

Glaring daggers at the doctor, my mother helped me to my feet, grabbed my hand, and speed-walked back to Jameson. Unnerved by the expression on her face, he jumped to attention and ran to hold the door open. My mother did not take the route back to the harem, and that alone had my pulse quickening.

"Tumidia? What occurred? Where are you going?" Jameson asked, losing his emotionless, professional mask. My mother must terrify him.

I hope that's a good thing, Field said.

"I am taking my daughter somewhere quiet while I have a conversation with the scarmaster," she answered brusquely, her skirts hissing along the floor like angry lionesses.

"Oh! Congratulations, but the scarmaster? Seems a little old for that."

"It's a stupid tradition that should have been abolished ages ago," she snapped as we took a right turn.

"It's a part of our culture..." he began hesitantly. "It doesn't hurt for long, and they're so young they hardly remember going through it. The gods bless those wh—"

She whirled to face him, face red with rage. "Come see me again when you've had cubs undergo the scarification ceremony—when you've had to wash blood and tears off their confused, hurt, and frightened faces. Come see me when you've had your cubs killed because you, as their sire, died trying to keep your place on the throne." Finally, she bared her teeth and spoke through them. "Oh wait, you wouldn't be able to. You'd be dead."

Color drained from Jameson's face, and though he continued following, it was at a greater distance and done in silence. I winced internally. He hadn't deserved to bear the brunt of all that fury, but I could tell that it was a bad time to test her, especially if she was caring for mothers of those recently culled. What a tragedy.

My mother only freed my hand when we arrived at a section of the castle that might have been used for outdoor storage. She pointed a finger at me and ordered, "Stay here until I get you! I'll be back in an hour or so..." She sighed as she gave me one last pained look and promptly left with Jameson, closing the door behind her. It seemed I was being hidden until she was done with... whatever she was about to do.

I immediately went into planning my future escape and took in the space where I'd been left. I didn't want to think about the scarmaster when there were ladders to be found. I walked around the stone-paved inner yard, looking for anything that could help me find a route out of the castle.

No ladders, Field grunted. *But there's a toolbox.* I snatched the box off the barrel and opened it to find some basic implements. *Hammer, chisel, mallet... nails... Let's hide this in a corner.* I followed Field's suggestion and looked for the least visible nook to conceal it. When I wandered around a corner, I spied a narrow gap in the wall.

What's this? I murmured to Field and placed the toolbox down to investigate it. It seemed like the giant walls of the castle had another wall running parallel so support beams could maintain its stability. The inner wall didn't go all the way against the perpendicular wall, leaving a small opening that I might've been able to squeeze through if I didn't have a female's butt.

What if we removed two bricks around butt level? Field asked, and the only reason why I didn't laugh was because that might actually work.

I snatched the mallet and chisel, but I hesitated when I held it to the wall. *This will be too loud if that back wall is the outer wall, Field. The guards likely circle the outside in shifts.*

Can we put something between the chisel and brick to deaden the sound?

I don't know... would fabric work? I could maybe bring a dress here... I wasn't sold on that idea. It'd be hard enough just getting back here without being seen... or scented. I groaned, feeling like we were so close to a solution. If we could get between the walls, we could either find a way to climb up and over with the wooden beams or make handholds. I didn't think we'd be able to make a big enough hole to crawl through without alerting the guards. If one walked past it, even if we put the bricks back, it'd be obvious what we were working on over the course of several days.

Augh! Field cried in frustration. *We're so close! There isn't any rope around here, is there?*

I doubt it. With how often females try to save their cubs, they probably leave very little out. I dug through the mess in the yard, but I didn't see anything that would work. *Be hard to find a forty-foot rope anyway. It'd take a long time to gather enough fabric to tie together something that'd hold.*

Well, squeeze the toolbox back there so no one can see it and remove it... in case they come for it.

That's a better hiding place, I agreed.

Let's say we jumped off the wall and told Javed to catch us... would we kill him on accident?

Field... we're not doing that.

Ok, fine... Let's say we ch— Field interrupted herself when we heard feet approaching the one door to the inner yard, and I immediately sat down to bury my face in my arms, forcing tears into my eyes. Fortunately—and unfortunately—I had a large number of things to be distressed over, so it didn't take much to make sure I was found crying. I didn't really have a reason to be in this nook of the yard unless I was hiding.

"Daughter?" my mother's voice called out, her footsteps approaching. She sighed, and I heard her say, "We need to return. Come with me..."

I looked up through my burning eyes and let her help me up while I made a weak attempt to compose myself. "Wh-what happened, Mother?" I asked timidly as she pulled me along the halls. She didn't reply. She still appeared angry, but she also looked tired now—a little worn.

Nausea coiled in my belly, and a cold sweat broke out on my forehead. We entered the Jong Harem to find Jameson addressing an older male in dark brown robes, two guards waiting behind him. It was as I'd thought.

Oh, look, Field gnarled, using sarcasm to hide her fear, *it's the pure elder and his pure fathers.*

Your comparison is most accurate, I murmured, completely consumed by my own fear. My body was exhausted already, and since I wasn't sure how much energy I had to cope with this, I let myself collapse by Jameson's desk. Conservation was the key during bad days at the village. If I was too worn to think properly, I wouldn't be able to maintain the web of lies I'd been weaving for years. Whatever this was—right here, right now—I knew I wouldn't be able to escape it.

Cruelty was a hard trait for me to discern, but I felt I was fairly decent at spotting it. We had an elderly man or male—I'd never know now—in our old village whose face was so dour and angry-looking that I'd at first sworn he must have tortured animals for a living, but he was actually rather benign in nature. This older male seemed like he might be a mix of the old man and the pure father—frightening both in face and in the unbreakable piety to his practice.

"Get off the floor, cub," the older male snapped, tightening the black sash that held back his long brown hair, so long that it fell to his mid-back in waves.

The door opened behind me as I stood, making me jump and knock over a pile of folders on Jameson's desk. "I'm sorry!" I stammered, but he just waved me off and sorted through the mess I'd made. When I glanced down, I noticed something startling.

I saw something I could read.

Look! Field shouted, pointing out what I'd just seen. I made a note to snoop through that pile later, but I was too spooked to be excited by it. *It said something about height and weight. Why would it be written in what our village used? Javed said it was a fake language!*

I-I don't know. Later, Field, I said to get her to quiet. The person who'd walked in was Roul, and he balked at the people crowded by the main desk.

"Looking for Oudine…" he informed, his brows drawn, and Jameson pointed to the pool where Oudine bathed. I was glad to see her awake and out of bed. Maybe Roul was here to check on her? He did mention she might be hungover. When he crouched by the pool, Oudine swam over to him, urgently whispering something and pointing to the scene around me. Other lionesses cautiously gathered from surrounding rooms, curious about what was happening.

"Let's commence the ceremony," the robed male said and ordered his lions to fetch a chair. "I'm Scarmaster Godefroid, and we will be welcoming a new member into our pride today." He must have been delivering this speech for decades, and I couldn't fathom how many times it'd been recited for doomed cubs. "Will the mother come forth?"

I stared at my mother as she approached him and felt the bitter sting of betrayal. I knew she'd probably tried and that she had no say, but I'd hoped she could've protected me from this.

I remembered Javed's brutal words when I told him my family wouldn't let anything bad happen. Perhaps she also would have surrendered if they ever decided I needed to be restrained and poisoned.

My mother stated in a tight, angry voice, "Today, my daughter, Alodie, will be accepted into our community and recognized as having completed her passage from young cubhood." Her nostrils flared with her scowl. "Obviously."

The scarmaster shot her a look, and one of his guards growled threateningly. Then it hit me that my mother hadn't said my name. Was Niusha not my birth name? I knew Raju and Nisha had also been given false names by whoever had abducted them. Maybe everyone's names were fake.

Still, I didn't like the name 'Alodie.' It didn't... suit me.

We don't need our birth name, Field remarked stubbornly. *I've always known you as Niusha. Javed knows you as Niusha. So do the cubs. You are Niusha.*

When my mother grabbed a cup of wine and handed it to me, my concern spiked. She fought to hold her head high as she said, "You may drink this to fortify yourself."

Nope. Don't want that, Field declined, and somehow she momentarily got control of me and dropped the cup, spilling its dark red liquid all over the front of my clothes and the stone floor. I gaped, shocked by what she'd done. That was new!

Field, we need to talk about what just happened! I squatted and fumbled for the cup. "S-s-sorry," I muttered and just set it upright on the floor, not wanting to stain Jameson's desk, though I didn't know why I cared. "I'm too nervous to keep anything d-down. Do I have to?"

"No," she said with a sigh and gestured to the chair. I nearly fainted in relief. Roul said wine could cause a miscarriage, and I had no idea how much a small amount of wine would do. Maybe it'd be fine, but I wasn't taking that chance if I could help it.

"What is he going to do to me?" I asked, forcing my shaking body to still. If I ran, I'd just be manhandled anyway—malehandled?

"Please explain." My mother prompted the scarmaster with a severe gesture. "She is not a cub. Give her some expectations."

"Simply put, cub," the scarmaster said, continuing to not address me as an adult, annoyingly enough, "I will incise the image of both your sire's and your dam's family line into your forehead."

I think fucking not! Field screamed, almost furious enough to come out and draw blood. We both knew better, and I hated that. So did she.

"What?" I hadn't noticed any scars on foreheads. I searched the faces in the room, trying to find any marks on their brows but saw none.

"Many of us have grown accustomed to makeup," my mother said and rubbed at her forehead to display hers. Her ornate scar wasn't extremely noticeable, unlike Javed's brand, but that didn't mean I wanted one.

"Well, if you don't display it, and I'm too old, why do I have to be scarred?" I asked, starting to panic. I didn't want this creature's claws on me! I didn't want to be touched by the same male who'd mutilated my beautiful Javed!

"Because this ceremony is what welcomes you into the community. It tells us who your parents are. It's tradition," the scarmaster retorted and gestured for his males to lead me to the chair. His last two words were said with cold, steely finality. I wasn't quite sure what happened to my brain at that point, but the fear ensnared both Field and me. I could almost see him bent over Javed's back, carving into him while my mate screamed.

My vision blurred from tears, my breathing turned ragged, and my heart threatened to thrum out of my ears. I looked over at the crowd that had gathered, briefly spying Oudine in a robe with Roul next to her. My distraught mother stood rigidly, her chin wobbling, her eyes watering.

Contrary to every plan I'd formed, I started trying to squirm out of the chair, out of the guards' grasps. My fright was further fueled by one of them grabbing and tilting my head back, keeping it locked in place. Part of my brain was trying to tell me this wasn't a big deal, but the other part of my brain didn't want anyone cutting me for any reason at all, especially not the person who'd tortured my mate.

"No!" I shouted and tried to squeeze once more out of the two male lions' grips. "No! I don't want this! Don't cut me!"

The scarmaster regarded me with disgust while sharpening his claw on some kind of stone. "You'd think a cub would be honored to have the symbol of a king on their forehead."

"I don't care who it is!" I tried to look over at the crowd when my alarm grew as frantic as my heart. "I came here to be safe!" I screamed through tears, still somehow holding on to the thread of my lie. "Are you so obsessed with tradition that you'll let him cut me for no reason? Just because that's how it's done?" I wailed and tried to jerk my head back as the scarmaster leaned over and ran his claw down my forehead. I yelped and hissed at the resulting pain. "Why would you even cut a cub? How bad are you at identifying your own that you need to hurt a cub to put your name on it?" I screamed, and the scarmaster growled a warning at me when he drew the next line. "I came here to be safe, but you're just a bunch of cub-killers and mutilators!"

I knew I'd gone too far, and it drew a variety of murmurs from the crowd. I kicked and screamed, but when one of the lions shoved a rag into my mouth, I gave up and let the scarmaster do his work. No one was going to save me; I'd already known that, but I'd hoped.

I drifted away as bloody water streamed down from my brow. The scarmaster would wipe the blood from my face with a wet rag every four or five cuts, and my forehead soon became a field of fire. I had no idea how Javed had tolerated getting his entire back scarred over and over again.

That was when I realized that I was acting pathetically. This was nothing compared to what he'd endured. These scars didn't have to change me. I could bear this burden if Javed could bear his with such strength. In dark irony, I accepted that we were a matched pair now.

It was probably over in fifteen minutes, but it'd felt like two hours. The scarmaster finally stood back and said, "Welcome to your pride, Alodie. Your community accepts and recognizes you now."

You mean that you accept and recognize us. Everyone else isn't blind, Field spat as he bowed humbly and left. *Look at that unassuming parade.*

I sat up slowly, helped by my mother and Oudine, who guided me to my bed. I stared at the wall while they cleaned and bandaged me, which was generous considering what I'd yelled at everyone. Numbness, betrayal, and embarrassment buzzed through me, a strange combination, but I didn't know how to process my emotions or what I'd just endured.

"He'll come back tomorrow to redo them," my mother muttered, anger blooming in her cheeks.

I flinched in dismay, but I wasn't sure why I was surprised. After I'd thought about it, Javed said he was worried my mark would scar if he kept redoing it. I guessed shifters healed thoroughly.

"What is this?" my mother inquired, lifting my hair aside so she could study Javed's puncture marks. When she tried to feel them, I blocked her. I didn't want her or anyone else touching them. It was too personal.

"She said those are called mating marks," Oudine whispered and shared what I'd told her.

"Tell her about the culling ban while you're at it," I rasped with a sore throat, suddenly feeling like I had enough energy for one act of petulance.

"Shh!" Oudine shushed me, looking worriedly about to see if anyone had overheard. "Th-there's no proof." My mother glared at her, demanding answers, so Oudine caved and relayed the rest. I guessed she did remember last night's conversation after all.

When Oudine finished talking, my mother went rigid and stood abruptly. It looked like she was going to run away to process all this, like how she'd reacted when Jameson told her I was still alive.

"Do I have to go to the dinner tonight?" I asked my mother before she could leave. "They said I'd be punished, but… I can't show up like this."

"I'll ask. I think since this is all unusual, you should be allowed to recover," she replied, her face softening just a little when she looked down at me. "Get some rest. I'll have food sent to you."

"Thank you, Mother."

That felt weird but good to say. Say hi for me.

"Field says hi," I added hastily.

She blinked in confusion, then once it dawned on her, she relaxed and smiled. "Lobelia returns your greeting, Field." She gently squeezed my hand before departing, calmer now.

Mother's name is Lobelia. Tumidia and Lobelia. Field hummed.

Oudine lay down next to me to offer a hug, and I curled up against her, too tired and too dried out to cry. How did I have the right to cry when Javed had gone through much worse? Oudine got up after a little while of stroking my hair and releasing the same little growl-purrs that I'd given Javed to soothe him. It wasn't as calming as his chuffs—no place was safer than being in Javed's arms—but it did comfort me. If Tumidia was my mother, Oudine felt like an aunt. Maybe she'd be my chosen aunt.

I'd miss them when I left.

"Curtains closed?" she asked, and I nodded, wanting to escape into the darkness for a little bit while Field worked on healing my forehead.

Then I heard footsteps approach her bed, and a familiar lion's voice murmured, "How is she?"

"About as well as anyone would be in her situation," she whispered sadly. "She's resting now. Her mother and I cleaned her up."

"That was brutal to watch. She certainly responded like someone who'd never heard of cullings befo—"

"Roul! Shush! I told you not to repeat that," she hissed.

"You're right. I'm sorry, Oudine. I'm just rattled. I apologize."

"It's not easy to watch a cub go through scarification, but there's something so much more disturbing about making an adult go through it too," she said beneath her breath.

It's painful to go through as well, Field muttered while I tried to sleep.

It hurt... The pulse in my brow also distracted me, throbbing painfully from the numerous small cuts.

"So how are you feeling, Oudine? I originally came to check up on you," Roul asked. I couldn't tell what their relationship was. I supposed they had none if there were no mates or spouses here. He seemed sweetly invested in her, though. It warmed my heart that she had someone who cared about her, especially after a culling.

"Shaken… Oh, you mean from drinking?" She laughed quietly, like she was trying not to wake me. Little did she know that many things were keeping me from falling asleep—conversations and people mating in the same room being two of them. Last night had been dreadful.

"Hungover?"

"No, Niusha—er, I mean Alodie—made sure I drank a hundred glasses of water."

"A hundred?" He chuckled.

"Sure felt like it." She paused and murmured, "It's not like I had anywhere to be. I need to go ask Jameson about my work schedule. There's been nothing for weeks. I didn't even have someone come during my heat! I guess I've been hoping no one would notice if there was a mistake or something." She laughed but then instantly sobered. "I've been enjoying the break; that is, if one can enjoy anything after losing their cubs…"

"Oh, Jameson wouldn't necessarily have the answer to all of that," Roul replied evasively. "I'm glad you're feeling better, so I'm going to g—"

"Wait, what do you mean? No, don't you go anywhere when I'm talking to you!"

Despite my original irritation at where they'd chosen to converse, I had to suppress my giggling. I was tired and in pain, but at least I was being entertained.

"You don't have any work because your schedule's been freed by… a friend," Roul answered, and I could almost hear the shrug in his low voice.

"Now what in all the stars is that supposed to mean?"

"Fine. You want to know? My bid finally went through for you since there was no king's bid this time, so I just decided to let you rest for the season."

"You what?"

He sighed. In a sincere, yet accepting tone, he said, "I think it's pretty obvious. Can't win the heart of someone with a broken one. See you at dinner." From the sound of departing footsteps and Oudine's bewildered gasp, I could safely say that the conversation was over, which was great because I could barely stay awake. I'd really wanted to hear how that ended.

What a romantic gesture, Field mumbled before I drifted off, hoping that their sweet conversation would help me avoid the nightmare.

Chapter 30

"Oh, here you are!" the voice of the svelte dragon-shifter crooned when he strode into the study, looking extremely pleased with himself. I didn't know how he always kept himself spotless in his line of work, but his black-and-brown leather armor was just as pristine as the last time I saw him.

I grunted to acknowledge his presence and continued to draw another uncertain layout of both the jails and the arena. I'd tried to forget it all for years, and now I was forced to dig deeper into painful memories. The effort was giving me a headache, or perhaps it was the fact that I hadn't really slept since Niusha had left. The chieftain of Gantsara had generously provided me with a room in his large home, but I couldn't bring myself to sleep in a bed… alone.

I was not only desperately missing Niusha, but I was afraid of having nightmares about her. It was hard enough to live with daymares, but I couldn't cope with my mind running wild at night with my greatest fears. Every time I closed my eyes, I'd see someone forcing themself on my mate. I knew I'd feel it across our stretched bond if it occurred, so I dreaded it'd hit any minute. It had me wound impossibly tight.

"And look who I picked up along the way," Leofwine added, and I scented him before I saw him. Quennel walked cautiously into the study and received my full glare.

I bet he's smug now that we caved and returned to the Proudless, Convict growled.

He knew it was the last thing we wanted to do. He pushed me too hard. I chose to ignore him and return to my migraine-inducing project.

"Yikes," Leofwine remarked, glancing between me and my old right-hand male. "Alright, well, now that we've got the ice for our scotch, I suppose I'll get down to business." I grunted again and gestured with a hand for him to continue. "Adelais and I found a number of villages in the jungle and south of it. Some of them were normal, but I found several hugging the southern range that were using drugs to manage their villagers. I procured a couple bottles and found some fresh samples," he reported and removed several leaves from a pocket. I slammed my palm down and gestured for him to immediately put them away.

"Shit biscuits!" Quennel snapped. "Put those away before you get us all intoxicated! Are you slow in the brain?"

Leofwine's lips pulled into a frown as he took a thorough sniff of a leaf. "This is nothing but a garnish," he said in confusion. "I think some of us make tea from this."

I snorted, gestured more violently, and added a furious growl this time. Leofwine eyed some pottery rattling on a shelf, likely remembering I could very well stun him, and hastily repocketed his evidence. I stomped to the nearest window to let in fresh air before I became lightheaded.

"Don't you do that again, you oversized pair of wings," Quennel grumbled and walked over to the window to clear his lungs.

"Interesting," Leofwine murmured, then gathered himself, returning to his previous demeanor and topic. "Anyway, because there is no one to ask for permission, I sent my mstovaris to bring some knights and retrieve those we deem survivors of abuse. Several surrounding villages agreed to accept them into their communities for rehabilitation. I think they hope to find some long-lost offspring among them. Oh, and since I personally watched individuals being trafficked from the village, I picked up their leader and left the small fry behind to undergo judgment from their very unhappy neighbors."

I sat back in my chair, and an ounce of pleasure found its way into my mind. It was good to see some justice finally occurring, but it served as a reminder of how brutally powerful the dragons were. This was the act of a single dragon and a cat-shifter. It wouldn't be wise to cross them.

I casually held up a note that said, *Well done. Where is this leader? You brought them here?*

"Yup! Already interrogated," he answered boastfully, wiping the back of his elongated claws on his leather armor and staring at them in satisfaction. "Wait until you get a load of this one. Those villages have been farming hatchlin—I mean, cubs—for decades, but when there was a change and slavers were looking for more slaves immediately, the villages began offloading adults too. The value of slaves shot up."

Leofwine paused patiently while I wrote down a question. I held up a note that inquired, *So are they all using them for blood farms? How is draining people sustainable? They are killing them either on accident or on purpose. Young shifters can't afford to lose any blood.*

The male sighed, crossed his legs lazily, and rested his cheek on his fist. He made a sweeping gesture with his other hand and said, "No, it's definitely not sustainable. Slave deaths are accidents, but there is a hurry to ship out a large amount soon. Seems like there will be an offer to provide blood to the bats, but it'll be poisoned with those plants you cats all seem allergic to."

Who? Why kill the bats? I asked on paper. *Have you shared this with them?*

"Seems like territory opened up in the north for the bat-shifters, completely out of the blue. Since it's north of the lions' original territory, I suspect they want to expand north. I get why; it's a very pretty slice of land, just overflowing with natural resources.

"Since the bat-shifters asked us for help," he continued, "we have no issues with defending their territory. We will build positive relationships where we can, especially if that means hunting down trash. It is amusing to note, however, that Luzia tried one of the plants and suffered no ill effects. At most, they might get an upset stomach from the 'poison,' but she sent some back with Ferrer."

Luzia's here? I asked.

"Yep."

Where did you lock up the slaver?

His face fell. "Oh… was I not supposed to feed Luzia?"

What! Convict blurted.

I rubbed my fingers over my tired eyes and heard a scream come from outside somewhere. Leofwine winced and stared guiltily at his hands. "Whoops," he mumbled. "I don't think he knew anything else anyway."

I sighed and took it as a blessing. It was, ultimately, one less thing off my shoulders, and the dragon-shifter had acquired some critical information. A low growl boiled in my chest as I realized that Niusha had been expected to breed her entire life… and she'd only ended up in a new place with the same expectation. Cubs… more cubs without a care for the mothers who'd birthed them.

"And just to end things on a positive note, when I brought up your lioness's name at one of the villages, I was accosted by a small army of cubs wanting to know where she was and how she and someone else were faring. They didn't have a name to give me, but I was asked to find someone called Volcano-Rooster-Ginger Muscles-Mountain-Cloak."

I couldn't hold back the twitch at the corner of my lip that threatened to turn into a nostalgic smile. Niusha's orphans must be doing well. It was good to hear news of them.

"Several of them begged to come with me, but I had my claws full." He chuckled, flashing his brilliant fangs. Then he stood and shoved his hands into his pockets. "I will get out of your hair now, Ginger Muscles. There is much work to be done and reports to be made. I'll be back in a bit." I nodded, and he strode out purposefully.

Glad the cubs are well, Convict murmured, still absorbing all the information.

"You always did seem to collect nicknames," Quennel said with a small smile. "We've got Uproar, The Last Word, The Final Say, The Great Convictor—all given to you by the people and rebels you've inspired." I snorted dismissively at that, irritated that he seemed pleased by my forced return. "Now we have Volcano, Rooster, Ginger Muscles, Mountain, and Cloak. That's nine so far? I must say that cubs are so much more creative than adults…"

I wrote one large message and held it up for him to read. *What do you want?*

He deflated a little and plopped back against the leather chair. After turning his head and scratching his greying mutton chops, he said, "I heard Niusha left. I'm sorry that she made that decision."

So sorry that you'd want it to happen again if it meant me returning to the Proudless? I inquired angrily.

"No, Javed," he said with wide eyes, slowly shaking his head. "You know I wouldn't wish such a thing." He pointed to my neck and noted, "You marked her, didn't you? You think I don't know what it's like to lose a mate to the lions? To lose a daughter?"

A drip of shame trickled past my anger and numbness, and I leaned back in my chair as well, feeling more drained by the minute. *We may be able to recover your mate, Quennel, but I'm not sure I'll be able to recover mine. Not if we fail again.*

"Aaron said you seemed more confident when you returned." Quennel tilted his head and took in my appearance. "Have you slept?"

I glanced down at my pen while I played with it and shook my head. I scribbled another note that said, *Can't bring myself to. Also trying to remember the layout of the cells and arena. At least one good thing might have come from that chapter.*

"Many good things came from it. Unfortunately, a lot of it came after your exiling. The people couldn't stay mad at you for long, and it wasn't everyone."

I sighed, unable to bring myself to care about that. The world was now in shades of grey without Niusha by my side. I stared out the window, noting that it was getting late in the afternoon. If I wanted to talk to her again, I'd have to leave soon.

It's not a matter of want; it's a matter of need, my tiger asserted. *I'm going crazy in here, Javed.*

Me too, I whispered. *But it's just as maddening to talk to her.*

But we found out she kept our cubs safe.

For now, I argued coldly.

Of course. Everything is for now! he snapped. *That's why we're going to finish what we started! We're going to crush the lions and save our mate!*

"I will leave you to your thoughts, Javed," Quennel said, getting up with a groan and stretching out his leg. "I'm sorry about Niusha, but we need to focus on what we set out to do. We owe it to the people who've shed blood for our cause."

I just stared at the older lion as he limped out, obviously tired despite the ride he'd gotten on the way over here. When he was gone, I departed the town once more. I knew we weren't supposed to link again until tomorrow night, but I was too tortured by the unknown. I needed to make sure that what I'd felt earlier wasn't real.

I wasn't even able to wait until midnight, and as soon as I arrived, I mind-linked her. I knew I'd woken her up as soon as she groggily replied. *Javed? You're back.* I felt her surprise, but anxiety slowly crept in across our bond. I hadn't been kind last time, and she likely thought I would continue with that behavior.

I got a bad feeling earlier today. I came to inquire about it. The words came out cold and formal, much more distant than I'd intended, and I sighed in frustration.

I... was slightly injured earlier, but I'm fine. Field is helping. Maybe that's what you felt. I don't know how, though. Aren't you far away?

Doesn't seem to matter, I replied shortly. She became more uneasy with me, and she had a right to be. *What happened?*

I felt her hesitation, and her fear spiked. She didn't want to tell me, which agitated me all the more. *The scarmaster cut my parents' family symbols into my forehead. Apparently, it's a rite of passage. I didn't want it, but I knew there'd be risks coming here.*

Crimson bled into the edges of my vision, and had I been within the castle walls, I would have slaughtered every lion in sight.

He touched her, Convict seethed privately to me, his rage mirroring the one boiling in my veins.

That creature cut our Niusha, I replied to him, feeding off his ire.

When we see him again, I'm going to bite his hands off, then you can kill him!

Done, but I'm considering letting him bleed to death.

I felt Niusha's fear spike further, and I tried to get some semblance of control over my emotions. It wasn't like I could do anything right now, and I didn't want to make her afraid of me, though I was pretty certain I'd already done that.

Niusha spoke again. *I found a location to escape from, but I need to find the right tools to manage it. I haven't searched the supplies yet, but mayb—*

You're changing the subject, I accused. *Was he older with long brown hair?*

Yes, she said shortly, clearly wanting to move on from the scarmaster. I focused on the bond, trying to get a clearer picture of her. She was in a little pain. She probably didn't want to think about it. Maybe if I rushed and tried to get her out sooner, he wouldn't be able to cut it enough times for it to scar.

I also found documentation that I could actually read, she informed me. *I need to get a better look.*

What do you mean you could read it? I asked, surprised. She wasn't talking about that rubbish her survival guide was written in, was she?

It was in the written language I learned from the village, she answered.

That's strange, I said thoughtfully. *That language is unlike anything used in our territories.* We were both quiet for a minute, then I remembered everything Leofwine had said. *Niusha, the dragons are liberating your villagers, and they're transferring anyone connected to trafficking to receive punishment for their crimes in another village.*

Really? She gasped in excitement. I held back a groan, deeply missing Niusha's passion as a source of joy in my life.

Yes, and the dragon said the orphans were asking about you. They seem to be well. They even wanted to come with him.

Oh! It's so good to hear that! She sighed in delight. *Oh, I miss them so.*

Then you better get out of there so you can see them, I said, unable to hold back a small smile, but then I noticed that Niusha was slowing becoming aroused.

Before I could ask about it, she said, *I want to get out of here so I can see you, Javed.*

Niusha, I asked, feeling uneasy. Was someone with her? *Why are you aroused?*

You wouldn't believe me if I told you, she said flatly. When I felt a flare of alarm, she quickly changed her wording and explained. *The harem I'm in has no privacy—except for curtains around the beds, and there's a million females in here. I'd like to see you handle being around sex noises when males come in randomly to breed with their assigned lionesses! There's only so much I can listen to without thinking of you. And no, I'm still safely unassigned.*

You should be assigned to me, I replied gruffly.

Well, it'd be great if you were here right now to help with that.

I don't need to be there to help with that, I said, mentally prowling around a notion.

What do you mean?

I hesitated for a moment. What was my idiot brain doing? Why was I torturing myself like this when I could still lose her?

I think you need sleep, furless. We need to get our fire back. Go on, just fucking enjoy talking to her. Maybe it'll help us sleep later. We can't save her if we're mad from lack of sleep, Convict grunted assertively. He seemed particularly stubborn about this, especially now that we had more information and more help.

I sighed and sat down against a tree, listening to the crickets chirp their own mating calls. *What are you wearing, Niusha?* I asked, unbuckling my pants to relieve the pressure that was slowly growing.

What am I wearing? Uh... I'm in a nightgown. It's actually pretty nice.

Mmm, I hummed, trying to picture her. *What color is it? How long? Are you wearing underwear?*

It's red, and I'd say it goes down to mid thigh? And yes, I am wearing underwear. Why are you asking all of this? She inquired so innocently that it turned me on like crazy.

I'm asking because I'm going to masturbate while I think about you and talk dirty to you, and I want you to do the same, I growled, rubbing anxiously at the bulge in my pants while I waited for her to join me.

I... masturbate?

Touch yourself the way I touch you. I'll guide you through it, I said as patiently as I could.

Oh... ok. I'm not alone, though. There's only a curtain here.

Then I guess you better be quiet. I grinned and felt my canines elongate. A tiny thrill came from her, and I opened my pants, groaning as my erection sprang free. *I'm already so hard for you. It practically tore through my pants trying to get out.*

Oh... that sounds... dangerous for your pants, she replied falteringly, and I nearly laughed through the bond. She was already terrible at this, my precious Niusha, the source of my madness.

Look down at yourself, my beautiful queen, I said while I idly stroked a finger up my hardening dick, teasing it and Niusha simultaneously. *Can you see your nipples through your gown? Can you see the peaks press against the fabric?*

Yes...

Touch one. Just brush your finger across the tip, like you're stroking it with a feather. Is it hard? I was satisfied to feel arousal spark in her, and I growled quietly, pleased that we could both enjoy this after all.

Yes, she breathed again. *It is.*

Now I want you to slide your palms down your delicious body and peel up the bottom of your nightgown, but do it slowly, like you're stalking prey.

Peeling... she said quietly and waited for my next instruction. I could almost hear her breathlessness.

You're such a good lioness, I purred to her and rubbed the head of my engorged crown, spreading the precum that'd risen from my excitement. *What do your panties look like? Are they wet with desire for me?* I already knew the answer to the second question.

They're white, but there's a bit of lace at the top and bottom. They are definitely... quite wet. I miss you.

The last line was more loving than sexy, but somehow it made me harder. I grunted through a pleasurable throb and wrapped my hand around my member. *I miss you too.*

What now? she inquired.

I want you to think about my cock—about how swollen and pulsing it is for you right now. I want you to think about it while you slowly slide your underwear down to your ankles and kick them off. Think about how much you want me and about how impatient you are to unclothe yourself.

Oh gods, she murmured. *I'm doing that now...*

Good. Just picture me there, pumping away at my erection while I wait for you, eager to lay eyes on your spread pussy.

What now? My legs are spread... did you want that?

Oh lioness, I want that more than anything, I groaned and spat in my palm to lubricate my dick. *I can't help but picture your perfect pussy nestled in those beautiful golden curls. I'd give anything to spread those wet folds with my fingers, but that just means you'll have to do it for me. But we're not there yet.*

We... We're not? she asked, her sexual frustration coming across loud and clear.

Oh no, we need to finish undressing you, I said, running my fist up my veined length and sighing in pleasure. My cock twitched when she whimpered. Oh Sky Gods, I even loved the noises she made over our mind-links. *Take your nightgown off,* I ordered firmly, changing the tone to stimulate her.

It's off, she murmured, still sounding so unsure about how she should be replying.

Excellent, I groaned. *I can practically see your lush breasts now. Gods, I'd die for just a taste of them. We can spend time here, or we can move on if you're uncomfortable.*

No, we can... spend time... here, she said after thinking about it. *This is... different.*

Good, because I'm salivating too much thinking about them. Touch your breasts for me. Are they warm? Are they soft? Are they covered in goose bumps from how I talk to you?

My mate forced herself through a moment of discomfort but eventually moaned over the link, clearly aroused now. *Th-they're all of those things. They feel heavy and full.*

I bet they do. Someday they'll be full of milk because of how many times you've milked my dick, I replied. *I'm still pumping my cock. You can milk my dick even from far away.*

Oh gods, I did milk you. I couldn't resist. You're too attractive. I never had a chance!

Pinch your nipples for me. Pinch and pull and push them for me. Play with what I can't, I ordered.

Ah! was her only reply, and I rubbed another rivulet of precum around my pulsing length, which now felt more like steel than flesh. *I wish you could see how rock hard I am for you this very moment. I want to drag my dick around your breasts and spread this precum that keeps weeping out. My cock is crying for your hot, sweaty flesh. It wants you to reek of your mate, your tiger.*

I want that, she lamented. *I want to be covered in you again to make all these males know I'm yours.*

Her referencing the other males nearly had me snarling out loud, and I needed to be just as quiet as her. *When you get back, Niusha, I'm going to keep you locked up, wrapped around me, and covered in my cum for weeks!* I hissed, making my warning clear. The flood of excitement that came across the bond told me she didn't hate that idea at all.

Wh-wh-what now? she asked through her ignited willingness to play.

Lick your fingers and pinch your nipple again. I want you to squeeze and pretend those are my lips like I'm sucking on you. I'm picturing it myself, and I could easily come by the sheer thought of wrapping my lips around your swollen, rouged nipples.

Oh! she cried.

Pinch them faster. I'm a ravenous tiger, you know that, I growled as my hand traveled quicker along my now-massive shaft. I groaned, wishing I could spill right now, but I wanted to come with her. The hot, aching pressure was unbelievable, and I couldn't wait to climax—to release my load while I pretended to ejaculate on my hot mate.

M-m-maybe someday... we... we... could do this for real. She gasped, stuttering all over herself in her pleasure. I was thrilled by her admission. From the massive throb of my dick trying to let go, I'd say I was a little too thrilled.

Only when you're ready, my queen, I grunted. *Gods, I want to explode so bad. I need you to touch yourself, lioness. Drag your other hand down between your legs. Find your pussy, then bring your finger back until you find a swollen little nub.*

My c-clit? she asked.

Your clit, beautiful, I verified and gripped my cock hard, willing it not to release yet. It felt too fucking good, though. It was colossal, like only Niusha could make it, and dripping an obscene amount of precum. *I'd give anything to be balls-deep in you right now. Did you find it?*

Yes! Ah...

Do you remember how I touch you? Do you remember how I rub around in circles, or move up and down to make you climax? I want you to do that. Touch yourself and think of me.

I... It feels good, but not as good as you doing it, she said in a voice tight with pleasure.

And it never will, I snarled, *but I'm there with you, in your mind, over our bond. We mated, you and me. I marked you. I'm just as much in that room as you are.*

Y-yes... Yes, you are! Ah... I'm picturing how you grind against me—all thick and veiny. She moaned, now completely engaged in our play.

I am both of those right now. My dick is still drooling for you. It's making a fucking mess.

Oh gods!

Follow the pleasure, my lioness. Chase it like the huntress you are! Claim it like you claimed me for your very own. I grunted, pumping cautiously at my erection now. Every stroke threatened to set it off as my sack drew in tight. *Fuck, Niusha! When you come, I'm going to fucking cover you with my load. Shit!*

Oh gods! Oh gods!

She couldn't even communicate through her efforts, and I was drowning under the hot, vulgar, and lustful energy I was getting from her over our bond. *Think of how many times I've fucked you. Remember how I force my fucking giant dick into you until I can barely pull it out!*

Oh gods! Oh gods! Oh gods!

That's it. I'm right there with you, fisting my cock while I think about fucking you. While I think ab—

Ah—! A giant flood of pleasure rolled across our bond, and I couldn't contain myself if I'd wanted to because my mate had found her release. I hissed through my teeth as I came, angling my dick away to release ropes of cum.

Fuck! I cried through my orgasm, and I was sure that Niusha was feeling my pleasure as well. For just a moment, it felt like we were together for the first time in days, and that was the peak of euphoria for me. All I wanted was to be with her, and tonight I'd gotten a small slice of that. Perhaps it would be enough to keep me going.

Oh Sky Gods, I murmured up at the stars as I caught my breath. *Please give me the strength to get through this. Please let me not be too late to save h—*

Uh-oh, she mumbled, startling me from my prayer.

What? I asked in alarm.

Her tone was mildly sheepish. *I might have woken the whole harem.*

Chapter 31

Niusha

Javed, I have to go! I scrambled to throw on my nightgown and underwear because I heard Oudine climbing out of her bed.

I'll meet with you tomorrow, he said in a low voice. I restrained a giggle at his attempt to return to his stern demeanor, and I could almost hear him clearing his throat. I knew he wanted to stay distraught and distance himself, but he continued to slip with his control like he had from the very beginning. Maybe he could forgive me after I left this place for good.

When he disappeared, I felt the same sense of loss I always did. I rubbed my chest at the ache and focused on my next immediate problem—waking the entire harem with my quiet, moaning roar.

I'm embarrassed, but at the same time, it was so good that I almost don't care, Field said, cackling. *If only Convict had a way with words.*

Give him more than a minute's chance next time, I returned with a smile.

What, and give him a minute to make a poem about penises and barbs? 'Oh, Field, your pussy is a rose to my penis's thorns.'

"Ni—Alodie?" Oudine said from outside my curtains. I didn't think I'd ever get used to being called that. "Are you ok? Did you have a nightmare?"

Field started laughing, and I needed her to stop. It was wrecking my composure!

"That was no nightmare noise," another lioness remarked sleepily.

I opened the curtains and balked to see every lioness in the room staring at me or peeking through their curtains at the scene—except for one bed. Someone was mating with Juliote, and I found it too distracting to come up with a lie.

"It reminds me of a louder version of what I've heard come from Juliote's bed sometimes," a dark-haired lioness murmured thoughtfully. The females crawled out of bed to gather near mine. For having been awoken, they were very chatty right now.

A lantern was lit, and I noticed Jameson regarding the females' activity. Did he ever sleep? He craned his neck to figure out what was going on, probably making sure we were ok. He scowled when his eyes fell on Juliote's curtained bed, and it seemed like he was checking the time. I'd never seen him that disgruntled before, but maybe we'd woken him up too. Did he sleep at his desk?

He jumped out of his seat and stalked toward her shaking bed. He rapped on the wall next to the curtains and barked, "Jachet! Hurry up. The lionesses are invoking room privacy. Finish or I'll rip your dick out of her myself!"

Oh shit! Field said. *For a short lion, he's a phenomenal guard.*

There was an annoyed snarl, and a male much larger than Jameson crawled out of Juliote's bed after about thirty seconds. "She was close," the lion grumbled irritably. Somehow, Jameson stared him down and pointed toward the door. Jachet made no complaint, likely because Jameson was the gatekeeper to the females. I wondered how such a small lion got such an important job.

The small ones don't get to breed, I think, Field said. *That's what my instincts tell me, so he's the least risky to place here... or something.*

The notion deeply irked me. *That's stupid, considering how they also kill each other over females. Poor Jameson has to watch it but can't have it. This place is cruel.*

Juliote's head finally poked out of the curtains, her hair a bird's nest. Her eyes lingered on Jameson's departure, and then her head swiveled to look at the chatting females. "Oh, why are we all gathered?" She crawled out in a wrinkled nightgown and settled by my bed.

"Something new happened," a female with bright blond tresses told her.

"What? Alodie's climax?" she asked, then looked up at me in surprise. "I didn't know you were put on the breeding list yet. Who did you get assigned to?"

"Wait, what do you mean her climax?" a lioness inquired with a frown. "Only males climax. Does she have both? I've heard that can happen."

My face flushed further. "I assure you I am without cock," I said hastily.

"You haven't had a climax? It's when you get an explosion of pleasure during sex," Juliote informed her, tilting her head in confusion. "The doctor told me not to share that information. Has anyone else here had one?"

Only one other female raised her hand. "Doctor told me to not share that too. I didn't know what it was…"

Juliote seemed at a loss for words. "Oh…"

"Um… you don't need to have sex to have one…" I said hesitantly and covered my face, unable to meet any eyes. "I was in here by myself…" Oh gods, this was embarrassing. I wished the Earth Gods could swallow me up and take me underground to hide forever. "I'm sorry I woke you," I mumbled through my hands.

"Wait, why would the doctor tell you not to share?" Oudine asked Juliote. She seemed incredibly upset about this, but Juliote shrugged and started nervously chewing on one of her nails.

"Because it takes pressure off the males and protects the king's 'masculinity,'" Jameson muttered very quietly from his desk, obviously venting to himself. He was leaning over paperwork again, likely thinking he might as well get something done while we were all up and chatting.

Many of the eyes that'd been fixed on me had now turned to Jameson. When Oudine cleared her throat, Jameson looked up and paled. "Did you… all hear… that?"

"Yes, and we won't tell if you explain yourself," Oudine commanded in her most superior lioness voice.

"Uh…" Jameson swallowed hard, looking like he'd fallen into a trap. "It's to c-control expectations. If others are better at pleasing females than the king, who usually doesn't care about pleasing, then it would make him look weak. Every male is ordered to breed and get out. You can't miss what you don't know about… It'd make the king look like a joke if females left his chamber feeling unsatisfied and started craving a different male. This is just one of the… general rules that breeding males have always followed…"

The room became full of hissing, seething lionesses, and Jameson looked like he'd rather be in the dungeon than here in this room.

"One of?" a lioness snarled, leaning toward Jameson from her seat. I could see her claws extending, and I couldn't be sure if she was aware.

"Shouldn't have worded it like that," he mumbled under his breath. The hearing that Field had given me was incredible. I'd never have imagined I could hear someone whispering from across a room this big.

"Alodie said that there are no cullings outside our pride and that cats have one partner who are called mates. Explain,"

Oudine growled aggressively. The females gasped; some looked horrified, some angry, and some disbelieving.

"Oudine… I will get executed…" Jameson pleaded, his eyes wide with terror. His composure sloughed off like snakeskin.

"All. Of. My. Cubs. Have. Been. Executed!" Oudine raged through her teeth in near-blind fury, jumping threateningly to her feet. The rest of the lionesses bristled and followed her example.

I didn't know what to do. This situation was out of control. Lionesses threatened him to talk, pleaded for information, and some simply cried, already deriving it as truth from his hesitation.

Jameson scrubbed his hands over his face and raised his palm, asking for quiet. The lionesses settled, but the room remained full of swirling, scalding energy. Jameson stood, opened the harem door to check the hall, then closed and locked it.

"I will probably be killed tomorrow, but I suppose I do not live an ideal life anyway," he shared in resignation, then sat on his desk, facing us. The lantern traced sad, grim lines down his face. "The lions are the only cats left who cull. What you've been told for decades is a lie. It's not an unavoidable instinct. The king just doesn't want to raise the offspring of the king he conquered and killed."

More of the females began sobbing and wailing, while others converged on them, cooing and comforting to quiet the despairing mothers. Everyone needed to hear Jameson's words. I got off of my bed and walked toward his desk, intent on looking through the folders right now. If he thought he was going to die, he probably wouldn't care about what I'd find.

"You have the mating mark?" Jameson asked me wearily as I plopped myself down on the floor to go through the files under his lantern's light. I nodded and moved my hair, showing him and the harem Javed's teeth marks. He hunched farther, like a lifetime of exhaustion had finally caught up to him. "Alodie speaks the truth, but many lions are also unaware of this." Jameson continued to explain what fated and chosen mates were, detailing what they didn't know about the Moon Goddess. The lions and lionesses weren't allowed to claim a single mate; all females had to be shared to prevent males from going without a breeding partner.

"I don't understand one thing," Oudine said, shaking her head and placing her clawed hands on her hips. Her canines were prominent now as she spoke. "If we have fated mates, why don't we have that intense recognition?"

"It's something that has been hard to understand." Jameson sighed. "We think it's because our beasts naturally form male-dominated harems. To keep the peace, the pull will be harder to notice at first, but they say once a lion and lioness mark each other, it's just as potent as any bond."

"Wait a minute…" Juliote gaped and pointed an accusatory finger at Jameson. "Are you mine?"

Jameson snorted through his nose and turned his gaze down to his claws. "It doesn't matter, Juliote. I'm not allowed to breed, and I'm going to be executed. There's no way this information won't spread, and once they figure out who shared it, I will be killed."

"What?" Juliote shrieked, then she jumped to her feet and pointed at the lionesses. "If anyone exposes Jameson, you're dead! Do you hear me?" In her ire, she didn't see the edge of the rug and tripped, but I believed her threat still stood.

It fell quiet in the room, for a long time actually. Occasionally, a lioness would ask poor Jameson about the other cats or recognition. He appeared to answer them as best as he could, sounding more depressed by the question.

After another tense moment of silence, one female announced, "I am discontent with my life here." She looked around at the others, who appeared to be in agreement.

"Me too."

"I as well."

"My lioness has been roaring and won't shut up."

My plan had already completely fallen to ruin, so I just focused on finding the form I'd seen. When I finally discovered something I could read, I placed a hand over my mouth in shock. My gaze flew across the page as I tried to process the implications.

"Jameson, where are the forms for the cubs who've just been culled?" I asked, and he jumped off his desk to sort through the folders in the large bookshelf. He dropped one in front of me, and my fingers flew through the profiles. Each one had notes in the village's written language. My finger skimmed across the text. I didn't recognize every single word, but I knew enough to understand what'd happened.

"I don't know what those say, so I can't help you," Jameson commented dispassionately.

"That's fine. I can read them. My village taught me these letters," I replied, and in my peripheral vision, I saw his head jerk in surprise.

"What are they?"

Instead of answering him, I asked the shaken females, "Did you not see your cubs' bodies after the culling? You didn't witness it?"

"We don't watch the cullings," Oudine said flatly. "We usually are there for putting the bodies to rest, but they didn't let us last time. Said they were diseased, and we couldn't be there for removal." She frowned. "That was painful."

"Well, I'm reading that your cubs were not killed this time. They were kept for trafficking," I said, trying to keep my rage as suppressed as possible. It specified blood farming in these notes, but I needed to think, and this was overwhelming me.

The room fell dead quiet, and I didn't know what to do. I had more information for them, but it would completely destroy my lie.

Field, help, I begged. *What now?*

We don't know if lionesses truly run together. There could be someone in here who'd give us up. But at the same time, if we did tell them, we could get help finding out where the cubs were taken, which could be where everyone else is.

I'm torn... I said, and I ran the back of my hand over a sweaty brow.

I think supplying the truth is worth the risk. It will speed up our progress. Remember, the longer we're here, the more danger there will be for us and our own offspring.

I had to keep remembering that. There were more lives at risk than three… or four. If I died while freeing them, my unborn would go with honor. I tried not to think about it, though. It'd crush Javed, so I'd have to do my best to save everyone.

If there is anything I know about us, Niusha, it's that we put what feels right over the risks. Remember the newborn. Remember Chirasmi. We must put honorable actions over our pride.

Honor over pride… I echoed numbly, and I raised my eyes to regard the lionesses who'd soon hold my life in their claws.

I hadn't planned on ever revealing the truth about why I returned to the pride, and I tried to dislodge the mental block I'd placed in my throat. Field had helped me decide on what was more important, and if these lionesses could help me find the kidnapped and trafficked individuals, then it was worth the risk of exposure. The added bonus now would be their potential reunion with their cubs, who'd been long thought dead. I tried mind-linking Javed to tell him about this critical development, but he was gone. Well, we were supposed to talk tomorrow night anyway.

I grabbed Jameson's chair while the room sat in stunned silence and seated myself by the guard, who was still perched on his desk. All eyes moved to me. The hunters in these females could sense the change coming like a storm. I sat neither hunched over in fear nor tall in self-assurance while I mentally prepared myself to speak. I'd never addressed so many individuals in my life, and what I had to share was difficult.

I took a deep inhale and exhaled slowly to gather my frayed nerves. "I'm not completely certain about how I was taken from this pride. I assume that maybe I was the first to be trafficked out, but I suppose it no longer matters. If your cubs were kept for trafficking, then you need to understand what it's like out there and what I've learned because my journey started with saving cubs that were about to be sold.

"Before I could be culled, I was taken to a small mountain village that had once been a place of comfort..." I told them everything—about how I'd escaped with the orphans when I realized they were going to be sold, about meeting the tiger in the jungle who'd saved us more times than I could count, and about the horrifying stories I'd heard about my own people. I told them about those who'd disappeared and about who was responsible. I told them about the blood farms and the lions' plans to poison their own neighbors up north just to take their territory. I told them about why I was here—why I was truly here.

"I suppose, like Jameson, my life is in your claws now," I said, trying to sound calm, but my voice shook as much as my body. I was a quivering, dead leaf seconds away from snapping off the tree. "If you can help me find the missing ones, I have a feeling they're where your cubs have been taken."

Another leaf seemed to have snapped off the tree before me because a lioness stuttered, "H-how do we kn-know you're n-not just u-using us? Only y-you can r-read that. Y-you could be l-lying!"

I raised my hands helplessly and was about to say that I couldn't prove anything, but another lioness interjected, "You know she's not. She came here knowing there was no escape. Only desperate people do that."

"What are you talking about? Desperate people lie all the time."

"That's true, bu—"

"She doesn't seem like she's lying, though... she was supposed to be culled herself..."

"But our cubs! If she can help us find our cubs, isn't that worth the chance?"

"I don't know if I could survive it if that hope proves false..."

There was a good deal of arguing among the lionesses, but all the same, I smiled at Jameson. "I guess if you're executed tomorrow, you won't be alone." I sighed, then laughed bitterly. His wan face managed a quarter-hearted smile, and we turned our attention to Oudine, who stood and growled for silence.

"I think we're tired, and we need to rest on what we've learned," she snapped. "There is to be no sharing of this information until we continue this discussion. If I discover you've broken this rule, I'll kill you myself. I will not have anyone get between me and a chance to see if my cubs still live! If what she says is true, it could be we're overdue to do more than simply take the lions to task."

The lionesses murmured their assents and shuffled off to their individual beds, looking decades older than they had an hour ago. Juliote stood and made a beeline for Jameson, who shrank back, spooked by her focused approach. She patiently held out her hand until he finally slid off his desk, his face a mix of confusion and wariness.

"What is it, Juliote?" he asked tersely, but his shaking pinky finger belied his nervousness.

"If you're going to die tomorrow—which you won't, by the way—then I'd like to know what mating with a fated mate is like."

"Juliote, I have never… I'm not allowed to… I cannot…" he protested, bumping into the desk behind him and unable to finish a single sentence. She appeared to have broken him.

"I don't care if you're inexperienced! I don't care if you're not allowed to. You either want me or you don't," Juliote argued. Jameson was trying like mad to keep his composure, but she was whittling him down to a twig, and he looked close to snapping.

His nostrils flared, and he jerked his head at her sweaty nightgown. "You were just with Jachet."

"Then maybe you should bathe me?"

I took that as my cue to put the files away and get back to bed.

I smiled when I heard her nightgown fall to the floor, and the sound was immediately followed by Jameson's gasp. I closed my curtains and crawled into bed, accepting that I'd be falling asleep to the sounds of sex again. I thought it was for the best this time; too much had happened, and the uncomfortable noises made for a preferable distraction.

"We'll be quiet," Juliote's voice said to the harem, and there were only several grunts in reply. No one seemed to care. I wasn't certain how any two fated mates could possibly be quiet. Javed and I had to do a lot of muffling when we mated. The sound of people quietly bathing was actually relaxing, but when they'd adjourned to Juliote's bed, they were anything but quiet.

I was immediately educated on what happened when lionesses did not report to work first thing in the morning. The rapping on the harem doors startled like thunder, and they swung open loudly, accompanied by a booming, furious voice.

"Lionesses! Heed your king!" the male roared, and though it was nothing like Javed's roar, it still unsettled the lioness within me. I sat up and tried to rub my eyes, but my claw had snagged on the pillow, and I smacked myself in the face with it.

Ah! What's the king doing here? Field cried. *Get up!*

Doubly awoken by king and pillow, I scrambled out of bed to follow Oudine's lead, but she was taking her precious time leaving her sheets. The majority of the lionesses hissed in irritation after he'd roared, and they petulantly rolled over in bed to ignore him. Was this because of last night? Was this some kind of protest? Fear sparked in my belly, and the hairs on the back of my neck stood on end at their display. How would he react to that show of disrespect?

"What in the everlasting fuck…" the king mouthed with wide eyes at their snub of his authority. He marched to the closest bed, yanked the curtains open, and snapped at a guard, "Take her to the cells!" The female who'd been sleeping in was dragged out rather forcefully, and I gaped at their roughness. Field nudged at me, like she wanted to come out, but I pushed back.

Knock it off, I warned her.

The resolve in the harem crumbled with the fall of a single female. The lionesses immediately poured out of their beds to protest his decision, begging him to not make an example of her, but they were ignored as much as they'd previously ignored him. I crouched by my bed so I wouldn't draw attention, and Oudine settled next to me.

The king strode down the line of beds, coldly ordering his guards to collect two more females to bring back to the cells. The lionesses were on their knees now, pleading, and that seemed to have been enough to bandage his wounded pride. I felt an urge to sneer at his fragile insecurity, which was bizarre because sneering wasn't a facial expression I made very often. I jerked and turned my attention inward when I realized that Field was trying to snarl through me.

Stop that! You can't just control my body whenever you want! I raged at her.

He's a bad king! she seethed. *He does not deserve his power!*

You're too fast, and you're too powerful, Field. I need you to realize that before you get me in trouble! You need to hold yourself in check! I can't! Do you realize how much damage you could do?

"If you're done protesting," the king growled angrily, pacing before the prostrating lionesses, "you need to get to work! If this happens again, I will send ten more down next time!"

The lionesses dressed and fled the room to belatedly pursue their duties. When one guard took the three lionesses who were bound for the cells, I finally noticed the other two individuals who'd arrived with the king. One I was happy to see, but the presence of the other one filled me with loathing and dread.

"Alodie!" the king called harshly, scanning the room for me. His eyes fell on my crouched form, and he glowered. Oudine nudged me anxiously, and my brain finally woke up the rest of the way. Oh gods, that was my name! I wasted no time standing before him, Keid, and Scarmaster Godefroid. I pretended to be completely terrified so I could hide the half of me that was enraged. I knew why Godefroid was here, but what about Keid?

One of the king's guards grabbed a chair and gestured for me to sit. I looked morosely at the seat for a second, then eased myself onto it. There was no getting out of this one, was there?

"Scarmaster, you are to pursue your task as you see fit, and when you're done, I wish for the witch to look at and remove that mark on her shoulder," the king said, then promptly left without addressing me at all. I gasped and covered my mating mark with my hand.

No! Field screamed. *You come one step closer, and I—*

"You can't!" I cried before I could think. Was that what I should have said? My brain stopped working. How was I supposed to play this? "You can't do that!" The idea of anyone even touching my mark was so much more violating than Mehr's unwanted touch. I couldn't handle someone removing it.

"Hold this please," Godefroid mumbled, passing Keid's chain to a strangely refreshed-looking Jameson, who also appeared like he wanted nothing to do with managing the witch's shackles. Speaking of which, it was the first time I saw her wearing the cold irons. I didn't like the sight, and it was a brutal reminder of how she was a slave and not a doctor's assistant.

The guards held me down again, but I saved my strength. My mind whirled with questions as I considered the possibility of losing my mating mark. I'd lose the only means of talking to my mate! I'd lose my contact with the outside world! Would Javed and I be able to redo it if the witch removed it? If someone else marked me, could I find someone else to remove it? What would it do to my soul? What would removing it do to Javed's soul? Would he feel it? Would it hurt him?

I'd never know if I cried because my face was covered in watery blood again. The scarmaster redrew his lines of fire across my forehead like a zealot, intent on scribing his stamp into me. There was no point to it. It was pride. The scarmaster took his pride from living flesh. The king took his pride from making people beg.

No one shows their pride the right way here, Field said tonelessly. *This is all being done so wrong. So wrong.*

I had nothing to say to her. I was already trying to cope with the scarmaster's torture. I just kept my eyes shut and dreamed of Javed until the lion's task was completed, trying not to think about how I was running out of time.

Chapter 32

Niusha

I heard the harem doors swing open once more, and I could scent my mother even through the bloody water that was being wiped off my face. Oudine was tending to me now, drying my face before applying soapy water to bloodstained skin. My forehead was a smoldering mess of searing pain, but I used that pain to fuel my anger.

"My cub," my mother mourned, coming to my side to hold my hand in her warm ones. She squeezed them to show her support, and I groaned quietly. I was suffering and stressed, but it was good to have her here. I didn't know if it was actually true, but I felt like I needed her right now. Tears of relief sprang into my eyes, and she crooned with growl-purrs to calm me.

Mother's here. Field sighed with some degree of contentment.

"Don't let them remove my mark," I begged her quietly, and when I could finally open my eyes, I saw that hers were flared wide open in outrage.

"What is she saying?" my mother snapped at Godefroid, who tilted his chin up at her hostility.

"The king wishes it gone. The witch will remove it," the scarmaster said with an uncaring shrug. Keid froze in place, looking overwhelmingly uncomfortable. Her cheeks were pinched as she stared at the ground, reminding me of a prey animal trying to remain unnoticed. Her breathing was quiet but very shallow, and she looked almost as unhappy about her task as I was.

"Why? It doesn't do anything," my mother argued hotly. "Why torture her, aside from it being your favorite pastime?"

I gasped quietly at her insult, unable to believe my mother's gall.

Bad at protecting us, but otherwise, she's a good mother, Field noted approvingly.

"The king simply gets what he wishes, you know that. None can have more influence over his females," the scarmaster replied, gesturing Keid toward me.

"His females?" my mother hissed, appearing to not like how he'd just described the harem. The scarmaster ignored her and stared meaningfully at Keid.

The witch cautiously lifted my hair to study the mark on my shoulder. When she touched the sensitive bite mark, I growled at the violation. The guards the king had left behind for the scarmaster came forward to hold me while Keid placed her palm down on my mark.

Field began to scrape at me from the inside, wanting to get out and stop this, but I resisted her influence. *Field! You coming out will get us mauled within an inch of our life or put in the cells!* I screamed at her, desperate for my lioness to calm before she got us killed.

Keid placed her delicate, pale fingers on my face to turn my gaze to hers. She then leaned close and mouthed something to me. I drew my brows in, and she mouthed the words again.

What did she say? I asked Field, hoping she was paying attention through her rebellion of one.

I'm not sure. I heard some tiny pops in her mouth where consonants were, but I think she said, "Trust me."

How could I trust anyone else but Javed with my soul? I tried to wiggle out of the guards' hands, panicking despite Keid's attempts to placate me. This was my soul! This was my link to Javed! I couldn't risk it for anything.

Oh, now you want to get free? Field scolded.

You were out for blood! I just want to run! I cried.

"Please!" I begged, not sure who I was begging. It wasn't like anyone had the authority to overrule the king. My mother began protesting with me and tried to push the guards away, but another guard came forward to restrain her. Keid's eyes watered, but her lips were set in a grim line. She took a deep breath.

And then I felt it.

A pain I'd never known before assaulted me, combined with a sense of the outer world growing silent, agonizingly small, flooding me with panic. Inside, my nerves screamed louder than when I'd almost lost my foot and assailed my emotions more brutally than Javed's coldest moments. It swelled like a hazy, stinging fog that curled out from my marrow and worked its way to the surface of my skin. It bled into my eyes, whooshed achingly through my ears, and turned bitter as it mixed into my saliva. It was everywhere but my soul, and this time, I fell blissfully unconscious… or perhaps I'd fallen blissfully dead.

A wet object dragged over my face, and for a moment, I thought maybe Javed was licking me awake, but then my memories caught up to me. I bolted to a sitting position but ended up cracking skulls with Oudine. Our resulting cries of pain was an ugly duet.

"Owww!" she howled and rubbed at her red forehead.

Though also reeling from hot pain, I fumbled for an apology, frightened by the sight of blood on her skin. "I'm sorry! I'm sorry!" I cried as my mother pull me back down to lie on my bed.

"Ah, you opened your cuts," my mother said, grabbing the cloth from Oudine to quickly dab at the other woman's forehead before tending to mine. Oh, thank the Sky Gods I hadn't cracked Oudine's head hard enough to make her bleed. That was just from me.

Then, I remembered. I fell into sobs, recalling what'd been done to me and my connection to my fated mate. Oudine and my mother tried to calm me, but I couldn't stop. I felt different, and the change disturbed me well past what any comfort could fix. I'd been completely violated, and I didn't want to li—

"Shh," Oudine whispered, shaking my shoulder to get my attention. "She didn't remove it. She secretly muted it! You can't see it anymore, but your mate can reopen it."

I immediately stopped crying and looked up at my friend's urgent expression. Despite the red mark on her forehead, she appeared lucid. I glanced over at my mother to verify, and she nodded slowly but remained displeased overall.

"Keid did something very risky," she said shortly and picked at the sleeve of her dress. "She slipped a note into my hand when no one was looking. She risked losing her hand for you. I'm assuming the shifter that marked you is more important than you let on. But even so, this was the third time I've failed to protect you."

I stared up at her for a moment, barely registering her self-loathing while I thought about what I wanted to do. There were too many losses being taken in the route I'd originally planned, and this path wasn't sustainable. I was at a crossroads, and I had to reevaluate.

I made a decision, and I decided that it was time to become aggressive. The lionesses gave in too easily, and they needed more than just a firm hand.

This close call lit a fire under our tail. We need to put our last item first, Field asserted, approving my decision. *I will try not to be violent until it's time, but I've been pushed hard, Niusha.*

I know, I said.

"Oudine?" Roul's voice called after the harem doors opened and closed. "I had a bad feeling, so I came to… where are you?"

"Bring him in," I ordered Oudine. "We all need to talk. Is the room empty?"

"Just Jameson and several lionesses," she answered and waved Roul in from my curtains. The large male climbed in, looking a little surprised to see my mother as well. He reached hesitantly toward Oudine's bruising forehead but frowned and returned his hands to himself.

It was fortunate that our harem beds were large because we just barely managed to fit everyone on mine. I stared at Roul and hoped I wasn't about to make a bad judgment call. Whenever I didn't have enough information, I had to trust my instincts, and those instincts told me that Roul was a good, reliable lion. He rebelled in his own small ways and seemed to genuinely care about the lionesses and their cubs. I'd deal with the repercussions if he was false.

Roul was about to ask a question, but I started first in a whisper. "What will happen to the lionesses that were taken to the cells?"

My mother frowned, unwilling to discuss it, so Roul answered. "They stay until they finish their three-month penalty or win their way out in the lioness arena." He nodded as my eyes shot open. "It seems like you've heard of the arena?" He scratched at the salt-and-pepper hair at his temple, then swept the darker strands from his brows. "It's not like the lion arena battles. Battles aren't fought to the death, just to the victor. Whoever wins gets to return to their harem but not before the king humiliates them one last time." He shifted uncomfortably, and his lip raised in a silent snarl.

"What does he do?" I asked, thinking about the poor lionesses who'd just been taken down to the cells.

"He mounts her in front of the entire arena, then sends her back to her harem. It's meant to reinforce the lionesses' place in society." Roul looked as disgusted with it as the stewing females by my side. “I don’t think it’s an effective method of punishment, and it’s obscenely outdated.”

“Those females didn’t do nearly enough to warrant such a horrible thing,” I spat out angrily.

“No one can tell the king what to do,” he said, scrubbing his hands over his face in frustration.

“I’ve made my decision,” I said under my breath, feeling the moment shine in a shimmering, angry light. “The lionesses will gather, and we’re going to take over the castle. The arena is open to the public for the lions’ battles, correct? Is that the same for the females? How well is the king guarded at this event?”

They didn’t seem to hear my subsequent questions.

“What?”

“You can’t possibly be…”

I waved their disbelieving comments away and pointed at Roul. “Oudine, did you update him?” I asked, staring pointedly at her. She grimaced and nodded guiltily. “Did you update my mother while I was unconscious?” She nodded again.

“I’m not ashamed of being a hypocrite…”

“That’s good. It saves time,” I said. “You may think I’m insane for thinking about this, but I think you’re all unbelievable for having put up with this for so long. I don’t know how you can stand a minute more knowing that your cubs are out there having their blood drained! The king did this to your cubs! Your cubs! He needs to go, and we need to change things… fast. Once he’s out of the way, we can dig through the castle to find the information we need.”

“I agree. I want my cubs back if they live. I will do anything if we have enough lionesses,” Oudine said, but my mother hesitated.

“I will see what support I can get from the other harems… but if this gets out, Alodie…”

“That’s why we need to be fast. I especially do not want those lionesses to be forced into such a disgusting punishment!” I insisted fiercely, Field’s face just behind mine in support, bolstering my aggressive assertion. “Now, answer my questions.

How many guard the king at this event, and when is the next lioness fight in the arena?"

Roul shook his head and took a deep breath, then glanced surreptitiously at Oudine before caving at her determined—but quivering—jaw. It seemed like he was willing to do almost anything to please her. "Yes, the event is public. It's meant to show off the king's power and great magnanimousness, even over his own people—not that it was ever questioned." He scoffed, then sent me a look of warning. "Security is doubled for public events, and the balcony from where he watches is surrounded by lions. It used to be three times that when we were dealing with a kingdom-wide rebellion. For your last question, if there are at least four lionesses in the cells, the arena happens once a week. The next one is tomorrow. That's too soon, Alodie." Roul tapped his claws anxiously on his legs.

"No, Roul, that's perfect." I closed my eyes, drumming my own fingers on my knees while I adjusted my strategy. "It gives the lionesses no time to second-guess. So he's guarded heavily. Lionesses are invited to watch?" I asked, and Roul grumbled an affirmative. "Is the winning lioness bound?"

"No, it would defeat the purpose of having 'tamed' her. There are guards at the arena doors, but the king and the lioness are given room for her humiliation and his 'blessing' of forgiveness. She just kneels and waits for it to be over with." Roul's voice was getting thick with revulsion. It was obviously something no one liked discussing.

"Would you say this is when he's at his most vulnerable at any time or day of the week? I assume he's always guarded at the castle," I asked.

"I suppose… yes."

"Here is my proposal," I said, formulating the last of my plan as my brain skimmed every nightmare I'd ever had of escaping my village. The only way through when there were too many eyes was to play along with the village. I had to get into that arena.

"Killing a king throws the pride into some degree of disarray?" I asked my last question before continuing.

"To some extent. Usually, the killing is anticipated because there is a formal challenge. If someone manages to kill the king outside of a challenge, it does cause hesitance and uncertainty. It can be chaotic at its worst, especially if there were not a lot of witnesses," Roul answered, brows deeply furrowed. He did not seem to like where my plan was headed.

"What I will do is nonnegotiable, and I cannot be swayed," I stated coldly, staring at both Oudine and my mother so they could see how serious I was. "You will gather the lionesses to watch the arena fight tomorrow. When I signal, the lionesses will take control of the pride by force of numbers. Roul will be established as an interim king to temporarily quell the lions, but you will answer to Oudine. Is that understood? Know that too much immediate change will result in a responding revolt." I directed the last of my statement to a shocked Roul. If he was who I thought he was to Oudine, he wouldn't be very hard to control. Gods, I hated thinking like that, but it was necessary.

I could see it all clearly, even through the uncertainties. My mind felt formed for this, though, somehow. So many years planning and strategizing, preparing and expecting. I could be so wrong, but what if I was actually right?

"This is all… very, very sudden," Roul protested under his breath. "How can you be sure the lionesses will even show up?"

"Simply tell them what I discovered. If they don't show up, and I am killed, they will lose the only lioness who can read the second language in their cubs' files. If they want to find their cubs, like I want to find them, then they must show up. I'm sure the news of what else the lions have been keeping from them will also ignite their desire for change. They must realize that they outnumber the males, and if the chaos I start tomorrow shocks the pride, then they will have an even greater upper hand."

"You are reckless, my cub," my mother murmured with reproach.

"But why do I have to be?" I retorted furiously and punched the mattress, crashing down on her like a jungle storm. "I have to be to prevent a lioness from getting raped! I have to be to shock you all out of your constant state of surrender and stupor! I have to be to save the next cub who's being drained this very second! There is no time left to not be reckless!" I snarled my last question, and Field added her voice to mine. "Now, you tell me. Do lionesses run together, or do they hunt together?"

She stared at me with wet eyes, but then she lifted her chin like the proud beast I knew lived within her. "They say we used to hunt together."

"Then we shall hunt for our pride once more."

Aaron

Before the sun had reached its peak, the soul-shattering roar of our leader rattled our town into a state of panic. It wasn't the call to arms or a shout for assistance; it was something much darker from its tone. It wasn't for us, though. The roar was so thick and heavy that even breathing became a slog.

I staggered away from the market booth I'd been perusing and leaned against a tent pole, clutching at my thrumming heart. I'd never been so affected by his roar from such a distance, and I glanced around in awe as the other townsfolk fell to their knees.

Something was wrong. Grateful for my low center of gravity, I leaned toward the chieftain's residence where Javed was staying and stumbled into a run. Quennel better be there. He was staying in the room adjacent to Javed's, and hopefully, he was already dealing with the issue.

I winced at the sound of glass breaking as I approached the chieftain's home, hoping I wouldn't walk in on bloodshed. I already had enough to deal with, and sorting out something else would topple my precarious pile of tasks.

I rushed in through the front entry and up the stairs to find Javed's door in a state of planks and splinters. Our beloved leader was crouched on the ground, thrashing against—or at—Quennel. Though his human voice was mute, his contorted facial expression told me that he was screaming at the top of his lungs. The older lion grappled with him, like he was trying to keep Javed from injuring himself, but Quennel wasn't nearly strong enough to subdue the tiger.

"Aaron! Get the sky-stealin' shit over here!" he called with wild eyes. I pounced onto Javed's shoulder to wrestle his hand away from his bloody skull, where he'd sunk his claws. The tears running down his face shocked me, and I feared discovering what'd driven him into such a state.

"What happened?" I shouted at Quennel, wishing for the hundredth time that our leader could speak.

"You know as much as me! Great monkey-toting shit balls!" The older lion grunted when Javed swung him off to rend his own desk into nothing but antique mahogany shards… with one hand. "I was trimming my blasted beard in the other room when his roar knocked me over! Nearly took a bleedin' eye out!"

I grimaced and held on as tight as I could, but between an aging lion and a snow leopard of average height, we were no match for Javed, not to mention the colossal force coming from Convict. I had a feeling I knew what was going on now, and I believed Quennel did too, but no one was able to speak it. There was only one thing that could drive a shifter this mad—to destroy their environment, their body—and none of us had a chance of controlling him right now.

"I need to knock him out," I warned as Javed tried to buck me off him, "before he roars again!" Quennel yelled his assent, so I raised my fist, hoped for the best, and delivered a hard blow to his jaw to snap his head to the side. Our leader dropped like a carcass, and I froze, listening for a heartbeat.

"Not dead." Quennel puffed and hopped up onto a foot. His fake one had found its way across the room, so I fetched it for him. We both collapsed on the leather couch, exhausted and shaken.

"What now?" I asked, staring at the tiger's blood-and-tear-spattered visage. Our leader wasn't who he was before, and I'd been thrown by his severe mood upon his return.

"You have a day to get the Proudless ready, Aaron," Quennel said breathlessly and looked up to find the doorway filled with other cats.

Their arrival interrupted my reply, and we moved so they could drag Javed's massive body onto the couch where he could rest off my knockout. The chieftain, his mate, and a number of Proudless ran off to get water, medicine, and other items. Fortunately, the chieftain was more concerned about our leader than furious at the state of the room. This wasn't necessarily why our great tiger-shifter was nicknamed Uproar, but it suited the moment just fine.

I didn't have to try too hard to remember the last thing Quennel had said. "A day?" I asked worriedly, rubbing my sweat-slicked hands against my trousers.

"He's going to their territory tomorrow whether we like it or not." He adjusted his false leg with a pained groan. "It's now or never. If he gets caught again, they'll suffer no qualms about executing him this time. Gather them all, Aaron—every single last one. It's either we give him all we've got, or we lose him forever when he goes alone. You're looking at a male hanging by his last thread of sanity, and none of us are strong enough to restrain him—physically or emotionally."

"There is never a way out," I murmured, thinking back to those who've suffered losses during our long, painful war against the lions. Feeling a mate's death, its severance… I'd never experienced it, but I'd seen others lose such bonds.

"There is one way, you know that, and we'll have to do everything we can to keep him from killing himself once he gets his revenge for his murdered mate. Tell everyone we're leaving tomorrow. Perhaps we'll get lucky with the opening of the arena," Quennel said, and his voice thickened with a sob when I turned to leave. "She seemed like a good female."

I ran off to find Mas'ud and his team of cheetahs, still chilled from how Javed had acted like a rabid animal. If watching him showed me only a fraction of how excruciating the experience was, I could see why the Last Word would rely on the last resort.

I pressed the cold cloth to my forehead as I ran the timeline by Oudine over and over until she repeated it flawlessly. We slowly included more females to learn our plan as the hours passed, and Juliote said she'd work with Jameson to break down the parties that'd need to be subdued first. There was a very strict and limited list of those the lionesses were allowed to kill but only if the named lions interfered with the takeover. Everyone seemed to agree that the king's advisor would be a problem, so he was placed on the list as well. I'd seen death aplenty by Javed's side, so I didn't take it lightly, but I also wouldn't lose sleep over it. It was either Advisor Eudes or the many cubs who'd been stolen.

The room flooded more and more with angry lionesses, ones who'd arrived to memorize the coup details on their harem's behalf. My mother had organized all the information and evidence, and though most of the proof was unprovable, the possibility of their cubs being alive was enough to convince almost everyone to get involved. My mother was also a respected individual who'd managed to do some good for the lionesses while she'd been one of the past king's favorites—one of them being lowering the culling age by several years to give more cubs a chance at survival. The turnover rate of the king's throne had—unsurprisingly—been depleting the population since the lions had merged all the prides into one.

There was a knock at the harem door, and a guard walked in to deliver a message to Jameson, who'd turned his conversation with Juliote into a harmless one about her schedule keeping her up too late. The lionesses did their best to appear calm as they conversed, and when the lion left the room, the females relaxed significantly. Jameson waved me over with a frown and gave the letter to me.

"I can't read anything but that strange script, Jameson. What does it say?" I asked, passing it back to him.

"You're being summoned to the king's bed tonight, and you're required to get your health checked beforehand," he said flatly. "Do what you will with that information, but if you don't show, you'll be in a great deal of trouble, Alodie."

"Do I just walk to the doctor's office?" I asked, pointing to the harem door. I didn't want to go, but I had a plan for this. It was up to the Sky Gods whether it worked or not.

"I'll escort you when you're ready," he said, and I jogged off to the room with the toilet stalls. After I was done with my harrowing, agonizing procedure, I placed a cloth liner on my underwear and limped to the doctor's office with the harem guard at my side. It was fortunate he was well practiced with holding a neutral expression, convincing everyone that he was an unwilling guard being forced to escort an irritable, cramping female. Well, I supposed I was both angry and in pain; that much was true.

I found my way back into the examination room where the doctor came in with Keid, and I handed him the order from the king.

"Health check… We should just do a pelvic exam and pass or fail her for the evening," Doctor Gris said to Keid, who simply nodded and washed her hands. "Undergarment off, please."

I removed the undergarment and placed it on the table, making sure the bloody liner was visible. The doctor saw it immediately and asked, "Did you start bleeding, or have you been bleeding since taking the abortive?" he inquired, removing the liner and tossing it into the trash.

"I'm not sure…" I mumbled, face heating from the topic. I didn't need to act this time either. "I had some spotting after, but it just started cramping a couple hours ago."

"Surprised the king didn't scent it," the doctor muttered to himself, and I knew I couldn't hide my racing heart from the lion. That was the mild flaw in my plan, but I hoped I could be convincing enough to be excused. I just needed a little more time with my acquired team. "Do a minimal pelvic exam, but I'm going to excuse her for another three days. Just make sure everything looks ok, Keid."

She nodded, and the doctor exited the room, leaving me alone with the witch who'd muted my connection to my mate. I didn't know how I felt about it, but I supposed I should be grateful that she'd found a workaround. I was still angry with her, but at the same time, I felt pity. Sighing heavily, I reclined on the examination table so she could do what she needed to do. My mind spun, overwhelmed by stressful thoughts and swirling emotions, so I took long, slow breaths to calm myself.

"You are desperate, aren't you?" Keid said quietly as she rose to wash her hands. I studied her while I sat up, waiting for her next words. She turned and leaned against the sink, looking utterly defeated. Her periwinkle eyes were blotched red as if she hadn't slept last night. "No sign of endometrial tissue and recent lacerations on the inner vaginal wall. A clever trick. Excruciating, but quite clever. A bit hard to fool a witch, though."

I fought to keep calm as I stared back at her, understanding that her hands were tied as tightly here as they were in shackles. "Are you going to share that?"

She shook her head, her white ponytail swinging behind her. "It does nothing for me to do so. I do not enjoy causing injuries. I don't even know how to remove a mark and don't wish to. I am an unwilling participant in these events." Just like Jameson, she hid her emotions quite thoroughly.

"Why are you here?" I whispered, seeking the truth the day before all this came to a stop.

"They wanted a witch to assist with the females since the last specialist passed away. They have many of us behind bars, but they picked me because I am 'scary,'" she said, delivering it numbly, but a muscle in her cheek twitched ever so slightly, "not because I'm particularly skilled in this field."

"You're hardly scary," I argued. "You're probably the loveliest woman I've ever seen… though it's possible you're only the second human I've ever seen… now that I think about it. I thought I was a human woman until recently."

"No, I'm not... not lovely," she said falteringly, slanting her head to the side with closed, tight eyes like I was offering her a spoonful of something revolting. She did not know how to accept compliments. "You're not a man. You don't kn— We're getting off topic." Keid had grown mildly angry now, but at least I got a glimpse of her personality. I wondered how she'd react once she was finally freed.

"Where are the other witches being held?" I asked, realizing this could greatly help my search. "I met someone named—oh gosh, what was the name?" I thought fiercely to remember the woman who saved my foot. "Tsisana! She's looking for her sis—"

"She's still looking for me?" Keid gasped, eyes instantly flooding with tears.

Oh, Field sputtered. *This is Tsisana's sister.*

I didn't know how they could be related when they looked so different, but maybe they only shared one parent? I knew so little about people. I jumped off the table after putting my underwear back on, and I gave Keid a fierce hug. She stiffened against me, but then shakily rested her palms on my back.

"If the storm gets loud tomorrow, find shelter, then I'll come find you," I whispered, then rubbed her shoulder and left the doctor's office. Being a very intelligent woman, she'd understand my somewhat cryptic message. She was human, like all witches, and I was worried about her fragility. Apparently they didn't heal like shifters did, so I wanted her to stay hidden until the worst of the coup had passed.

Chapter 33

Javed

There were voices outside of the darkness, but I held my hand against their notes and pushed, looking for any purchase with which to prevent my return from slumber. I knew what waited for me outside of oblivion, and I didn't want it. I was fine here in the void, where emotions were as meaningless as the black abyss.

"Unlike the matter in our skies that block the starlight, the darkness in your eyes is but an illusion, fateful son," a female's voice said, cutting through my denial. "It is a glowing morning. The Sun God has risen and so have the lions."

My eyes snapped open, compelled by the reminder that I had people to kill. I was numb, but I knew that as soon as my memories returned, my mind would leave me. I didn't care.

I took this moment to regard the dark-haired female who sat in the leather chair by my couch. Her umbral eyes stared in a reserved manner, but her gaze was not cold. It was an impartial distance brought from too much wisdom. Those eyes had seen more than I could imagine.

Wolf, I thought to myself. *This is a wolf-shifter. Where is Quennel?*

"He's here," the female said and gestured to a corner where my second-in-command sat, picking nervously at his mutton chops. His remaining leg quivered with either anxiety or impatience.

Can she hear me? I thought to Convict but realized he was hibernating. Right, he had gone mad, frothing at the soul. I'd follow him shortly.

"We can hear you," she said. "We are the Sky Gods. This is our vessel. We've come to offer you a blessing."

I don't want anything from you, I said to the person before me. I didn't care if it was the Sky Gods Themselves; the only thing I wanted was revenge, then sweet oblivion. I stood up to leave, but the female's hand slapped down on my chest and shoved me back into the couch. It was done so casually that I felt like a weak cub again.

"Then you need not accept it. You are experiencing crippling symptoms, and I simply offer you sanity to see your task through," the female replied calmly. Her eyes were so unnaturally dispassionate that a chill swept down my spine. Something enormous was in there... something too vast to belong in any living body. Perhaps I was speaking to my creators after all.

Which is what? I inquired, fending off the madness to get my question answered.

"Finish what my catalyst started, Last Word," the gods bade.

Catalyst? I snarled my question, but my eyes watered with the realization. They were talking about Niusha, weren't They?

"Your mate, yes. You need to finish what she started. We have many preferred beginnings and endings and have designed you both accordingly. We desire success in this matter. You failed to humble our lions because invading their den was not yours to start, only yours to finish. That partnership is how you were both meant to work."

We were never meant to work. The Moon Goddess had made a mistake, I snarled, not necessarily meaning the words, but my heart was nothing but dust, and it didn't care. *She cruelly put us in an impossible situation!*

"We cannot speak freely. To do so would interfere too much with Fate's work, but we can say that Niusha's job was to provide you with a breath. You cannot roar without a breath."

I thought about everything Niusha had done. She had been reckless, yes, but she'd been decisive and proactive. She'd saved the cubs initially, but I'd ultimately needed to escort them all to safety. What had she done to the lions? Had she weakened them somehow? Was that why she'd been killed?

I'm already going, I said to the Sky Gods. *Nothing has changed anyway.*

"Be sure that you do," They said through the female. "You have a gods-given duty. Don't let her push go to waste, Last Word. We won't have any further threats to our bat-shifters. Make our children behave. You will be rewarded upon completion of your task."

You won't find me when it's over, I replied darkly and left the room with a silent Quennel at my heels. The gods did not attempt to stop me this time.

Unless They could bring my mate back from the skies where her spirit rested, I didn't want any reward. I desired the void. I'd gladly leave to join her in the stars. Perhaps we'd be fated again in a better era.

Hours after my return from the doctor's office, two guards arrived at the Jong Harem. One of them handed a note to Jameson, who read the contents with a grim expression. Seeing that I was already looking at him, he waved me over to talk, and I quickly said goodbye to Oudine and Juliote before joining Jameson at his desk. If this was what I thought it was, I wouldn't be returning to this room ever again. I just hoped it was what I thought it was.

"Alodie," Jameson said with a nod, then he gestured to the two guards who moved to flank me. "This is your escort to the cells where you will be held for a period of three months unless you win your freedom in the arena." He placed the note on his desk and reported, "This is punishment for multiple disturbances you've created, including disobedience toward the scarmaster, avoidance of your introduction to the pride, and finally, ignoring the king's summons."

"I did not ignore it. I was excused," I complained to Jameson. "The doctor excused me!" I was anything but upset about it, though. This meant I didn't need to create more trouble to get thrown where I wanted to be. As much as I'd tried to control my plans since arriving, my chaos was somehow working better for me in the long run.

"Unfortunately, the king did not believe the report," Jameson said curtly and nodded to the guards to remove me from the harem. "You are noncompliant and must be tamed."

Field could only laugh, filling my mind with deep cackling. Had the rules here always been so strict or was this simply how the new king chose to operate? There seemed to be little to no room for mistakes, and explanations went completely ignored.

I glanced up at the guards who prompted me to leave with them, but their eyes lingered on the rest of the harem. Perhaps they'd expected more of an outcry from the females because the males seemed unnerved by the quiet, searing heat of their glares. I gave the lionesses one last look and left without a word.

I then allowed myself to act how I felt, which was scared. I knew what I was going to do, but there were still factors that I hadn't been able to set in stone yet.

Don't doubt us, Field said, though she sounded nervous as well. *Our plan is as good as it's going to get at this point. I'm relying on you to get us where we need to be.*

I will, Field.

The guards marched me out of the castle toward another colossal structure that was—aside from the entirety of Edeletrots—larger than any town or village I'd seen. It had to be the outside of the arena, and I supposed that the cells were built into it. An urge to dig my heels into the dusty flagstone clawed at me, but I maintained my pace with the lions who hadn't tried to handle me thus far.

We passed two lions posted at the arched entrance to the arena and turned right into a side door. More worked or kept watch inside, but they were a lot more relaxed than the ones on duty. Stares landed on me as I was walked past, and voices muttered speculations about what I'd done wrong. I had to wonder how many of them approved of the lions' bloody expansion of their territory or if any of them felt guilty about lying to their female population. What had these males been told about the other cats? What had they seen with their own eyes?

That was the problem, really. The only person who was keeping track of all the lies was the king—perhaps his advisor too. It was hard to say who else. This entire kingdom needed their own cup of purity removed from the table. Whether the lionesses succeeded or not, tomorrow would slap the males with withdrawals, a brutal introduction to reality. That reality was the simple truth that no matter how hard one tried to maintain them, all lies expired.

If I failed to move the kingdom to the females' control, at least I'd have started something that someone else could eventually finish. There was no way that the lionesses would accept any culling after this, and perhaps they would free the trafficked people themselves while looking for their cubs.

The guards led me through another door that opened to a dark stone hall lined with cells. Doorways let in a little daylight, but the hall was otherwise lit by ensconced candles. Surprisingly, I passed cells enclosing lions, noticing that almost all of them seemed to be in some kind of soldier's uniform. There weren't a great many of them, but I'd make a note to see what they were in here for later. Perhaps there were some who were sympathetic to the other cats' plights and refused to follow orders… or perhaps that notion was simply a fantasy.

At the very end of the hall were five cells that held a lioness in each. I recognized the three who were taken from the Jong Harem, but there were two who looked like they'd been in here for quite a while. One had withdrawn, curled up in the back of her cell, but the other had a feral edge to her. She snarled at the guards when they put me into an adjacent cell, but they largely ignored her.

After they left, one of the lionesses whispered to me, "Alodie?"

I still wasn't used to that name, but I nodded and settled as close as possible to the others. Another woke and crawled groggily to grab the bars of her own cell.

"What are you doing here? Did they… find out?" a female whispered worriedly.

"No," I murmured, brushing a strand of hair from my face. "This was intentional, and I need to ask you all for a favor."

The three lionesses from the Jong Harem nodded, though one looked perplexed.

The aggressive lioness barked out a laugh. "What could we possibly have to offer? Never seen you before, by the way."

After a guard passed us, I whispered, "I need you to concede to me in the arena tomorrow. I'm working with a plan, and there's no point in hurting each other..." I hesitated, not sure how much I should share with these lionesses since we were in such a vulnerable and fragile position.

"Like scraps I will," the wild one sneered. "I want out!"

"You'll just end up in here again, Polemia," the other unfamiliar lioness murmured from her defeated position in the back of her cell.

"Shut it, Douceline!" Polemia hissed and lunged at her bars to startle her neighbor, who flinched and curled tighter.

Polemia will be a problem, Field murmured darkly to me. *I'm not sure I even trust her to keep our plan a secret. She might do anything to get out of here, including selling us out to the lions.*

I won't be sharing the plan then. I sighed. *If we have to fight her... Field, I'm worried. She's... tough-looking.* I stared at Polemia, who shook her bars one last time and jerked angrily from them. Her light brown hair had slightly matted, and her skin was dirtier than Douceline's, like she'd protested against using any bathing water they'd given her.

"Polemia," I said sternly to get her attention. "If I get out, you'll get out. Think about it." I pushed my fear aside and stared her down through the bars, but she just curled her lip up in another sneer.

"If we fight, you'll lose. You'll all lose. Think on that," she snarled back at me.

Field snorted. *We just have to defeat her then.*

Why didn't I ask Javed for those self-defense lessons instead of getting all jealous? I bemoaned.

She might just be a big talker. We knew this could happen.

I had hoped it wouldn't.

The night in the cell had been miserable, and I'd followed the lead of the other lionesses, choosing to shift into Field's form to stay warm. When dawn arrived and melted the chill in the air, I quickly changed back and threw my dress on before a guard could pass by and see me naked. A laugh came from Polemia's cell, and I glanced over to find scorn on her face. It struck me that I hadn't really expected to continue receiving judgmental looks after arriving at the pride. It seemed that no matter where I went there was always someone I could disappoint.

Polemia leaned toward me and said mockingly, "How can you expect to get out of the arena if you can't even stand someone seeing you naked? King's not gonna ride you fully clothed."

I was torn on a response. My claws extended without warning, and when I thought about snapping back at her, I realized that all my aggression was coming from Field. I frowned and turned inward to address her.

Are you going to be able to keep your head clear, Field? I asked, tension pulling every single one of my muscles.

I'm just getting ready to dominate her, she snapped. *Her attitude has no place in a pride.*

Don't forget why we're here, Field. She's not our true enemy. I didn't want to lose myself to instinct and hurt anyone. I'd felt bloodlust before, and it was unsettling. I stood and paced my cell, shaking my arms in an attempt to settle my nerves and loosen my body.

Don't get lost in denial again, Niusha! Her aggression toward me was unexpected, and she continued snarling out her message, enraged. *We absolutely have to focus on fighting. It's the only way we can get to our goal! You need to get riled up! Everything relies on this! We've never fought before! This is going to get sloppy and dangerous!*

"Hey! I'm talking to you!" Polemia yelled, interrupting my conversation with my lioness. I glanced up at her and raised my brows. I'd forgotten what she'd said already.

"I need you to concede, Polemia," I reminded, trying to maintain my calm, but she only made a big show of laughing and returned to strutting around her cell.

It's almost like she's high on acpoama, Field muttered. *How do you get through to someone like her?*

I don't know if she's the problem, I replied with a sigh. *This place is bad for the mind.* My eyes followed the wild lioness's restlessness until I finally allowed an unsettling warning to pop out of my mouth. "It's not too late to change your mind. The missing cubs are relying on you."

Polemia froze, and her gaze snapped to mine. I licked my lips and wrapped my arms around myself. If I couldn't trust her with my plans or talk sense into her, perhaps she could be rattled out of her blind rage.

"The who?" Douceline asked, but I didn't reply and neither did the three lionesses from the Jong Harem. I decided to ignore her and nodded reassuringly to the females who already knew me. Even if I hadn't asked them to concede, they didn't seem keen on fighting at all, and I smiled internally; the lions were not going to get a good show today.

Footsteps approached from down the hall, but it didn't sound like the usual guard on his rounds. I heard the sweeping of cloth escorted by two sets of clanking armor. Once I got his scent, I scowled. There was no way he was ever touching me again.

The Scarmaster Godefroid stopped in front of my cell, and he leaned close to the bars to get a look at my forehead. A growl burst from my chest, but as much as I hated how Field occasionally took control of my body, I didn't admonish her this time.

"It's healing too fast. Might as well do it beforehand so the king can see," Godefroid said with a frown and gestured for a guard to open my cell. In the blink of an eye, Field made me lunge at the bars and roar. Godefroid stumbled back into his escort, blanching at my outburst. He blinked several times, then waved the cell guard away with a hand and a nervous laugh.

"You're not touching me again!" I hissed at him, wanting to take that truth and shove it down his throat.

The scarmaster gave me a look of disdain, pressing his lips into a thin, displeased line. "I'd report this atrocious behavior, but you're already locked up. Don't make things worse for yourself, Alodie. The dungeon is another place I work."

Field and I immediately thought of Javed, and she flew into a murderous rage. She took over my body again, snarled, and reached for the scarmaster's throat. I could tell that Godefroid had spent his entire life down here because he knew just how far to stand from the cells. Field's claws—my claws—were merely an inch from his chest, but they might as well have been miles away.

"I seem to have upset your lioness quite a bit," Godefroid said, staring at me with curiosity. I tried to wrench back control of my body, but Field's rage brutally reinforced her grip.

"We know f-full w-well the 'work' you d-do here!" I spat, able to use my own mouth at least.

"I have no idea how… unless tales of my skill have made it past the wall. How intriguing," the scarmaster said with an antagonistic smirk. His eyes flickered between mine, searching for something. He took a sharp breath and said, "Perhaps you've heard of my work on the Proudless's old leader? I can't take all the credit. There were a number of other lions who wanted to write something. I mean, with all the space he had to offer, how could I ref—"

Field roared and lunged again, making me split my chin open on the bars. Tears blurred my vision, and I redoubled my efforts to suppress her. Her screaming within my mind distracted me so much that I could barely focus. I'd been pushed too far away from my own body.

Field! I shrieked at her. *Stop! You're hurting me! Don't let him do this to us!*

Her strength faltered when she tried to process what I'd said, and I finally wrested back control of my body. The scarmaster wore a fascinated expression, but the guards at his side fidgeted uncomfortably. Was it unusual for him to taunt females?

"You know of him, don't you? You must've if you were out there," the scarmaster accused with a grin. He rested his chin on the heel of a palm and wrapped the other arm around himself, posing like I was a creature to be studied. "Certainly, you must know he deserved it… killing those three innocent people."

I didn't allow anything to show on my face when he'd guessed. He was merely speculating—likely wanting me to ask about his greatest 'work' yet. Field was not making my display of apathy easy, though.

Field! Stop! I yelled at her when she pushed again. *Don't let him rattle us! We're not in the arena yet!*

"I don't want to hear your excuses for what you do, mutilator!" I snapped at the scarmaster, nearly cutting my tongue on my elongated canines. The bloodlust returned, and I suddenly craved sinking my teeth into his jugular.

No, no, no. I blinked hard and shook my head in an attempt to calm. I needed to save my energy, so I stumbled back and fell to my knees by the stone wall. No… it definitely wouldn't do to exhaust myself before my task was complete. I waved the scarmaster away, but unsurprisingly, he didn't leave.

"Someday, you'll witness the male arena battles. We just don't have enough captives right now to pit against each other," Godefroid said with a sick look of nostalgia on his face. "It's too bad we sent him into exile. They were originally going to execute him, but I didn't want all my art to go to waste… I spent such a long time on it."

I turned my head to the side, feeling an urge to vomit from those words. Sensing my weakness, Field wrestled for control, but I blocked her. She was out for blood now and absolutely incapable of rational thought.

Please! Don't exhaust us before the fight's begun! I begged her. *We'll come back for him! I'll let you kill him yourself! Please, Field!*

My offer somewhat appeased her, but I was reeling from the loss of control. My head spun, and I braced myself with a hand on the dirty floor to keep myself from collapsing. It was hard enough to listen to the scarmaster's words.

"—ver seen such fighting in my life. It's so incredibly satisfying to watch your artwork out there in the arena winning battles! He'd never take the life, though. No, no, no, he never would. Could you imagine the king's frustration? My frustration?"

I stared lifelessly at the dirt under my fingers, waiting for the scarmaster to talk himself out and leave. The other lionesses would occasionally growl, irritated by his presence and nonstop chatting. I regretted ever speaking to him. I didn't want to hear any of this.

"At first, I tried to torture him into behaving, but no matter how I cut his skin, he wouldn't kill his opponent. No, the king was quite unhappy about that. It didn't make him look good to open the arena and have no deaths. So did you hear what we had to do?" The scarmaster looked eagerly at me, but I jammed my fingers into my ears.

"At first, the king grabbed a random spectator from the stands. If he didn't kill his opponent, the king would kill the spectator. The tiger just froze like a stupid gib, so the king killed the spectator!"

I couldn't block his voice. I could still hear him despite my plugged ears.

"The next time we opened the arena, the king picked out a female tiger, but the tiger just wouldn't kill his opponent! It was madness! You should have seen how furious the crowd was! The tiger wouldn't kill his arena opponent to save the life of an innocent female. A female of his own kind! What a leader!" The scarmaster laughed, and I barely made out Polemia's screaming for him to shut up.

Tears started rolling down my cheeks, and I pressed my fingers harder into my ears. Why was he doing this? Why was he telling me this? Was he just trying to unsteady me—the troublemaker—before my arena debut or did he somehow know that Javed was my mate? He couldn't know!

"The final time, the king grabbed a cub an—" Godefroid said, but I desperately began humming to hide his muffled voice. I couldn't. I couldn't listen to this! Not only was this not his story to tell, but I didn't want to know what happened to that cub—not right now. I hummed and sobbed for ages to keep the horror at bay.

Poor Javed. My poor, poor Javed. With eyes shut tight, I cried and hummed louder and louder to make sure I wouldn't hear anything else from the scarmaster. I was already shaken, and I had to stay as sturdy as possible, so I rejected all sight and sound for as long as I could.

I wasn't sure if it was ten minutes or several hours later, but I was eventually startled out of my escape by a prodding finger. I blinked up at a guard, who gestured for me to stand and follow him out of the cell. He began unlocking the doors to the other females and said, “Attention lionesses, the arena is open, and the fights are to begin momentarily. Please wait for your names to be called.”

The prospect of going out in front of thousands to do this hit hard and fast. My stomach threatened to lose its contents once again, and I couldn’t stop the shaking that possessed my arms and legs. Not only was I already emotionally exhausted, but my lioness had retreated, and I desperately needed her.

“Starlight preserve us,” I whispered and kept an ear out for my birth name.

But… the thought of them using my birth name sparked a realization, and in that moment, clarity returned. I took in a deep breath and squared my shoulders. They would call for an Alodie, but they were going to get a Niusha.

They weren’t expecting a Niusha.

Chapter 34

Niusha

When the first two names were called, I slumped in relief. I adjusted my seating on the wooden bench by the arena doors as Douceline and Emelisse stood. Both of them shook with nerves, and Douceline was biting her lower lip particularly hard, making it turn white. To my alarm, the guards handed over short robes, making the two females strip to don them.

Seeing the shocked look on my face, the lioness next to me, Nadalinde, murmured, "If they ask us to shift, the robes make it easier." She'd turned green by the time the two lionesses finished preparing for their fight. The chatter of the crowd leaked through the doors, a thicker, heavier sound than I expected. I couldn't imagine what it would be like to finally step past that doorway, but I could only hope that not as many people had shown up for the lioness fights. If they weren't to the death, they couldn't be that exciting… right?

Emelisse poked Douceline gently, and I overheard her whisper, "I'll concede to you… I… I don't want to f-fight."

Douceline twisted her lips, and her brows drew inward. "Are you sure? I don't mind conceding either..." Emelisse nodded and shifted nervously as the doors opened for them. The guard explained the rules, which were to fight until the other was incapable of moving. I could only guess what that meant; maybe one could pin their opponent down, and that would count. The last thing I wanted to have to do was knock someone out or permanently injure them.

The two lionesses disappeared past the door, which closed once more. The audience cheers grew louder, but after a minute, complaining and booing filled the arena. Both lionesses returned through the door with red faces, and Emelisse was escorted back to her cell. I tried to catch her eye in an attempt to comfort her, but she wouldn't look at anyone.

Soon, Emelisse. You won't be in there much longer, I thought to her in a silent promise.

Douceline took her seat again and folded her trembling, clawed hands in her lap. She continued to bite at her lower lip but hadn't noticed she'd drawn blood. Worried I was doing the same, I licked my own lips to check. Nothing. Good. Admittedly, it would be a bit embarrassing to draw first blood on myself.

Nadalinde started in her seat when her name was called along with Polemia's. I reached to give her hand a squeeze before she stood, and she sent me grateful smile. Polemia sized her up, then shook her head in false pity. Nadalinde simply averted her eyes and stared down at the ground until the doors groaned open. I wondered if she'd only concede once they were inside because she wasn't saying anything to Polemia. I couldn't blame her considering the hostility that was radiating from the aggressive lioness.

Nadalinde released a sudden sob when the guard ushered them through to meet the crowd. Polemia followed her and flexed her fingers, like she was waking up her lioness. A moment later, the audience began cheering again, and I glanced over at Noémy in a silence inquiry. She sandwiched her lips between her teeth and shook her head.

"She chose to fight..." Noémy whispered through a worried frown, and we both stared at the door for what might have been fifteen minutes. The longer the fight went, the more worried I became for Nadalinde. Why had she chosen to fight? I told them all to concede so no one would get hurt!

I tried to get clues from the crowd's noises and grimaced every time it sounded like someone was injured. It had me growing unbearably jumpy, and I nearly fell out of my seat when Polemia stumbled through the door, breathing heavily and covered in scratches. A guard carried Nadalinde past us, who was cupping her knee with an agonized expression. Whimpering, she looked around, and when she found me, she mouthed, "I tired her out for you."

My eyes flooded and my lips parted in horror at Nadalinde's sacrifice. I hadn't wanted that! Polemia was my challenge only! Mixed in with the sadness and shock was anger. I stared with pinched cheeks at Polemia, who settled on the bench and dabbed at her cuts with a wet cloth. I couldn't blame her for fighting, but I was furious all the same. This entire show was pointless! It obviously didn't even work to curb behavior, and Polemia was the prime example of that... according to Douceline.

I waited for my name to be called along with Noémy's, but to my surprise, she was called out with Douceline. When they left for the arena, Polemia looked at me with a sour expression and said, "They're giving you an edge to win. King must really want time with you, but don't get cocky. You still have to face me."

"Do I really have to?" I asked plainly. "You really don't care about the cubs, do you?"

"What the scraps are you even talking about?" she yelled, then hissed at a guard who told her to be quiet. I shook my head in exasperation and kept my mouth shut when the guard gave me a look of warning. I supposed he really didn't want to deal with an agitated Polemia, and I held in a dry laugh. Now he knew how I felt.

In a repeat of her first fight, Douceline came in through the doors with Noémy, who apparently conceded. The crowd complained louder, voicing their grotesque craving for violence. I sighed and crossed my legs, leaning down to stare at the ground. I'd been told that conceding was allowed, but what if too many of us did it? Would the king interfere like he had with Javed's fights? Was this making the king look weak?

One thing at a time, I said to myself. I couldn't change anything now. I tried to nudge Field while we waited, but she was still silent. *Field,* I called, growing concerned. *I need you to come back. We might be next. Field!* Nothing happened. She remained quiet, and I suppressed a stressed whimper.

I held my breath, and when my name was finally called, I flinched embarrassingly. Douceline stood with me to prepare and undressed without discomfort, while I shuffled aside to strip and throw on the robe. Polemia laughed at my shyness, making a flash of irritation burn in my chest. Knowing it was a waste of energy, I tried to release my annoyance with a puff of breath. I had only one thing I needed to focus on, and it certainly wasn't letting Polemia drain me.

My heart was skittering like a rabbit's by the time the arena doors opened, and the view beyond the entrance had cold terror shooting through me like ice and thunder. A colossal wave of people surrounded the expanse of the fighting grounds. There were too many heads… too many eyes!

Too many... I gasped inwardly. *Field!* I called, trying not to let tears of fright and panic spring into my eyes. *Field, I need you!*

At her continued absence, I took an involuntary step backward as if that would prevent me from fainting, but Douceline reached over to steady me.

"I'll concede," she whispered, her body quivering as well. At this point, my nerves were almost completely shot, but it somewhat comforted me to know I wasn't the only one seconds away from peeing.

We walked to the middle of the fighting grounds, which wasn't a short trip by any means. The presence of the audience crushed us, and that alone was confusing and completely unexpected. Yes, I'd been nervous addressing the Jong Harem, but the number of people here made me feel like a giant python had coiled over and around my shoulders. The weight was almost unbearable, and my legs and ankles all but turned into limp saplings.

"—ho is a new member of the pride!" a lion announced to the crowd from his spot about fifty feet from us. I was certain he was talking about me, but I had little to no ability to concentrate on his words. My eyes scanned the open dirt grounds and found it matching what Roul had shared. There were two guards at the door I'd passed through and another two at the other end of the arena, guarding a second exit. Along the wall stood several more lions, but they were pretty far from me. I recognized one as Roul, who'd gotten himself assigned as promised. A sigh of relief escaped me. The plan had stayed alive during my absence.

When the horn sounded for the match to begin, Douceline fell to her knees and cried, "I concede!" The audience erupted into angry shouts, furious that—once again—they wouldn't get to witness a fight. The lion announcer looked over his shoulder at us and tried to quell the anger pouring from the stands. A commanding voice was shouting amongst the chaos, but it was a roar that interrupted everyone.

"There will be no more concessions for the remainder of the fights!" the advisor snapped from the balcony and briefly discussed something with the king before relaying the next proclamation. "The lionesses will fight or other means will be used to inspire violence!"

I stared up at the balcony where Advisor Eudes and King Leudbal watched. The two were surrounded by males who were likely other lions of import. Guards waited behind them as well, and I hoped that the lionesses would be able to handle everyone in order to get to Eudes. Hope was all I had. The only thing I had control over was doing my part.

When I turned back to Douceline, she climbed to her feet and came running at me with a growl. I blanched and stumbled back, startled by her charge. She grabbed my shoulder and wrist in an attempt to grapple me down to the ground, but I quickly realized she was just trying to communicate something.

"Punch my head! I'll make it look real!" she whimpered and shoved half-heartedly at me. I pushed her off, sick to my stomach. I didn't want to hurt her, but like with everything I'd gone through before, I reminded myself that people were relying on me.

I lunged at Douceline who ducked to avoid my punch, making me stumble from the force of my own swing. "Douceline!" I shouted at her in surprise and irritation. "What are yo—"

She ran backward from me, apologizing. "I'm sorry! I didn't want to get hit! I mean…"

"What do you want me t—"

"Try again! I promise I'll do it!"

I balled my hand into a fist, making a second attempt to punch her, but she winced and pulled back, making me miss again. Looking at the aghast expression on my face, she blanched, turned, and ran, yelling more apologies.

"Douceline! What?" I shouted and started running after her. Her whimpers tore at my heart, but the laughter and jeering from the audience had me growing furious. "This isn't a fucking joke!" I hissed at them as I ran, using a curse word that was more satisfying than anticipated.

I caught up to Douceline, grabbed her shoulder to turn her, then punched her left cheekbone, making her head whip to the side. She collapsed into a ball, and I dropped next to her in a panic, worried I'd actually knocked her unconscious.

"Douceline! Douceline!" I cried, shaking her shoulders. When she exhaled a whisper for me to stop, I slouched and sent a prayer of thanks to all the gods, not that they had any control over this... I didn't think.

I could barely make out the announcer's words as the guards moved around me to pick up the defeated lioness, but I imagined he was probably calling out Polemia—the only one left to fight. It turned out he had. I nursed my right hand as I approached her; I hadn't expected the punch to hurt as much as it had.

Field, I called out to my lioness when Polemia and I finally stood face-to-face. *Field! Come back to me! It's time to fight Polemia!* There was a moment of recognition, but Field remained tucked away in my mind, back in the shadows. *You have to come out!* I yelled, fearful. *I need you! You have to stop brooding over what the scarmaster said! You're letting him win!*

The horn blew sooner than I expected, and Polemia's claws scraped through the air. I stumbled back to avoid them and tripped, falling hard on my tailbone. Polemia laughed at my yelp of pain and leaped to land on me, but I rolled over and scrambled to my feet. I felt her claws swipe through my hair, making my heart lurch from the near miss. She'd aimed for my scalp!

She charged at me again, and I panicked, unable to think of anything I could do in response. My blank brain wouldn't let me recall what I'd seen Javed do, and I certainly couldn't use any moves that Field had as a lioness.

"The cubs!" I squeaked, unsteadying her for a moment. An angry but very confused expression strained her features, and her arms twitched with uncertainty.

Taking advantage of her imbalance, I reached for her wrists and tried to grab them before she could cut me. My body suddenly remembered how I'd killed the snake before it could bite Javed, and the reflex I'd rarely used before let me catch both her wrists. Then I remembered Javed mentioning using someone's body weight against an attacker, but since I didn't know exactly what to do with Polemia's lunge, we tumbled down together.

Maybe it was because of my time in the jungle or maybe it was because Nadalinde had already worked on tiring her, but now that we were wrestling on the ground, I realized that I was stronger than her. Polemia screamed in outrage when I finally rolled on top, then put my weight on her hips and wrists to subdue her. She was a wriggling force of profanity as I kept her anchored, and I looked around for the announcer to see if this counted as a victory.

"Did I win?" I yelled, out of breath. After a minute of eternity, the announcer verified that Polemia had lost, and I stood to get off of her. Not accepting the outcome, she snarled and swiped at me—violence in her wild eyes. I rushed backwards, shocked, but the guards quickly caught up and hauled her to the cells.

You'll be out soon, Polemia, I promised her, bending over with my hands on my knees as I gasped for air and nursed a rib cramp. When I finally steadied, I noticed that the king was no longer on the balcony but was walking into the arena, headed straight for me. I would have been elated at reaching my goal, but I wasn't ready at all. My lioness was nowhere to be found.

aved

Had I been in my right mind, I would have found the roaring of the arena to be a stunning force that'd bring me to my traumatized knees. As it was now, I felt nothing. Niusha's death had been a sick gift of numbing, allowing me to stalk through the arena halls without pause. All I could do, and all I wanted to do, was to find my quarries and finally kill them all. The king was dead. The advisor was dead. The scarmaster was dead. Every lion who'd carved their pleasure out on my back was dead. If they thought I'd forgotten their scents, they were dead wrong. Dead.

"This is not what it was like years ago," Quennel whispered, trying to keep up with my long strides. Even if I could, I wouldn't have said anything. I had nothing to say to anyone. My checklist only included getting revenge for my dead mate and leaving this world to join her. I didn't even know why the Proudless had followed. I wasn't here to lead them, but they seemed to have expected that. Quennel, Mas'ud, and Aaron in particular were all acting like cub-sitters.

I turned a corner and noticed a large number of lionesses crowding several lion guards, flirting like they were all in heat. The distraction worked just fine for me, and I slipped past the flustered guards. The majority of the lionesses stared past the lions at me and Quennel, and something in their eyes struck me as odd. The hungry, sharp, and focused gazes reminded me of predators on the hunt, not frolicsome females looking for a bit of fun. I saw myself reflected in their stares.

"Too many lionesses out and about..." Quennel muttered anxiously from behind me. I ignored him, assuming it was simply because of the lioness fights. The last time we were here, it was during the male fights. "They're acting strangely."

Suspicious or not, the distractions they caused worked well for me. The march to the king's balcony was clear, and had I cared, I might have been suspicious. Rounding a corner, there were six females with the last two lions guarding the balcony doors. I strode up to them with my claws out, but when the females looked over their shoulders and saw my obvious intent, they hastily subdued the guards themselves. I stared in slack-jawed shock as the females dragged the gagged, struggling lions back down the hall and out of sight, keeping us in their wary gazes throughout the entirety of their retreat.

"What in the everlasting snow-shitting fuckfest was that?" Quennel hissed to himself as I placed a hand on the balcony door. I stared where the lionesses had disappeared and had the strange sensation that Niusha was here with me in spirit. What had she done here? Had she been the cause of this? An electric chill sizzled down my spine, and I pulled reflexively at my hood. I would not let her sacrifice and efforts go to waste.

I eased the balcony door open and scanned the filled seats but then scowled when I noticed the king's empty chair. He wasn't here. Where the fuck had he gone? I bristled in fury and was about to rend the door into splinters but froze when I heard a number of people approach from down the hall.

"Javed!" Quennel whispered, pulling on my cloak. I turned to see lionesses march toward us, but they suddenly parted when Mas'ud came barreling through them. Though the cheetah's appearance startled the females, they weren't concerned enough to stop their own advance.

"Javed!" Mas'ud caught up to me and held on to my arm while he caught his breath. "Niusha's down there! She w-won the fights!"

I snarled and pushed him off me, enraged by his claim. Niusha was dead! He dared to play with my emotions like this? He dared to speak her name in such a blatant lie? If there weren't lions and lionesses everywhere, I would have roared him into the ground and turned him into a pile of paralyzed flesh!

Mas'ud grunted when he hit the floor. "It's true!" he said as he scrambled to his feet and held out a hand in supplication. His remaining eye rounded in frantic insistence.

"She might have many sisters who look just like her, Mas'ud," Quennel said sadly, pulling the cheetah out of my immediate reach. "Someone named 'Alodie' won." He eyed my claws and moved between Mas'ud and me.

"No! It's Ni—" Mas'ud stated, stopping midsentence and moving farther aside to let the lionesses pass. Whatever they had overheard, they didn't seem to care about any of it. I used them as a wall to hide my entrance into the balcony and stalked to the edge behind a curtain to see if I could find the king on the arena grounds. I wasn't going to prey on anyone else until I got to him. He'd be a much harder target if the chaos started early.

When my eyes fell on the center of the arena, every muscle, every organ, and every cell in my tortured body spasmed with shock. It was impossible. There was no way that what I was seeing was real. I leaned forward and started to hyperventilate. My pulse soared. I felt like I'd been struck out of nowhere by a falling tree.

Niusha was down there.

That lioness… that lioness in the center of the arena was Niusha. I couldn't scent her across the large distance and through all the bodies, but I knew that female. I knew that lioness. That was my lioness! That was my female! That was my fated mate down there!

I gripped my chest—right over my heart—and dug my claws into the muscles. Pain radiated and worked hard to gather my wits. I couldn't believe it. Everything that'd accosted my body the other day told me that she'd died! She'd died! Niusha had died, hadn't she?

I bit my lip and growled when I saw that the one by her was the king. He dragged her to the very center and finally ripped away her robe, exposing her naked body to the crowd. I stared in disbelief at her neck. Her mark was gone. Her mark had disappeared! How?

The blood that'd been coursing through my body drained from my face when I suddenly realized what was about to happen. I almost froze from fear, uncertain of my ability to get down there in time. The king was about to rape my mate! He was going to force himself on my mate in front of everyone!

The blood returned in a boil, frothing my mind. I relapsed into madness and jumped over the balcony railing, risking life and limb to get to her in time. I dug my claws into bricks and ledges to slow my descent just enough to not die. If I broke a leg, I'd just take over Convict's body and suffer the consequences later.

"Field! Field!" Niusha was screaming as the king forced her onto her hands and knees. None of the guards interfered to help the king, who was struggling to hold her while untying his pants. I tore through a banner, unable to keep my eyes off the horror show, and fell hard to the ground. Then I stumbled to my feet and raced across the grounds, but what happened next almost made me stop in my tracks.

With a scream that turned into a roar, Niusha twisted and rolled onto her back under the king, raising her right hand in an arcing slap. By the time it hit the king's throat, it had turned into a lion's paw, and Field's momentum continued, ripping out his royal throat. The complete shift was so fast that I might have missed half of it in a blink. No big cat, except for maybe a cheetah, could shift that quickly.

Upon seeing her, Convict ripped his way out of me and barreled to his lioness, who'd pushed the dying king off her like a cotton doll. Convict aimed to finish the job, but another lion joined the slaughtering and tore out the rest of the king's throat. My tiger went for the king's belly instead and ripped it apart, then lashed out at the other lion, furious his quarry had been stolen. Unexpectedly, his claws met with Field's coat as she intervened, rending deep gashes into her side.

Convict stared in shock as she roared in pain. *Why?* he cried, but she didn't react at all. Field's eyes had turned a frightening shade of feral, and she ran off toward the left exit, growling with unbridled rage. Convict didn't spend another second on the lion, who'd shifted back into his human form. The moment we turned away, the lionesses surrounded him protectively and tried to make announcements over the chaos, but neither Convict nor I cared to pay attention to it.

Follow her! I screamed to Convict, terrified that we'd lose them both all over again, but he didn't need any urging. He sped after Field, dodging the lionesses who'd flooded the crowd from the shadows and started taking prisoners. Mas'ud's cheetah arrived at my side, but we ignored him too, focused only on following Field's scent.

We chased her into the dungeon until we discovered her motive—her prey. Field had her jaws around the scarmaster's leg and was bringing him toward us, snarling furiously as she dragged her half-shifted prize. Godefroid was tangled in his clothes, unable to fully shift and defend himself. He screamed when he fully reverted to his human form and tried to kick Field off his leg, but she shook him violently until the cracking of his bone echoed down the hall. Field released him, staring meaningfully at Convict as she did so, and my tiger didn't waste the present.

Godefroid rolled onto his stomach to crawl away, but my tiger pounced on him and dug into his back, making the male screech in agony and shock. Convict raked through cloth, through skin, and finally through bones and organs, ripping everything out of the scarmaster with psychotic ferocity. He didn't stop until he'd clawed completely through the lion to the ground. Accompanying his pants and growls were the squeaks and scrapes of claws sliding across blood-soaked stone.

Field tore at the scarmaster's arms, needing to rip apart his body almost as much as us. Convict joined her in a heartbeat, shredding the rest of his body until there wasn't anything recognizable left of the male who'd tortured us and mutilated our mate.

After her blood thirst was sated, Field wobbled tiredly, looking confused and lost. Convict sobbed and leaned into her, breathing hard. *Field... Field...*

They stayed like that for a moment, panting wearily and recovering from the murderous craze. Convict butted heads with her, rubbing possessively against Field to let her know he was there. The lioness's traumatized gaze simply darted about while she caught her breath, anxious and alert. A heavy, reverberating groan then forced its way out of her chest, and she fell to her belly, shifting smoothly into Niusha.

Mate... Niusha... we're here, Convict uttered in disbelief. He leaned his head into her shoulder, then returned me to my body. I fell to my knees and scooped my female into my arms, crying madly. A scream, though silent, raked its way out my wailing throat and bellowing chest. She was alive! Alive!

Her head lolled into me, and she moaned upon seeing her blood-soaked hands. The shock in her eyes jabbed my heart, and I crushed her shaking form close. She only allowed it for a couple heartbeats before struggling to stand.

"J-Javed… is that… you?" she craned her neck to stare up at me. I nodded emphatically and pulled her closer, burying my face into her neck. "I… I have to go to…" she mumbled and gestured away from me. "Help me…"

I jumped to my feet, but I wouldn't let her go. *Where?* I asked, knowing that if I had my voice, I'd be mute anyway from my traumatized state. *Where?* I repeated. That was when I realized she couldn't hear me. I sobbed once in emotional pain and frustration, then put her down. Weakly, I gestured that I'd follow her.

Mas'ud had been waiting, apparently, and came forward to say, "Javed… the females appear to be taking over the pride, but they're struggling… What should… What do we do? We weren't expecting this. Our Proudless are hesitating, and it's making us vulnerable."

"Support the lionesses. Protect them," Niusha commanded without hesitation, snapping back to alertness and pointing in the direction of the arena. "Find Roul and Oudine; they'll tell you where we need the most help. Roul's the one who attacked the king after F-Field ripped his neck."

Mas'ud looked worriedly from her to me, as if he wasn't sure he should be taking orders from Niusha, but I gestured to where she'd pointed and growled at him. He got the message extremely quickly and dashed out, shifting midair to get there faster with his cheetah.

"I'm so tired," she whispered and leaned against me. I huffed a question, and she nodded, understanding my inquiry. "I have more… to do." She rubbed her sweaty brow with a forearm while looking for a place to rinse her hands. Quickly, she found a bucket and dunked her hands in to wash off the blood. "We have a small kill list… I need to find the advisor and see if the females got him yet. I need to check in with my mother, and later I need to find Keid. After that… we'll be raiding the offices to find where the trafficked people went. They could be right under our noses here…"

She wobbled toward me, causing me to reach out and embrace her again. She caved and joined me in another moment together… just the two of us. I winced when my fingers brushed the wet gashes on her ribs. I'd help her with that in a minute, but now, she needed me as much as I needed her in my arms, and I was going to give her everything I had.

I'd been so wrong, and she now had my complete, unconditional support.

Chapter 35

Niusha

I allowed myself to be lost in Javed's embrace for a while. I was tired, wound up, slightly disoriented, and in a great deal of pain. I tried not to complain about the gashes because I didn't want Javed and Convict to feel worse about them. The events in the arena had been chaotic, and Field hadn't been in her right mind. Honestly, I was just glad Javed and Roul hadn't ended up clashing.

I'm s-sorry, Field said as Javed rocked me slowly against his warm—but bloody—chest, squeezing tight and chuffing into my hair. I absorbed the relief I received while listening to Field, and the tingling from the mate touch momentarily soothed all my pain. *I'm so sorry I wasn't there for the fights... I'd been so outraged—so blown out of my mind—by what that... that... sadistic lion said that I didn't trust myself to come out and not kill the first person I saw. I would have killed a lioness, Niusha. I would have killed Douceline or P-Polemia!* She sobbed wildly in my head, her tears spilling from my eyes.

You came through for me, Field, and you didn't kill anyone we hadn't planned on killing, I comforted. *Please don't cry. Please, please don't cry. We need to calm for the next step...*

I'm so glad our mate's here!

I sniffed away some mucus and smiled. We both were glad. Everything was much easier with them by our side. Not only was life generally a million times better with Javed and Convict, but the safety they provided gave me space to think, and right now, I had a lot of responsibilities to manage.

Javed pulled me away from him, wiped his bloody hands on a nearby rag, and brushed my tears off my cheeks. He smiled down at me, looking a little worried, then frowned when he saw the split on my chin. He licked his thumb and started cleaning the blood from my face in his usual fashion. I submitted to the grooming, feeling a great deal of comfort from the normalcy. His heart-stoppingly handsome face turned its attention to my ribs, and I spied his guilt-ridden cringe.

"It's ok, Javed. It's not that bad. It was an accident. Let's just… find a bandage, ok?" I said and rubbed his shoulder in an attempt to make him feel better. He sighed, kissed the top of my head apologetically, and helped steady me.

There was a medical kit in the guards' break room, and Javed cleaned all my injuries thoroughly. He finally added some ointment, pads of cotton, and wrapped bandages around my rib cage. We discovered robes in a cabinet, and he helped me don one, then gestured a severe 'no' with both hands.

I nodded. "I won't shift again. I promise."

Javed grunted in satisfaction, found a large robe for himself, and gestured for me to lead the way. I grabbed his hand and left the cells, striding into the light to retrace my steps back to the castle. The area outside the arena was just as bloody and chaotic. Other cat-shifters had collided violently with some lions, but what really surprised me was seeing the lions fighting among themselves. Anxiety had me biting my lip again, and I wondered if some of them had sided with the lionesses because they supported their movement or because they simply accepted Roul as the new king. I supposed it didn't really matter at the moment.

It was bound to get messy, Field murmured, and I hummed an agreement.

We found my mother in the place I learned was called the 'throne room.' Roul and Oudine were already there, and when they spotted me, they ran over immediately. I could see that my mother and Oudine wanted to embrace me, but they stopped short, hesitating at the bulk and presence of my mate.

"It's him!"

"That's the Proudless's leader!"

It seemed that everyone here knew who Javed was, and in hindsight, if he'd fought for so long in the arena, of course they'd all know him. Before my mother or Oudine could say anything—not that it looked like the gaping lionesses could—I introduced him properly.

Raising my chin, I announced, "This is Javed, my fated mate and father of my cubs. He's here to help m—"

"You're pregnant?" my mother cried and darted forward to grab my shoulders. I blanched under her wild-eyed outburst and started nervously when she placed a hand on my stomach. "Niusha! You're not supposed to shift when pregnant! I know why you hid it, but why didn't you tell me?"

Shit! Field blurted.

"I..." I didn't know what to say to that. I hadn't known! I looked over at an alarmed Javed, who clearly hadn't known either—or had just forgotten.

"You could have lost them! We need to find Keid!" She grabbed my hand and whirled to march out of the room.

"Wait, wait!" I gasped, trying to pull out of her grip. "We need to check in wi—" I started saying, but Javed growled in displeasure from behind me.

"See?" my mother snapped. "Even your mate knows better! You two, escort us!" She pointed at a couple robed lionesses, who hastened to flank us. Javed snorted from behind as my mother tugged me along the corridors.

"I don't know where she would be now…" my mother uttered as we hurried to the doctor's office.

"I told her to hide, but I didn't tell her why," I said. Entering the office, I noticed that almost every cabinet was open and empty. It looked like the lionesses had already raided the supplies to treat the wounded. No lion or lioness remained either, but I kept my eyes and ears open for any sign of Keid.

Finally, I heard it. A nervous heartbeat fluttered from the next room, and I chased it to a cabinet under the sink. I called her name before opening the door, not wanting to scare her. Keid's frosty pink face stared up at me, her wide eyes looking more lavender in the dark of the room.

I helped the poor woman out of her hiding place, but my mother saw fit to snap at her. "Keid! I assume you're the one who helped hide her pregnancy. My foolish daughter shifted, and I need to know if she lost her cubs!"

"O-oh. I will check, Tumidia," Keid stuttered. My mate growled at my mother—likely for calling me foolish—which made Keid back up and bump into the examination table. She drew me over so she could check on my cubs… far from him.

"Don't start with me, Javed," my mother snapped at him, and for some reason, I burst into nervous laughter.

Keid advised me to quiet down so she could focus, and I stilled, allowing Field to continue laughing for the both of us. Fortunately, the woman didn't need me to undress and had to be using some form of witchcraft to tell.

"They're fine," Keid announced and straightened. "What… what is happening out there?" She pointed to the door with drawn brows, no longer able to hide her fear and worry. After I breathed a sigh of relief, I explained the takeover, and she fell into a chair, utterly shocked.

"You'll be seeing your sister soon," I informed with a smile. "We'll try to find her for you, unless you'd rather leave first and look for her. You're free, Keid." The witch covered her face and bawled, heaving gut-wrenching sobs from exhaustion and disbelief. I held her close for a minute to let her get some comfort, then asked my burning question. "Do you know where the witches are being held? Perhaps the trafficked ones and the cubs are in the same area."

She wiped mucus from her nose and looked up at me with a shake of her head. "They're down a floor under the arena, but the last time I was there, I didn't see any shifters. It was just witches. That was over a year ago, though… I think. It's been so long."

I stepped back and hummed thoughtfully. Now that my body was free from the hug and available, Javed wrapped his arms around me, clearly relieved his offspring were safe too. I wanted to celebrate that fact, but my mind was so distracted by current events that I had a hard time focusing on any one thing.

My mother said, "I'll send some people down to release them. Keid, I think you should go along to explain the situation. I don't want anyone lashing out at my lionesses."

The witch wiped tears from her cheeks and nodded feverishly. "They won't be strong enough to attack anyone, but I promise I'll keep them in line. Is an exit out of the arena accessible?" The poor woman palmed the wall for balance—pale, overwhelmed, and reeling.

"They'll be escorted out, yes. If you all stay nearby for a day, we can provide you with food and medical supplies to get you on your way. Anyone needing more time to get their strength is welcome here under supervision. I can't imagine there wouldn't be someone out for revenge," my mother replied briskly.

"That's… generous." Keid cleared her throat and lowered her gaze.

"It's not. I imagine we have a great amount of reparations to do. I'm relying on other guidance here," my mother said, weariness weighing down her face and shoulders. As quickly as her fatigue had shown, it disappeared, and she stared meaningfully up at Javed. He grunted in acknowledgment.

"Keid… are you able to fix Javed's muting?" I asked, pulling away from my mate so she could look at his neck. She stood, wobbled nervously, and bravely approached my tiger-shifter. The line of symbols fell under her scrutiny, and she tilted her head in consideration.

"I didn't do this… I don't know. I need to consult with some witches. Can I get back to you on this? I w-won't leave, I promise. I o-owe you, Niusha," Keid stammered, quickly stepping away from Javed.

"Of course. I trust you," I said, placing a hand on her tense shoulder. For some reason, seeing Keid this frightened made me feel stronger. I'd been so scared and felt so helpless when I had the orphans, but this time, I finally had the power to safeguard. And now with Javed by my side, I felt like we could do everything we'd set out to do.

When we arrived at the throne room, my mother ordered a group of lionesses to escort Keid to where the witches were being held. I heard Javed growl and turned to see him crooking his finger at Mas'ud, who'd arrived with a large number of Proudless while we were gone. After receiving a short series of frustrated gestures from Javed, Mas'ud nodded and gathered his cats to assist the lionesses.

Oudine and Roul approached, and the lion said to me, "I think we're ready to search the offices for information on the cubs, but we'll need you to read anything we can't. I don't know if we'll find more of that… strange script you found."

"I want to go as soon as possible," Oudine said, anxiously moving her weight from one foot to the other, "in case they try to hide the information or move them out."

Roul reached for her hand, and when she accepted it, he squeezed it. A flash of warmth blossomed in my chest to see such affection. The lionesses here deserved better, and I knew Roul would be good to Oudine if she accepted him.

I nodded, also feeling urgency for Oudine's sake. A thought occurred to me, though, and I turned to Javed. "Is Quennel here? He can try to mind-link his mate if she's here, right?"

Javed jerked his chin toward the wall, where the older lion rested with a wet cloth on his brow. He'd removed his false leg before lying down, and my heart suffered a pang of sympathy. He must be so exhausted. My mate squatted and gently woke Quennel, who snorted and sat up in alarm. Javed calmed the jumpy lion and gestured to me.

"Hey, Quennel," I greeted with a soft smile. "Ready to look for your mate and daughter?"

His eyes flooded with tears, and he grunted as he buckled on his false leg. "Shite, yes! Oh lioness, it's so good to see you lived after all…" Javed helped him up, and the lion hobbled over to me to deliver an emotional hug. Quennel seemed a lot older in the moment, quivering as he wrapped his tired arms around me. I patted his back, and he stepped away, wiping his red and swollen eyelids.

"Let's go," I prompted, and Roul led the way out of the throne room. Quennel had a hard time keeping up, sweating and wincing with every step, so Javed lifted him off the ground and into a carry. The older lion was a whirlwind of profanity for a minute until he gave up and let Javed have his way. I hid a smile behind a hand, finding Quennel's pout too similar to Chirasmi's when she'd turned fussy.

However, my smile was wiped off my face when we rounded a corner. In front of the office we'd intended to raid was Advisor Eudes, already in his large lion form and radiating hostility.

"Advisor!" my mother screamed, sobbing at the sight of several deceased lionesses who'd already tried to kill him. I went to her before she could collapse in grief and tugged her out of the way.

The advisor's malevolent gaze was drawn to Javed, who slowly put down Quennel and shrugged off his robe, growling deeply in response to the advisor's challenge. Roul began undressing too, but Javed violently gestured for him to back off his prey.

I saw it on his face. He needed this. He desperately needed this.

Javed

Let me out, let me out, let me out! Convict snarled from within, desperate to wrap his maw around this lion's neck and hear the snap of a breaking spine. After all, this male had gotten to hear my agony with every word he'd carved into my skin. It was only fair.

He hadn't been the king's advisor when I'd been here, so I supposed he replaced the old one upon the last king's death. It was just as well that he was on the lionesses' potential kill list because he definitely was on mine. I didn't know his name, but I hadn't forgotten his scent. I hadn't forgotten any of their scents.

Convict lunged the same time the advisor did and snarled in tandem with our quarry. The advisor came in low, needing to keep his weight balanced on one front paw while Convict sprang forward with both paws in the air. The lion received two ugly, clawed slaps to his face while only managing to graze my tiger's arm.

The lion dashed to the side, flanking us in an attempt to target our neck or spine. Convict was large, but he was still agile, and his powerful back legs sprang his hindquarters out of danger. We received cuts to our shoulder, but Convict's claws slashed through the lion's mane, grazing his jugular.

How do you want me to kill him? my tiger asked.

However you please, I replied, deferring to his desire, and Convict grunted in satisfaction. He didn't want to play around anymore. There weren't enough people watching for Convict to want to make a show of it, and we didn't have anything to prove to Niusha, who was relying on our help today.

The advisor tried to get around us again, snarling violently from rage, humiliation, and pain. Convict held his roar back—not wanting to stun him and make it too easy—and slapped the lion's face again with his left paw, keeping him away from our face while Convict placed his right paw on the lion's withers.

Because Convict considered it the ultimate 'fuck you' to any lion he killed, he opened his maw wide, pushed past the mane to clamp over the nape, and bit hard. Thick lion manes offered some protection but could not ultimately stop a well-placed bite or scratch. If Convict's mouth could fit around his target, it was simply going to get crushed.

The satisfying crack of a spine breaking hit our ears, and the dead lion fell limp, never to lay claws on me ever again. Convict removed his mouth from the corpse and stepped back, shuddering in pleasure. I quickly shifted back to my human form, ignoring the stinging pain from my aggravated wounds.

One more down. How many left? my tiger inquired.

Not sure who's still alive, I answered. *Stay on the alert. If we scent them, we'll kill them.*

Niusha slammed into my chest, hugging me fiercely while I caught my breath, and I patted her back with my forearm, not wanting to get more blood on her. Roul picked up a shirt that had likely been discarded by this advisor and tossed it to me. I nodded to acknowledge his thoughtfulness and wiped my hands clean. I desperately needed a shower, but thankfully, the lioness who was currently clinging to me had not complained yet.

After I threw on my robe, Roul and I simultaneously grabbed one of the dead lion-shifter's legs and dragged him out of the way. We moved the lionesses with more respect, and Niusha's mother had managed to compose herself by the time we forced open the office door. We flooded the room and searched the records for information on where the trafficked individuals might be.

The other female, Oudine, handed a heavy box to Niusha that she found in a filing cabinet, and my mate dug through it. I peered over her shoulder and noticed that a lot of it was written in what I'd originally thought was a fake language. I made a mental note to show these records to Leofwine if I was able to contact him. Perhaps the script was created for trafficking so the average person wouldn't be able to decipher sensitive material. So far, everything seen here spoke to wider use. The fact that this secret was taught to the villagers told me how unstable their village elder had actually been… or foolishly confident.

Niusha pulled out what looked like a blueprint and handed it to me. "What is this? Is it a map?"

Roul, Oudine, and Niusha's mother came to study the blueprint while a waiting Quennel seated himself. Roul pointed at the top, then at the bottom third of the page. "Isn't that the arena? Does this here mean there's another basement level?"

It seemed to be the case, and I let them discuss it while I glanced back at Quennel. He'd been quiet, but I couldn't tell if it was from pain or anxiety—probably both. I wanted to see him reunited with his family and given a room to recover in as soon as possible. I looked back at the blueprint and frowned when something occurred to me. If his family was here, why couldn't he sense his mate?

I wrote a question down and showed it to Oudine, frustrated that I couldn't communicate directly with Niusha. I wanted to mark my mate again as soon as possible, but we hadn't found the time and privacy to do that yet. Also, I still needed to know how she'd lost my mark.

Oudine glanced at my question, furrowed her brows, then asked the others, "Is it possible that the witches could've hidden the presence of these people, like how Niusha's mark was muted?"

Well, that answered one of my unasked questions.

Niusha's mother considered it. "Maybe. Let's go to the arena cells. Keid should still be there. Does it show how to reach that floor?" Roul nodded.

My lioness then grabbed the blueprint and handed the box back to Oudine. "Can we get someone to secure these documents and this office?"

"Yes. We absolutely need to do that," Oudine agreed.

"I think we should move everything important to one highly guarded location for now."

"I'll take care of it," Niusha's mother said and departed swiftly with the box. I suspected she also needed a moment alone to mourn the deaths of those lionesses. This was going to be a sad day for many, but if we found the missing people, there'd be a lot more to celebrate than grieve.

I carried a grumpy Quennel to the arena, noting the location's convenience for moving slaves in and out of the territory. Though it had been built within Edeletrots's grounds, it was accessible from both the castle and the exterior wall, which was how the fights had been made available to outsiders.

"I've never been here," Oudine muttered to Roul as we entered the first-floor cells. A large number of human women were already resting here, likely witches who were just freed by Keid and the others. I watched lionesses and Proudless run around with urgency, fetching water and treating the sick while we passed down the crowded hall.

Roul already knew where the witches were held and guided us down to the basement so we could search for the last floor. I gagged and pulled my robe to my nose when the stench of waste and rot hit it. I glanced around and noticed everyone else doing the same, but some of the witches being liberated didn't seem affected. They were either used to it or just didn't smell it as strongly as shifters did. I'd heard their noses weren't very good in general.

Niusha found Keid and jogged up to her, obviously wanting to get in and out as soon as possible. "Keid," my mate called through the fabric of her robe, "we found a blueprint that says more people might be a floor below us. Do you know if there are any spells that could prevent someone from sensing their mate if they're here?"

Keid's pale eyes flickered down the hall, and she shifted nervously before answering. "Whatever my witches might have been forced to do, they get immunity, right?"

"I don't think we can promise anything, but if it was forced, I can't see how they'd be held accountable," Roul said slowly, tactfully.

Keid didn't look particularly happy with that answer, but she sighed and nodded. "Yes, an area can be dampened," she said, gesturing vaguely down the busy hall. "If you find the symbol that c—"

"Vail! Vail!" Quennel screamed, thrashing in my arms to be released. I hastily placed the lion on the ground, and he lumbered down the hall, squeezing past witches who were hobbling toward their own freedom. I grabbed Niusha's hand and followed him, growling sharply to make everyone ahead clear the way.

Quennel pushed through the last group of witches and approached a stone door that a very, very old witch was scraping at with a long nail. The scent of rot was much stronger here, and I fought with all my might to not dry heave again.

Great Sky Gods, bring the rain to give these people a bath, Convict complained.

When Quennel growled at her to move out of the way, Keid yelled, "Leave her alone!" and dashed forward to gently pull the old woman from him. The quivering witch patted Keid on the arm but didn't say anything. Keid then leaned toward the door and pointed at a scratched-out symbol. "See? She was just helping! They're right here!"

She reached for the doorknob but not before Quennel yanked the heavy door open and descended the flight of wide stone steps. He was a lion on the rampage for his mate and wasn't listening to anything. I couldn't blame him. I gripped Niusha's hand tighter and reminded myself that my mate was alive. Niusha was alive.

The third floor was a dark stone hall that hid a flurry of activity behind closed doors. Fists were thumping behind almost all the doors in the hall, pounding as frantically as the excited heartbeats making them. Quennel roared when he approached the second door on the left, released the simple lever that locked it, and swung it open.

Quennel's mate, Vail, burst out and fell into his shaking arms, nearly crashing them both into the ground. Oriel was attached to her mother's leg, her face covered in tears, snot, and trauma. I blew out a breath I didn't know I'd been holding and leaned against the wall, my legs all but turning into quivering, wilted reeds. We'd found them.

I started opening the other doors to see what the situation was here. The first couple rooms held adults who'd been trafficked. Most of them had been restrained, their arms bleeding into buckets and jars at a very slow drip. Their arms looked like they'd been cut and healed over and over, as if their abductors were trying to keep their sources of blood alive. Niusha gave a dismayed cry once she recognized people from her old village, and ran to their aid, unable to stop from freeing them first. When Roul took charge of leading out the trafficked people, Niusha and Oudine joined me in opening the rest of the doors.

I'd tried so hard to keep it together this entire time, wanting to stay strong for Niusha, but when I saw room after room of cubs dripping blood into buckets, I nearly lost my remaining strength. There were so many of them. Hundreds of cubs were here, and the only ones not being bled were the sickly or those younger than maybe one or two years. I searched blindly for a wall to lean against—just for a moment—and listened to Oudine unleash the most ear-piercing roar I'd ever heard in my life. The sound was the absolute epitome of rage, despair, and relief. I'd likely never hear such a sound again in my life… and I hoped I never would.

My mate also reeled and palmed my arm, her cheeks paling and eyes rounding. "I… I need to go get the lionesses… I need… my mother needs to see this," she uttered numbly while Oudine hurried to care for the palest cubs, ripping strips of fabric from her clothes to apply pressure to their wounds.

"The cubs are alive… They're alive!"

Chapter 36

Niusha

The walk back to my mother was like treading through the muggiest evening. A fog had not only descended on my mind, but shock was slowly crawling back into all my faculties. My legs swung like iron despite the emotional weight that'd been removed from my shoulders. What I'd set out to do was done. I'd found the cubs and the trafficked people. I found them. They were alive—the cubs, Quennel's family, Tsisana's sister, and my old villagers. They were all alive…

The lions must pay, Field said quietly, a steely edge to her tone. She'd nearly sprung out of me once we saw the young lions and lionesses laid out, dripping. Some had hurt themselves trying to get free, so I knew there'd be other wounds to treat. It'd been traumatizing to discover, and those cubs were going to need substantial care after this.

We'll sort out the ones responsible, I said to her as Javed and I marched up a flight of stone steps. Though it was momentarily quiet, I could barely hear the slapping of our feet on the hard surface. My distress was much too loud. My heart thrummed angrily in my ears, calling for more violence.

Those who knew about it too, she added coldly.

This is going to get muddy... I replied, worried about all the grey areas the lionesses and supporting lions were going to have to navigate.

"Mother," I choked out as I entered the throne room, ignoring the people talking to her. "We found them. They're under the arena. Send... send... send lionesses and... if there are any d-doctors. Under where the witches were being held." I wasn't sure how I got out those words, but I immediately embraced my mother and dissolved into tears.

It struck me hard how lucky those cubs and I had been. I'd only survived my culling because someone trafficked me from the castle, and these cubs only survived because a king had deemed their blood too valuable to waste. If only the cubs of other cullings had been so fortunate. I still couldn't fathom why I'd been taken. Perhaps they wanted to breed lions into slavery. I wasn't sure if I'd ever know, and I had to either let that go or question it another day.

My mother didn't release me as she barked out orders, and the room ignited with urgent shouts, hopeful cries, and relieved sobbing. We were both shaking, and it felt like the last of our energy was fading. Shaking as much as it had all day, I feared my body had been damaged and would never return to normal.

My mother held me a while, then patted my back and put me at arm's length. "We still have work to do, Alodie." She rubbed at her eyes, ones that so closely resembled mine, and forced a comforting smile. I didn't know how she did that—how she found the energy to console on top of everything else we'd seen.

Despite that, I opened my mouth to ask her to use my other name, but I realized that might be hurtful, so I'd save that conversation for another time. Maybe I'd only allow it from her, but it simply felt wrong. My rescuing from Edeletrots had blessed me with a second chance. This place had aimed to kill a helpless Alodie… only for a Niusha to rise in her supposed wake.

My mother straightened and gestured to the new arrivals, who were, without a doubt, not cat-shifters. "We have some important guests, Daughter. How they knew to arrive at this moment, I do not know." She leveled her stern gaze on the group and pursed her lips.

A female with umbral eyes stepped forward and gestured to my mate. "This is the one," she said in a strong, silvery voice. I knew instantly that this was a person of some authority, and I stepped closer to Javed while he simultaneously reached for me.

"What do you mean by 'this is the one?'" I asked anxiously, edging in front of Javed despite his gentle growling at me. He pulled me back again, and I frowned up at him in displeasure. We desperately wanted to protect each other—even more since being reunited—and it might have been comical had I not been so concerned and exhausted.

"We are the Sky Gods," the female stated formally, gesturing to herself, but before I could voice my confusion, she went on to say, "and this is our vessel. We are here to verify that our will has and will be executed."

"Executed?" I asked in alarm, feeling my canines extend without warning. I worried at my hands, which were now sporting claws. My body was responding excessively to a word that had multiple meanings, and it probably wasn't being used in the way I feared, but I was on edge. I was on edge and exhausted. At this point, to put it mildly, my worn state was making me stupid.

"We are not here to kill him, Catalyst," a petite female said through a curl of orange hair brighter than Javed's. "That could have been done easily. The Sky Gods asked to borrow my children to assist him should he accept his reward."

I swallowed past a stubborn lump in my throat, uneasy hearing such morbid confidence coming out of this delicate female. I tried to get more information with my nose, sniffing with Field's help.

Like the dark-eyed female, this vessel scented a bit musky, like a dog but spicier. She definitely wasn't a cat. None of them were.

A large male with brown hair made his introduction, his tousled locks mismatching his royal garments. "I am King Keyon, the king of the dragon kingdom. Let's… speak plainly. I realize this must be overwhelming, and I don't at all mean that in a condescending manner."

I sniffed discreetly as he spoke, noticing he smelled similar to Leofwine, who was actually here as well, leaning against a column while talking to Adelais. They weren't looking at us, which was just as well. That female cat-shifter put me on edge.

"The Sun God asked us to come and offer medical treatment that only I'm capable of. Javed, I believe?" the female next to King Keyon asked and held out her hand for Javed to shake, which he accepted. She was almost as pale as Keid, but silvery blond hair streamed out from under her low veil, which also hid what appeared to be a thorned crown. With how the king tensed at her proximity to my mate, I realized this was the queen. I relaxed slightly and actually felt safer with that knowledge. They seemed like compassionate people regardless of their immense power and influence. I felt that truth in my gut.

I glanced up at Javed to see his reaction, but his face had turned as rigid as his body. He waited impatiently for them to explain more, and I squeezed his hand to remind him of my presence. Like I always had and always would, I started asking questions for him.

"What treatment? And why? How are such important people here for one person?"

The Sky Gods said, "We asked him to come, and he did, though it was of his own accord. We've been waiting for the right souls to be born for a long time to calm our feuding children. Niusha, our catalyst and our breath, and Javed, the last word and the final say, have begun the long process of bringing order to this kingdom—though it seems to be lacking leadership." Her words, well, Their words, were said without scorn. There was an odd detachment in Their tone, but it was somehow rich beyond measure. Whatever was inside this vessel didn't seem like it could possibly fit. The effect was so overwhelming that I had a hard time paying attention to Their speech. Not even the room felt big enough for Them.

"A kingdom with a king within a kingdom with no king," the smaller redhead remarked with disdain, looking around in near-parental disappointment. She was much more emotive, aggressive even, but seemed to carry as vast a presence as the Sky Gods. The more I took in this encounter, the more it staggered me.

"This is the Sun God," the Sky Gods introduced, gesturing to Their companion. I clung tighter to Javed with my increasing tension, our hearts racing each other's. "Do you wish to have the memories removed from your skin? We assume you wish for the return of your voice as well."

I gasped and looked to see Javed's reaction. His face had hardened into a cold, stony mask, and a muscle in his jaw twitched as he glanced surreptitiously around the room. Was he embarrassed? Was he anxious at having what he'd hidden so desperately called into attention? He raked his slightly bloodstained fingers through his messy locks, though I wasn't sure if he was consciously or subconsciously trying to hide the brand on his forehead.

At that gesture, and with the subtle, pained expression that flashed across his face, I could tell that he felt deep guilt as well. I thought about what the scarmaster had said and gripped his arm firmly. Those three weren't on him. Those three deaths weren't on his shoulders. Back then, three people were going to die in the arena no matter what he decided. We needed to have a long talk about that soon.

"Whatever you're feeling, you deserve what you've earned," I said, standing in front of him and tilting his head down to meet my gaze. "You've saved more than you've been forced to take. Many deaths were not on your hands, do you understand? You're worthy and therefore worthy of reward."

I knew it was going to be a struggle to convince him, and Field pushed her way forward, letting him see her presence in my eyes. It was an odd sensation, but she needed him and Convict to sense her will. Despite my attempt to be gentle, Field aimed to bully them into accepting their reward.

I set my jaw as firmly as his. Being supportive, defiant for him, and defiant against him was a hard stance to balance. Javed's position seemed to weaken, and his eyes slid from mine. His expression turned begrudgingly questioning, and I opened my mouth to speak.

"Is it safe?" my mother asked sharply before I could utter any words. "I won't have my daughter's mate put in danger."

Javed seemed annoyed by her statement, likely not appreciating her controlling attitude. I sighed and rubbed his arm. "Your decision," I whispered up to him. "Only yours."

"He'll have to be hurt before he's healed, but my child is capable. He will be asleep for the duration," the Sun God said in a tone that suffered no questioning, yet I had questions still.

"How? How will he be hurt?" I inquired with a scowl. I didn't like the sound of this at all.

"He'll..." The veiled female paused with a grimace, then glanced around and lowered her voice. "He'll have to be flayed a little at a time and healed bit by bit. He won't feel it, though! We have a couple of coven mothers here to help and someone who'll keep him asleep throughout the entire process. He'll wake without any pain."

"I'd prefer to start as soon as possible," said another male who stood behind everyone. He didn't look like anyone I'd ever seen. Though as intimidating as the other males in his own dark, kingly attire, he still had delicate features, and I noticed that the pale silvery ears that stuck out from his black hair were pointed like the bat-shifters' ears. However, this was no bat...

The scope of this uneased me. Was Javed so important to these two gods? Was I? I furrowed my brows in thought, not understanding any of this. I'd come from such a strange place and ended up somewhere stranger. If I hadn't felt Their overwhelming presence, I'd have absolutely questioned Their claims of godhood. I rubbed an eye, wondering about everything that'd led up to this. My actions were mine, weren't they? My thoughts raced, and I closed my eyes, distress flooding me.

"Calm, Catalyst," the Sky Gods said in a tone much like my mother's. My eyes snapped open, compelled to stare at the female who somehow housed the skies under her skin. "It is simpler than you think. You both are as we intended, and you've done well to help our children—your people. You will continue to do so as that's simply your nature. There is no need to question something finite. You put yourself and your cubs at risk for hundreds more. Your mate suffered greatly for the greater good. Allow good to come to you."

I turned to Javed once again and simply let him know I supported whatever he decided. He knew how I felt about his appearance. I'd made it clear he was beautiful to me.

His gaze drifted to somewhere far away, and his strength drained before my eyes. He slouched before kings and gods, looking so very, very worn. It was like the last five years of his life were catching up to him. My mate scratched the tip of his nose with his wrist and moved his stare to the floor. After an excruciatingly long wait, he glanced back up at the umbral-eyed female and nodded his assent.

"Then let it be done," the Sun God commanded the group. "Is my will clear, children and children of others?"

There were a number of nods and agreements from the visitors, then the redhead's potent demeanor withered. In an instant, the godly presence dissipated and left a wide-eyed vessel in its wake. The female fidgeted impatiently, and I offered her a hesitant smile of acknowledgment, which she returned just as awkwardly. She clearly wanted to leave as soon as possible.

"Leofwine," the dragon king called out, turning to face the dragon-shifter who was currently feeling up Adelais. His head snapped around, and he raised his brows in query, not bothering to remove his mischievous hands from where they were roaming. "Get someone to take these vessels home, please. They will be tired from hosting."

"Also," I spoke up, leaning forward to gather everyone's attention, "I want one of our witches, Keid, to oversee the healing, please." It was a request, but I put as much firmness into it as I could. I trusted her to some extent and wanted someone I knew there.

"I'm... I'm so sorry, but n-nay," the veiled queen denied with a gentle wave of her hand. "I swear to you he's in the best hands, though!" Her large brown eyes carried confidence and care despite her stammer.

"We can't let anyone watch," the king added, immovable on the matter.

I opened my mouth to object because I was absolutely, certainly, without a doubt going to be there, but Javed gently yanked on my arm and shook his head. I started to protest again, but the tiger-shifter repeated the motion with more urgency. His dark orange locks danced around his forehead brand, the symbol that tormented him. "Then mark me before so I c—"

Javed moved closer to make his silent message loud and clear. He gripped both my arms, stared deep into my eyes with his jungle-teal gaze, and repeated his headshake one last time—slowly, intensely, unrelentingly. The beautiful male mouthed the word 'no' and placed a long, slow, soft kiss on my forehead. I gaped as he turned to follow strangers so they could slowly rip off his skin. I couldn't bear the thought of more injury coming to him while he faced it alone, even if he was asleep. When he disappeared from sight, I fell to the floor and into tears. I didn't think I had more left to cry and yet here they sprang.

My mother allowed me a moment before urging me up and insisting we get back to work. I didn't feel shame in crying, but she was right. Though I could move my body to perform tasks, my mind was stuck on my mate and how much I desperately wanted to follow him.

"Do you remember when you did this for me?" Oudine asked, handing over a drink of cool water.

The warm morning sunlight filtering into the hall scattered off the metal cup in my hand and flitted across the wall like a spooked star. I yawned widely and nodded, barely placing a hand over my mouth in time for politeness' sake.

She added wryly, "You're not drunk, though. You're just parched from crying."

"I still don't understand why all you make yourself sick and silly with such a potion," I muttered into the cup. Oudine chuckled weakly, and I forced a smile onto my face before looking back at the hospital door. I'd been sleeping next to it every night, memorizing every curve in the wood's grain and waiting anxiously for my mate to appear.

She spoke again but her tone had fallen timid, like she was about to make a confession. "I know your mother harps on about how you're waiting out here, but I don't think she's ever had someone like you do. I think… I think I understand better now."

I leaned back against the wall and brushed her hair aside to find the very fresh bite Roul had left on her marking spot. The punctures were still swollen; they must have made the decision late last night or early this morning.

"I had a feeling." My smile this time was easy, genuine. I liked good news, and this one in particular warmed my weary heart. "Fated or chosen? I suspect fated from how he mooned over you all this time."

The lioness chuckled and nodded but still blushed in bashfulness. "Seems the goddess above had plans this entire time. It also makes sharing responsibilities easier. Much has changed already, and we've been relying on each other more than expected. Roul is... spoiling me. He was overjoyed that I hadn't lost my cubs and has floated the idea of us all moving into the king's chambers... b-back home, I mean. The old grounds." Her eyes focused on somewhere far, far away before they flickered back to mine. "The concept of living away from the harem—with a family, in a family—is strange to me, but being with Roul and my cubs... it makes me feel safer for some reason. My cubs, Niusha... My cubs." She shook her head in disbelief and lifted the arms she'd wrapped around herself to pull me into a near-crushing hug.

I held her just as tightly as she dissolved into her daily breakdown. Nearly all the lionesses who'd reclaimed their long-thought-deceased cubs were in similar states—laughing one moment and sobbing the next. The day we'd found the cubs was also the day I'd started drowning in gifts from thankful pride members. The only gift I desired though, was for Javed's treatment to be done. I worried for him despite the gods-given assurances.

I pushed away the deep pain that came from his absence and asked, "So the lions agreed to leave and return to their—er, our—original territory?" I'd missed all the meetings yesterday, unable to focus on anything but Javed being locked in the hospital with kings, queens, witches, and those possibly not of this realm.

Oudine nodded and sniffed wetly before responding. She pulled back, wiped mucus and tears from her upper lip, and said, "Since this castle is in a central location, the other cats want to establish some form of equal representation here. They're a little lost, though, since so many have resisted the concept of a kingdom due to us lions.

"We have other news too. We're expecting the lycans and wolves in a week or so for talks. They seem keen on improving their relationship with us now that lions aren't in a place of dominance. The gods knew they never got along. I thought for sure we'd return to war when one of our older king's daughters died there."

"I know nothing of our history." I sighed, and as reluctant as I was to discover more horrors, I made a mental note to learn it all. Then, I grimaced at a thought. "Please tell me the cats have at least moved on from Javed and me?" I bit my lip in anticipation.

She chuckled, sniffled, and shook her head. "No, but they're all trying to agree on a fallback plan, the lionesses are demanding you, and the other cats want him. It's nearly universal since you're a mated pair, and they believe you're the only ones capable of being completely unbiased. You've both earned the majority of the trust available, which wasn't much to begin with." Oudine snorted and patted my back affectionately. "There's not much else they're currently able to agree on."

I collapsed against the wall and stared miserably at the hospital door. "He'll hate that," I whispered to her. "He just wanted to disappear, Oudine. He never wanted that responsibility again."

"No one will force you to stay, you know. As much as I don't want you to disappear, you have to know you're free to build your family in pretty much any cat territory you wish." She grimaced. "I don't want to be the one to tell your mother that, though. Please don't make me do that."

We both laughed manically at her comedic begging, suffering from tired nerves. I slapped my thigh as I tried to breathe, but the sound of a door opening blew the rest of the wind from my belly. My attention fully centered on the witch at the hospital entrance who was gesturing for me to follow, and I nearly clawed my way up the wall to get to my feet.

"Javed?" I asked her breathlessly as she led me to an examination room, barely noticing the eminent team who'd treated him. The witch didn't reply; she merely opened a door and allowed me into the room.

My mate, naked from the waist up, was leaning over the counter by the sink, staring down into a hand mirror that rested flat on the polished surface. He blinked a couple times and looked up at me with an odd expression on his face. I'd been expecting… well, I wasn't sure what I'd been expecting, but it wasn't the surreal look of peace on his face.

Javed, my staggeringly handsome male, was calm as he smiled at me, breathing evenly and appearing perfectly fine. There was nothing in his face or body language that suggested he was in any pain. In fact, he'd never looked so… healthy and relaxed. I opened my mouth to say something, anything, but I was at a loss—even for a singular greeting.

However, my lip twitched when I finally noticed it. Of all the potential changes, I hadn't anticipated them giving him a haircut. I burst into laughter and approached, lifting my hand to run my fingers along his shorter locks. Then I brushed the strands aside to get a full view of his clear brow.

The brand was gone. The raised welts that had plagued his emotions for so long had finally been removed. As they'd promised, the memory of those three had been wiped from his skin. He didn't need the brand to remember them, and I was certain he'd never let himself forget.

I stroked the skin that furrowed under my thumb, the wrinkling from his tender expression. "As it should be," I whispered to him. "Are you happier?"

He took a deep breath, closed his eyes, and nodded. I placed a gentle hand on his shoulder to urge him to turn for me. As he rotated, I bit my lip, tearing up at the clear skin on his broad back. I traced my finger down his shoulder blade in disbelief. Smooth. All the scars had been taken from his flesh.

"I can hardly believe my eyes," I murmured. How was such skill possible? "I can't see anything, Javed. I can't even tell where the new skin begins." I leaned closer, trying to find the edges where they'd begun removing his skin before replacing it, but there was nothing. I couldn't comprehend it, and utter nonsense blurted out of my lips, "Looks like the healer had the last word this time."

Javed burst into chuckles, and the unexpected, foreign sound startled me. I recoiled with wide eyes, and he turned to face me again, his sensual lips slightly parted as he laughed. Nothing could describe the beauty of his laughter. The rich tone suited him, and now I desperately needed to hear him speak. Why hadn't he said anything yet?

"Talk to me!" I urged, moving closer and palming his chest. My gaze flickered to his neck and found the line of symbols completely gone. Its removal meant he could talk, right? "Oh my gods, Javed, please!"

His eyes gleamed and his cheeks raised as he took on a glowing smile. Shaking his head, he simply claimed my hand and led me out of the room. I protested initially, then started babbling nervously as he remained silent.

"Javed? Is your voice not back? I don't understand... Why aren't you talking to me?" I asked. I'd waited days for his recovery, drowning beneath all the unknowns!

We marched past Oudine, who brightened at the sight of us, but then cocked her head when she noticed his silence. Javed froze at a turn and looked left, then right, visibly confused.

"Do you want to leave? The main hall is this way..." I pointed to the right, puzzled. He nodded, squeezed my hand, and turned in that direction.

The silence was getting to me, and too much had happened to keep words from tumbling out of my mouth. I started telling him what'd happened in his absence, too nervous from his refusal—or inability—to communicate. "When th-the Proudless assisted the lionesses, the lions realized that they'd lost control of the kingdom. Many blame the lionesses for making them vulnerable during the Proudless invasion because the timing was so suspicious. It was hard for people to believe that the external and internal uprisings weren't connected. To be fair, in a way they were connected..." I frowned when I noticed he was walking us to the main gates. Were we leaving?

Forcing myself to be patient, I continued my update. "We've had to promise reparations, move back home, and make concessions to keep our lions and lionesses safe during this power shift, which made a lot of people upset. When it was brought to light that the king we'd killed had faked the last culling and used the cubs to farm blood to poison the bat-shifters—which was to steal their northern territory—most of the rage turned toward the king's closest circle." I gasped for air, trying to summarize the complicated mess. I was barely keeping it all straight myself.

Javed nodded and hummed an agreement, which surprised me.

"You knew?" I asked as we cleared the gates and strode up a golden hill. The dry grass bowed under a small breeze, or maybe it was in homage to the male who'd finally healed.

He nodded again, but rocked his hand to communicate a 'somewhat.' I twisted my lips as I stared up at him. Why wasn't he talking?

"W-well, the bat-shifters returned with a larger delegation from the dragon kingdom," I continued, "and said they'd tracked blood trafficking back to the castle, which explained why we had adults there… as well as some from my village." I sniffed with a heavy heart, recalling the familiar faces that were so pale and drawn from blood loss. It had been too close. Sushila had needed emergency care, but no one had died. Niraj also seemed a lot more attentive to her after she'd returned from the hospital. No doubt this experience would continue to change them both, and everyone would discover their true nature when they were fully off the purity. They all had their own stolen offspring to search for now.

I placed a hand to my forehead, trying to organize my thoughts once more as we walked toward a shaded copse of trees. We were leaving the castle far behind, and I could barely see the witches' encampment nestled against Edeletrots's walls.

"Anyw-way," I said, my hands growing sweaty in his steady grip. "The dragons had waited until our uprising to approach, refusing to interfere in our infighting per their p-politics. The lionesses have given them permission to follow leads with an escort since they still wish to hunt down the rest of the trafficking rings. In return, they're willing to offer advice and a small amount of financial support as the lions return to their homeland

and the cats establish some form of a c-central government here at the castle."

Javed tensed, and I just let the words stutter out of my mouth. "Th-they want you to l-lead the kingdom, Javed." We'd stopped in the middle of the copse, the scenery peaceful but the moment tense. The cool breeze that curled over the hill brushed through his hair, letting the orange strands dance. Perhaps they were celebrating being free from the cloak for good. "I m-mean the non-lions. The lionesses want me, so… they're both insisting we take a leadership role to represent everyone fairly." The anxiety I saw in his teal eyes had me panicking. "Please say something if you can," I begged, but he was frozen as he stared at me.

Not knowing what else to do, I stood on my tiptoes, pulled his head down, and planted my lips on his.

Chapter 37

Javed

Niusha was kissing me. She was kissing me! Oh, how I'd longed for this moment. I'd wanted those lips the very second I saw her.

Disbelief stunned me—but only for a heartbeat—and I melted into her, letting her offering comfort me a minute more. Her lips were soft but stiff, so I pried them open with my tongue to take over the lead, to show her the pleasurable dance a kiss could be. I wanted to erase any negative notions she feared of the act that Mehr had tried to brand on her. That scar wasn't visible, but no doubt it was still there like mine.

I massaged her sweet lips, unable to hold back my groans. I'd spent so much time not filtering my human noises that they now sprang out without warning. She responded with an aroused whimper that sent fire billowing through my veins and had my abdomen cramping with desire.

I walked my Niusha back into a tree, crushing my body against hers in a hungry embrace. She pressed her hips against mine, which just made my fire burn brighter. When the tiger inside of me threatened to growl and mount her, I released her lips and let us both catch our breaths. This wasn't why I'd brought us out here.

She was so lovely. Her lids were heavy, and her face was flushed, alive with want. When I cleared my throat, her eyes cleared as well, and she blinked up at me in sudden alertness. Her lips parted like she was about to speak, but I interrupted her. Using the long-lost tools of my throat and mouth, I spoke the first word in years, praying that my voice wouldn't crack or fail on me.

"Niusha," I said quietly to a stunned face. Her brows drew in over her gaze, and in those sparkling eyes, I could see how profoundly moved she was. I brushed away a tear that hung from her lower eyelash and spoke again, needing a little more practice before I said what I really needed to say. I didn't want to fuck it up. It was too important and would be a treasured memory for decades to come.

My beautiful Niusha curled her fingers into my chest muscles, desperate for more. I wouldn't deny her anything, not ever again. "I wanted to bring you out here because… I wanted you alone to have my first word. I wouldn't have any at all if you hadn't come stumbling into my corner of the jungle with a troupe of cubs at your paws."

A laugh burst from her lips, and more tears streamed down her red cheeks, the whites of her eyes rouging from salt water and emotion. She rubbed them and then breathed out an absolute bevy of compliments. "Gods, Javed, your voice is like cream. So smooth, so compelling. Not too deep, not too high. It's beautiful. It's right in the middle, and it... it practically sings to me!" She shook her head in awe. "It's no wonder you amassed an army so easily when you were younger. You must have had so many females, and probably some males, swooning at your feet."

I chuckled as I continued to brush away her tears. I'd heard such words before, but they meant more coming from my fated mate. I'd sing like a bird if it was what she wanted. "You have my words like you have my heart, Niusha," I said more softly, gathering the courage and confidence for my next sentence.

Her face sobered with a tender, adoring expression. "You have mine too, Javed..." she whispered as she stared unwaveringly into my eyes. I held that ardent gaze and placed my hands over hers, moving them to the middle of my chest.

"I love you," I said, sharing the most important words I'd ever speak in my lifetime. Her body softened against mine, and her head tilted back, like I'd just slid a piece of chocolate into her mouth. Her physical response gave me confidence, and I relaxed slightly, even though she hadn't responded yet.

She slanted her head and brought my face down again to meet her lips. Her kiss seared with a deep passion, seeping into the very marrow of my bones and further stimulating a part of my body that was becoming as hard as one. When she released me from her lips, seemingly unbothered by the act that had made her so anxious before, she voiced her own feelings.

"I love you too. Oh Javed, I love you so much! I've missed you so!" she confessed in return, her chin quivering with emotion. "I couldn't stand being apart. It was so hard. I'm so, so—"

I placed a finger on her lips before she could apologize, then stroked her hair to offer comfort. "Don't apologize, my love," I murmured. "I've learned much, and I know you're simply a force of nature. Don't ever be false to yourself. Please..."

She nodded but pushed slightly against me to move from the tree. "I am always making mistakes," she whispered, though I suspected she was talking to herself.

"Yet look where we are." I pointed back to the castle. "In the time I've known you, you've liberated orphans and helped in uniting an entire region."

"It was reckless," she countered, cringing at the view. The place now held traumatic memories for us both.

"Because we work better together," I explained and made her look at me again. "It's what the Sky Gods had in mind, I think. Give yourself time. We both have healing to do. Please... do that with me?"

Niusha bit her lip and nodded reluctantly. Then she pressed tenderly against my chest, urging me back toward the tree. I let her guide me down so we were sitting, facing each other. "I don't ever want to be apart again," she choked out and crawled onto my lap in a straddle. I swallowed heavily as my heart began thumping against my sternum, adamant in communicating its growing passion.

I stared sadly at the spot on her neck where my mark used to be, and she placed her fingers on it, her gaze tracking mine. I asked, "How…? How did it get muted? Can we not…"

Her wavy locks swayed as she shook her head. "Keid was supposed to remove it, but she muted it to hide it... like I mentioned. I don't even know if removing a mark is possible. Anyway, she said you just have to bite me again to fix it."

An aroused growl threatened to bubble from my chest, and I rumbled, "Do you want me to, Niusha?"

"I love it when you say my name." Her eyes closed in bliss. I placed my hands on her hips, making my mood known if she couldn't already tell by how hard her seat had become. It had her fully alert, and she finally answered, "Yes! Yes, I do. Please, Javed. I miss you. I miss you so much. I miss you being inside my body and soul in so many ways."

The words were a trigger, and we fumbled with each other's clothes, her hands working on my pants while I pulled up her skirts and yanked her underwear to the side. With our garments pushed away enough to join, I lifted her and lowered her onto my waiting length, letting her hands guide me to notch against her slick entrance.

Our eyes met as I pushed her down, parting and easing her channel to take me into her wet heat. Something happened in that moment to slow us, and when her soft bottom rested against the tops of my thighs, we just stared at each other in silence, only letting our heartbeats speak.

"Be mine forever," I begged in a whisper, pleading into her stunning blue-grey eyes. "Please, Niusha. Don't ever leave me again. I'll follow you anywhere, just never leave me again."

"I'm yours, Javed," she breathed out, placing her hands on my cheeks to draw me into another kiss. "I'll never leave your side again. I love you too much. You're a part of me." She hesitated, then brought one of my hands to her breast—a move that engulfed me in fire. She sent me a timid, meaningful look and kissed me once more.

A pathetic whimper escaped my throat, and, as though we shared the same mind, I began to pull her up the same time she started lifting herself. The beasts in both of us knew that now was the time for lovemaking, not feral mating. The tiger in me was already extremely satisfied with having planted my offspring in her. Oh gods, the cubs were safe. My cubs. Our cubs…

Our moans echoed in each other's throats, like we shared the same voice for just a moment. If I wasn't so at peace, I'd be crying from how moved I was. My heart basked in the euphoria of our love, as pleased as my cock was in her buttery, hot pussy. No, more so.

I allowed Niusha to set the pace while she rode my lap, pressing my shoulders back into the bark. I'd sat behind her so many times under the branches of a tree, but this time she was facing me under one, and I didn't feel the fear of being seen. In fact, my soul exalted with every look she gave me between kisses. Her gaze weakened my temperance, which wasn't much to begin with, and I caved.

"I can't!" A hot wave of lust had me gasping, and I leaned forward to split her soft flesh with my canines, biting hard into her marking spot. She jerked violently against me as I released my venom, letting it seep all the way down into her soul. It reopened the path to her very being, and I stayed adamantly in place, giving her all that my venom glands had so our souls would stay united forever.

Her core clamped around my rock-hard erection as she orgasmed from my venomous, bloody onslaught. I roared into her skin as she convulsed around me, her claws stabbing into my back. I hungrily devoured the pain that came from her pleasure, knowing the more it hurt me, the deeper she'd fallen into ecstasy. My grip on her hip bones tightened, and I grinded up against her, unable to hold back a moment more. She was squeezing too tight. Her womb, though already nurturing life we'd made together, was begging once more for my seed.

I released her from my bite, and I thought she was about to faint against me, but she moved up my slickened length to dig her canines into my marking spot. I screamed, and the pleasure of her bite—though unnecessary since I still had her mark in my skin—sent my senses spinning. I came hard into her, rocking violently as I unloaded rope after rope. I vaguely remembered yelling her name when I hit the peak of euphoria, tugging her tight against me so that we were nearly one being.

We'd fallen to the side, convulsing, writhing, worshiping our union for what felt like ages and mere seconds. The joy our souls found together was feverish this second time. We'd nearly lost each other, and taking back our love and future had kindled an unfathomable high. She knew just how precious she was to me, and I her. It was singular. I'd never find another. Neither would she. I'd never want another. Neither would she. Her death would be my death. She was my reason for being, and I'd never fucking risk losing her again.

By the time my cock had finished its claiming inside her, we were a gasping pile in the tall grass. She was bound tight in my arms, and I flexed her into me, unwilling to let go of her and this moment. I savored her scent as I nuzzled in her milk-and-coffee tresses. She smelled beautiful. Everything about her was beauty personified. She made my soul beam, mirroring the peaceful smile on my face.

"You're my home, Niusha," I whispered into her hair, and she tilted her sweaty, flushed face to look up at me. "I'll go where you go." I swallowed heavily as I made a big decision. "If you wish to stay here and work," I said and cleared my throat, unwilling to let it go hoarse, "I'll stay. I'll support you."

She blinked and brushed away a strand of her hair, brows drawn in concern. "You said you never wanted lives in your hands again…" Her own hands slid up my back, and she winced when she discovered the trail of blood she'd caused. "Oh no, did I cut you aga—"

I interrupted her, unbothered by her enthusiastic scratching. "Scars made by your pleasure are the ones I'd gladly show off." Then I returned to the topic at hand, now seeing the potentials, scary as they might be. "But no, it's different now. Maybe now… Maybe we're in a better position to help lives now. Save them. If we have support… we could reunite families. I was thinking about the cubs, Niusha. Your other cubs… Gerhard, Sam, Jam, and Tahmina. They'll want their families if we can find them. Chirasmi should be with her mother soon."

A look of guilt crossed her features, and I knew she'd temporarily forgotten about them. In all the chaos, I couldn't blame her. She'd started a hurricane over the last week.

"I'm sure they're happy where they are," I added hastily, "and I know you left them in good hands. Maybe they can even stay with us here if they'd prefer while we look for their families…"

"I'd love that," she admitted in a thick voice. I kissed her forehead softly, putting all my love into comforting her. "They wouldn't be the only ones staying," she said with a weak laugh, and I leaned back to give her a questioning look. "Lots of lionesses and lions found fated mates among the Proudless while you were being treated." She chuckled again. "Many don't want to return to pride life, so they've been allowed to stay here if they're interested in working as representatives. The gods know there's plenty of space now. One of those bat-shifters went a little nuts because he scented his mate and couldn't find her. The poor guy. He's been causing a scene." She snorted and palmed her face, the corners of her mouth curling into a sympathetic smile.

"To think of all those souls who never would've met without you," I murmured, stroking her cheek.

"Us… I think," she corrected thoughtfully. "Us, Javed." She placed a hand on my chest, tracing the contours of my muscles. "Aaron's torn. You'll have to speak with him. He found himself fated to a frisky little lioness, but he's loyal to you. If you stay, he'll want to stay and work here. I wasn't going to say it before and guilt you into making a decision… but since you seem ok with staying…"

I chuckled and scrubbed a hand over my chin. "Aaron works too hard. He needs to learn to relax," I said with an amused grin. "Though that's probably my fault. I hope she'll teach him how to do that. I'm happy for them."

"Oudine and Roul have to leave..." Her smile saddened. "They're leading the lions back to old territory, but my friends Jameson and Juliote are wanting to stay here and help. Jameson will get to escape the prejudice he lived with, and I asked for him to get a respected position when things become more organized. He's a good male, and she's sharp. I know he and Juliote will be dedicated to positive change." Niusha blinked sleepily at me, and I rubbed her upper arm in affection.

I was unable to believe I was lying here in the cool grass, talking to my mate about changing the world with cubs on the way. It was all I'd ever wanted before I'd been captured. I couldn't let the bad affect the future. It was in me to help as much as it was in her. Even if I felt the urge to run, deep down, I wouldn't be acting true to myself, but I knew I couldn't do it alone. I wasn't strong enough without her. I could only do it with Niusha at my side.

Then I felt her discomfort. Not meeting my gaze, she informed, "My mother is… ah… staying too."

Run, Convict said. Apparently, he hadn't been quiet about it because I heard Field's bold laughter in my head. Niusha's mother was a bit like her, but time had turned Tumidia into a tough matriarch. I couldn't lie; her mother did intimidate me a little.

"I'm sure we'll survive," I said with a small grin, which had her melting in relief. I was saying it mostly to Convict though, who was being a big old tabby cub again.

You're the cub, furless, Convict spat back at me, making me laugh at his snippety response.

"Why so cranky, Convict?" I leaned in to nuzzle Niusha's nose.

Why so cranky? Gee, I wonder. I don't get to see Field until they deliver our cubs, and now I'm stuck dealing with her mothe—

Careful finishing that sentence, sweetie, Field's voice interrupted, sounding very much like a future matriarch herself. *I very much adore my mother. I'll forgive you this time, though.*

So very generous, he muttered, but his tone faded from impulsive sarcasm to deep humility. *Why?* His cringe was palpable.

Because I love you too, idiot, dick spurs and all.

Niusha and I burst into laughter. I very much looked forward to their love growing like it had for Niusha and me. I pulled my mate close again and sighed in happiness. She was my favorite paradise. She was where I belonged. Forever.

Seen. Heard. Home.

I was finally home.

The End

Author's Notes

Those who have been reading my books since day one know why this book was written. This book is another step taken in my exposure therapy, and it's too difficult to revisit my assault, so I'd recommend reading the Author's Notes in *The Mistake and the Lycan King*, *The Dragon Knight and the Coveted*, and *The Packless and the Fae Prince* if you wish to know.

Why did Niusha risk it?

Why did she go to the lions when everyone yelled at her not to? Why did she put the issue with the lions and the others above herself, her mate, and her unborn?

Niusha was my desperate drive to understand myself better and the risks I take to do so. When I went into therapy for the first time and had my first real epiphany, it changed the way I saw my life. My world seemed bigger because something finally made sense, and to see progress, albeit tiny, made recovery actually seem like a real goal. In order to live my life, to truly live it, and target my wounds, I needed to understand why I was the way I was. Why I hurt the way I did. Why I hated or liked the things I did. There were so many different things about me. Niusha's struggle with her identity, the core of her being, is a reflection of mine.

The assault, the abuse, and the resulting PTSD made me terrified that I'd always live a life of running away. I ran from everything. I ran from confrontation, from groups of people, and myself. I couldn't accept myself. I hated who I was. I hated being weak even though I had always idolized fictional warrior women.

Feeling weak had me desperate to find safety, and that manifested in my sleep. From early childhood to now, I have suffered, and still suffer, from chronic nightmares—just like Niusha—where I'm escaping the place of my abuse. Once I clear the property, it's a mad dash to a corner where I can finally get out of sight and disappear into the hills, terror on my back. It's all here, in this book. There are variations, but this is the one I focused on.

Exposure therapy is not without risk. Niusha fought recklessly to get answers. But she did believe in herself when not only her mate didn't, but many of my readers didn't. The lions are like trauma. It seems too big to fight, too dangerous, too painful, but is it impossible? One wouldn't know until they did it, and many would take the risk to try out of sheer desperation. Exposure therapy is painful, it's risky when you go through it alone, and I try my best to not consider it outright torture (not a great word choice either as it's a distorted thought).

As Niusha put dealing with the lions first, I put my trauma first. How could she live her life with her mate and offspring with the lions hanging over their head? How could I love someone, grow, and have a family of my own someday with my trauma hanging over my head? I saw her not singularly as naive and selfish, but as a person who didn't see a way forward without addressing the biggest threat. My life was at risk. It still is. My trauma was too dangerous for me to ignore. It still is. Therapists used to call people with my case impossible to treat, and many of us had an assumed countdown. I don't think I have to explain what happens when you get to zero.

But I can't let the lions win.

The effects of sexual assault on a woman's sexual well-being:

This story was also a return to the ghost hands I'd started processing with Elpis in *TDKatC*. What was new here was Niusha's combined horror of climaxing to a nightmare. As a child, I'd have a nightmare where I was being assaulted by a man, and upon waking up, I'd notice a weak pulsing between my legs. I had no idea what it was, and it scared me. Something about it felt deeply violating, disturbing. For years I woke from nightmares like that, not understanding what my body was doing.

As I got older, I learned that I'd been having what they call nocturnal orgasms. Knowing that I'd unwillingly had them with these nightmares… There is no word strong enough to explain how that made me feel. The closest ones would be shame, horror, humiliation, confusion, generally sickened… and a deep sense that something was wrong with me. I hated it. I didn't want it. The nightmares were not something to ever associate with that physical response, and that ultimately contributed to clinically diagnosed anorgasmia. I'm still struggling with this in therapy. I still feel ashamed about it. I also know it's not my fault. I didn't choose it.

Why lions?

In regards to why the situation was built around a bloody lion expansion, it's me venting familial ties to the Belgian occupation of the Congo, now the Democratic Republic of the Congo, and I must be vague. I grew up listening to stories of eating fresh fried bananas by the water, having pet tarantulas in the lawn, family surviving malaria during a pregnancy, seeing dead bodies roll down the river… Some stories I could digest at a young age. Others I had not been ready to hear.

I'd stumbled into closeted skeletons I didn't have the strength to push off me. Scars built upon scars. Trauma stacked. That is all I will say here.

The Congo lion still exists in the DRC, though its population is threatened. The lion is also found in Belgian's coat of arms. Lions also provided an emotionally distant opportunity to process the power dynamic between males and females. This novel, however, does not realistically depict actual lion prides.

If you want to learn about the history of the occupation, research with caution. There are things that cannot be unseen.

Scarification:

In regards to this practice, I will not share my personal feelings here. My books are about healing and not a place for debate. Scarification is an extremely controversial tradition that is done to very young children and adults alike. I have not seen it done in person, just through videos, and I will not comment on cultural and religious beliefs. Adults have expressed that they wished it was never done to them. Adults have also expressed pride in their markings. For those horrified about the practice, know that it is a dying tradition.

The debate:

I want to note that in regards to the debate of who would win in a fight, a lion or a tiger, I personally find the obsession somewhat sad, too full of nuance, pointless, and morbid. Let it be known that both lions and tigers are beautiful, incredible creatures that should be equally protected from poachers and habitat loss. As of right now, the lion conservation status is vulnerable and tigers are considered endangered.

Fun facts (to clear the palate):

The drugs mentioned in the book, netacaria and acpoama, are actually based on catnip and silvervine. I got the name netacaria from catnip's scientific name 'Nepeta Cataria' by combining the first and last letters of each word: (Ne)pe(ta) (Ca)ta(ria). The same mostly goes for silvervine, which is an alternative cat stimulant: (Ac)tinidia (Po)lyg(ama). I made the effects the drugs have on the cat-shifters loosely based on the effect catnip has on cats, which in turn has been compared to LSD use in humans. Though that theory seems to be unproven, I chose to give netacaria and acpoama the effects of LSD in both its long-term use and withdrawals. I also put the substances in their bug repellent because there was a 2021 study that the compounds found in catnip and silvervine were found to repel mosquitos. I take all studies with a grain of salt and simply use them as inspiration to feed my imagination. Research and lore building calms me after writing difficult chapters.

Convict's name is not a reference to a person convicted of a crime. It's a red herring. Convict, as an intransitive verb, refers to the act of finding a defendant guilty. Convict and Javed were not a criminal in the jungle but an exiled seeker of justice.

Field's name is not a reference to an open expanse of land. Field, as a transitive verb, is the act of responding to something. Field, the lioness, does not ignore matters.

If not for the unwavering support of my reader family and publishing team, I would not have been able to publish the Author's Notes in this particular novel. I've been especially vulnerable here, not liking to talk about family history or the nightmares, but this is continuing the documentation as it is apparently what sets this series apart from other novels. That being said, if any of this is familiar to you, and if it helps you not feel alone, that is enough to keep me going. I may feel shame, someone else may feel shame, but there is nothing to be ashamed about. We did nothing wrong. We simply lived. We are doing the best we can. Out of the page of this book or through the glass of your screen, I'm reaching out to you in solidarity and love. We're doing the best we can.

Starlight preserve you,
Asha Nyr

www.ingramcontent.com/pod-product-compliance
Lightning Source LLC
Chambersburg PA
CBHW020602310726
48979CB00008B/1305/J

* 9 7 9 8 9 8 8 5 3 5 0 8 9 *